EVOLUTION

IV

THE EXLIAN SYNDROME SERIES

BOOKS BY SETH RING

THE EXLIAN SYNDROME SERIES

Advent

Dark Dawn

Apex

Evolution

Shattered Glory (coming in 2026)

Light's Ascension (coming in 2026)

THE IRON TYRANT SERIES

Chain of Feathers

Crow's Fortune

Healing Skies

THE SOUL CALLER SERIES

Soul Caller 1

Soul Caller 2

THE DREAMER'S THRONE SERIES

Dreamer's Throne 1

Dreamer's Throne 2

Dreamer's Throne 3

Dreamer's Throne 4

STANDALONE (NOVA TERRA)

Mad Master Alchemist

THE TOWER SERIES

Forge Master

Reforged

Arcanist

Ignition

Bloodline

Avatar

Challenger

Marauder

THE BATTLE MAGE FARMER SERIES

Domestication

Germination

Cultivation

Fermentation

Transformation

Preservation

Separation

Conservation

Culmination

THE TITAN SERIES

Nova Terra: Titan

Nova Terra: Greymane

Nova Terra: Kingbreaker

Nova Terra: Guardian

Nova Terra: Liberator

Nova Terra: Earthshaper

Nova Terra: Stormbringer

Nova Terra: Stone King

Nova Terra: Catalyst

Nova Terra: Worldbearer

EVOLUTION

THE EXLIAN SYNDROME SERIES

IV

TESS I 0000004

DETECTED

SETH RING

BLACK STONE PUBLISHING

Published in 2025 by Blackstone Publishing
Cover and book design by Larissa Ezell

Printed in the United States of America
Originally published in hardcover by Blackstone Publishing in 2025

First paperback edition: 2025
ISBN 979-8-8746-9510-1
Fiction / LitRPG (Literary Role-Playing Game)

Version 1

Blackstone Publishing
31 Mistletoe Rd.
Ashland, OR 97520

www.BlackstonePublishing.com

EVOLUTION

IV

THE EXLIAN SYNDROME SERIES

Mark couldn't help but hold his breath as the sensor scanned his watch. Part of him feared the blare of the siren and the flashing red light that would declare him a fraud, but instead, a familiar ding settled his heart in his chest, and a blinking green light indicated there was no problem with his identity. Of course, the name that flashed up was Jonathan Leeds, but the face was his. Shaking off his lingering worry, Mark stepped through the doors of the train and looked around for a seat.

He was headed to the southern side of New Emery, and in the distance, he could see his destination already, a behemoth looming over the other buildings. Only a few days had passed since Mark had escaped from the Tomb, a secret underground prison for empowered, and he had just gotten word that the hunter license that Noah had arranged for him was ready.

As Mark sat, he scanned the Exlian network, looking for anomalies, a habit ingrained during his time in the wilderness and reinforced by his eventful stay in the Tomb. Nothing caught his attention, but that didn't stop him from casually sweeping the train car as well. A young man in a uniform at the other end of the car shifted position, and déjà vu flickered through the back of Mark's mind.

Life hadn't gone his way the last couple of years, to say the least. He'd finally become empowered, gaining superhuman abilities like the rest of his family, but his lifelong dream of joining the Defense Force had been shattered, and his assignment to the Engineering Corps had ended with the almost complete obliteration of the Black Mountain Battalion. Remembering the empowered men and women he had served with for a few weeks, Mark couldn't help but clench his fist.

Though it had only been a brief moment, his time with them and the subsequent events at Felwer Mine had forever seared the Black Mountain Battalion into his memory. To say nothing of the fact that he carried both Sergeant Fletcher's and Lieutenant Kami's powers in his body. Though he had managed to kill one of the two men responsible for the team's deaths, Captain Calder was still alive. A fact Mark was determined to rectify.

Of course, that would mean both finding Captain Calder *and* avoiding being thrown back in the Tomb . . . With a soft hiss, the doors opened, and shaking his head, Mark joined those spilling out onto the station platform. It was busy, filled with people coming and going, many of them dressed in mana suits. This station served as the area's primary hub, connecting the southern gate with the rest of the city of New Emery.

Rather than head for the city gate, like many of the others in the crowd, Mark walked toward the giant building a few blocks away from the station. He had seen enough images to immediately recognize the headquarters of the Hunters' Association. Unlike most of the large buildings in downtown New Emery, it had no guards at the front. Then again, anyone insane enough to try to cause trouble there would immediately find themselves surrounded by hundreds, if not thousands, of empowered who made their living hunting Exlian in the dead zone outside the city.

Feeling a faint pressure on his shoulder, Mark glanced over and saw Mime gazing at the crowds through half-lidded eyes as she perched there. For a moment, he considered asking the alien cat to get down, to prevent anyone from drawing a connection between Jonathan Leeds and his old identity as Mark Fields. Then again, Mime had an uncanny knack for going unnoticed, so he decided not to worry about it.

The headquarters was even busier inside than the bustle outside, and almost forty minutes passed before it was Mark's turn to see one of the receptionists.

"What do you need?" the middle-aged man behind the counter asked, not even looking up as Mark approached.

"I'm here to pick up my license."

"Hmm. Scan your watch."

Holding up his watch to the scanner, Mark heard a hum, and a screen in front of him flickered to life.

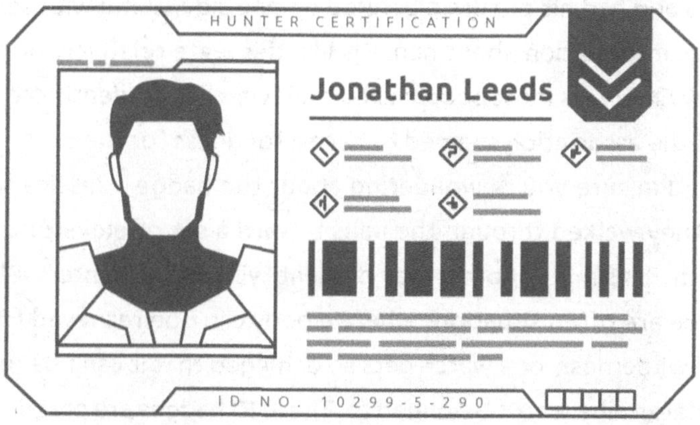

"Is that you? Make sure all the information is right, and then hit 'Accept.'"

It only took him a moment to scan the information, and after he accepted the prompt that popped up, the attendant finally looked up. "Well, Mr. Leeds, welcome to the Hunters' Association.

If you're interested in getting a tour of the association office and having someone explain how all of this works, I'd be happy to assign someone to you. It'll cost you one hundred credits."

Mark almost refused, out of habit, but then remembered that his account was flush. "Sure, that'd be fine."

Looking back down at his console, the attendant read over some names, then tapped one. "Great, Jessica will be over in just a second. If you don't mind stepping to the side while we wait for your badge to print, I'll help the next person in line."

A few minutes later, a young woman in her twenties was standing next to Mark with a pleasant smile permanently affixed to her lips. "Hello, sir. My name is Jessica. I'll be your guide for the next half hour. I'd be happy to show you the various amenities the association offers, as well as answer any questions you might have about the process. If you'll follow me, we'll start somewhere a little bit quieter."

The badge she handed Mark was about the size of a playing card and had his picture plastered on one side, along with some basic information about him. IDs like this were relatively rare in New Emery, as most people used their watches as identification, but the association seemed to have a fondness for them.

"I'm sure you're wondering about the badge," Jessica said as they walked through the halls toward a set of elevators. "In truth, it's simply another way of identifying other hunters. Plus, there are often situations where a body can't be retrieved from the wilderness, or a watch gets so damaged that it can't be used to determine who it belonged to. These ID badges are practically indestructible. There's been many a case where a hunter has been eaten by an Exlian, that Exlian has later been killed, and the badge was recovered from the monster's stomach. But enough about that . . . If you'll step into this elevator, I'd be happy to take you to the upper floors."

Mark followed her inside, and soon the doors opened to a much quieter hallway on the second floor.

"You came through the main entrance of the association, which is where you would be doing the majority of your trading as a level-one hunter," Jessica went on. "Most of the people downstairs were not new hunters but level one, and the goods and services they have access to are handled at the first-floor desks. As a level-two hunter, you have access to services provided on the second floor."

His forehead furrowing, Mark took another look at the badge he was holding and noticed two lines next to his name. "Can you explain how these levels work?" he asked as they entered a large open room with a series of desks.

"Sure. As I mentioned, downstairs is where all of the level-one services are. Level-two services are available here. Above us, on the third floor, are level-three services. That continues all the way up to level five, where the strongest hunters are served. Hunters in the D rank and below are level-one hunters. Hunters in the C rank are level two, B rank is level three, A rank is level four, and the association's two S-ranked hunters are served on level five. Of course, that's only the most basic way of categorizing the levels. Hunters who have an excellent track record can increase their level by contributing to the association. In your case, because of your strength and the generosity of your license's sponsor, you've been assigned to the second level. As you successfully hunt Exlian, you'll have the opportunity to upgrade your level, either through trading resources or by accruing enough contribution points."

Gesturing for Mark to follow, Jessica led him over to one of the nearby kiosks.

"Contribution points are a private currency used within the Hunters' Association. As you know, the association is not a monolithic organization. It simply exists to facilitate and coordinate hunters, providing a safe and stable way for them to take on and complete requests. When a request is issued, it's put into the database, and a hunter of the appropriate level can view and accept said request. If you'll scan your watch or your badge here, I'll show you what I mean."

After a moment of hesitation, Mark held out the badge, touching it lightly against the scanner. His information flashed across the screen, and then three buttons appeared.

"At the top, we have 'Active Requests.' You see that's currently zero because you don't have any. Underneath that, we have 'Requests,' the list of requests that are available. And at the bottom, we have 'Current Account Balance,' which again is zero because you haven't accepted any requests yet. Go ahead and select 'Requests,' and I'll show you how to take one on."

As soon as Mark selected the button, a massive list populated on the screen, and as he scanned it, his eyes widened in surprise. He continued to scroll through as Jessica gave him a basic explanation.

"Requests can be just about anything, but the Hunters' Association specializes in operations outside of the city. We are not a mercenary organization, no matter what the rumors might suggest. What this means is that any official request in our system will take you outside the city walls. It could be as simple as trying to find or retrieve something, or it could be scouting or treasure hunting. You might find a request to locate mineral deposits or particular resources that a group in New Emery is interested in developing. There are also hunting requests for specific kinds of materials. As dangerous as the Exlian are, they are also a treasure trove in the hands of the right people. We get a lot of alchemical requests, requests for complete corpses, and occasionally live specimen requests. Though at the second level, you won't have to worry about any of those.

"You'll notice a symbol indicating that the request is locked next to some of them. This simply means that there is a requirement that you don't meet, whether it's the amount of experience or the number of people in your group. Whenever a request is issued, the association assesses it and assigns a solo rank and a group rank. If you were, say, a level-four hunter, you might be able to take some of these requests. But as a level-two hunter, you'll only be able to take them on with a group, which serves as an excellent segue into the next most important part of being a hunter, namely groups."

Leaving the kiosk, Mark followed Jessica out of the large room to an even larger cafeteria, where he saw dozens of hunters lined up at a buffet. Half of the room was taken up by tables, while the other half held more comfortable seating arranged in small pods, many of which were filled.

"This is the cafeteria. It's a place where groups gather and where individuals who don't yet have a group can meet with existing ones. You'll likely spend the majority of your time in the association here as you wait for your missions to be approved. Past the cafeteria, we have a number of other facilities, including a training room, an assessment center, and the store, where you'll turn in your materials and buy new gear."

Jessica paused by the store. "There are a tremendous number of other small things the association can help you with, but all of them require contribution points. For example, we have a lawyer here in case you get into any legal scrapes. But like everything in the association, the kind of service you'll receive is based on what level you are and how many contribution points you have."

Noticing that Mark was looking past her, Jessica glanced over her shoulder and smiled when she caught sight of the impressive-looking mana suit in the window. "The association has just about everything. That's a brand-new Titan IX, from the

Borner family. Everything just depends on how many contribution points you have."

"Well, it sounds like I need to earn some," Mark said, chuckling.

By the time Mark said goodbye to Jessica and walked back out of the association building, he felt like he had a good grasp of what his new life was going to look like. Getting back on the train, Mark headed for his new apartment, located in a quiet suburb on the eastern side of the city. After scanning his watch to get into the building, he took the elevator up to the fourteenth floor and entered the one-bedroom apartment. It was a small space, and when the curtains were pulled tight, it reminded Mark of his apartment in the Tomb. Because of that, he kept the curtains open at all times, inviting in as much sky as he possibly could.

Noah seemed to have thought of everything, as the apartment was fully furnished, and there was even cat food for Mime. Of course, Mime was much more interested in the steaks Mark had picked up the day before.

"All right, all right," Mark said, after a few minutes of Mime's withering stare. "Just hold on, let me cook them."

As he heated up the pan, his watch vibrated, and a message popped up.

SKY

Are you free tomorrow? We should get some breakfast.

Hesitating for a moment, Mark dropped the two thick steaks into the pan and listened as they sizzled. He wasn't sure exactly why, but he felt a strange resistance whenever he thought about meeting with his friends, particularly Sky. It was silly, but it was almost as if he didn't know how to face them anymore. What made seeing Sky particularly awkward was the blooming connection between him and Phoenix. Though he tried to convince himself that it didn't really matter, his missed date with Phoenix had been weighing heavily on his mind. After a few minutes, he flipped the steaks and took a deep breath before sending a reply back to Sky.

JONATHAN

I don't think I can do breakfast. I just picked up my license, and tomorrow I'll be getting my power assessment early in the morning. Then I need to go pick out a mana suit, which will probably take most of the day.

SKY

Great, how about I come with you? I don't have anything else going on.

The reply came so quickly that Mark realized Sky must have been sitting there staring at her watch, just waiting for him to reply.

JONATHAN

Sure, that'd be great. Why don't we meet at 7?

Grimacing as he watched the message to Sky send, Mark dismissed the screen and focused his attention on his meal.

It wasn't long before the steaks were ready, and he served them up on two plates at the small table between the kitchen and the living room. Mime, crouched on the table next to her plate, ate with relish, carefully slicing off thin strips of meat with a single claw and gulping them down without bothering to chew. Mark ate slower, his mind full of conflicting thoughts about his friends, especially Sky.

When he was finished, he got himself a big glass of water and retrieved two data sticks from his bedroom before sitting back down at the table. He had gotten one of the data sticks from Master Lemuel, and it likely contained information about his new identity's background. The other had been given to him in front of Master Abrams's grave by Jason, the master's old disciple, and Mark had no idea what was on it.

After a moment of hesitation, he headed back into his room and got another data stick out of a small hidden pocket in his bag. He had retrieved this one before the facility in Felwer Mine had been destroyed. Bringing it back to the table, he placed it next to the others, then retrieved a small device with a data stick slot in it. According to what Noah had told him, this device would allow him to display the contents of the stick on a projected screen instead of on his watch, without running the risk that someone else would intercept it.

For good measure, Mark took off his watch and stuck it in his room under his pillow, closing the door to ensure maximum privacy. He hesitated for a moment but eventually settled on the stick Master Lemuel had given him.

As he'd suspected, it turned out to be information about Mark's new identity. According to what he read, Jonathan Leeds was an only child, orphaned during the last major wave. His parents had been regular members of the Defense Force and had been overrun in the attack on the southern wall. Jonathan had skated by in school without drawing much attention and, after receiving some military training, had worked as a bodyguard for the Javesi family. When he'd had enough of that, Jonathan had decided to retire and try his hand at being a hunter. In recognition of his service, the Javesi family had assisted him in buying a level-two hunter's license, the one he had just picked up.

After he finished reviewing the information on the data stick, Mark removed it and hesitated once more as he tried to decide which stick to look at next. Ultimately, he chose the one from Felwer Mine. Just like the first data stick, it slotted in easily, and its contents were soon displayed on the virtual screen.

At first, Mark didn't really understand what he was looking at. The files contained an endless sea of numbers and many terms he didn't understand. But as he continued to scroll through the information, a few things caught his eye. The first was the project name, Lilith. The second was a set of names buried in a list of active participants in the Lilith Project: Erol Javesi and Edward Graham. He knew who Edward Graham was, of course, as he had grown up seeing the scientist's face on his virtual screen almost every day, but he didn't know who Erol Javesi was, besides the obvious connection to Noah.

Turning off the projection, Mark went to his room and retrieved his watch to do a quick search. Erol Javesi, an entrepreneur and politician, had risen to the level of city councilman, much like his son, Andre Javesi. Why Noah's grandfather had been a member of the Lilith Project, Mark wasn't sure, but he was determined to find out.

Putting his watch back under his pillow, he went back out to the kitchen and continued reading. It took Mark almost an hour to make heads or tails of what the Lilith Project was about, and when he reached the end of the document, he sat back and sighed, rubbing his forehead.

"You know," he remarked to Mime, who was sitting next to him, "I'm wondering if it would be better if I had just left this data stick there to be buried."

Mime cocked her head sideways, staring at him with bright eyes.

"These crazy people were running experiments on nests, trying to see if they could create controllable monsters. It seems like the facility was attacked before they could succeed, but we know that the attackers were people from New Emery, not Exlian. It reminds me of the rumors about that orphanage where Sky used to live, Saint Vincent's. And why do I get the feeling that something like that is still going on?"

Disconnecting the data stick, Mark hesitated, then went to retrieve his watch. Sliding it onto his wrist, he stood in the doorway of his bedroom. After staring at his watch for a long moment, he tapped on the virtual screen. "Maestro, can you hear me?"

When nothing happened, Mark let out the breath he had been unconsciously holding. He thought it was likely that Maestro, the mad scientist who ruled the Tomb, was keeping tabs on him, but he wasn't sure how closely. It was reassuring that he couldn't tell when Mark called his name. But before Mark could put his hand down, the screen shivered, and a small pop-up appeared.

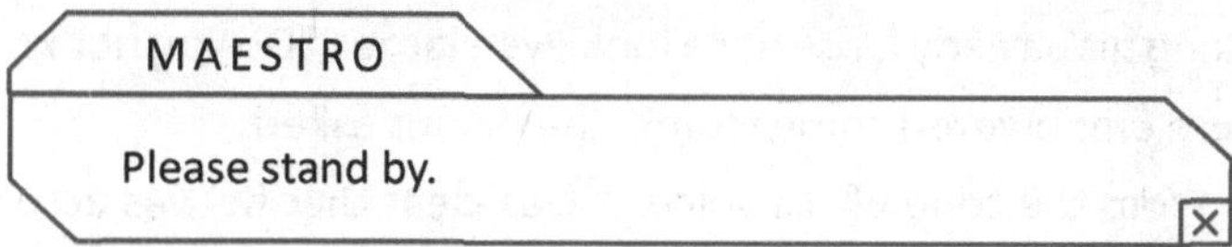

Less than thirty seconds later, the screen shivered again, and Maestro's face appeared, taking up the entirety of the virtual screen. "Hello, Mark. Do you need something?"

"Ah, I . . . I'm sorry to bother you."

"If you're sorry, then get on with it. I have a lot to do, and I'm in the middle of an experiment."

"Right . . . Have you ever heard of a program called Lilith? A secret project to try to make controllable monsters."

Though the expression on Maestro's face remained carefully neutral, Mark caught a faint twitch in the mad genius's eyelid and knew he had struck a nerve.

"Lilith, huh? Where did you hear about that?"

"When I was out in the wilderness with the Black Mountain Battalion, I was deployed to a base that had been abandoned at Felwer Mine. There was a facility down there, a massive testing facility, that had been studying an Exlian nest." Mark held up the data stick. "I pulled some information from the facility, and honestly, I can't make heads or tails of it. I was wondering if you had any information."

Maestro's eyes grew slightly bigger when he saw the data stick Mark was waving. "I want that. I've been looking for information regarding the initial empowerment project. The information you hold might be a clue. In fact, one of the first tasks I was going to ask you to help with was to dig into the current empowerment projects. But it seems like you're one step ahead."

"Hold on," Mark said, rubbing his forehead. "What do you mean, empowerment projects? You mean what they're doing with mutants?"

Raising one eyebrow, Maestro leaned in closer, the camera making his already large nose look even larger. "Do you not know where empowered come from?" the genius asked.

From the tone of his voice, it was clear that he was actually asking if Mark was stupid. But since Mark genuinely didn't know what he was talking about, he simply shook his head.

"Mark, all of the abilities empowered humans possess come from the nests. From the integration of Exlian DNA into human bodies."

"Wait, you're saying we're all experiments?"

"To one degree or another, yes," Maestro replied. "They feed it through the water system: trace amounts of Exlian DNA along with an agent that neutralizes some of the more aggressive tendencies. The result has been the awakening of mutations in the population, what you would call naturally empowered. Of course, the initial experiments didn't go quite as planned, and the rate of natural awakening is relatively low, but thankfully, the gene therapy the population has undergone has allowed for the absorption of skill gems, which is the only reason we're still alive. The Lilith Project is where this all started. I want that data stick. I'll send someone to pick it up. Now, I really have to go. But if you find anything else like this, don't hesitate to let me know."

"But . . . wait!"

With a shimmer, Mark's virtual screen returned to its normal appearance as Maestro hung up. Doing his best to control his annoyance, Mark closed it with a wave, trying to digest the information he had just learned. If Maestro was telling the truth—and he had no reason not to, at least as far as Mark knew—that meant that everyone in the entire city was subjected to gene therapy without their knowledge. They were all little more than science experiments. Clenching his fist, Mark stared at it, watching as his arm transformed into a bone blade. Of course, while he didn't appreciate having been an unwitting test subject, the results weren't all bad.

He walked back out into the kitchen and took a seat at the table, where he was just about to slot the last data stick when he heard a faint beep at the door. When he went to see who it was, he found a small flying robot, the kind generally used for deliveries, hovering in the hallway.

"Here for pickup," the mechanical voice said, reminding Mark of Mr. Robot.

Just then, his wrist vibrated.

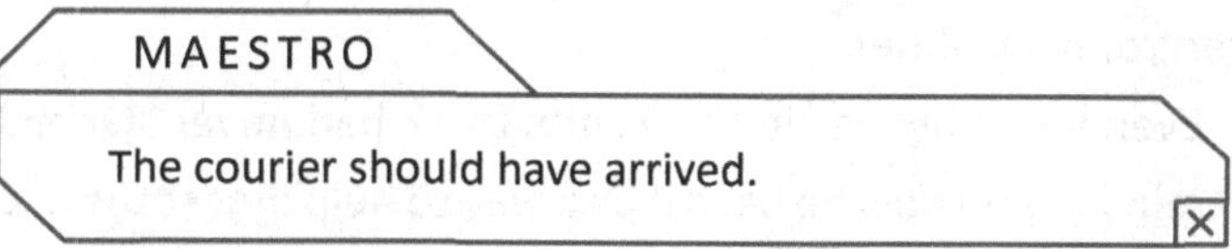

Realizing what was going on, Mark went back inside to retrieve the stick from Felwer Mine, then handed it over to the robot, who slipped it into a small chamber in its body. There was a flash of mana, and the data stick was gone, obviously transported to Maestro's side. Mark was about to step inside and close the door when the courier reached into its body and pulled out a vial of shimmering silver liquid shot through with threads of crimson that gave off an intense sense of bloodlust.

"Payment for services rendered," the robotic voice said, handing the vial to Mark. Without another word, the robot turned and flew off, maneuvering out of the window at the end of the hall and vanishing into the evening sky.

Back in the apartment, Mark sat down to examine the serum. He could sense the intensity of the mana it contained. In its unmarked glass tube, it looked similar to the other serums Maestro had Mark consume down in the Cradle, the part of the Tomb where Maestro ran his experiments. So after hesitating for a moment, he decided to just take it. Mark pushed the couch back against the wall, giving himself lots of space, then drank the potion down in one gulp. The silvery liquid slipped down Mark's throat, evaporating before it arrived at his stomach and transforming into a ferocious wave of energy that tore through his body.

Rather than fight it, Mark deliberately relaxed, accepting the energy as it bathed his muscles and bones with a burning feeling that quickly spread throughout his body. Once the initial wave of energy had settled, Mark stood up and began to move through his martial kata, executing the Cutting Palm technique to the full extent of his abilities.

Even while he was in the Tomb, Mark had never slacked on his training, and now he used it as a way to help digest the excess energy the serum contained. Though he had no idea what he had drunk, he trusted that Maestro wouldn't try to harm him. But as the burning sensation grew increasingly painful, that confidence started to waver.

Mark could feel a faint presence building in his chest, reminding him of the phantom war bear that had tried to consume his spirit in the Tomb. Rather than allow the presence to continue gathering, Mark focused his mind even as his body continued to move through his martial forms, launching a mental attack against the presence before it could solidify. His bones and muscles began to tremble, producing faint roars that he recognized as a war bear's battle cry, as Mark struck out, scattering the presence over and over again.

Finally, just as the burning pain in Mark's body was growing too intense for even him to manage, the war bear's spirit collapsed, dispersing through him, bringing with it a soothing feeling like being immersed in a warm, comforting bath. Bringing his kata to a close, Mark sat back down, wiping the sweat from his face as he settled into a calming meditation.

For the next six hours, Mark didn't move as the energy contained in the serum finished its work. When it was finally done, he let out a tired sigh and flopped over backward, sensing the changes inside him. Everything about him felt stronger, denser, as if his entire body had been solidified. He was just about to get up and head toward the shower when the virtual screen on his wall came to life and Maestro's face appeared.

"I've sent you a potion. You'll want to be careful when . . . Huh."

Even through the virtual screen, Maestro could see the changes in Mark's body, and he trailed off, realizing that his warning was too late.

"Well, I was going to tell you to be cautious when you took it, but clearly we're already past that point. There was a reasonable chance that it would clash, as this serum was much stronger than the previous one. It seems that there wasn't any issue, however. How do you feel?"

"I feel great," Mark said, clenching his fist. "I feel strong."

"You should. You should find that your stats have been upgraded marginally, increasing your fortitude and your strength by a small degree. The main focus of the serum, however, is to reinforce your skin, improving both your regeneration and your mana shield. You'll have to test the effects out yourself, but I believe you should be having an assessment tomorrow, right? Use that as an opportunity to get used to your new powers."

Glancing off to the side, Maestro grimaced.

"I have to go, but the information you retrieved and sent me was fascinating and has shed considerable light on a few mysteries I had been pondering. I think I'll be able to use this information to track down other points of interest. When I do, I'll let you know where they are. You can go and check them out for me. In exchange, I'll continue to supply you with serums to increase your strength."

Mark opened his mouth to reply, but before he could, Maestro disconnected. Seeing Mime walk over to sit next to him, Mark sighed and scratched her behind the ears.

"You know, I'm not so sure that I like the fact he can just pop up wherever and whenever he wants," he grumbled.

Mime just closed her eyes and leaned into his scratches.

After taking a shower, Mark returned to the kitchen table to look at the last data stick. Before he did, he glanced down at his wrist, pushing the mana in his arm to form a circuit. Even though he didn't have an activator, he could replicate its effect. A moment later, his status screen popped up.

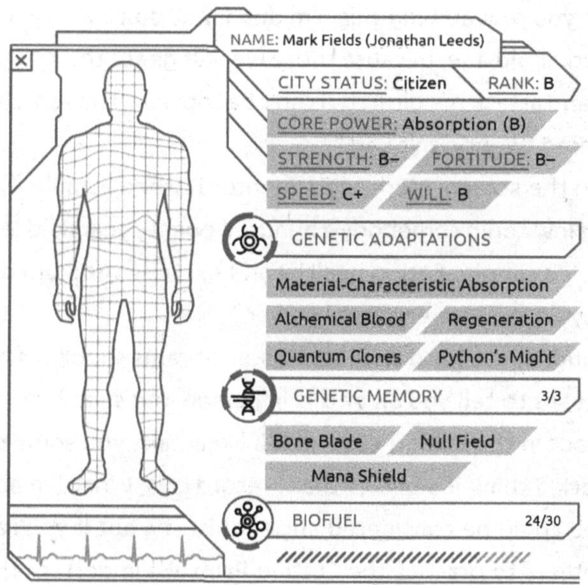

Just like the other serums he had taken, this one had increased Mark's stats. It had bumped him into B rank, though it hadn't helped his speed at all. Both his strength and fortitude had been directly elevated, climbing from C+ to B–. His will had grown as well, though Mark could tell that had nothing to do with the serum. He had absorbed the necroseed of a baeloth in Felwer Mine, and it continued to change him.

Marveling at how much he had grown since he'd first awakened his powers, Mark turned his attention to the last data stick, tensing as he slotted it in and watched the screen flicker to life. His breath caught in his throat as he saw Master Abrams appear, a scowl on the old man's wrinkled face. The familiar sight of Abrams's grumpy expression caused Mark's heart to ache, and he quickly reached out to pause the video. Getting up, he walked to the kitchen sink and filled a glass with water. Trying not to crush it, Mark took slow sips until he had calmed down. It wasn't until he had drained the glass that Mark felt collected enough to press play once more.

"If you're watching this, I'm dead, but don't worry. I probably died of old age, because those weaklings are too cowardly to come and attack me directly. I can't be too mad, though. Living to a hundred twenty isn't bad."

On the screen, Mark's lost mentor flashed a smile. "I know, right? How could somebody a hundred twenty years old look this good? It's simple. Eating healthy and exercise. And of course, a healthy dose of supernatural power."

Laughing at his own joke, Master Abrams shook his head. "I had meant to tell you all of this in person, but seeing as you got stuck out in the wilderness and it'll likely take you some time to get back, I think it's better that I record this. What I'm about to tell you could be considered ancient history, but if you're going to continue to practice the Cutting Palm, it's important that you know. Contained on this data stick is the history of our martial art, as well as the names of all of your predecessors. In truth, I don't really care if you continue the line of the Cutting Palm. Apart from you, it's unlikely that anybody will be able to master it.

"As for why, it's really pretty simple. Whatever they're pumping into the water supply these days is doing something to people, doing something to their brains, changing them in subtle ways that make them incompatible with the final level of the Cutting Palm technique. Of course, why you're different, I have no idea. I've never seen anyone make progress like you do, and if you can't master the Cutting Palm, then it might as well rot in a corner, because there is no hope for anyone else. Like I said, I don't care if you master it or not, so don't feel pressured. I'm about to die, so it's not going to matter to me anyway. I'm just happy that the art is not dying with me." Master Abrams's expression relaxed, and he seemed to grow lighter, as if he had been carrying a heavy burden and now it had slipped away.

"I should have introduced you to the others and helped you become a member of the Order of Blood, but the rule is that you can only become a member once you've mastered the last stage of the Cutting Palm technique. You can read more about the order's history and why it exists in the information I included. All you need to know is that there are three other members left: Lemuel, Paris, and Orin. Originally, there were ten of us, but no more. The Order of Blood is divided into three different groups.

"Master Lemuel and I practiced the physical arts, Master Paris is the last ghost practitioner, and Master Orin is a seer. Like me, they don't have anyone to pass their legacies on to, so I would expect those legacies to die with them. Now, don't tell them I said this, but if you're especially nice to them, there's always a chance that they'll pass on their arts to you. Anyway, there's no need to feel sad after I'm gone. Like I said, I've lived a long life, much longer than I had any right to, and seeing how quickly you've mastered the Cutting Palm gives me hope for the future.

"Good luck, kid."

Mark sat in silence for a long time after the image had faded, and only after Mime nudged his hand with her nose did he sigh and begin to read through the files on the data stick. They read like a history textbook and revealed much Mark hadn't known before, giving him a clearer picture of the past.

According to what he read, the first attacks on New Emery had come almost a hundred years ago, in the form of mutated creatures that swarmed toward the city. At the time, empowered humans didn't exist, and no one had any clue what those creatures were. The military found its weapons largely ineffective, and the attack was only defeated after a group of martial artists from different disciplines had banded together to drive the monsters back.

That first wave had shaken society drastically, and it was only thanks to that alliance of martial artists that humanity had survived the following years. Thus was the Order of Blood established, as a bastion against the increasingly ferocious waves of monsters roaming the world.

For a time, the martial artists formed the backbone of society, until, around seventy years ago, a group of scientists who had been studying the monsters suggested that it might be possible to learn to wield mana, as the monsters did. The martial artists, fearing the corruption of their arts, turned down the suggestion, but over time, the idea gained such support that there was no way for them to keep people from experimenting.

Martial arts required talent, dedication, and years of work, while the empowered could wield mana as soon as they gained their abilities. After the first few empowered appeared, martial arts quickly fell out of favor as a new class of power-wielding people took control of the city.

The original alliance of martial artists, called the Order of Blood in honor of the blood shed in defense of New Emery, was forgotten, and one by one, the powerful martial disciplines were abandoned in favor of the much easier empowerment. This trend was solidified when the first children began to gain abilities, practically guaranteeing the martial traditions would be ignored.

Now, of the original twenty transcendent martial arts, only four remained. The Cutting Palm, passed from Master Abrams to Mark. The Northern Glimmer Sword, a blade-based martial art practiced by Master Lemuel. The Frozen Specter Art, practiced by Master Paris. And the Mysterious Star-Gazing Eye, practiced by Master Orin. The other martial arts had been lost, the majority of them taken to the grave, as the masters who practiced them died without apprentices.

It was a rather depressing history, and as Mark sat at his kitchen table, he felt a new weight on his shoulders. Obviously Master Abrams hadn't wanted to pass on his burden to Mark, but it was impossible to learn the history of the Cutting Palm and not feel a sense of responsibility.

Unfortunately, Mark wasn't yet a master of the Cutting Palm, as he had yet to learn the third and final stage. According to what Master Abrams had said, it wasn't actually something he could practice—it would only come with enlightenment. That didn't stop Mark from trying, but no matter how he tried to imitate the three different strikes he had seen, one from Master Abrams, one from Master Lemuel, and one from Jason, he couldn't seem to find the trick to projecting his mental energy with such force that it would directly harm the physical world.

It was now early in the morning, so he decided to give up. Almost as soon as his head touched the pillow, he was asleep, immersed in his usual dream of the wilderness. He still appeared in the base outside Felwer Mine, and after casually dispatching the screamer that lurked there, Mark headed out to explore.

Recently, he had been mapping the areas around the base, hunting Exlian whenever he encountered them while he explored the mountains and valleys. In truth, he didn't know exactly what he was looking for, but he could feel a faint tug at his spirit, driving him to continue searching. Over the course of six hours in the dilated time of the dream, he managed to explore half of a valley he had never been in before. Then the dream ended, and his eyes snapped open.

Sitting up with a yawn, he grabbed one of the nutrient pouches from beside his bed and gulped its contents down before standing up and stretching. Since he didn't have a whole lot of space in the apartment itself, he headed down to the gym attached to the complex and worked out for a couple of hours, being careful not to reveal his powers. He still found himself getting more than a few strange looks, so he decided that in the future, he would just go to the training room at the association headquarters.

After he had showered, he heard a knock at his door. Opening it revealed Sky standing in the hallway, dressed in street clothes.

"You sure you don't want some breakfast?" she said as she walked into the apartment. "Come on, let me buy something for you. I still owe you a fortune, so we can count it as interest. Besides, you treated me all those times. It's the least I could do."

Mark had fully expected to feel awkward facing Sky given the interest he had previously shown, but as soon as he saw her, all his awkwardness seemed to melt away, replaced by a warm happiness. "Let's get breakfast, but we'll have to make it quick. I don't want to be late for my appointment."

An hour later, they arrived at the Hunters' Association after grabbing a quick bite to eat at a stall near the train station. Sky looked around with considerable interest while Mark checked in at the kiosk. A few minutes later, one of the attendants arrived and asked if Mark was Jonathan Leeds. About to shake his head,

Mark felt Sky's elbow jab him and turned his headshake into a cough. "Ahem. Yeah, that's me."

"You can follow me. However, we don't allow just anyone to observe the assessment."

"I'm not just anyone," Sky said quickly, looping her arm through Mark's. "I'm his sister."

Looking at Sky and then back at Mark, the attendant raised his eyebrows. The two of them looked nothing alike, but Mark, prompted by the pressure on his arm, nodded to confirm Sky's claim. Though the attendant clearly didn't believe them, he just snorted and led them back through the hallways to a large training room with half a dozen combat rings. One of the rings was occupied by a man and a woman who appeared to be sparring, but otherwise, the room was quiet.

The attendant directed Mark to a set of machines in the back. "We'll be testing your basic stats, as they determine your rank. We don't test powers here, since they're too variable. The second portion of the assessment will be combat. You'll be asked to spar against one of our trainers."

"Sounds good," Mark said, rolling his shoulders to limber them up as he stepped in front of the strength-testing machine.

It was a relatively simple device with a horizontal bar that he could use to test his strength, as well as a striking surface. Gripping the bar, Mark began to pull it toward him, feeling increasing resistance as he tugged it toward his chest. After he had pulled it as far as he could, he returned it to its resting position, then stepped underneath it, lowering his body into a squat before explosively pushing the bar upward.

Noting something down, the attendant directed him to strike the target, and after shaking out his arms, Mark stepped forward, unleashing his heaviest punch. His fist slammed into the target with a dull thud, the machine absorbing all his strength. To Mark, it felt like he had punched a pillow, as if the power he had generated had vanished into an abyss. It was an unsettling feeling, and Mark had to suppress the urge to unleash a Cutting Palm strike. The machine had no display, so Mark couldn't tell how he had scored, and the attendant didn't seem concerned with it either.

After the strength test was done, Mark was taken to another machine that tested his reaction speed, and then he was asked to sprint a hundred meters as fast as he could. The fortitude test required him to step into a chamber that used air pressure to test the resilience of Mark's skin by pressing in on him from all sides. It was uncomfortable for a few seconds, but Mark found his body rapidly adjusting, even when the pressure grew almost unbearably strong.

Mark was most curious about how they were going to test his willpower, and he was surprised when it turned out to be the simplest test of all. His hand was hooked up to a series of clamps, and when the attendant flipped a switch, a thin current of mana ran through Mark's fingers into his palm. To Mark's knowledge, no one other than himself could see mana, but that didn't mean that they couldn't control it. The higher an individual's will, the finer their mana control. Of course, Mark could not only see the flow of mana but, with a thought, could influence it in ways other empowered couldn't. Worried that might mess with the reading, he instead tried to relax completely, allowing the mana to run its natural course through his palm.

When the last test finished, the attendant produced a short report, which he showed to Mark. "Here are your stats. We have strength, fortitude, and will all in the B rank, while speed is C ranked. This puts you at the low end of the B rank, which is higher than we initially anticipated. I see that you're still a level-two hunter. In order to become a level-three hunter, you'll need to accumulate five thousand points."

"Do I have to spend the points to become level three?"

"No, it works on an accumulation basis. No matter what you spend them on, or even if you choose to keep them, you'll qualify by reaching the threshold. Now, are you ready for the combat test?"

Mark nodded, his eyes still fixed on the report. It didn't give much information and matched his own status readings closely, though Mark had a feeling that it didn't accurately capture his abilities. For example, the assessment had measured his raw strength and punching power but hadn't taken his Cutting Palm into account at all. He'd also been punching without using his bone blade transformation, and he was confident that would have let him strike even harder. He hadn't activated his Python's might either, with which he could exert one and a half times his normal strength. Similarly, the test of his fortitude hadn't included his regeneration or his mana shield.

As he was thinking, Mark followed the attendant to a nearby ring, Sky trailing behind him.

"If you'll wait here for a moment, I'll go and get the trainer," said the attendant before hurrying off.

Sky stepped close to Mark, lowering her voice conspiratorially. "How did your stats go up so much? Weren't you D ranked before?"

Mark's lips twitched as he tried to figure out how to explain all that had happened to him in a simple sentence.

"Going out into the wilderness and then spending some time, uh, away really accelerated my growth," he said, slipping the report into his pocket.

"I'll say. I'm barely at the upper end of D ranked, and you're already B ranked? That's kind of crazy."

To Mark, it felt as if his strength had grown normally. But hearing Sky's incredulous words, he realized just how abnormal it was. A year and a half ago, he was D ranked, and now, he was solidly B ranked. Considering his potential had been judged no higher than C, it was truly bizarre. Most empowered would take years to go up a single rank, let alone two. Then again, most other empowered didn't grow by directly consuming Exlian . . .

Before he could reply, the attendant came back, leading a middle-aged woman with curly brown hair tied back in a loose ponytail. Her features were sharp, her eyes sharper. And as she looked Mark over, he felt a faint prickle, as if her gaze were a needle stabbing into his skin. The intensity of her gaze caused Sky to retreat half a step behind Mark, and it put him on guard.

"This is Instructor Sarda. She'll be testing your combat skill."

"A pleasure to meet you," Inspector Sarda said, holding her hand out toward Mark.

Taking a step forward, Mark calmed his jumping nerves and shook her hand. He found himself having trouble getting a read on the instructor and wasn't sure if the faint sense of intimidation he felt was because of her higher rank or her abilities. Figuring he would soon find out, he climbed into the ring after her, facing off with around fifteen feet between them.

Standing solidly in the center of the ring, Instructor Sarda looked over Mark again. "Your profile says that you're a close-combat fighter. Is that correct?"

"It is."

"And what sort of role do you see yourself playing in a team?"

"Well," Mark said, scratching his head, "I'm not completely sure, but I think that I could be either a tank or a melee striker. Most of my abilities are oriented toward defense."

"In that case, I'm going to attack. Do your best to defend."

Stretching out her hand, Instructor Sarda clenched her fingers around a rod made of mana that appeared in the air in front of her. Mark had seen this ability before, when his friend Danny had summoned a mace. The weapon, made from pure mana, would be practically indestructible and could be summoned and dismissed at will by its wielder.

Instructor Sarda darted forward, heading straight toward Mark, her rod lifting into the air. Suppressing his impulse to attack, Mark was still shifting into a defensive stance when the instructor blurred and he lost sight of her. Instinctively, his body twisted toward the left, his arm lifting to block the blow that came at his head. There was a meaty thwack as Instructor Sarda's rod slammed into the mana shield that materialized above his arm, sending a tremor of force through the shield, shaking Mark's stance. Instead of fighting it, he let the tremor roll through him, softening his stance ever so slightly to absorb the impact.

Then, as she withdrew her rod for a second strike, Mark borrowed the rebounding force and lunged forward, his hand reaching for the instructor's shirt. She reacted instantly, shifting the trajectory of her weapon to knock Mark's wrist with the butt end of her rod while flicking a rapid attack straight toward his throat. Mark didn't even blink but continued surging forward. At the last second, fearing that her rod would crush his throat, Sarda pulled the attack back and rapidly distanced herself. Realizing from her glare that she had misunderstood him, Mark stopped instead of continuing to chase after her.

"Is everything okay, Instructor?" he asked.

At first, she just looked at him, as if biting back a scathing rebuke, before sighing and gesturing with her weapon. "What would you have done if I had hit your throat?"

Realizing what the problem was, Mark held out one arm and, using his other hand, carved a deep gash in his flesh, causing blood to well up. Instructor Sarda's eyes widened, then widened even further when she saw the wound he had just caused rapidly vanishing.

"I have an incredibly high level of regeneration," Mark said. "Enough to heal just about any wound that doesn't immediately kill me. But even without the regeneration, your attack wouldn't have hit."

Taking two steps forward to stand in the center of the ring, he held out his arms to either side. "You can go ahead and attack. Doesn't matter where. I'll show you what I mean."

Though hesitant, the instructor stepped forward and jabbed with the end of her rod, stabbing straight toward Mark's heart. Just before the rod reached his chest, a mana shield appeared, blocking the blow. That didn't deter her, as Instructor Sarda took a step forward and to the side, borrowing the counterforce to swing her rod around in a rapid loop, slashing toward Mark's shoulder. Again, her blow glanced off a barrier that materialized at the last moment.

Unable to believe what she was seeing, Sarda unleashed a swarm of rapid strikes, only to find that each one was blocked before it could hit Mark. For a full three minutes, she hammered away at his body, and by the end, she was breathing heavily as she exerted her full strength to try to crush him. Finally, with a disgusted click of her tongue, she tossed the rod away. As soon as it left her fingers, it melted into the air, and she crossed her arms over her chest and stared at Mark.

"What do you think, Instructor?" Mark asked with a smile. "Have I passed the assessment?"

"I'd say," Instructor Sarda said, suppressing a laugh. "You're a walking wall. My attacks are only B ranked, but against somebody at this level, you're practically invulnerable. How do your shields fare against sharp attacks?"

"The same," Mark replied with a shrug, following Instructor Sarda out of the ring. "The only way to get through them, at least to my knowledge, is overpowering force."

"Do they just block physical attacks?"

"No, they block mana as well, though the stronger the attack, the longer the shields take to recharge. Against C-ranked attacks and below, they'll block practically any number. Against B ranked, it's possible to overwhelm them. And against A ranked, well, hopefully, I never have to find out." Mark delivered his words with a wry smile, causing Instructor Sarda to laugh.

"Well, you passed the assessment with flying colors. Here, take my contact number. I know a number of people who are looking for tanks, and I'd be happy to pass your name along to them, if you're interested."

"Sure, that'd be great," Mark said, exchanging information with the instructor. "Thank you very much."

With a wave, Instructor Sarda left, and after confirming with the attendant that everything was in order and that he could now take missions, Mark and Sky left the training hall.

"And here I thought I was strong," Sky said, shaking her head. "You know, I've always wondered why you were willing to give me that skill gem, but now it makes perfect sense. An inbuilt shield and regeneration? That's a ridiculous combination."

"I don't know. Flight is pretty good," Mark said as they walked down the hallway toward the store.

"Sure, flight is good, but if I ever got into a direct fight with you, I wouldn't last two seconds."

She was right, of course, so Mark just offered a smile.

The store was massive, filled with all sorts of different equipment and gear that hunters might need as they ventured out of the city to complete their requests. Mark's primary interest was in finding a mana suit. He had been thinking long and hard about the various kinds of suits he might use and was hoping to find something that would enhance rather than detract from his powers.

The store had an entire section for mana suits, with four different kinds on display, along with numerous accessories that could be used to customize them. Unlike the military, which preferred standardized suits, hunters were known for customizing theirs, tuning them to fit their specific power sets. Mark was planning on doing the same thing. He had no idea what had happened to the suit he had cobbled together out in the wilderness, but even if he'd still had it, he figured it would be a better idea to get something a bit more professionally tailored.

The four suit types ranged from the massive Titan suit, which stood close to ten feet tall and couldn't fit through a doorway, to an incredibly slim suit that reminded Mark of the gear a researcher might wear in a laboratory. The other two suits were in between, but all of them had extra mechanical arms and various attachment points where weapons and other gear could be added. Noah had been quite generous in filling Mark's bank account when he established this new identity, but as Mark looked at the price tags for the various suits, he couldn't help but grimace.

Seeing him, an attendant hurried over with a wide smile.

"I need a new suit," Mark said, and pointed at the lightest one. "I'm looking for something like that."

The attendant was professional and barely showed his disappointment. Instead, he stepped forward and began enthusiastically detailing the features for Mark. "This is the Cloud III, a suit designed for researchers and anyone else who needs to be able to deploy scientific instruments while out in the wilderness. Unlike our previous Cloud versions, this one has added plating on the chest, legs, and arms. Even more importantly, it has a four-week run time, even at the highest energy-usage levels. The entire thing barely weighs sixty pounds, and you've got four anchor points, two on the back and two on the ribs, where additional mechanical arms or other kinds of equipment can be attached. Would you like to try it on?"

"How thick is the armor?" Mark asked, leaning in to get a better look.

"Between the cloth, plates, and padding, it's only three-quarters of an inch thick. Of course, this maximizes your freedom of movement, but it does sacrifice some of the defensive capability of the suit."

"That's fine," Mark said. "In fact, it's practically perfect. Does it come in a color other than white?"

"Of course, we can get it in any color you want."

"What about camo patterns?"

"Sure, let me grab the book that has all of the different color options."

"You know," Sky said as the attendant walked back toward the desk, "if someone told me they were going to buy a mana suit with as little armor as possible, I'd say they were crazy. But given your shield, I guess it makes sense."

Running his fingers along the cloth-covered armor plates, Mark nodded. "Three-quarters of an inch is just about perfect. The shield materializes just over an inch away from my body. This means that I'll be able to activate the shield without interfering with my armor. Plus, I need a suit that will still allow me to use martial arts, which means complete flexibility. A lot of suits won't allow for specific movements, so that's important. Plus, this suit's a lot lighter than the others, which means that even in the event of an emergency, when I can't run the mana system, I'll still be able to move around. What about you? What kind of mana suit are you using these days?"

"Not even a full one," Sky replied with a rueful smile. "My power won't activate if I have a suit over fifty pounds, but my unit gave me a modified suit that's fairly typical for couriers. It's really just there to give me a bit of protection and a stabilization platform for my crossbow. I think my suit weighs fifteen pounds in total, my crossbow weighs another five, and I have maybe five pounds of gear in addition. So overall, my kit is really light. But the good news is that my weight limit is slowly increasing as I get stronger."

"That is good news. Do you know how high it's going to be when you hit A rank?"

"*If* I hit A rank," Sky said, shaking her head. "I'm still not convinced that I'm going to be able to do it. But supposedly, with every rank I go up, it's going to more than double. I'm low C right now, so by the time I hit B rank, it'll be a bit over a hundred pounds. And at A it'll be closer to two hundred fifty."

"Which means you'll be able to use a full suit and fly around. Terrifying."

The attendant soon returned with a booklet for Mark to flip through. After a bit of consideration, Mark settled on a gray color that would shift with the lighting conditions, growing darker the less light was present. Mark didn't bother with any accessories, though he did spend money on customizing the suit's helmet, adding the mask Master Lemuel had given him to the faceplate. The suit he was getting was largely stock and, according to the attendant, would only take four hours to put together, so Mark and Sky headed for the large cafeteria to get something to eat while they waited.

"Hey, thanks for coming with me," Mark said as they sat down with their food. "I'm sure you have a lot to do, so I really appreciate it."

"It's fun," Sky said with a smile. "Way more fun than sitting alone in my apartment, which is what I'd do if you weren't around. It's my day off today anyway, and these days when I'm not patrolling, I mostly just sit around."

"You're working with the Defense Force, right?"

"I am. Most days I'm on patrol, making sure that there are no issues around the city. Sometimes they have me monitoring specific buildings or individuals inside the city. But for the most part, I'm just making loops around New Emery."

"How long does it take you? I mean, to make a complete loop?"

"Well, depends," Sky said, poking at her food with her fork. "At full speed, maybe five minutes. But at that speed, I can hardly see anything. The world blurs a bit too much. It takes me roughly an hour to make a normal loop and double-check that each of the watchtowers is fine and doesn't need any help. So I'll normally do that four or five times a shift. I'm probably the fastest of the couriers, so occasionally they'll deploy me to send a message to one of our forward bases."

"You mean outside the city?"

"Yeah, just on the edge of the dead zone, though. For the most part, the dead zone doesn't have any real threats, or at least any flying threats. But I still find it rather nerve racking to leave the walls. But what about you? I know you're going to be a hunter now, but are you planning on joining a group?"

"For my first few requests, at least," Mark said, tearing a chunk of bread from his roll. He hesitated for a moment and sighed. "If I'm honest, I don't yet feel like I have my bearings, so I don't know. I'll give this hunter thing a try for a while, but I'd also like to maybe see about working as an alchemist."

"You could always do both. I mean, it would allow you to practice alchemy and hunt for your own ingredients."

"That's true."

Silence fell over the table as the conversation reached a lull, and just when Mark was trying to think up something to say, Sky looked up from her food, tucking a strand of her hair behind her ear. "Have you heard from Noah at all?"

Caught off guard, Mark looked at Sky blankly, catching a faint blush on her cheeks. "Noah? Uh, I mean, a bit? We message back and forth. Don't you have his number?"

Sky's blush deepened, and she poked at her food with her fork. "Yes, but I can't just message him for no reason."

"Why not? You message me for no reason all the time."

Rolling her eyes, Sky recovered her composure, making Mark wonder if he had been seeing things. "Sure, but you're not incredibly hot, Mark."

"Hey! I'm not that bad looking."

Though he protested, Mark couldn't help but feel a bit of relief. He hadn't known how to broach his change in feelings with

Sky, but it was becoming clear that he didn't have to. Earlier Sky had pretended to be his sister when she could have claimed to be his girlfriend, and now she was showing her interest in his friend, making Mark confident that she wasn't expecting anything romantic from him.

"Excuse me, are you, uh, Apex? Jonathan Leeds?"

Looking up, Mark saw a handsome man around thirty standing a few feet away, his arms crossed over his chest. He wore a jumpsuit with an unusually thick weave and had a shock of brown hair that poked up in every direction. There was something incredibly solid about him, as if his legs borrowed strength from the earth, keeping him firmly planted in place.

Half rising from his seat, Mark nodded. "That's me. You are . . ."

"You can call me Terra. I lead Earthbond, a hunting team. An instructor, Sarda, said you might be looking to join a team. You mind if I sit?"

"No, please. Have a seat," Mark said.

With a smile and nod toward Sky, Terra slid into the seat next to Mark. "Do you go by Jonathan or Apex?"

"Apex."

"It's an impressive name. I like it quite a bit," Terra said. "Obviously, Terra's a nickname for me as well. Tom's my birth name, but everybody's been calling me Terra for so long that that's what I'm used to. It's not often that Instructor Sarda recommends a hunter, so I thought I'd see if I could beat the crowds that are no doubt headed your way and catch you early. As I mentioned, I'm the leader of the Earthbond team. We have a total of four people, down from six after our last mission. The team consists of me; a werecat named Apora; Zem, who's our scout; and a speedster who goes by Brightblade. I'm a level-three hunter. The others are all level two. I'm the only B-ranked member of the team, and the others are C ranked. So we could really use another B-ranked empowered, especially a tank."

Mark listened quietly, tearing pieces of his roll off as Terra continued to describe the team. Their previous mission had been a success, albeit a mixed one, as two of their members, a pair of brothers who worked as frontline fighters, had died. Noticing how Mark's gaze shifted when he mentioned it, Terra rubbed the back of his head.

"I hate to say anything bad about fellow hunters, especially ones who are dead, but the brothers weren't very smart and split up with the rest of the party while they went to explore a building. They ran into a small swarm of mantises, and by the time we got to them, they had been ripped apart. Given how foolhardy they often were, it was only a matter of time. We managed to kill the mantises and retreat back to the city, and now we're stuck here until we can find somebody else to tank for us."

"What sort of missions do you normally take?" Mark asked, picking up his cup.

"We tend to focus on extermination missions," Terra replied, gazing directly back. "We find that they're the most efficient. These requests normally come from the Defense Force when they locate groups of Exlian moving in toward the city. We're usually one of the teams that head out of the gate to deal with them. Sometimes we'll take requests to disrupt gathering Exlian before they can swarm. We try to confine our targets to C-ranked Exlian and below, but the dead zones are unpredictable. Since we're operating as part of a larger group, however, we can always call in backup if we stumble upon a target that's out of our league."

Terra gave Mark a very steady feeling, and he found himself inclined to agree to Terra's request. When he glanced over at Sky to see what she thought, she gave him a short nod.

"All right, I'm in."

"Excellent, I'm glad to hear it. We were waiting to find a tank before deploying, so we've got something lined up immediately for tomorrow morning. Why don't you grab your gear and come and meet the team?"

"About that, I'm actually waiting on a new mana suit," Mark said. "The one I was using before got scrapped. It's supposed to be done this afternoon."

"Great, that works out perfectly. Once you pick it up, how about you meet me and the rest of the team in the training room? It'd be good to get a sense of your fighting style, and I'm sure the others will be excited to meet you."

Standing up, Terra reached across the table to shake Mark's hand, then hurried away to find the rest of his team.

"Well, look at that. Not even a day goes by, and you're already plugged in," Sky said with a grin.

"We'll see if it lasts."

If she noticed the faint bitterness laced in his tone, Sky didn't say anything, instead changing the subject to talk about recent events in the city. For the most part, Mark listened quietly, his thoughts occupied by this new team he was joining.

Around half an hour after Terra had left, Mark received a file that contained the profiles of his four new teammates. Terra was a B-ranked earth controller, able to manipulate dirt and stone to form instantaneous fortifications. His power set seemed to be focused on controlling the battlefield, and he could not only attack and defend but also trap opponents in place.

The second member of the team, Apora, could transform her body, gaining animal characteristics that allowed her access to special abilities. In her case, the C-ranked werecat gained increased agility and sharp claws that could tear through metal. The team's scout and ranged attacker was Zem, a young woman with bright-red hair who used a military-issue repeating crossbow loaded with all sorts of different bolts. The speedster of the team, Brightblade, wielded a pair of double swords.

A few hours later, after watching his bank account rapidly empty and acquiring his new mana suit, Mark said goodbye to Sky, geared up, and headed for the training room. Walking in, he saw Terra waving in the distance and headed over. His new teammates were already dressed in their mana suits. Terra was in a large one that bore brown and yellow markings and boasted heavy armor. Apora wore a very light suit, specially customized to allow her to take advantage of her transformation. Similarly, Zem was dressed in scout armor, while Brightblade wore the more standard knight's attire. When they saw Mark's practically armorless suit, they exchanged glances, and Apora spoke up in a gruff voice: "I thought you said he was a tank. He looks more like a researcher to me."

"He is a tank," Terra said. "At least, that's what Instructor Sarda said."

Mark wasn't offended by the skeptical looks; in fact, he had expected them. After all, he was standing there in less armor than any of the others, despite the fact that his role would be to stand out in front of the group and absorb enemy attacks.

"Hello, everyone, my name is Apex. I'm relatively new to this whole hunting thing, though not new to killing Exlian. A pleasure to meet you all."

There was a scattered chorus of hellos, and then Terra, still looking at Mark's armor, gave him a half-hearted smile. "Well, since you'll be joining us for this next mission, why don't we go ahead and do a bit of sparring, you know, so we can get used to your combat style."

"Sure." Looking thoughtfully at the others, Mark nodded. "I think that's a good idea."

"And how would you like to do this?" Terra asked.

"I think the best thing would be to have all four of you attack me," Mark replied with a straight face. "It'll help me get a good sense of your combat rhythms and, hopefully, allow me to demonstrate my abilities."

"You want all of us to attack you? Like, at the same time?" Apora asked. "Are you sure about that?"

"Yeah, I think that's going to be the most efficient way to do this, though it'd be nice if we had somewhere a little bit bigger. I'm afraid we might damage the training room if we really get into it."

Just then, Instructor Sarda jogged over.

"I've got a place for you," she said with a wide smile. "We can use one of the combat halls in the back. I'm between classes, so you guys can use the space."

"Great, that would work well," Terra said. "Thank you."

"Oh, sure. Happy to help," the instructor replied, falling in beside Mark as they made their way out of the hall and down a flight of stairs.

Instructor Sarda led them to a massive, empty room the size of a warehouse, and as soon as Mark walked in, he sensed a subtle layer of mana coating everything. Blinking, he activated his mana sight and saw that the walls, floor, and even ceiling were covered in an incredibly dense, complex mana pattern, with lines running everywhere.

"This is one of the combat halls," Sarda said. "This is where I run my classes and give people training, which you can pay for if you ever want to polish up your skills. The floor and walls are practically indestructible, and any damage you do cause will self-repair, so you can really cut loose in here. Be careful, though, because there are no safety measures. You spar at your own risk, but you're welcome to go ahead. We'll just need to be out of here in an hour and a half."

"I think that'll be more than enough time," Terra replied.

"Won't you be at a disadvantage?" Mark asked, looking down at the hard cement floor. "Don't your powers work better when you have access to earth?"

"You don't need to worry about it," Terra replied. Reaching

out, he snapped his fingers, and a spike of hardened earth rose up in front of him. "The combat halls can simulate almost any environment, so a person with elemental control can use their abilities freely in here."

"That's good," Mark said, taking up his place across from the others. "I'm ready when you are."

Still looking rather unsure about the arrangement, Terra glanced at the others and then turned back to Mark, opening his mouth to say something. But before he could get any words out, there was a hiss, and a crossbow bolt ripped through the air, heading straight for Mark. He had been expecting more talk and was caught off guard by the sudden strike, but he noticed that the attack was headed for his shoulder, rather than his heart. So he simply lifted his hand and brushed the bolt aside. With a crackle, the mana-infused tip hit the mana shield that formed around his hand, and then the bolt diverted, flying past him to slam into the wall.

At the same time, Apora let out a sharp yell and bounded forward on all fours, rapidly covering the distance between her and Mark. Brightblade was right behind her, his body moving with supernatural smoothness as he lifted his swords to attack. Rather than focus on the two fighters hurtling toward him, Mark kept his eyes on Zem and Terra. Zem's crossbow had already reloaded, and she crouched next to Terra, readying her next shot. Meanwhile, Terra had thrust out his hands, and Mark could see him muttering something under his breath. A faint surge of mana coiled around Mark's feet, a sure sign that Terra was trying to manipulate the ground beneath him.

Mark waited until the last second, then suddenly darted forward and to the side, taking himself out of range of the stone that suddenly rose to envelop the space his feet had been a moment earlier. His impeccable timing disrupted Apora's leap as well, forcing her to shorten the distance she was traveling. Abandoning any sort of defense, Mark activated Python's might and threw his fist toward Apora's chest. Her claws caught his arm first, but just when she thought she could rip through the armor, a mana shield appeared, and her claws failed to find purchase and slipped off.

In the brief moment before Mark's fist slammed into her, she managed to twist her upper body, preventing him from landing a clean strike. But he didn't slow down, taking another step forward and unleashing a kick even before his punch hit. Despite suffering only a glancing blow, Apora was hammered down into the ground, and a moment later Mark's foot caught her in the stomach, sending her rolling across the floor.

It was at that moment that Zem's second arrow and Brightblade's swords arrived. Realizing they were going to strike at exactly the same time, Mark shifted his body, ensuring that the swords struck first, giving him a tenth of a second before he had to deal with the arrow. Though that tenth of a second wasn't long, it was just enough time for Mark's mana shields to recharge, causing both attacks to bounce off him harmlessly. By this time, Brightblade had realized that something was going wrong, and he rapidly retreated, slipping out of Mark's range before he could strike.

Cracking a grin, Mark took off running straight for Terra and Zem. Terra summoned a wall of spikes that rose up in front of Mark, but rather than jump over them or try to maneuver around them, Mark simply slammed into the spikes at full speed, crushing the hardened earth and sending clods of dirt flying through the air. When he emerged on the other side, slightly slower but none the worse for wear, Terra's expression grew ugly.

Because the mana shields only appeared when attacks were about to strike Mark's body and then promptly vanished, they were surprisingly hard to spot, and as long as he avoided being hit by multiple attacks at the same time, the mana shields made him almost completely invulnerable. With them as well as his strength and fortitude, Mark was little different from a war bear, and he could see the same sort of dread a war bear might cause settling on the others.

As he closed the distance between him and Terra, Apora hit him from behind, but Mark simply ignored her, and her claws once again slipped off him without ever truly touching his armor. Realizing what he was trying to do, Brightblade slipped between him and Terra, his swords stabbing toward Mark's legs and shoulder. Rather than dodge, Mark lifted his hands.

Flicking the point of one sword aside, he simultaneously dodged the strike heading toward his legs. He shifted his body and slammed his palm into Brightblade's side. There was a faint crunch, and with a grunt, Brightblade staggered away. Mark followed up with a fierce chop, but Brightblade was too fast, stepping back out of his range before his attack could land.

Mark felt a faint sense of threat and spun around as Zem, only ten feet away, launched another bolt straight at the middle of his chest. He focused, reinforcing the shield there. The bolt struck with a solid thwack, forcing Mark back a few steps before it dropped to the ground, splintered.

"You've got to be kidding me," Zem muttered, shaking her head and standing up. "That was point-blank range."

Rather than continue to attack, Mark just shrugged and looked at Terra, who had already lifted his helmet's mask.

"Are you just completely invulnerable?" Terra asked, staring at Mark as if he had grown two heads.

"My ability is similar to a war bear's," Mark said. "It's an autonomously deploying mana shield."

"So that's why you kept adjusting how you were hit," Apora said, walking closer with a long, loping gait. "You needed to make sure you weren't being struck simultaneously in multiple places."

When she saw the others looking at her, she grimaced and rubbed her chest, where Mark's fist had slammed into her. "A war bear's mana shields are almost impossible to break without overwhelming force, but they can only deploy one place at a time, which means if you can strike a war bear in multiple locations simultaneously, you have a chance to hurt it."

"That's right," Mark said. "That's why I tried to deal with each attack one at a time."

"I figured that out too," Brightblade said, "though it didn't help me much. What I want to know is, How are your attacks so sharp?" As he spoke, he lifted his arm to reveal the side of his suit, where one of the armor plates had been cracked. "It was like getting hit with a war pick."

Holding out his hands, palms up, Mark wiggled his fingers slightly. "I practice something called the Cutting Palm. It's a martial art. It allows me to transform my bare-handed attacks into the equivalent of a mana blade."

"I've heard of that," Brightblade said, sheathing his swords and coming close to look at Mark's hands.

"Normally, it's a lot more lethal," Mark said, "but only when I'm bare handed. I'll probably modify this suit so that it doesn't have gloves, or at least make them removable. I just picked it up, though, and I haven't had time."

"Okay, so this clears up a huge mystery," Terra said. "Here I was wondering why on earth you were using such a light suit, but I imagine having a heavy one would get in the way of your autonomous shield; is that correct?"

"Yes, the shield only manifests close to my skin, so having anything heavier than this would mean that my armor would get broken before the shield is hit. And besides, with my fighting style, I need the maneuverability. I admit it's going to look rather odd when we leave the city and I'm running around with the rest of you, but I'm confident in my strength."

"As you should be," Zem said, patting her crossbow. "You just took a bolt at point-blank range and barely even blinked."

"So what do you all think?" Instructor Sarda asked, walking over.

"I think we found our new tank," Apora said, giving Mark a nod. "I like your fighting style, and so long as we don't run into any terror-ranked Exlian, you should be able to block anything that they throw at us."

"Even better, you can be aggressive," Terra said, "which means you'll draw even more attention, as Exlian like to focus on the largest threat. However, I feel like we barely even got to show you our abilities. Instructor Sarda, do you mind if we continue to use the facility, at least for a little bit?"

"Oh, go ahead. We've still got plenty of time."

"Thank you," Terra said. "Let's show our new teammate what we can do, folks."

Though they hadn't gotten a chance to show off much thanks to Mark's astonishing defensive ability, he had gotten a hint of how strong the team was, and for the next hour, as they demonstrated their various abilities and talked through how they liked to handle different situations, Mark found himself quite impressed. Of course, his last team had consisted of the S-ranked Winter Wolf, the insane killer Joker, and two other very strong empowered. Comparatively, the Earthbond team wasn't that impressive, but they were more than strong enough for Mark to trust them at his back.

Terra's earth control was sharp and precise, allowing him to drastically change the battlefield in a short time. He could raise a labyrinth from blank ground, transforming an area into one giant, deadly trap as he launched attacks from the labyrinth walls. He could also "entomb" a target by creating a hole in the ground beneath them while the displaced earth rose up on all sides to trap them. Then he could attack at will or simply keep them locked away.

Apora and Brightblade had similar fighting styles, relying on speed and agility to launch their attacks. While Brightblade used typical mana swords, a thin layer of mana shrouded Apora's claws whenever she launched a strike. The primary difference between them was how they defended themselves. Brightblade moved in short, sharp bursts, pausing briefly between movements to reorient himself. As a C-ranked speedster, he moved as fast as a high B-ranked empowered, but the rest of his stats were low C. Of course, his mana suit made up for those deficiencies, providing him with increased strength and fortitude.

On the other hand, because of her transformation, Apora had to use a specialized suit, which didn't augment her body nearly as much. While Brightblade favored a hit-and-run style of fighting, keeping distance before moving in to strike swiftly and then retreating once more, Apora relied on her natural agility and inhuman flexibility to fight in melee range, tearing her opponent to shreds with her mana-empowered claws.

Zem, like Terra, had no desire to be in close combat and instead maintained a healthy distance from her target, launching bolt after bolt from her mana-empowered crossbow. It was a large and bulky thing that could reload automatically and cycle through a few different types of bolts. Mark had never seen anything like it, and he found himself fascinated as he watched new bolts appear to replace the ones that Zem had just shot. He sensed a brief flash of mana that reminded him of the teleportation box he had first seen down in the Tomb in Mr. Robot's chest, then later in the courier drone Maestro had sent to deliver his serum.

In a break during her demonstration, Mark asked Zem how the crossbow worked. "Where are those bolts coming from? The crossbow's not making them, is it?"

"No," Zem said, flipping the crossbow over to show Mark the rectangular box attached to the bottom. "This has a dimensional-transfer function. I've got specialized magazines at home that are loaded with bolts. I'm honestly not sure how exactly this works, but I can swap between them by rotating this dial. Once I have the bolt selected, I simply press this button here to complete the mana circuit, and it pulls the bolt in and loads it up much faster than doing it by hand. Plus, I don't have to carry all of the bolts with me. The crossbow can fire about five hundred before it needs to recharge, which is usually more than enough.

"My preference is to swap between armor piercing, which are these explosive-tipped bolts; shock, good for missions where we're trying to capture rather than kill; and stealth bolts, which are practically silent, making them good for ambushes. I have about half a dozen others that I can use as well. Things like coil bolts, which allow me to send strands of wire across gaps; shriekers, which have a remote-controlled noise generator for distractions; things like that."

As she spoke, Zem selected the armor-piercing bolts and pressed the button. Mark watched in fascination as the mana circuit in the bottom of the crossbow flared to life, causing the bolt to materialize before being pushed into position.

"That's pretty incredible," Mark said. "I wouldn't mind having a crossbow like that myself."

"Unfortunately, you can't buy them in the Hunters' Association store, but I can show you the shop that makes them," Zem said, engaging the safety and leaning the crossbow against her shoulder.

"I wonder why the Defense Force doesn't use devices like this. It seems like it would be really helpful in defending the walls."

"Because they're not efficient enough," Apora said, canceling her transformation. "They're good for hunters, but they don't load fast enough for a full-on assault."

"I don't know," Zem said with a shrug. "Some of the new ones are getting really fast."

"I'm starving," Brightblade said. "Why don't we go get something to eat?"

"That's a good idea," Terra replied. "It would be good to spend a little bit of time chatting about this upcoming mission. Come on, I know of a good place nearby. We can grab something to eat there."

"Not the cafeteria?" Mark asked, still watching as Zem skillfully took apart the crossbow and stored the pieces in a case.

"The cafeteria? Ugh, no," Apora said with a grimace. "It won't take you long before you'll find that the food they serve there is practically not worth eating."

"Apora's right," Terra said with a laugh. "There are actually dozens of small restaurants that have sprung up in the surrounding area, because most hunters who have been around for any length of time pretty much refuse to eat in the cafeteria."

After all their gear had been stowed and everyone had changed out of their mana suits, Terra led them out of the Hunters' Association and down the street to a small café, where they found a table in the corner and ordered their food. Mark had long since stopped caring what he ate, as long as it was in high enough volume to keep his biofuel meter full. So he chose the biggest thing on the menu without paying attention to what it was.

After they got their drinks, Terra turned the conversation to their upcoming mission, laying out the details for everyone. "There's been a spate of new sightings, mostly murder scorpions, south of the city. They seem to be moving in force. Thankfully, we're still dealing with the scouts rather than a wave, but it's still a good idea to be on our toes. After all, we never know when the wave is actually going to come."

"Ugh, murder scorpions? I hate murder scorpions," Brightblade muttered.

"Of course you do. Everybody hates murder scorpions," Apora chided, shaking her head.

"We'll be part of a whole bunch of different teams who are being recruited for this task," Terra said, ignoring his teammates. Tapping his watch, he projected a map onto the table and pointed at a section that had been marked in red. "We've got four square blocks to clear. This will be our search zone, and our goal is to make sure that there are no murder scorpions in that area. We lucked out this time, and there are no skyscrapers. However, records indicate that there was a garage here at one point. The upper two floors have collapsed, leaving only two floors aboveground."

"What about underground?" Zem asked, picking up her glass.

"Unfortunately, there are two floors underground too," Terra said, tapping on the garage's symbol with his finger.

"Oh, come on. Of course there are," Apora said, shaking her head. "I hate going underground, especially after murder scorpions."

"It shouldn't be so bad this time," Terra replied, glancing at Mark. "With Apex here, we shouldn't have to worry about close combat. As long as we approach it slowly and don't get surrounded, we'll be fine."

"Isn't 'approach it slowly and not get surrounded' always the plan?" Brightblade asked, causing the others to laugh.

"Well, yes," Terra admitted, "but now that we have a stable tank, we don't have to go as slowly as before, and we're much less worried about being surrounded."

"Fair point."

Turning to Mark, Terra smiled at him. "Do you have any questions?"

"Seems straightforward enough," Mark said, doing his best to memorize the layout. "I'm assuming we'll be starting in that block and clearing that area first?"

"Yes. If we don't, there's a good chance that the other Exlian will retreat to that location. Exlian, especially murder scorpions, like underground spaces. If we start there, we should be able to kill the majority of them. Then it's just a matter of hunting the rest down."

"That's always the most annoying part," Apora said. "Luckily, we have Zem and her radar."

Seeing that Mark was looking at her, Zem gave a half shrug. "One of my abilities is a danger sense. It allows me to pinpoint the location of the most dangerous thing in the area."

"Normally, it'd be good for running away," Terra said. "However, we use it to identify groups of Exlian and move toward them."

"Clever," Mark said, leaning back in his chair as the waiter arrived with their food.

He had just picked up his fork when he felt a faint tickle in the back of his mind, and his senses sharpened. Closing his eyes in a long blink, Mark focused on the psychic network, doing a quick scan of the surrounding area. Almost immediately, he got a faint hit, not nearly as bright as the typical Exlian but more illuminated than the gray marbles that represented Terra and the rest of the team. Whatever it was, it was behind him and to the left, likely standing right outside the restaurant's window. Putting his fork down, Mark pushed himself back from the table.

"Terra, do you know where the bathroom is?" he asked, glancing around.

"Yeah, if you take the hall back from the front door, it's over there," Terra replied, and with a nod, Mark got up, casually scanning the room.

He caught sight of a woman quickly pulling back from the front window, as if worried he might see her. Careful not to change his expression, Mark walked toward the hallway where the bathroom was, keeping track of the woman through the psychic network. When she started to retreat as Mark got to the front door, he split with a shiver, stepping left and right simultaneously. Mark went to the bathroom while his clone followed the woman, who had already disappeared around the corner. Mark's clones were, to all intents and purposes, no different from himself, so he had no trouble using the Exlian network to track her, though he had to stay out of sight, because if she saw him, the clone would cease to exist.

Thankfully, the woman seemed intent on not being seen as well. She made her way through the maze of back alleys until she arrived at a run-down laundromat and slipped inside. Mark's clone, getting close, couldn't help but frown. There were six other people in the building, three of whom had a faint presence in the psychic network, just like the woman did. This was the mark of a mutant and brought to mind the mad Prophet of Salvation. Mark didn't like the idea that he was being watched, especially by an organization as dangerous as that.

But before he could learn more, someone stepped out of a doorway down the street and glanced in Mark's direction. With a faint pop, his clone vanished, and the real Mark, who had come back from the bathroom and sat down at the table, shivered slightly as his divided mind merged back together. Not getting the chance to reabsorb his clone before it vanished meant that Mark was limited to what it could pass along through his watch, rather than the clone's firsthand experiences.

I really need to figure out a way to make my clones permanent.

"Apex, do you still need to get any gear, or are you good to go?" Terra's question interrupted Mark's thoughts.

Shaking his head, Mark finished the last bite of his food and put his fork down on the edge of his plate. "I should be good to go."

"Excellent. In that case, we'll plan on meeting tomorrow morning at six a.m."

"All right, sounds good." Pushing himself back from the table, Mark stood up and smiled at each of his new teammates in turn. "I'm looking forward to it. I'll see you all tomorrow." Accompanied by a chorus of goodbyes, he left the restaurant and, after hesitating for a moment, chose not to make his way to the laundromat where the woman who had been watching him had disappeared.

The last thing Mark wanted right now was to get involved any further with the mutants. Unfortunately, he had a sneaking suspicion that he wouldn't have a choice. Of course, it could have been just a coincidence that the mutant woman had been standing outside the restaurant. Just because she had looked in the window didn't mean that she had been looking at him. But even as he tried to make excuses, Mark knew that he was only fooling himself.

Dallas, the mad Prophet of Salvation, had spoken of five meetings, two of which had already happened. Mark was not looking forward to the next one. The farther away he stayed from the mutants and their cult, the happier he would be.

Thankfully, he didn't notice any other mutants as he made his way to the train station and caught a train back to his apartment. Once there, he plopped down on the couch, earning himself an annoyed look from Mime, who had been sleeping, sprawled out on the center cushion.

"Sorry for waking you, Mime," Mark said, reaching over to scratch her belly. "Are you going to come with me tomorrow?"

Rolling over on her back, Mime just gave Mark a calm look, as if to remind him that she was always nearby. Which was true, though he didn't quite understand how it worked. After spending a little bit of time petting Mime, Mark turned his attention to his preparations.

While he was away, a number of different boxes had been left at the building's front desk, and now that Mark was home, they had been carried up and delivered to his door. Among them was a variety of equipment, all things he might find useful out in the dead zone. Normally, hunters traveled light, as they rarely expected to be outside the city wall for more than a day or two at a time. Given his previous experience leaving the city, though, Mark had no interest in risking getting caught without gear.

Then again, it wasn't practical to carry a massive pack on his back filled with tents, lights, dried food, and the like. Instead, Mark organized all his gear into small groups of items that he might use at the same time. And then, after everything was laid out on the table, he pointed at each group in turn, watching as his shadow stretched its tendrils up and swallowed it. Ever since he had discovered this ability in the Tomb, it had become his favorite, and he found himself using it constantly.

Once everything had disappeared, Mark practiced retrieving each group, causing them to appear and then disappear from the table in rapid succession. It was a tremendously useful ability, and he had been experimenting with it in his downtime. So long as his shadow could reach an object, it could be absorbed and retrieved at will. Furthermore, Mark could control its placement to a significant degree.

Of course, he couldn't very well use his shadow where others could see it, so when he arrived at the gate early the next morning, already dressed in his mana suit, a small pack rested at the small of his back. Through extensive testing the night before, Mark had discovered that his shadow could deposit small objects inside the pack, which would make it look much more natural when he retrieved his energy bars.

Mark was the first to arrive, but the rest of the team showed up a few minutes later, and after doing one final check, Terra led them to the gate, where they scanned their IDs and left the city. As soon as they stepped out into the dead zone, Mark could sense the others tensing. He, on the other hand, felt as if a weight had suddenly been lifted from his shoulders, allowing him to relax. He hadn't noticed just how much pressure being in the city put on him. But now that they were outside the city wall, Mark suddenly felt free and easy.

"Let's move ahead two blocks, and then we'll pause to go over the plan one last time," Terra said, speaking through the team channel.

They set off at a swift pace, Mark jogging out front, his eyes scanning back and forth across the street for any sign of the Exlian. At the same time, he kept a close watch on the psychic network, but he didn't see any sign of the enemy. It only took them a few minutes to cover the two blocks, and then Terra called for a halt, leading them to a small alcove in front of a building, where they paused to get their bearings.

"All right, we're off to a good start," Terra said, projecting the map into the air for everyone to see. "We're about twenty blocks from our designated zone, and we'll need to be careful as we get closer. Reports of murder scorpions have been increasing. Zem, what do you have for us?"

"Let me check it out," Zem said, closing her eyes.

Mark felt rather than saw the trace mana that spread from Zem in a wave, and immediately his expression stiffened as he felt it bounce off him. Zem jumped up, her eyes snapping open as she stared over his head, her breathing growing hurried. The rest of the team reacted immediately, shifting into a defensive formation, their eyes scanning past Mark as they tried to spot the threat Zem had just identified.

"Wait, that can't be right," Zem said, half to herself.

Closing her eyes, she used her ability again, but she seemed to find the same result.

"What's it telling you?" Terra asked.

"It says that there's a major threat that way," Zem said, pointing back toward the city.

"But I don't understand. There shouldn't be any powerful Exlian this close to the city wall."

"Not unless we're about to get a wave," Brightblade said grimly, biting his lip.

Mark sighed, stood up, and walked around to stand on the other side of Zem. "Do me a favor and use your ability again."

"Uh, sure." Zem closed her eyes for the third time, and this time, when she received the feedback from it, she only flinched and backed up a step instead.

"Somebody want to explain what's going on?" Terra asked, his gaze hard as he glanced between Zem and Mark.

"Uh, the threat just moved," Zem said. "I think I might be picking up Apex."

"Why would you pick up Apex? He's not an Exlian," Brightblade said.

"No, but if he's a bigger threat than the closest Exlian, my ability would trigger on him. It's just, I've never seen this before."

Mark just shrugged, unsure what to say. He suspected that Zem's ability was working just fine. Either it didn't differentiate between human and Exlian, simply identifying the most dangerous individual in the area, or it *did* differentiate between humans and Exlian, and Mark counted as both. Regardless, as long as he was next to her, he had a sneaking suspicion that her ability simply wouldn't be helpful, and from the frustrated look on Terra's face, it was clear that he wasn't the only one who had made that connection.

"I'm sorry," Zem said, shaking her head. "I'm not quite sure what to do."

"Don't worry about it," Apora replied, her eyes gleaming as she looked at Mark. "This actually makes me feel a lot better. I'd much rather have the most dangerous creature around on my side, as opposed to facing off against them as an enemy."

"Apora's right," Terra said, nodding. "All this means is that we're much more likely to succeed in our mission. We'll just have to hunt the old-fashioned way. Everyone, stay on your toes. Let's move out."

With Mark leading the way, the team took to the streets once more, cautiously making their way farther from the city. Mark noticed a faint hesitancy that hadn't existed before, but he chalked it up to the team being worried that they wouldn't be able to spot Exlian as easily. Of course, he could have reassured them by sharing details about his abilities, but Mark didn't relish appearing any more abnormal than he already did. It was clear to him that the team was already wary, and that wariness had only been reinforced by this new discovery.

The dead zone was quiet, and the only sound besides the rhythm of their feet was the odd creak when the wind pushed against a sign, setting it swinging. Though Mark had never been through this part of the dead zone, the sights were familiar.

Smashed buildings, ruined cars, massive gouges torn in cement from Exlian claws, and the occasional crater where some sort of explosion had devastated the city.

Mark had already memorized the route to the four blocks the team had been assigned, and he stuck to it, leading the way with a calm pace as he kept an eye out for Exlian. He occasionally caught sight of drones on the periphery of the psychic network, but it didn't take much to maneuver around them, and less than an hour after they had left the gate, they arrived at their destination.

Mark could see the half-bombed-out parking garage in the distance, as well as a couple of other four- or five-story buildings. One of the blocks they had been assigned was a park and was relatively flat, while another looked to be a commercial district with dozens of small shops.

Glancing at the overgrown park and then at the stores in the distance, Terra pointed at the parking garage. "We'll stick to the plan and start there. Remember, there are two underground floors, which I suspect is where we're going to find the majority of the Exlian. Since we don't have Zem's ability at our disposal, at least for the moment . . ." Terra paused and glanced at Zem, who shook her head, making a point of not looking at Mark.

With a sigh, Terra continued, "Since we don't have Zem's ability, we'll proceed extra slowly. Apex, I'm afraid we're going to have to use you to bait out our targets."

"No need to be sorry," Mark said, shrugging. "That's what I'm here for."

He was clearly much more confident than the others, and as he led the way toward the parking garage, the rest of the team lagged a few steps behind. Mark didn't let it bother him, as strong excitement was stirring in his heart, and part of him simply couldn't wait to find the Exlian.

The parking garage was a massive structure, with two stories belowground and four stories above, though the top two floors had been mostly demolished, leaving a massive pile of rubble resting on top of the building. Mark located a spot where they could climb up to access the second floor, and after a quick discussion with Terra, the team chose to make their entrance there, hoping to avoid being attacked from multiple sides at once.

After climbing up the slab of fallen concrete, Mark paused at the top, his eyes narrowing as he picked up faint signatures in the psychic network. There had been a time when hibernating Exlian could hide from Mark's awareness, yet as his strength grew, so too did his connection with the psychic network, and now Mark found himself able to identify them.

Four murder scorpions were tucked away in crevices in the

collapsed ceiling, and he could sense half a dozen others down below, on the ground floor of the parking garage. As soon as Mark stepped inside, he could sense the Exlian's attention turning toward him. They seemed more wary than anything else, and Mark thought he felt a faint tremor in the psychic network, as if the murder scorpions were warning him off, claiming this as their own territory.

He ignored the warning, of course, and instead vaulted over the short wall into the parking garage. The warning tremor grew stronger, but instead of backing down, Mark narrowed his eyes and took a heavy step forward, sending out a tremor of his own. Immediately, there was a loud shriek as the four dozing Exlian awoke and tunneled out of the ceiling.

"We've got incoming," Mark said, speaking for the benefit of the rest of the team, even as he began to advance.

Apora and Terra had already entered behind Mark, and Zem and Brightblade came in right after them, immediately seeing the four murder scorpions. Two of them dropped to the floor, now scrambling toward Mark as quickly as they could, while the other two were scuttling over the cracked concrete ceiling to try to pincer Mark from above and below.

He responded by accelerating abruptly, his shields flaring around his body as he slammed into the first murder scorpion. About two feet tall and three feet wide, it had four large razor-sharp claws and a long segmented tail that ended in a vicious stinger. It met Mark with its claws wide, snapping down on his body in an attempt to clip his arms and legs right off. Instead, it found itself unable to close its claws, thanks to the mana shields that appeared around Mark.

Undeterred, the scorpion swung its stinger toward Mark's chest, but with an almost casual gesture, he brushed it aside, his fingers running over the end of the tail. The armor plating cracked and then ruptured, causing the creature to let out a wail of pain as it fell back.

The second scorpion jumped toward Mark, eager to succeed where its companion had failed, but just before it slammed into him, a bolt seemed to materialize out of thin air, sinking deep into its mouth, significantly slowing its momentum. That gave Mark just enough time to dodge the scorpion above him that tried to clip his head in half with a sharp claw. While he knew the scorpion wouldn't be able to get through his mana shields, Mark couldn't help but feel a little bit uncomfortable with the idea of a claw clamping down on his head. He danced backward, even as stone spikes pierced through the scorpion's belly, emerging from the broken concrete ceiling.

In the next moment, both Apora and Brightblade arrived on either side of Mark, striking out fiercely against the murder scorpions. There was no way to hide the fight, and Mark could sense more scorpions starting to rush up to the second floor. They didn't bother with the stairs, instead climbing through holes in the floor and up the outside of the building.

Realizing that they would soon be surrounded, Mark surged forward, blocking a swinging pincer with his foot, even as his fingers sank deep into a scorpion's head, killing it in a single blow. That didn't stop its tail from battering against Mark's chest in a dying reflex. The first three blows glanced off his shields. The fourth happened to arrive a fraction of a second behind a claw strike from one of the other scorpions, and despite Mark's attempt to dodge, the stinger pierced his suit and stabbed into his skin.

He could feel a burning sensation as venom rapidly pumped into his body, followed by a faint weakness. Yet instead of slowing down, Mark continued his frantic melee against the scorpions, relying on his regeneration and poison immunity. The burning sensation faded, but Mark had learned his lesson. When he killed the next scorpion, he quickly distanced himself, avoiding its thrashing.

The rest of the team fought a lot more cautiously than Mark, who spared no thought for his own safety as he dispatched three of the four scorpions. The fourth was killed by a well-placed explosive bolt from Zem's crossbow, and the team had just enough time to gather up before the other murder scorpions climbed over the walls and charged toward them.

"Retreat to your six," Terra called out. "Apex, guard the front."

Apora and Brightblade led the retreat, overwhelming a charging murder scorpion with a swift flurry of blows, while Mark positioned himself to intercept the other three rushing across the parking garage toward them. Their retreat bought them a few seconds, and planting himself firmly, Terra thrust out both hands, palms down, and made a grasping motion, arcane-sounding words tumbling from his lips. As far as Mark knew, the words were nonsense and simply provided a repeatable framework that Terra could use to manipulate mana in the same way each time.

There was a faint hum as mana began to gather around them, and then, just before the murder scorpions launched themselves toward Mark, the concrete floor between them twisted and grew, walls shooting up to create a rough labyrinth.

The Exlian let out shrieks and raced into one of the open passages, but instead of a clear path, they were met with stone spikes that burst from the walls, hindering their progress. The spikes weren't quite sharp enough to pierce through the tough Exlian exoskeletons, but they slowed the enemy, which was what Terra was aiming for.

With his hands still outstretched, Terra dropped one of the walls, revealing a trapped Exlian. Brightblade flashed forward, bringing his sword down on the monster's head. One by one, Terra and the team eliminated the Exlian in this way, first trapping them in place, then striking them while they were defenseless. Since the others seemed to have everything well in hand, Mark focused on watching their surroundings, making sure no other Exlian were coming their way.

After the last of the Exlian had fallen, the team rested for a moment, then gathered the scorpions' stingers and venom glands, the two most valuable parts of their bodies. Mark was hesitant to leave the rest of the scorpions' corpses behind, as a number of other body parts could be used for alchemy, but ultimately he decided to let it be, figuring he might be able to sneak away and come back later.

With the top two floors clear, it was time to proceed down into the basement. When they arrived at the entrance to the lower levels, Mark called for the team to stop. He could sense dozens of Exlian down below and realized that if they had started the fight on the ground floor instead, they likely would have been completely swarmed.

Thankfully, the majority of the Exlian they were fighting were D ranked, which meant they posed little threat to the Earthbond team. However, Mark sensed three much more powerful mental signals on the lower levels, indicating the presence of C-ranked murder scorpions.

"I don't like the look of that passage," Mark said as they gathered at the top of the stairwell. "I'm guessing that there are a lot more of them down there."

"I'm not going to be as helpful," Zem said, "since we'll be fighting in close quarters."

"Don't worry, I can make up for it," Terra chimed in.

"All right, but don't overdraw yourself. If need be, we can always retreat to the stairs and use that as a choke point to fight them," Mark replied. "If everyone's ready, let's go."

Creeping down the steps into the darkness, Mark didn't bother with a light, but he was soon reminded that the others would need one when Terra nearly tripped on a loose piece of rubble. Reaching into his bag, Mark had his shadow deposit a small clip-on lamp, which he attached to the front of his suit, tapping it twice to turn it on. It cast a soft reddish glow over everything in front of him, adding a rather harrowing tint to the already creepy stairwell.

The others had gotten lamps of their own out, and after everybody had turned their lights on, the team continued down the stairs. It appeared that the stairwell wasn't used by the Exlian to move between levels, because at the bottom, the door was firmly shut. Mark could sense almost twenty warrior-ranked Exlian beyond it, all of which were watching him warily through the network to see what he would do. There were almost a dozen drones as well, which were putting themselves as far away from him as they possibly could, clearly much more frightened of him than their larger, stronger compatriots.

Arriving at the door, Mark paused, unsure how to explain how he knew what was on the other side to the rest of the team. After a moment of hesitation, he decided not to and instead looked at Terra, as if waiting for a command to open the door.

Terra looked at Zem in turn, who closed her eyes and once again tried her sensing ability. Despite the fact that there was a swarm of Exlian on the other side, Zem shook her head and smiled wryly, pointing at Mark.

"Sorry," Mark muttered, his quiet voice carrying clearly over their voice channel.

"Not your fault," Terra said. "If anything, it's a compliment. Expect enemies on the other side, team, and let's go."

Giving Terra a thumbs-up, Mark turned and kicked the door in, blasting it off its hinges and sending it flying across the garage floor. The Exlian reacted instantly, letting out shrieks of anger as they rushed toward Mark and the others. In the brief moment before the Exlian reached the doorway, Mark noticed with some amusement how the smaller ones stayed back, allowing the three larger murder scorpions to attack first.

Stepping through the doorway, Mark met them with a fierce flurry of blows that tore apart the first Exlian's claws. As the creature recoiled in pain, Mark pressed forward, dodging a venomous stinger as he crushed the monster's head. As it entered its death throes, his foot snapped out, slamming into the side of its carapace and sending it skidding backward. Striking out blindly, its tail pierced the carapace of another murder scorpion, which turned with a hiss and tore the already dead corpse into pieces with a few swift snaps of its claws. Mark took the opportunity afforded to slam into the other scorpion, landing a palm strike on its side. As it stumbled, his palm lightly touched its armored carapace. His fingers dug in, and twisting his wrist sharply, he tore a massive chunk from the monster's side.

As it hissed and tried to retreat, an explosive bolt slipped into the gap, sending shards of Exlian flying as it exploded, tearing open the wound Mark had made. Apora and Brightblade had entered the room and were already engaged with the Exlian, while Terra and Zem stood by the door, using their ranged abilities to keep the others from being overwhelmed.

Mark bounced between opponents like a cannonball, using the force of his impacts to disrupt the Exlian swarm's rhythm. Everything his hands touched was cleaved apart, no matter if it was the hard chitin carapace or softer flesh beneath. He used his whole body as a weapon, leveraging his mana shields to transform his fists, elbows, knees, and feet into deadly bludgeons and interspersing Cutting Palm strikes between the shielded blows.

Though the fighting was rather frantic, it wasn't particularly dangerous, at least for Mark. He threw himself into it with vigor, crushing and gouging and ripping apart any Exlian that came close. The only concern he had was that he was using biofuel at a tremendous rate, but he found that easy enough to remedy in the darkness. His shadow surreptitiously swallowed chunks of Exlian flesh that fell to the floor, rapidly refilling his biofuel.

As the number of murder scorpions dwindled, the drones began to throw themselves into the fight as well. They were even easier to kill, but with each one that died, the death cry echoing in the psychic network grew stronger. Mark soon realized what they were trying to do. Around forty feet away from the door, a hole had been gnawed through the floor. As he fought his way forward, Mark realized that it didn't connect to the second basement level but instead plunged farther down into the earth. A bad feeling rose in his heart, and he was about to call for the others to retreat when a loud chittering noise rose from the hole. It swept across the basement floor, and a mental signature as bright as the sun appeared at the edge of Mark's range.

Eyes narrowing as he quickly assessed the new threat, he realized that it was a B-ranked Exlian, a murder scorpion that had evolved far beyond its companions. The other Exlian, sensing it drawing closer, threw themselves against the team with renewed ferocity, doing everything in their power to prevent Mark and the others from running away.

Terra was the first to notice something off, and he called for Apora and Brightblade to retreat, raising a wall of stone spikes to drive back the murder scorpions chasing them. Mark retreated as well, though at a more measured pace, killing two more scorpions on the way. There was a tremor underfoot as the B-ranked scorpion pushed its way up the narrow hole, and then a massive claw rose over the edge, landing with a thud that cracked the concrete.

"What is that?" Brightblade asked, his eyes widening.

"Trouble. That's what that is," Apora hissed.

"Looks like a B-ranked murder scorpion," Terra said grimly.

"Should we retreat?" Zem asked, glancing over her shoulder at the narrow doorway they had come through. "It probably won't be able to follow us up into the stairwell."

"Yeah, but if it breaks to the surface, we're going to have even more trouble with it," Terra said. "I doubt we can outrun it, so our next best option is to fight it down here, where it can't leverage its size."

Slicing the tail from the last of the smaller murder scorpions,

Mark crushed its head with his boot and kicked the flailing corpse aside. "Terra's right—we'll have a better chance down here than we will on the surface."

If the rest of the team noticed the faint excitement in Mark's tone, they didn't say anything. He suspected that they were too distracted by the monstrous creature that had just emerged from the tunnel. It was staring at them ravenously, its mouth opening and closing, as if it couldn't wait to taste their flesh.

Rolling his shoulders a few times, Mark shook out his arms and legs and got into his combat stance, ready to fight the giant scorpion. The others weren't so sure, but after Terra took a step forward and extended his hands, they groaned and got into position.

The scorpion was so big its back barely had a foot of clearance. This was to the team's advantage, as it meant that the monster would have trouble getting its tail into play. It couldn't strike from overhead as it normally did, so it had to swing its tail around its body to attack.

Of course, Mark didn't discount the tail entirely, and he was quite wary of the scorpion's claws, which he suspected would be able to break his shields. A B-ranked Exlian typically required a whole team of B-ranked empowered to bring down, as its strength, speed, and fortitude were much closer to the A rank. Since it also had a vicious nature and nearly supernatural willpower, it was impossible to put it down without killing it.

For a moment, the underground space was silent as man and beast stared at each other, each waiting for the other to make the first move. Finally growing impatient, the murder scorpion took a step forward, and Mark charged at almost exactly the same time.

The scorpion reacted by swinging a claw toward Mark to clamp down on him, but he twisted his body, falling nearly horizontal. One hand slapped the ground, carving a deep gouge in it, as he shifted the direction of his momentum, practically sliding along the ground underneath the claw. He bounced back to his feet and unleashed a strike that tore through the side of the scorpion's mouth.

Jerking its head up to get away from the pain, it slammed its back into the roof of the garage, causing the space to tremble. Infuriated, the monster shifted its tactics. It took a step forward, scraping its carapace along the ceiling, and then dropped, intending to crush Mark with its tremendous bulk. But he danced backward, keeping himself low as a bolt flew past his ear with inches to spare. It sank deep into the scorpion's mouth and then exploded, tearing apart one of the monster's mandibles and scorching the flesh that Mark's strike had exposed.

Mark heard a shout from behind and felt the space beginning to constrict as Terra controlled the floor and ceiling, sending out spike after spike in an attempt to trap the monster in place. Apora and Brightblade arrived a moment later, dodging past the Exlian's claws and landing coordinated strikes on its body. With a shriek, the scorpion twisted, snapping stone spikes that left white scratches across its carapace as it swung its claws wildly, attempting to smash the annoying insects attacking it into paste.

Brightblade was able to escape the attack, his body blurring as he dashed directly backward, moving so fast he almost seemed to teleport. Apora wasn't quite so lucky, as she had been midair when the monster began to move. Realizing that she was about to get pasted by a claw, Mark kicked off the scorpion's face and grabbed her around the waist, pulling her close to his chest just before the claw slammed into them.

He felt his mana shield flare and then crack, and a considerable amount of force shook his body, nearly making him lose his grip on Apora. As they tumbled through the air, she managed to get her feet underneath them, and they skidded to a stop. Thanks to Mark getting in the way, she had hardly felt the impact at all, and she quickly helped him to his feet.

"Thanks," she said, flashing a smile, as Mark blinked and re-oriented himself.

"It's what I'm here for," Mark said, shaking his head to clear it.

Hearing a scream, he looked at the giant scorpion, which was trying to force its way through a forest of stone spikes to reach Zem, who kept sending bolt after explosive bolt into its body. Using two of its claws to shield its head, the scorpion was thrashing with its other two claws, snapping the stone spikes Terra continually raised. With every motion the monster made, the parking garage trembled, and Mark could tell things were starting to destabilize.

"We need to move," Terra yelled. "This entire place is going to come down. Get back to the stairwell."

"I thought we didn't want to fight it on the surface," Zem yelled back.

"We don't, but we won't be able to fight it at all if the ceiling collapses on us."

Thanks to Terra trapping the monster, everyone was able to gather quickly, and as they began filing through the door, Mark brought up the rear. The scorpion, peeking at them through a small gap between its claws, saw they were trying to leave and redoubled its efforts. There was a grinding sound as its carapace ripped, but the monster didn't stop and slammed a claw into the cement to find purchase so it could pull itself forward. Then the stone spikes gave way, and it abruptly accelerated, heading straight for the doorway.

"Go," Mark yelled, his eyes fixed on the approaching monster.

As the others sprinted up the staircase, Mark hesitated briefly. The human part of his mind was screaming at him to run, that it was madness to try to fight the monster in this environment. The slightly less human part was screaming the opposite, that now was the best time to kill the monster in front of him. It had challenged Mark, and to run would be to admit that it was stronger than he was.

The others had just turned the corner when Mark decided it would be better to move out of the oncoming monster's way. But his moment of hesitation had cost him, and a flailing claw slammed into the wall, sending a shock wave through the concrete that shattered the stairs into hundreds of pieces. As concrete exploded around him, Mark realized that his path to the surface had been sealed.

There was another way to get up to the surface, a ramp that led from the basement to the first floor, but it was on the other side of the garage, and he'd have to pass the B-ranked Exlian to get there. Cursing himself for his foolishness, Mark abandoned all thoughts of running and instead launched himself forward, attacking as fiercely as he could.

The scorpion, caught off guard by Mark's sudden assault, tried to slow its momentum but failed, running full tilt into his palm strikes. With every movement of his hands, wounds appeared on the scorpion's face as his fingers cleaved through carapace and flesh alike.

Mark was standing just inside the stairwell, making it impossible for the scorpion to bring its claws to bear without backing up, so it tried to backpedal, intending to crush Mark with one of his claws. But now that the others weren't around, Mark had no qualms about pulling out all the stops. Not giving it time to retreat, he surged forward, transforming his arms into bone blade and stabbing them through the monster's carapace with such force that the tips of his gloves shredded, leaving his fingers exposed.

One of the scorpion's mandibles had already been blasted apart by an explosive bolt from Zem's crossbow, and with one hand dug into the monster's back armor, Mark attacked the scorpion's mouth, cutting the other mandible free and causing the creature to rear its head back, roaring in pain. At the same time, Mark commanded his shadow forward, and with a gleeful shake, it pounced.

With the shadow eating its way up from underneath the scorpion and Mark tearing massive chunks of flesh from its face, the monster quickly realized that if it couldn't distance itself, it would soon be dead. Unfortunately, no matter how it thrashed, it found itself unable to retreat, as it got caught in the remnants of the stone spikes jutting from the ceiling and the floor.

Though he appeared to be attacking with a mindless ferocity, Mark wasn't simply swinging wildly. Instead, his strikes cut through the scorpion with precision, carving into its head so that he could target its brain. Like normal scorpions, the murder scorpion had its brain at the base of its head, where the skull connected to the body, rather than near the top. In smaller scorpions, this didn't matter much, as a single strike could pierce all the way through their bodies to reach their brains. But the giant scorpion had heavy plates that made it almost impossible to reach the brain without digging through the top of the scorpion's head, which was exactly what Mark did.

Though it lacked mandibles, the scorpion still tried to bite at Mark, and he could feel his mana shield activating intermittently as it attempted to gnaw off his leg. Just before he broke through to the monster's brain, he felt its entire body jerk, crashing to the side, as his shadow devoured its last remaining leg on its right side.

Mark nearly lost his grip, but he managed to stabilize himself, only to feel a tremendous force slam into his side. As the scorpion's body had shifted, it had created just enough space for its tail to squeeze in, and as fierce pain began to assault his leg, Mark looked down and saw the scorpion's stinger had punched a hole through his mana shield and his suit, piercing all the way through his leg to emerge from the back.

Venom began coursing through his body almost immediately, but Mark just gritted his teeth and turned his attention back to the task at hand. With two more heavy slashes, he cut apart the flesh hiding the monster's brain stem, and then, with a final strike, he crushed it.

The Exlian immediately began thrashing, though its death throes were much less fierce than the others', as more than half of its body had already been consumed. Clenching his teeth so hard he feared his gums might bleed, Mark grabbed the twitching stinger and tore it free from his leg, paying little attention to the blackish blood that poured out of the wound.

Gasping, he rolled over, falling from his perch on the dead scorpion's head and slamming into the ground with a bone-jarring thud. A laugh escaped his lips. He could feel a constant rush of energy surging through his body as his shadow continued to devour the scorpion, and along with it, he could feel his strength rising incrementally.

By the time he caught his breath, the wound on his leg had healed almost completely, and the burning pain of the scorpion's venom had faded. Curious, Mark opened his status as his shadow finished devouring the rest of the scorpion, and saw a notification blinking at him.

Excessive exposure to B-ranked murder scorpion venom has caused your body to adapt. Minor Poison Resistance has advanced to Major Poison Resistance.

The rate at which Mark's body adapted was genuinely terrifying, and he couldn't help but wonder if there would come a day when he was immune to all toxins. But poison resistance wasn't the only benefit he had gotten from the fight. Though there hadn't been a change reflected in his status, Mark could tell that his strength was inching from B– to B.

Huh. All I have to do is eat three or four more of these guys, and I'll be good to go.

The thought caused Mark to laugh again, but knowing he couldn't hang around, he stood up and took stock of the situation. The entire place was trashed and looked like it was going to come down at any moment. Though he looked a fright and bore gashes all over his suit, Mark was none the worse for wear. His biofuel was maxed, and he felt stronger than ever. Any remaining Exlian had long since fled, so Mark began to make his way through the rubble, heading for the other exit. Along the way, his shadow swept up the remains of any murder scorpions it could find, transforming them into trace amounts of strength. As Mark was getting close to the exit, he heard the voice channel crackle to life.

"Apex, are you still alive?"

Hesitating for just a moment as he tried to figure out how he was going to explain this, Mark settled on what he thought was the most believable story. "Yeah, I'm coming up via the ramp."

"All right, we'll meet you there."

When Mark emerged, he found the rest of the team huddled together in the distance, watching carefully just in case any Exlian came up after him. When they saw he was alone, they hurried over.

"What happened?" Apora asked, taking in Mark's nearly ruined mana suit.

"Scorpion's gone. Maybe it was badly wounded, but after it crushed the stairwell, it retreated."

Of course, Mark left out that he had killed it before it could escape. The others didn't need to know that. Making a show of being tired and shaky, Mark sat down on the ground.

"What happened there?" Brightblade asked, pointing to the

tear in Mark's suit where the stinger had gone straight through his leg.

"Suit ripped, got caught by the scorpion's stinger as it retreated."

"You're lucky to be alive," Terra said. "We all are."

After some discussion with the rest of the group, Terra decided they should return to the city rather than continue exploring the other zones. Mark protested that he was perfectly fine, which earned him strange looks from the rest of the team. When Zem pointed to his practically ruined suit, he finally relented. The team headed back toward the city gates, though not before harvesting what little they could from the murder scorpions they had killed on the upper floors.

There was nothing left of the giant scorpion; Mark's shadow had seen to that. The others were understandably loath to head back down into the basement. So they abandoned the corpses on the lower levels, which was just as well, since Mark's shadow had devoured those too.

On the way back to the city, whether through ill fortune or something else, they ran into two groups of Exlian drones accompanied by warrior-class Exlian and were forced to fight. In both cases, Mark, having spotted them early, was able to ensure that the team was in a relatively defensible position. The fights went smoothly, with Mark blocking at the front while the others attacked from behind. As annoying as it was to constantly get pulled into fights, they were able to harvest quite a few materials, which improved Terra's mood considerably.

As they got close to the gate, Mark noticed a large group of hunters and soldiers emerging. Terra led the team off to the side to wait until the group had finished exiting the city. As Mark watched them gathering into small groups, he felt a nudge.

"Do you see the one in that black suit with the spines coming off its back?" Zem whispered in the team channel. "That's Hex."

"Hex?"

It took Mark a moment to realize Zem was talking about one of the five strongest empowered in the city. Ranked fifth, Hex was a master of energy control, wielding a strange, dark mana known for being able to bypass defenses and rapidly drain the life of her targets. Ostensibly the weakest of the five S-ranked empowered, she was still strong enough to single-handedly defeat at least a dozen people in the A rank.

"Whoa, isn't that the Seer?"

At Brightblade's exclamation, Mark turned his attention from Hex, looking back toward the gate, where a massive mana suit had emerged. Heavily armored and covered in an array of weapons, the Seer was an unmistakable sight. Though she normally went by her real name, Sora, most people called her the Seer, as her abilities allowed her to peek into the future. She was S ranked as well and was widely considered the third-strongest empowered in New Emery, after Ra, who wielded perfect control of light, and a man named Kain, whose power granted him almost complete invulnerability.

To see two of the top five empowered together was impressive, though Sora and Hex were known to often work together. Mark could sense the excitement of the rest of the team, but he found himself slightly underwhelmed. Probably because he had begun to realize that there were many powerful people in the city, and even more underneath it.

Maestro was an S-ranked empowered as well, though he wasn't listed on the public rankings. Winter Wolf was the same. Before she had been sent to the Tomb, she had been A ranked, though low. But after she'd undergone Maestro's treatments, her abilities had risen. And if the display she had put on during their mission was anything to go by, her powers were firmly in the S rank. How she would stack up against the top five empowered, Mark wasn't sure. But he had a sneaking suspicion that Winter Wolf would be able to hold her own.

Mark also suspected that other S-ranked empowered lived in the city, carefully hiding their strength for one reason or another.

After Sora and Hex and their team had disappeared into the dead zone, Mark followed Terra and the others back into the city, heading straight for the Hunters' Association, where they wrapped up their mission.

At first, Terra was worried that they would have to use the extra material they had gathered to offset the fact that they hadn't actually completed their mission. But when the zone they had been assigned was scanned, he was surprised to discover that the number of Exlian in that area was well below the target range. Considering they had only killed the Exlian in one of the four blocks, it was strange. Mark suspected that the other Exlian had gotten the message and, after the death of the giant scorpion, had chosen to retreat. Regardless, the lack of Exlian in that zone meant that their mission was successful, and the additional materials they had gathered could be sold for extra profit. Mark's share of the reward was sent to his account, and after the team had gotten out of their mana suits, Mark approached Zem.

"Would you mind showing me that shop you were talking about? The one where you bought your crossbow?"

"Oh, sure, I can do that."

Saying goodbye to the others, Mark and Zem left the association headquarters and caught the train heading toward the center of the city. He couldn't quite tell if Zem was naturally reticent or if she was nervous for some reason. But all attempts at small talk were met with quiet one-word answers. So eventually he gave up, and they rode in silence.

Zem only brightened when they arrived at the shop, a large three-story affair with weapons of all shapes and sizes. The third floor held the ranged weapons, and Zem's enthusiasm overflowed as she introduced Mark to all the different kinds. Most empowered preferred bows or crossbows with mana-tipped arrows, though some used guns that shot energy blasts. An auto-loading crossbow like Zem's occupied a prime spot in the middle of the store, and when one of the attendants saw them loitering around it, he hurried over.

"Hello, welcome to Cavvod's Armaments. I see you're looking at the Nova Stinger Mark III. Are you interested in trying it out?"

"Is this the one you have?" Mark asked Zem.

"No, I have the Mark II. This one just came out a few months ago."

"So you're familiar with the Nova Stinger series, then," the attendant said, beaming. "The Mark III has an even smoother loading action, shaving off three-tenths of a second. Additionally, it's been outfitted with a slightly superior scope, allowing for better accuracy at long ranges."

Noticing that Zem didn't look particularly impressed, Mark waited for her to speak up.

"Most people who pick up a weapon like this are going to end up customizing it for themselves," she said quietly. "So the stock features aren't considered that big a deal. The faster reload time sure is nice, but most people aren't proficient enough to take advantage of it."

"How much is something like this running?" Mark asked the attendant.

"Four million credits for the base model, another one and a half for the scope."

"Does it come with any of the boxes to store bolts in?"

"It comes with one base. If you want extras, each is five hundred thousand credits."

The price was a good bit higher than Mark had been hoping, as he didn't actually need a crossbow. While he didn't mind the idea of carrying around a ranged weapon in the dead zone, he much preferred to fight with his hands in close quarters. And considering his habit of rushing straight into the enemy as fast as possible, a bulky crossbow would simply get in the way.

Instead, what he was most interested in was the mana circuit the crossbow contained. An idea had been brewing in his head for a while now, and the opportunity to study the auto-loading feature of the crossbow would help a lot. He had considered asking Zem if he could borrow hers for a few hours, but he was afraid that if he took it apart, he wouldn't be able to put it back together. However, four million credits was just about everything Mark still had, after he deducted the cost of repairing his suit.

With a frown, he checked his watch, doing some quick mental calculations. If he repaired his suit himself, he might be able to save some money. But it would also mean that he couldn't buy materials for alchemy. After considering it for a while, Mark determined he could postpone the potions for a bit. Still frowning, he glanced at the attendant and then turned his attention to the crossbow on display. "All right, I'll take one."

Caught off guard, as he'd been fairly sure Mark was going to decline, the attendant stared for a moment and then nodded rapidly. "Of course. Will you take it with you? Or would you like me to deliver it? I'm happy to deliver it for free, and I'll even throw in a set of bolts for you, including a sample pack of some of our newest offerings."

"You can deliver it," Mark said. He paid, wincing as he saw his credit balance dropping precipitously.

After arranging for the crossbow to be sent to his apartment, Mark thanked Zem and said goodbye, catching the train back home. The sun was starting to set as he prepared dinner for himself and Mime, and he had just sat down when his watch buzzed, alerting him that the men who were delivering his crossbow had arrived. Buzzing them up, he had them place the large crates in the living room, and after thanking them for their help, he sent them on their way with a tip.

He was so excited to look at his new purchase that he left his dinner on the table. Two crates had been delivered, one holding the crossbow itself with half a dozen different types of bolts, the other holding the large box where the bolts would be stored.

Since Mark only had one, he ignored the dial on the crossbow and instead began testing the loading function. The process it used was relatively simple, though the mana circuit was anything but. Each crossbow had a unique serial number embedded in the circuit, as did the ammo storage boxes, allowing them to link without any fear that a crossbow might pull from the wrong box.

In a discussion with Zem, Mark had learned that there was no limit to the range of the autoloader, meaning that the box could sit safely back in the city while the empowered holding the crossbow could wander all over the wilderness, confident that as long as there were bolts to load, they would appear without fail. Deciding it would behoove him to begin writing down a few of the things he was observing, Mark turned to go get a piece of paper and caught sight of Mime halfway through his food.

"Hey! What are you doing? That's my dinner."

Giving him an arch look, Mime pulled the plate closer, shifting around it so her back was to him. Ignoring his grumbles, she continued to eat, and with a sigh, Mark grabbed a nutrient pouch from the fridge, holding it between his teeth as he got his paper and began writing his notes. Despite the exertion that afternoon, he still had plenty of biofuel left thanks to the murder scorpions he had consumed, so he wasn't particularly worried about missing dinner.

The more he delved into the mana circuit, the more complex he realized it was. What looked like one circuit was really several, all interconnected through specialized links that allowed the mana to flow through them unhindered. At first, the complexity left him scratching his head, but it wasn't long before he began isolating the various pieces, running test after test to identify exactly what each circuit did. His idea was simple: If he could replicate the activator, why couldn't he replicate the teleportation effect as well?

That would make it possible to summon his gear from anywhere, but he already had his shadow to carry any number of items. Instead, what he was curious about was whether he could figure out a way to send himself through space. It was a mad idea but one that didn't seem entirely outside the realm of possibility.

He spent the majority of the night studying the circuits before, at close to four in the morning, finally forcing himself to go to bed. As soon as he appeared in the dream, Mark jumped down from the building he was standing on, landing with a heavy thud. Almost immediately, he heard a faint whiz from his left and dodged, wincing as a blast of sound scorched the air beside him.

By now, killing screamers was practically second nature, and a few moments later, Mark was standing over the Exlian's corpse, watching as it began to fade away. There were no other Exlian in the area, which suited him just fine, and rather than head out of the run-down base to explore the surroundings as he normally did, he began recalling the mana circuits he had been studying.

Taking a deep breath, Mark closed his eyes and focused his mind. Mana gathered, and he formed it into the crossbow's main circuit, which functioned as a target, determining where the bolt would appear and how it would be oriented. He positioned the target circuit a few feet in front of him, hanging in the air. It took a fair amount of concentration to keep it together, so he split his mind in two, forming a mental clone to hold the circuit open.

Though he was practically certain that what he was about to try wasn't going to work and would likely kill him in the dream, Mark didn't hesitate, inscribing the second mana circuit on his hand. This was the circuit that marked the object that needed to be shifted, and it was found in the ammo case. As he finished it, he split off his mind again, now keeping two mana circuits active while he formed the third and final circuit, the trigger that should, in theory, cause the object marked by the second circuit to teleport through space to the location of the first.

As soon as it was finished, he triggered it, not giving himself time to consider, and then let out a sharp scream as his hand was torn from his arm. Just before he lost consciousness, he saw his hand appear a few feet in front of him, blood dripping from the severed wrist. Then everything faded and his mind reset, placing him once again on the top of the building, his wrist still stinging slightly.

The pain quickly dissipated, however, and Mark couldn't help but do a little dance as excitement consumed him. Clearly, he had much work to do, but the basic principle was sound. Of course, this was something he could only practice in this mental world, as in the real world it was likely to result in gruesome death.

Though his attempts ended in painful failure after painful failure, Mark threw himself into his testing with abandon. He had lost count of how many times he had died in this dream world, his body torn apart by Exlian, and this, to him, was no different. His fear of death had long been ground away, and pain was nothing but a temporary annoyance, one that his mind had become numb to.

At first, he focused his tests on understanding how the marking circuit identified what to bring with it, and soon he realized that the circuit was locked to a specific size. This led him to the realization that he really needed to understand more about mana circuits in their entirety, and after his six hours in the dream were up, Mark immediately bounced out of bed and rushed to his InfoWeb terminal, pulling up every bit of information he could find on mana circuits and how they were built.

Terra had mentioned that they would have the next few days off before picking up another mission, and Mark spent them locked in his apartment, poring over books about the initial development of mana circuits. The deeper he delved, the faster his studying became, and soon Mark was splitting off different clones to read different texts, forming half a dozen versions of himself to study the subject.

Some of his clones read textbooks or delved into scholarly articles, while others sat around the kitchen table, feverishly working out calculations and attempting to redesign the mana circuits, and still others experimented with the crossbow and ammo box. Various observations were made after each test. When night came, Mark left his clones to their work and lay down in bed, eagerly entering the dream to begin testing everything he had learned that day. Though he hadn't yet succeeded when his watch buzzed, alerting him that Terra had found a new mission, Mark could tell that he was making progress. He had figured out a couple of key pieces of information and was now in the process of tuning the marking circuit so that it would include his mana suit and entire body.

Rather reluctantly, he paused his research and headed to the association to meet up with the rest of the team. They had agreed to meet after breakfast to go over the details of the mission and do some team training. When Mark arrived, Terra and Apora were already there. Zem and Brightblade arrived not long after, and they sat down together at a table in the cafeteria.

"The mission I picked this time is a little bit less variable, at least hopefully," Terra said, passing out the details. "It's a simple retrieval mission. We need the glands and blades from four mantises."

Mark, who found himself slightly distracted, since he still had clones working back in his apartment, scratched his head. "Mantises are the ones with the big bone blade arms, right?"

"Yes. They have four legs and a tall upper torso with three-foot blades on arms that extend from their back. They're typically D ranked, though we're looking for C ranked."

Whether Terra had picked this mission because he wanted to avoid the excitement of the previous mission or for another reason, Mark wasn't sure. But it reminded him that he had yet to fix his mana suit.

"I'm sorry, but would it be possible to delay our mission for a day or two?" he asked, rather embarrassed.

"Sure, this one's not particularly time sensitive. But why? What are you thinking?" Terra asked.

"Well, I kind of got distracted with something, and I need to fix my mana suit."

Remembering the giant tear in the leg, Terra nodded. "Yeah, sure. That's no problem. How long do you think it'll take?"

"It shouldn't be more than a day. All I'm really doing is patching the hole."

"What do you mean, you're patching the hole?" Brightblade asked, resting his forearms on the table. "Don't you mean the repair shop is patching the hole?"

"Actually, I was considering doing it myself. I'm a bit short on funds."

"He bought a swanky new crossbow," Zem supplied helpfully.

"Do you know how to repair mana suits?" Apora asked, staring at Mark skeptically.

"Yeah, well, the thing is that because of my fighting style, my suits tend to get trashed pretty quickly. That's one of the reasons that I just buy a cheap one," Mark said, feeling more embarrassed by the moment. "If I had to buy a new suit or even send it into the repair shop every single time I went out, I'd be sunk. So I've learned to do some basic repairs on my own."

"I guess that makes sense," Apora said. "I know there's a workshop you can rent here in the association. If you don't mind, could

I watch you repair it? I'm a bit curious about that. I've been thinking about doing some modifications to my suit, but I don't know anything about working on them, and I don't really want to pay for somebody else to try out experimental mods."

"Sure," Mark said, with an easy nod. "I'd be happy to show you what I know."

"All right, then it's settled," Terra said. "We'll plan on leaving after Apex's suit is repaired, either tomorrow or the day after that. Everyone else can use this time to either train or prep anything they need to."

Together with Apora, Mark headed for a kiosk to book time in one of the workshops. They were able to get into one right away, and Mark carried his torn suit with him. The workshop, though rather dated, had just about everything he needed, including a significant stock of basic suit parts that could be purchased on the spot.

Overall, apart from the massive hole in the leg, Mark's suit was in relatively good shape, and after fixing gashes on the arms and chest, he focused his attention on the suit's leg. Had he been fixing it properly, he would have replaced the entire thigh plate, but instead Mark chose the cheapest patch he could find, a soft reinforced cloth, not bothering to try to match his suit's material. Then he showed Apora how to use the tools to shape the patch and fix it in place. It looked ugly but only cost him a little bit over 2,000 credits.

Apora was an eager student, paying careful attention to everything Mark did and asking a considerable number of questions, which he answered as best he could. Occasionally, she would pose a question that Mark didn't know the answer to, and they would pause to look it up together and try to figure it out.

After he had finished his repairs, Mark met the rest of the team for training, putting the suit through its paces. In reality, he would have been perfectly fine venturing out of the city without a suit at all, but he knew that would only earn him strange looks. Even the S-ranked empowered wore suits when they left the city, and the sight of someone in the B rank running around without one in the wilderness would no doubt raise some red flags.

After he was satisfied that his suit wouldn't have any issues, Mark returned to his apartment, where his clones had been continuing to study the mana circuits. As soon as he stepped into the apartment, the clones stopped what they were doing, stood, and walked toward him, merging into his body, bringing with them all their new knowledge and the calculations they had done. As all that information merged into him, Mark sighed and shook his head. His tests were progressing well, but he had a feeling that it would still be some time before he'd be able to teleport himself smoothly.

That night, in his dream, he confirmed this. The modified marking circuit was a lot better than the original, but occasionally he would find himself leaving a piece of a limb behind when he tested it, resulting in a bloody death. He wasn't quite sure why this was the case, but he trusted that as he continued experimenting, it would become clear.

Since the mission this time didn't seem particularly fraught, Mark elected to leave two clones behind in his apartment. One to continue researching mana circuits, and the second to continue modifying the teleportation circuits. Running two additional clones didn't create that much of a burden, though Mark found himself slightly more distracted than normal as he joined the rest of the team and proceeded out of the city into the dead zone.

Instead of leaving from the south, they took the western gate, entering the territories where Mark had spent most of his time as a trainee. Seeing the familiar buildings brought back memories of his first mission with Noah and Phoenix, but Mark pushed them aside and focused on the mission. Over the course of the next four hours, the team hunted down a dozen mantises before finally finding the four C-ranked ones they needed. They gathered the materials after killing them and retreated to New Emery, turning their materials in at the gate to a representative from the association, who would ensure they got to the appropriate individual.

Since their mission had been relatively easy, Terra announced they would only get one day off before their next hunt, and Mark hurried back to his apartment, eager to integrate what his clones had learned. Between his study of mana circuits and hunts with the Earthbond team, Mark's days were full and, apart from the occasional message from Noah and Sky, largely the same. He kept at least two clones active at all times, rapidly deepening his knowledge of mana engineering while continuing to test new iterations of the mana circuits in the safety of the dream. Otherwise, his waking hours were split between meditating, practicing his martial arts, and venturing out of the city to hunt, and his nights were spent testing everything he had learned during the day.

As the days slipped past, transforming into weeks, then months, Mark could feel his strength growing little by little, and one day he realized that the weather was getting colder. He had been out of the Tomb for a full four months. Ever since their first mission, the Earthbond team had had no particularly close calls, and Mark had settled into a rhythm that saw his points steadily ticking up. Each mission netted him approximately 100 points, and over the course of four months, Mark had participated in forty-five different missions. He had already passed 3,000 points, enough to unlock the second level of association membership. Of course, Mark had been on the second level from the start, and he would have to wait until he had 5,000 points before he could reach the third.

His stats were growing as well, thanks to the Exlian he had managed to devour, and his strength had finally broken through to B. More importantly, at least in Mark's mind, he had finally figured out the trick to his new marking circuit. The previous night, he had successfully deployed it, managing to teleport himself entirely intact six feet forward ten times out of ten. Mark had also managed to merge the trigger circuit with the new marking circuit into a complete teleportation circuit, which made activation easier. The next step was to figure out how to keep the teleportation circuit active while shifting the target circuit's location, allowing him to do more than teleport a few feet forward.

That evening, as Mark was buried in his calculations, he felt his watch vibrate, and a message popped up. It took him a moment to work out who it was from, but when he realized that Maestro had sent it, he put down his pen and read it carefully.

MAESTRO

I've submitted a request to the association, locked to you. I need a few mutated Exlian hearts. It's a relatively new type of Exlian called an earth rat. They have a particular affinity for earth mana, which gives them a better-than-normal burrowing ability. Our scans have located a den of rats that have a particular mutation I'm interested in studying. I'll send you the location as part of the details of the mission. The sooner you can get this done, the better. The buggers run quickly, so it might be best to bring a team with you.

Sitting back in his chair, Mark thought for a moment and then called Terra. After a moment, the call was picked up, and Terra's face appeared above Mark's watch.

"Hey, Apex. It's unusual to get a call from you at this time of night."

"Yeah, sorry. I just got wind of something and wondered if the team would be available tomorrow. I know it's short notice, but somebody had a specific request. I haven't gotten the details yet, but if you're interested, we could meet up tomorrow and go over them."

"A custom request? Sure. I'd be happy to look at it, if nothing else," Terra said. "Do you want me to get the rest of the team together?"

"Up to you. If it's not something that we're interested in as a team, then there's no point in bothering everybody. And I know that Brightblade said he had some stuff to do tomorrow."

"Sure. Well, I'll put the word out, and anybody who wants to can show up."

"All right, thanks. I'll see you tomorrow."

Ending the call, Mark put the matter out of his mind and returned to his calculations.

That night in the dream, Mark repeatedly tested his finalized teleportation circuit, proving that it worked consistently. After close to a hundred tests, he was confident that he wasn't going to accidentally leave a piece of his body behind, and moved on to the next stage of his testing.

So far, he had only been teleporting directly forward, using one mental clone to establish one mana circuit on his body and a second to establish a target circuit five feet in front of him. Now, he began to try to shift that target, moving it farther from him and to either the right or the left. It had been relatively simple to move directly forward, and each time he teleported, it felt as if the world had just shifted slightly toward him when he blinked.

He found it much more disorienting when he began to move the location of the target circuit, and after each teleportation, he had to stop and reorient himself. Thankfully, as he practiced, he began to get used to the sudden shift in his view and was soon moving around the ruined base smoothly. Teleporting up to a rooftop, he paused and surveyed the landscape. He still had around an hour left before the dream would end, so he decided to try something new.

While Mark was confident in the two mana circuits he had developed, there was a third that he had been trying, a brand-new circuit that combined the others, tying his targeting to his eyesight. His intent was to create a circuit that would allow him to jump forward through space to any place his eyes could reach.

Of course, Mark had no illusions that his first attempts would succeed, and indeed, when he built and activated the new mana circuit, he felt a tearing pain as his eyes jumped clear out of his head, plunging him into darkness. Thankfully, a moment later, his eyesight was restored as he respawned on the top of the building where he always awoke. The sensation was awful, and Mark decided to spend some time reworking the mana circuit before trying again.

After getting up, doing his morning training, and having breakfast, he headed for the association, where Terra and Apora waved hello. "Hey, Apex, Terra says you might have a mission for us."

Sitting down at their table, Mark sent the details he had retrieved to their watches. "The client is looking for as many mutated earth rat hearts as we can find. They've located a den that shows signs of mutation and want us to grab them."

"Uh, Apex, regular earth rats are all C ranked, right?"

"I know."

Giving him a strange look, Terra continued, "Mutated earth rats are all going to be B ranked. Don't you think that's a little bit outside of our scope?"

After pausing to consider the question, Mark shook his head. "No, I think that we should be fine. Earth rats aren't particularly aggressive. I mean, they're Exlian, of course. But as long as we kill one of them, they're liable to run away."

"Only so they can ambush us later," Apora said. "Didn't you hear about the team that discovered the earth rats? They thought they had scared them away, but they were ambushed six times before they made it back to the city. It was only once they were in New Emery that the things stopped attacking them."

"Okay, so 'less aggressive' is relative," Mark said. "We'll just have to kill the entire den from the beginning."

"I really don't think that this is a good idea," Terra said, shaking his head.

"Hold on," Apora replied. "This might actually be doable."

"What are you talking about?"

Highlighting a section of the request, Apora sent it to Terra and Mark. "It says that the client is willing to provide five Wraith Walk potions that will allow us to retreat back to the city without any trouble."

Reading over that section, Mark nodded. "That's right. Wraith Walk will keep the Exlian from being able to track us, so as long as we strike quickly, we should be able to retreat without any trouble. The mission will be considered a success even if we only get one heart, so I think it's worth doing. We can take down a B-ranked earth rat without too much trouble; then we pop the Wraith Walk potions and retreat. Easy."

"Apex, missions in the dead zone are never easy," Terra said flatly, "but this might be doable. I should be able to track them through my earth mana affinity. We ambush the strongest one, and then we run."

Closing his eyes and crossing his arms over his chest, Terra was silent for a long minute, and Mark just let him think. Finally, Terra nodded. "All right, we're in."

"What are we in for?" Zem asked, walking over with Brightblade trailing behind her.

"We've got a new mission, to hunt some mutated earth rats," Mark said, shifting over to make room for the others to sit down.

"Mutated earth rats? Aren't they B ranked?"

"We have a plan," Terra replied. "This is going to be a quick, though likely not easy, run, and before you get too bent out of shape, check the reward on this."

Since Mark had never actually considered turning the mission down, he hadn't bothered to look at what sort of reward was being offered. He glanced at the top of the information packet, and his eyes went wide.

Even Brightblade let out a low whistle. "A thousand points and half a million credits per heart we retrieve? Don't earth rats have more than one heart?"

"Yup, three."

"Sign me up."

Everyone else was just as excited, and two hours later, the team had suited up and headed to the gate. Most other teams had already left, so there was no queue when they got there, and it wasn't long before they were standing among the buildings in the dead zone, going over the plan once more. The Wraith Walk potions were loaded into vials and slotted into their suits, ready to be injected at the push of a button when the time came. After he was sure that everybody was ready, Terra gestured for Mark to lead the way forward, and they made their way swiftly through the maze of crumbling concrete buildings toward the den.

Though they moved quickly, Mark was careful to avoid any Exlian he spotted, not wanting to tangle the team in a fight. Eventually, they arrived at their target location, an old grocery store, where the earth rats had made their den. As they approached, Mark could sense the Exlian gathered together inside. Among them were six presences that were considerably stronger than the others.

Pausing about half a block away, Mark carefully counted. There were at least two dozen C-ranked earth rats along with the six B-ranked ones, which was a force much bigger than the team could handle. As the others crowded around him, Mark considered how he was going to communicate the challenge. His main concern was that if they simply pushed into the den, they would end up swarmed. Although earth rats weren't particularly large monsters, their numbers would easily make up for any size disparity.

At the same time, another part of him simply wanted to plunge forward, throw himself into the mass, and devour them all. Tamping that impulse down, Mark was just considering how to approach the situation when he noticed a group of drones coming from the team's right. The earth rats spotted them at the same time, and a large group of them broke off, rushing toward the new interlopers. The drones sped up, and Mark detected a couple of more powerful Exlian mental signatures with them, an indication that this was an intentional incursion into the earth rats' territory.

Realizing that he was witnessing infighting between two different Exlian groups, Mark sensed an opportunity. Two B-ranked and three C-ranked earth rats were all that remained at the den, which made it a perfect time to strike. Mark tapped Terra on the shoulder and gestured ahead.

"Let's go," he said, and before the others could argue, he took off, moving swiftly through the rubble that dotted the street toward the grocery store's entrance. What had previously been a large set of floor-to-ceiling windows had long since been broken, and Mark rushed through them, heading straight for the earth rats' den, which was located in the back right of the store.

Shelves were strewn about, anything edible long since consumed. There were no lights, but Mark didn't need them. As the rest of his team hurried to keep up, he heard the chitter of the earth rats as they detected his presence and surged forward to attack. Each about the size of a small dog, they were quick, moving unimpeded over the twisted metal shelves to throw themselves at Mark. One of the B-ranked earth rats led the charge, while the other lurked at the back of the group, undoubtedly waiting for an opportunity to launch a surprise attack.

Mark, transforming his arms into bone blades, dodged under a leaping earth rat, carving a mortal wound through its neck and along its soft belly. At the same time, his foot snapped out, catching another rat in the side of its head, sending it tumbling into one of the few remaining shelves, which fell over with a loud bang. A third rat latched onto Mark's leg, its sharp teeth failing to pierce his mana shield, and an arrow fired from Zem's crossbow caught the fourth rat in the eye, piercing its brain and killing it instantly. The momentum carried it back to where the last rat was crouched, and as its dead companion fell to the ground and began thrashing, the final earth rat screeched and attempted to burrow into the ground, only to find that the earth, which normally parted before it smoothly, was completely locked up.

Terra, anticipating the rat's retreat, had stretched out his hands and begun fighting for control of the earth mana around it, preventing an easy escape. Brightblade and Apora reached it a moment later, their attacks scoring wounds on its back, causing it to hiss in pain. It tried to turn tail and run, but Mark had already gotten around behind it, and after a few frantic minutes of fighting, it finally succumbed to its wounds and died.

The fighting had been swift, and the entire time, Mark had been keeping an eye on the war happening in the distance. As soon as the final earth rat fell, Mark got to work cutting open the corpses and retrieving the hearts. Though he had never dissected an earth rat, he was intimately familiar with Exlian anatomy and had no trouble extracting each rat's three hearts.

Typically, an earth rat's heart was only worth around 10,000 credits, but the B-ranked hearts were worth 500,000 a piece to Maestro, and Mark could practically see the credit signs flashing in Brightblade's eyes when he stuck the sixth heart in the special box that would preserve it.

"Let's get going," Terra said, after storing the box in his bag. "From the size of this den, there are probably more of these things out there, and I don't fancy getting ambushed by them on the way back."

"You say there are more of them? Shouldn't we stay and kill them?" Brightblade asked greedily.

"No, we should get back to the city," Terra said. "I could barely stop one from burrowing, and that's while you guys were attacking it. If we have to face more than one of these things at a time, it's going to be a nightmare."

"As much as I hate to admit it, I agree with Terra," Apora said, her claws glinting as she pointed at the corpse of one of the B-ranked earth rats. "If Apex hadn't hit the first one with a lucky attack, we might still be fighting. Their bodies are unnaturally tough, given their size, which probably has something to do with their mutation. We got what we came for; we should retreat."

Looking at Zem and Mark hopefully, Brightblade saw that they agreed with Apora's assessment, and with a sigh, he nodded. "Fine, we'll go back. I know it's the right choice, I just . . ."

His voice trailed off, and Terra, patting him on the shoulder, led the way out into the street. "Everybody pop your potions, and let's go."

Reaching for his waist, Mark activated the injector. He felt a needle pierce his arm and a cool sensation rush through his body as the Wraith Walk potion took effect. Within seconds, he could feel his body beginning to fade, though he knew that was only an illusion. Rather than actually transform him into a wraith, the Wraith Walk potion erased his scent and heat signature and dampened his presence, making him easy to ignore.

How exactly the potions worked, Mark had no idea, but he

made a mental note to ask Maestro for the recipe so he could try to make more of them. A Wraith Walk potion cost close to a million credits, which was quite cheap when you considered the fact that they could save a hunter's life out in the wilderness.

Terra looked around at the team to make sure everyone had activated their potion, and then headed toward the city, with the others following close behind. Mark kept an eye on the psychic network, just in case they ran across any Exlian. To his surprise, Terra seemed to be able to anticipate the Exlian, and twice he had the team pause and hide in a building to wait for a group of drones to pass before continuing. Mark wasn't sure exactly how he did it.

They were around twenty minutes from the gate and had relaxed considerably when Terra suddenly stopped for the third time. Immediately, Mark scanned the area. At first, he didn't see anything, as there were no Exlian anywhere close by. But after a moment, he spotted a group of ten humans lurking in a building that their current route would take them right past.

"Something's off," Terra said after a moment, "but I'm not sure what."

"More Exlian?" Apora asked.

"No, the footfalls seem too heavy for that."

It was then that Mark realized Terra was picking up vibrations, which was an ingenious use of his abilities.

"Suits?"

"I think so, but they're not moving right now, which probably means an ambush."

"What about one of those two buildings up there?" Mark asked, his eyes scanning the path ahead.

After examining the buildings Mark was pointing at and not seeing anything, Terra shook his head. "Can't tell, but we might as well go around. Let's backtrack and take another route."

The team had just begun to retreat when they heard a shout,

and the people Mark had located rushed out of the building ahead of them. Only a hundred feet separated them, a distance that someone in a mana suit could cross very quickly. With a single glance, Mark took in the suits of the people rushing toward them. They were all nondescript, with no clear markings, each obviously customized, identifying the group in front of them as hunters. However, from the way they brandished their weapons, it was clear that they weren't interested in talking to Mark and the others. Instead they were out for blood.

"Raiders," Terra spat, his voice grim. "Retreat!"

Even as he spoke, Terra thrust both hands forward, conjuring a maze of walls between the team and the approaching raiders. This bought them a bit more time to fall back, and he led the way, racing into a nearby building to ensure the raiders wouldn't be able to surround them. Mark, who had been behind everyone before they turned around, moved a bit slower than the others. He naturally fell to the back of the group once more, positioning himself between the team and the oncoming raiders. Zem delayed slightly as well, aiming at a raider who had jumped onto the walls that Terra had created and was now racing across the top of the maze.

Stabilizing her crossbow, Zem fired off a shot. As mana flared in the crossbow and it reloaded, she turned and ran. The bolt was utterly silent and hard to see, catching the raider off guard. At the last moment, sensing danger, he tried to throw himself to the side, only to slip on the narrow wall. He tumbled to the ground as Zem's bolt whizzed past.

Still bringing up the rear, Mark kept a close eye on the raiders, who soon broke free of the maze and began to close the distance as well. It seemed that all their suits were built for speed, similar to Brightblade's. Mark didn't get a particularly dangerous feeling from any of them, which was reassuring, but they moved with trained confidence, a clear indication that they were not new to this kind of work. Terra continued to do his best to slow the enemy down, sealing doorways after the team had run through them and erecting earthen walls to break the line of sight. They had just passed through the building and emerged onto another street, however, when Mark sensed danger.

"Get down!" His yell came a second before the hum of a mana blast, and Apora, who had been targeted, barely managed to twist out of the way. Turning a back handspring, she looked in the direction the attack had come from, and caught sight of sunlight glimmering off the barrel of a mana rifle. Zem, who was only a few steps away from Mark, was targeted next, but just before the blast hit her, a shadow fell between her and the attack as Mark shoved her out of the way. There was a crackle as the mana bolt slammed into the shield that appeared over his back, and the force of the blow sent him stumbling forward, tripping over Zem's prone body.

"We need to get under cover, fast!" Terra yelled, raising two tall walls on either side of the team to block the enemy's line of sight.

A moment later, two more mana bolts slammed into the walls, sending gouts of dirt flying as they punched through and burrowed into the ground.

"Go! Don't stop!"

The team raced for another building, and glancing over his shoulder, Mark caught sight of the raiders bursting out of the one behind them. In addition to the ten enemies pursuing them, there were at least two with long-range weapons positioned on top of buildings with good lines of sight to the areas around them, which would make escape difficult. The raiders had clearly planned this ambush meticulously and likely had considerable experience in this sort of thing.

"Terra, are you able to send a distress signal?" Zem asked as they raced across the ground floor of the building they had entered.

"No, it looks like we're being jammed."

Glancing down at his own watch, Mark realized that the signal wasn't going through. Thankfully, they were able to communicate with each other, but he noticed that even that signal was a little bit fuzzy. Starting to wonder if this was more than just a simple ambush, Mark followed Terra and the others as they raced down an alleyway behind the building, soon arriving at another street.

"I can give us cover," Terra said, "but I don't know how much it's going to help. As soon as they see the walls going up, they're going to punch them full of holes."

"You called them raiders," Mark said suddenly. "What do you mean by that?"

Thrown off by the abrupt question, Terra gave Mark a strange look but still answered. "Raiders are hunters who prefer to target humans instead of Exlian. They scavenge suits and any Exlian parts that a team has collected. Sometimes they'll hold teams for ransom or force them to smuggle goods into New Emery."

"Isn't that all illegal?" Mark asked.

"It is illegal, and clearly, they really care," Brightblade said sarcastically.

"I guess I'm just wondering how they move in and out of the city. Or do they live outside? Wouldn't the guards at the gate spot them if they keep coming in with extra suits covered in blood?"

"Not that simple. Most of them have legal identities that they use to enter and exit the city. They then swap into the other suits to raid."

"As fun as this conversation is, we need to go," Zem said. "They're probably closing in."

"They already did," Mark replied. "They've got us surrounded on three sides." Not bothering to explain how he knew, he pointed back the direction they had come. "The team behind us is split to the right and the left. If you head back the way we just came, you'll be able to get out of the encirclement. I'll draw their attention this direction while you guys make a run for the city."

"Are you sure that's a good idea? Wouldn't we be safer if we were all together?" Apora asked, clearly uncomfortable with the idea of Mark going out on his own.

"No," Mark said before Terra could respond. "I'm tough enough to survive everything they throw at me, and fast enough that I should be able to outdistance them eventually. You guys don't have any time, so get moving as soon as I get their attention. I'll meet you back in New Emery."

Turning on his heel, Mark dashed out of the alleyway, not giving the team any time to respond. As soon as he emerged, there was a crack, and a mana bolt slammed into the shield that appeared over his shoulder. Stumbling to the side, he felt the whip of another bolt scraping by his head and breathed a small sigh of relief that it hadn't hit him. He lowered his body into a crouch and darted for the other side of the street.

Behind him, he could sense Terra, Apora, Zem, and Brightblade retreating back along the alleyway. Just before Mark made it across the street, the wall in front of him exploded outward, and a brute with skin the color of stone reached for him with both hands.

Though he was running full tilt, Mark reacted instantly, shifting his weight and transforming his arms into bone blade. Ducking under the giant's grab, he tore into the brute's side, carving deep gashes in the stonelike skin that covered his opponent's ribs. Hearing a grunt of pain, Mark hammered a kick into the brute's legs, but he was barely able to make the man stagger.

There was a yell as one of the suited raiders appeared,

swinging a mana sword at Mark, who blocked it with a raised arm. The brute, swinging around, slammed an elbow into Mark, who lifted his hand and used the mana shield that appeared to absorb the blow, borrowing the force to throw himself backward.

All around him, others were emerging, and though a few of the raiders started to chase the rest of the team, a stone wall had risen across the entrance to the alleyway, preventing them from pursuing Terra and the others. That was exactly what Mark had been hoping would happen, and now he charged out of the raiders' encirclement, taking three heavy strikes as he forced his way through.

As the raiders' weapons bounced off him, he could see their bewilderment. Though a heavily armored mana suit could defend against the strike of a mana sword, Mark's suit was anything but, and the raiders clearly anticipated chopping straight through it. Instead, their weapons were turned aside by Mark's mana shields, buying him the few seconds he needed to break free from their encirclement and begin running.

Furious, the raiders yelled and gave chase, so Mark ducked into a nearby building, smashing straight through the double doors. Seeing a stairwell, he darted for it and raced up, one of the raiders only a few steps behind. When Mark got to the second landing, he spun, his foot lashing out, aimed at the raider's head.

Though caught off guard, the raider still managed to duck underneath Mark's kick. He then lunged forward, stabbing at Mark's waist with his mana blade. Mark didn't bother blocking, instead relying on the mana shield that manifested just before the blade reached him. Planting his foot firmly, he brought his hand down in a chop, tearing straight through his opponent's chest. The armor, which should have stopped the blow, parted like water around Mark's fingers, and blood burst from the gash, drenching his hand.

The raider tumbled backward down the stairs, and Mark

turned and raced up another floor. The other raiders had nearly caught up, and Mark continued his mad dash until he arrived at the top floor. He entered a room and saw the outer wall had been torn open. A dozen feet away was the concrete wall of another building, its small glass window still intact. Mark didn't hesitate, running forward and diving across the gap between buildings.

With a crash, the window broke, and he could feel glass scraping against him as he tumbled into the empty room beyond. Jumping to his feet, Mark reached behind himself, grabbing the heavy crossbow that materialized out of his shadow, even as he settled into a crouch. The first raider who tried to follow let out a sharp scream as a crossbow bolt slammed into his head, completely halting his forward momentum and sending him tumbling five stories to the ground below, where he landed with a sickening crunch.

The second raider had already begun to jump before the first one fell, and he made it into the window before the crossbow reloaded. He barely managed to block Mark's second shot by positioning his mana blade in front of his chest, but with a crack, the blade snapped. Then Mark's foot slammed into his head, sending him tumbling back out the window.

The remaining raiders wisely chose not to try to jump the gap. Having bought himself a moment of respite, Mark calmed his breathing, using the psychic network to track his enemies. A couple of them began to climb up onto the roof, intending to attack Mark from above, while some of the others headed back down the stairs, hoping to catch Mark if he tried to descend.

Thinking for a moment, Mark tossed the crossbow back into his shadow and began to retreat, making next to no noise, thanks in large part to the Wraith Walk potion, which was still active. He estimated that he still had another half an hour before it faded, which, in his mind, was more than enough time to do what he needed to.

Mark, who was growing surer by the minute that the raiders

were targeting him intentionally, retreated out of the room with the window and quickly stripped off his suit. They probably had some way of locking onto his position, and the suit was the most likely culprit. Of course, if they were using a power, there wasn't much that he could do, but if they had managed to put some sort of tracing mark on his suit, he could at least deny them that. After he removed it, his shadow rose up and enveloped it, and Mark, dressed in his skintight bodysuit, crept toward the top floor.

"Mime, can you shield me?"

Rather than receive a clear response, Mark felt a subtle shift in his mind, and an understanding of how to bend his shadow around him to shield his mental energy appeared. As he paused for a moment, Mark's eyes gleamed in the darkness, flashing red as his presence faded even further.

Coming around the corner, he saw a small room with a ladder that led up to a roof hatch. He could sense three raiders above him, positioning themselves around the hatch, and with a shiver, his body split. There was a long moment of silence, and then abruptly, the hatch bulged upward as it was torn free from the roof, creating a gaping hole. A raider dropped down through the hole, slamming into the floor, his weapon raised as he scanned for threats. Seeing nothing, he took a heavy step forward as another raider landed behind him, this one more lightly armored.

"Let's go," one of the raiders said, his voice raspy.

A sharp twang sounded in response, and a bolt fired at point-blank range slammed into his helmet, fracturing the armored faceplate. With a shout, he staggered backward, bumping into his companion, who was distracted by movement from both his right and his left. Thrown into confusion when he caught sight of a Mark on each side, one of which vanished with a pop, he failed to react in time, allowing Mark to land a blow on the back of his neck that severed his suit and his spine.

The last of the raiders, who had just jumped down from the roof, landed on the corpse of his companion, lost his footing, and tumbled to the side. Even as he struggled to get to his feet, the first of the raiders heard another twang, and a second crossbow bolt drove through the crack in his mask, shattering his cheekbone and snapping his head backward. With a scream, he fell to the ground, bleeding out.

When the raider who had just jumped down managed to get his balance, he saw Mark standing at the end of the hall near the stairs, holding a crossbow. Yet as soon as the raider caught sight of him, Mark vanished, and the crossbow tumbled to the ground. Unable to make heads or tails of what was going on, the raider didn't notice Mark's real body coming up behind him.

Mark grabbed the raider's head and wrenched it swiftly to the side, analyzing the remaining threats. Though the raider tried to resist, Mark's B-ranked strength allowed him to overpower his opponent instantly. There was a sharp crack, and the man's body twitched before falling still. Only a few seconds had passed since the fight began, and Mark's brutal efficiency had ensured that he had come out of it unscathed. Glancing at the corpses, he retrieved his crossbow and was about to leave when a thought struck him.

"Can you absorb them," he asked, "and take their powers?"

No, they're too weak.

His shadow's response confirmed something Mark had begun to suspect. His ability to absorb new powers from dead people only worked if they were stronger than him. Now that he was B ranked himself, he couldn't absorb abilities from anybody B ranked or lower. If he wanted to add any new abilities, he would have to find empowered who were stronger than him.

Abandoning his original idea, Mark waved his hand, and his shadow eagerly pounced on the corpses, rapidly gobbling them up and restoring the biofuel he had spent. Ignoring the faint crunching sound, Mark considered whether to head up to the roof or move down and confront the raiders who were climbing up from below. Six of the enemy had been eliminated, leaving four of the original ten who had charged them. There was also the brute who had been stationed behind them and the two ranged attackers, bringing the total up to seven enemies that Mark was aware of.

Returning to the stairwell, Mark cautiously made his way down, paying close attention to the psychic network. It wasn't long before he spotted the enemy entering the building. There were four of them, the brute in the lead. As they rapidly climbed the stairs, Mark considered the best way to ambush them. Currently shrouded by the lingering effects of the Wraith Walk potion, he was virtually undetectable unless directly looked at. Armed with his crossbow and a few other weapons, he felt confident. He estimated that none of his opponents were above the C rank, which gave him the upper hand.

Deciding to use a similar approach to his previous ambush, Mark concentrated for a moment. His body shivered and split into three different copies. One of them pulled out his crossbow while the others found hiding places. He didn't have to wait long before he heard the pounding footsteps of the raiders, led by the heavy thudding of the brute.

When the brute's head appeared, Mark eased out his breath and pulled the trigger of his crossbow. A bolt tore toward the brute's chest. To his credit, the brute managed to react before the bolt hit, lifting his arm to block with his heavily shielded gauntlet. The bolt slammed into him, cracking the armor plating on his mana suit but failing to pierce through. The sudden force nearly knocked the brute down the steps, but he managed to grab the railing, keeping himself from tumbling back into his companions.

With a low roar, he surged forward, practically throwing himself up the staircase, and arrived at the landing a second later. Yet as soon as he did, a figure dropped from above, plunging down through the center of the stairwell. Though the brute didn't see Mark, he sensed the motion and started to turn. Before he could, another bolt glanced off his chest armor, causing him to stumble backward toward the railing.

Mark reached out as he fell, fingers digging deep into the brute's armor. The momentum slowed Mark slightly, pulling him toward the side of the stairwell. But instead of stabilizing himself, he kicked off the concrete stairs, throwing himself backward and pulling the brute after him.

One of the other raiders glanced over and for the briefest moment saw the brute tumbling through the railing, his weight crushing the metal as Mark's tug pulled him over. The raider caught sight of Mark as well, though only for a split second before there was a faint pop and Mark was gone, leaving only the brute tumbling through the gap in the stairs.

With a scream, the brute flailed, trying to find purchase. But he was falling too fast, and Mark's tug had pulled him clear of the staircase, making it impossible for him to find a grip. The other three raiders arrived at the landing a moment later, and distracted by their companion's fall, they didn't notice Mark crouched at the other end of a short hallway, his crossbow leveled.

The twang of the crossbow was drowned out by the brute's scream and the loud crack as he slammed into the concrete at the bottom of the stairwell. The force of the fall was so great the entire building trembled, and one of the raiders suddenly jerked, his body stiffening as Mark's bolt pierced through the back of his mana suit, slipping in through a gap between his shoulder and backplate.

As he let out a loud yell, the others spun around, no longer worrying about their large companion who had fallen back down to the bottom floor. Mark had already retreated, but they caught sight of a flicker of movement around the corner, and the two unscathed raiders let out loud shouts as they raced down the hallway, weapons drawn.

The raider who had been hit by the bolt staggered, gripping the loose railing as he tried to keep himself on his feet, but before he could decide whether to follow his companions or retreat down the stairs, Mark climbed the steps behind him. Grabbing his leg, he yanked, pulling his feet out from under him and causing him to fall face-first to the ground. The attack was so sudden the raider hardly had time to scream before he slammed into the concrete floor.

Mark was on him in a moment, cutting through the back of the suit and severing the raider's spine, killing him instantly. Shaking the blood from his fingers, Mark dashed toward the hallway, even as the two raiders who had rushed forward found themselves ambushed from both sides.

Upon turning the corner, they hadn't seen Mark and had advanced about halfway down the hall, cautiously checking the rooms on either side. Then they heard their companion's scream and turned. As soon as they did, the doors on either side of them burst open, and Mark appeared from their right and their left. Yet even as they turned their heads to look, he vanished again with the same strange popping sound.

A moment later, Mark came around the corner at a full sprint, practically flying as he kicked off the walls. Distracted by the ambush, the raiders didn't manage to react to this new threat in time, and Mark's hand tore through the first raider's suit, cutting his arm off just below the elbow. As the raider jerked in shock and pain, Mark's other hand found his neck, tearing open his throat.

The last raider managed to bring up his mana blade, but Mark ducked under his wild swing, and a moment later, he too lay dead on the ground. Mark immediately turned and headed for the stairs as his shadow rose up to envelop the two corpses, swallowing them whole to preserve their armor for later. By the time he turned the corner, nothing remained in the hallway save for the two broken-down doors.

He rushed to the steps and glanced down the stairwell. The brute he had thrown over the edge was nowhere in sight, and with a quick scan of the psychic network, Mark spotted him slowly making his way out of the building. Scooping up the third corpse at the top of the stairs, Mark hurried down, his feet making no noise thanks to the Wraith Walk potion, despite the fact that he was running full tilt.

As he moved, he assessed his situation. Besides the brute, there were three other attackers, at least that he was aware of. The two ranged attackers, as well as one raider who was still watching the top of the building he was in.

By the time Mark made it down to the first floor, the brute had already staggered out into the street, clearly badly wounded from the way he weaved as he walked. The fact that the brute had survived the fall at all was a clear testament to his unnatural strength and fortitude.

Mark wasn't about to let an enemy go, but it also didn't seem wise to rush out into the street, into the line of sight of the two hidden snipers. As he got to the door, Mark paused for a second, then stepped forward and stepped back at the same time, his body splitting as a copy of him rushed out after the staggering brute.

Despite the fact that the brute was all the way across the road, with his back toward the entrance, Mark felt a slight shiver as his copy popped into nothingness, a clear indication that someone had caught sight of him. Glad that he hadn't just sprinted out into the street, Mark lifted his crossbow, took aim, and fired.

At the last moment, the brute, sensing the attack, dropped to his knees and bent forward, which caused the bolt to skip off his backplate, letting out a sharp whine as it vanished into the alleyway the brute had been heading toward. Clicking his tongue, Mark reloaded the crossbow and tossed it behind him, where it was swallowed up by his shadow. At this point, chasing after the brute was likely a no-go, at least until he got rid of the two snipers. Killing both of them was probably a long shot, but Mark knew that if he wanted to freely maneuver, both would need to be eliminated.

He retreated farther into the building, leaving a copy of himself armed with the crossbow to watch the building's entrance. Mark headed for a window on the side of the building, quietly opened it, and slipped out into the street. As he did, he analyzed the direction of the ranged attacks, trying to pinpoint one of the snipers. He had a rough idea of where they were, and he moved quickly through the tangled alleyways.

Only two buildings were tall enough to provide a good line of sight, and Mark headed for the taller of the two. It only took him a couple of minutes to get there. Wary that the sniper might have booby-trapped the inside of the building, Mark moved around to the back of it and began scaling the wall. His fingers gouged holes in the cement to provide him with a firm grip as he climbed up. The building was six stories tall, and when he got to the fourth floor, he began to wonder if his approach was really such a good idea. A glance down showed a dizzying drop, and a thread of nervousness wormed its way into his heart. Taking a deep breath, Mark resisted the urge to slip into a nearby window and continued to climb.

By this time, he had already spotted the sniper through the psychic network, a dull-gray marble sitting at the top of the building. Slowing down as he got to the roof, Mark made as little noise as possible, helped by the remains of the Wraith Walk potion. When he finally grabbed the edge of the roof and pulled himself over, he caught sight of the sniper lying prone on the corner, cradling a long mana rifle as he slowly swept the streets where Mark should have been with a pair of binoculars. The sniper was wearing a dull-gray mana suit that blended in with the cement and had a cloak that broke up his silhouette. Judging by his gear, the man was clearly a professional, but that didn't help him much as Mark arrived silently behind him.

Just before Mark struck, the sniper seemed to sense something and threw himself to the side, his body twisting as he let go of his rifle and reached for a mana blade. Before he could draw it from its sheath, Mark's hand fell, tearing through his suit and piercing his neck, nearly decapitating him in one swift stroke.

The fight was over almost before it began, and ignoring the acrid smell as blood began to pool under the sniper's corpse, Mark grabbed the rifle and settled down in the sniper's original position. His eyes scanned the nearby rooftops as he looked for the second sniper. Unable to see him, Mark did spot the broad-shouldered brute, who had regrouped with the last raider a few streets away from the building where they had fought Mark.

Figuring that dealing with them would be easy, Mark refocused, but after a full minute of searching, he still couldn't find the second sniper. Wondering if maybe there wasn't one, Mark sent a command to the clone he had left behind, and a moment later he saw himself emerge from the doorway of the building. Almost immediately, Mark felt the clone vanish with a pop.

He saw a slight movement in the window of a building four blocks away. Had he not been paying careful attention, he would have missed it, and it was only after watching the window for another few minutes that he caught sight of a faint silhouette shifting position to get a better view of the front door of the building.

The sniper, undoubtedly confused, was half exposed, and letting out his breath, Mark lifted the rifle, focusing the scope on the window. He was by no means an expert with ranged energy weapons, but Mark's physical control was tremendous, allowing him to keep the rifle completely still as he drew a bead on the sniper.

Worried that targeting the sniper for too long might alert the enemy, Mark quickly squeezed off his shot, and with a faint thrum, the rifle jumped in his hands. The bolt of mana crossed the distance almost instantly, punching a hole through the window to hit the sniper hidden beyond. The sniper vanished, though Mark had no idea whether he was alive or dead.

Staying in a low crouch, Mark rose and shifted to another part of the roof. If the sniper wasn't dead, Mark had just exposed his position, though since he was higher, it would be much harder for the enemy sniper to hit him. From his new spot, he scanned the window where the enemy sniper had been, but didn't see any sign of movement, so he turned his attention to the brute and remaining raider.

They were still hunkered down a few streets away from where Mark should have been, but judging from their panicked movements, they most likely knew the other sniper had been hit. Taking careful aim, Mark targeted the smaller of the two raiders and squeezed off a shot. The bolt of compressed mana punched a neat hole straight through the raider's mana suit, obliterating his heart along with a good portion of his chest. As he crumpled to the ground, the brute turned and sprinted for cover, helped along by a second shot that barely missed his shoulder.

Shifting positions once more, Mark turned his attention back to the sniper's location but still didn't see any movement. Since he could no longer see the brute, who had entered a nearby building, Mark dropped the sniper rifle into his shadow, and after absorbing the sniper's corpse, he quickly made his way back down to street level, this time taking the stairs.

Along the way, he surprised a small group of four drones that had wandered up to the second floor, likely drawn by the gunfire. His Wraith Walk potion was starting to fade, but Mark was still shrouded from the psychic network, allowing him to ambush them and tear them apart before they knew he was there. As their psychic screams echoed in the network, Mark hastened to leave the building, winding his way rapidly through the alleyways as he moved toward the other sniper's position.

Though he had seen the bolt hit, he had a suspicion that the other sniper was still alive, a suspicion that grew stronger as he got closer to the position where the sniper had fallen. Keeping a close eye on the psychic network, Mark saw more Exlian beginning to move into the area and carefully skirted around a group of drones led by a mantis.

The detour cost him a little bit of time, and when he arrived at the building where the enemy sniper had set up, he heard the sounds of fighting. A moment later, an obviously wounded man rushed out of the building. He was missing one of his arms, which had been blown off at the shoulder, and held a bloody mana blade in the other. There was a loud chittering behind him as three drones rushed out of the doorway and pounced on him. Watching for a moment longer, Mark swiftly turned away, even as the wounded sniper let out a scream and went down under the Exlian's claws.

Only one member of the enemy team remained: the brute. Mark knew that if he wanted, he could simply walk away, retreating toward the city and leaving the wounded brute to the Exlian, which were swarming the area. Yet something in Mark wouldn't let him retreat, driving him to end the fight and ensure that no danger remained. Strangely, the fact that Exlian were approaching didn't worry Mark one bit. Instead, he found himself practically ignoring their presence.

At one point, coming around a corner, he saw a group of drones emerge from a building down the street. Yet despite the fact that they were only a hundred feet from each other, the drones simply glanced in his direction and then turned away, continuing about their business as if they had nothing to do with him. Mark wasn't sure if it was because of the technique he was using to shroud his presence from the psychic network or for another reason, but reassured that the Exlian wouldn't be an issue, he sped up, heading toward the place where he had last seen the brute. When he arrived at the hiding spot, he found it empty, the brute having long since retreated.

"Mime, can you track him?"

Materializing from Mark's shadow, Mime glanced around

and then nodded. She took off like a flash. Mark followed closely behind her as they wound their way through the ruined city. Only a few minutes later, he spotted the brute cautiously making his way between two buildings. There was a group of Exlian on the brute's left, five drones and three warriors. Speeding up, Mark approached the brute from behind and a moment later caught sight of him crouched at the end of an alleyway behind an old metal dumpster.

Mark, who was still dressed in nothing but his skintight suit, paused at the other end of the alley, doing a sweep of the psychic network once again. The reason the brute hadn't continued forward was that the Exlian had begun moving down the street. Of course, though he was hidden for the moment, Mark knew that the Exlian would spot the brute almost immediately when they came in range. The direction the wind was blowing would carry his scent to the monsters without fail.

For a moment, Mark considered whether it would be better to just let the Exlian do the job for him. But just then the brute glanced backward and caught sight of Mark at the other end of the alleyway. With a shout of surprise, he rose to his feet, turning to face Mark, his face pale. There was a loud screech from the street as the Exlian spotted him and began to rush over.

Realizing his error, the brute charged toward Mark, judging him to be the weaker of the two threats. With a faint sigh, Mark stepped forward to meet the charge, kicking the brute's ankle as his foot landed to disrupt his balance. Caught off guard by the power behind Mark's kick, the brute swung his arm wildly to compensate, allowing Mark to take advantage of his unbalanced state.

Mark slipped around the strike, and his chop broke through the brute's helmet, tearing a gash across his eyes that caused him to scream. The pain distracted the brute, making him unable to regain his balance, and as he crashed to the ground, Mark's other hand chopped down, ripping apart the armor on his neck and cutting through his throat.

It only took a moment for the brute to bleed out, but Mark's attention wasn't on the dying man. Instead, he turned to the end of the alleyway, where three mantises had appeared. Rather than retreat, Mark took a step forward, his eyes gleaming, even as the large body behind him sank into his shadow.

The mantises, catching sight of Mark, abruptly stiffened and began to slowly back up. Mark's eyes narrowed, and he took another step forward, causing them to retreat even faster, vanishing from the mouth of the alleyway. By the time Mark made it to the street, they were gone, along with the drones that were with them.

If Mark had to guess, he would peg them as D ranked, which, in part, explained why they were so hesitant to attack him, though this wasn't a courtesy they would extend to any other humans. Unsure whether he should be pleased or creeped out, Mark shook his head. There was nothing he could do about it, so instead, he focused on his next move. The team of raiders was dead, and Terra and the other members of the team had retreated back to New Emery, so Mark decided to retreat as well, though not before sweeping the battlefield to collect the remaining bodies and pick up his fallen crossbow.

The first thing Mark did was pull his mana suit out of his shadow and climb into it. The truth was that he felt much more at home without it. But walking into New Emery in nothing but his bodysuit would undoubtedly raise questions. Mime jumped up onto his shoulder, and Mark reached up to scratch her under the chin.

"Maybe we should try coming back without a team," he said, looking around. "It'd probably be a lot easier to maneuver."

Mime gave him an amused look and nodded emphatically, then closed her eyes to enjoy his scratches. After taking a moment to orient himself, Mark headed back toward New Emery at a swift jog. His biofuel meter was full, his body bursting with energy. In many ways, he felt like a perpetual motion machine, as if he could run forever. Given enough Exlian, or people, for his shadow to consume, he thought it probably wasn't far from the truth.

As he jogged, he carefully assessed the fight he had just been through, weighing each of his choices along with the results. This was the first time he had truly used his clone ability in combat, and it had worked like a charm, allowing him to attack from multiple angles, to distract and disorient, and ultimately to overcome a larger group by himself.

Of course, it only worked in an environment where he could remain hidden, and if he had gotten into a pitched fight out in the open, it would have done him no good. The clones could only exist for a fraction of a second under other people's gazes. But that was enough, especially when fighting in close quarters. The crossbow had also performed well, and Mark was already considering new strategies. The fact that his clones could access his shadow just like him was a tremendous boon that would allow him to operate as his own team out in the dead zone or the wilderness beyond.

When Mark arrived at the gate, the fact that he was alone earned him a few strange looks from the guards. But after explaining he had been separated from his team due to an attack, the guards waved him through without any further questions. Mark didn't mention that they had been attacked by raiders, allowing the guards to assume it had been Exlian that had caused them to separate.

As soon as he stepped back into New Emery, he checked his watch and realized that a number of messages were waiting for him, most of them from Terra. Mark sent a quick reply to let his team leader know that he had returned to the city and was heading to his apartment to rest, arranging to meet the following morning.

After arriving back at his apartment, Mark took a quick

shower, then started to go through his spoils. The mission he and the others had undertaken had been successful, but Mark's true gain was nearly an entire team's worth of mana suits that he had collected from the corpses of the raider team. His shadow had consumed the corpses themselves, leaving only the gear behind. At his command, it was laid out neatly on his living room floor.

The brute's suit was the largest, taking up the most space, while the other suits were stretched out next to each other. All the suits were damaged, at least slightly, but most of the damage was located in or around the throat, where the helmet connected to the main body of the suit. The damage would undoubtedly lower the price Mark would get from selling them, but since the main armor plating and power systems were largely unharmed, it wouldn't be by much.

The brute's suit was in the worst shape; it had multiple heavy cracks in it, thanks to his four-story tumble down the stairwell. A couple of the suits had so little damage Mark was confident that he could actually repair them himself. Along with the suits were numerous mana weapons, most of which Mark would sell as well. He wanted to keep only a couple of them, like the sniper rifle.

After he was done organizing all the armor and weapons, Mark turned his attention to the watches he had recovered, checking them to see if there was any interesting information and transferring the linked accounts' contents into his. Though none of the raiders had many credits, Mark managed to scrape together a couple hundred thousand in total, the majority of them from the brute. None of the raiders had owned any property, which was a bit of a shame.

After he had finished transferring everything they owned, Mark reset each watch, wiping it clean of all information. The brute's watch he left active after finding a map embedded in one of the recent messages.

The map indicated a location outside the city, roughly an hour from where they had been ambushed. According to the message, this was the team's staging ground, a secure bunker the brute had established as a place for raiders to gather. There was no indication of who had hired the raiders or if they had been hired at all, and Mark wondered if he had been overthinking it. During the fight, he had been convinced that they were hunting him; he'd even gone so far as to remove his suit just in case they had planted some sort of tracking device on it. After he read through the brute's messages, however, it seemed much more likely this was just a regular raiding team that had spotted them and set up an ambush.

Figuring he might need the watch in order to get into the hideout, Mark tossed it back into his shadow without resetting it. He went to the kitchen to get a drink of water, thinking carefully through his next moves. Selling the raiders' suits wasn't something that he could do through legal channels. After all, if he simply walked into the Hunters' Association and dumped out a pile of eleven suits, he'd undoubtedly draw some unwanted attention. Of course, plenty of less-than-legal channels could be used, but Mark didn't actually know where to find them.

He was just wondering how to approach this problem when he felt his watch vibrate.

He saw a message from Maestro asking him when he was available for a call. Mark replied that he was available immediately, and a moment later, he saw Maestro's face pop up.

"How did it go? Was the mission successful? Were you able to retrieve the mutated rat hearts?"

"We were. We got six in total. There were still more at the den, but we figured this was good for the moment. We were able to sneak in without having to fight the whole group, which made things much easier."

"Good. I'm glad. You can deposit them the same way. I'll send a courier to you. Payment will arrive once you hand them to the courier. I also have another serum coming your way. This one should help smooth out some of the rough edges from the last one."

"Rough edges? What do you mean?" Mark asked, genuinely unsure what Maestro was talking about.

That earned him a long stare. "Are you not experiencing nightmares? Huh. All of my data suggests that you're experiencing constant nightmares when you sleep. Speaking of which, the fact that you only sleep for two hours a night and yet operate at near-peak efficiency is rather ludicrous. But the two hours you're getting should be plagued by nightmares of constantly being eaten by a war bear over and over and over again. In fact, I keep expecting you to bring it up, but you never do."

Scratching his nose, Mark shrugged. "I haven't been having any nightmares, though I do tend to dream a lot."

"Well, in that case, this serum might not be helpful," Maestro said. "You know what? Let's hold off on this round, and I'll retool it. Tell me, how's your glitch ability coming? Have you had any success?"

Reflecting on the question, Mark shook his head. "No, not much progress. I've been a bit distracted with some other things."

"Oh, like what?"

Figuring it wasn't very wise to expose all his secrets but unsure what Maestro knew already, Mark decided it wouldn't hurt to share what he had been attempting.

"I'm trying to understand mana circuits better," he said, "to see if I can figure out how to replicate that teleportation effect that you use. I bought one of those repeating crossbows that uses the same technology in its loading mechanism, and I've been trying to get my head around that."

"Ah, I wondered why you were doing so much self-study. Well, I have plenty of information that I can send your way, but the truth is that you'll only be able to work with mana circuits if you have some way to detect mana. Do you have some way to detect mana?"

Carefully controlling his heartbeat, Mark tried his best to keep his expression neutral.

"Sort of," he said. "It's a bit wonky, but I feel like I can detect where mana is by comparing it to where mana isn't, right? So like, understanding mana concentration, maybe?"

A look of realization appeared in Maestro's eyes, and his eyelids quivered slightly as the arms behind his chair began to dance, signaling his excitement. "I wonder if this has something to do with your glitch ability. After all, it's the ability to push mana away from a given area. Technically, this is a manipulation of mana, so it makes sense that you'd be able to sense the difference between where mana is concentrated and where it is not. If we could make your glitch ability more precise, you might have an actual mana control ability. Ooh, this is fascinating. Quite fascinating. I'll retool your next serum. Expect it within the month. I have much research to do."

The screen shimmered as the call closed down, leaving Mark staring at the empty space, wondering if what he had done was foolish. Granted, any help he could get from Maestro on controlling his null field was welcome. Mark just hoped he didn't accidentally send the mad genius down a dangerous path because he wasn't revealing the truth of his abilities.

"Shoot. I meant to ask him where I could sell the mana suits," Mark muttered, contemplating whether he should call Maestro again.

Before he could, his watch buzzed.

MAESTRO

If you're looking for a buyer for any extra gear you collect on your adventures, you can talk to Ivan.

Attached to the message was the address of an out-of-the-way shop in the southern part of the city. With a wry smile, Mark could only shake his head.

JONATHAN

Thanks. That's just what I was looking for.

It was rather unnerving to have Maestro following his every move, but at least Mark was aware of it. Maestro could undoubtedly have simply manipulated Mark from the shadows, but the fact that he not only had initiated direct contact but was upfront about constantly keeping tabs on Mark made things a little bit easier.

It was getting late, but Mark figured that any sort of shady operation likely had twenty-four-hour service, so he ordered a moving truck through the InfoWeb and, when it arrived, loaded the salvaged suits into it. After climbing into the passenger seat, he gave the driver the address, and they headed to the south side of New Emery.

It was clearly not the first time that the driver had done something like this, because he avoided the main roads and proceeded with due caution, making sure to stay out of sight of any patrols. When they arrived at the address Mark had been given, the driver got out a cigarette and pointed across the street. "I'll be smoking over there. Just give me a ring when you want to leave."

Hopping out of the truck, Mark watched him walk across the street, then turned his attention to the nondescript building in front of him. At one point, it had been a mechanic's shop, but the sign was so faded that it was impossible to tell what it had been named. The windows were dim, and as Mark got closer, he realized it was because they were covered with thick curtains. Knocking, he sensed someone stirring inside, and a moment later, a slot in the door popped open, and two eyes peered out at him.

"Yes? What do you want?"

"I'm here to see Ivan," Mark said. "I was recommended."

"Huh."

There was a pause. The slot slid shut, and the door opened, revealing a wall made of flesh. Startled, Mark looked up and then looked up some more, realizing that the man in front of him must have gotten down on his knee to look through the door slot.

"Come in, but if you make trouble, I'll crush you."

As the eight-foot-tall brute stepped back and gestured with a dinner-plate-size hand for Mark to enter, the rest of the room was revealed. There was an old counter with a middle-aged man sitting behind it, a large ledger in front of him. He had glasses perched on the end of his nose, and he peered at Mark over them. His salt-and-pepper hair traced a thin horseshoe around the back of his head, leaving the top to gleam in the bright lights.

"You say you come recommended, huh? Well, I'm Ivan, and I don't know anybody who would recommend you."

Stepping into the building, Mark gave Ivan half a shrug. "I don't know if you know him or not, but he certainly recommended me."

As Mark spoke, he gestured down with his finger toward the ground. At first, Ivan just stared at him blankly, and then realization dawned. "Oh, I see. Well, that is certainly a high recommendation. What can I help you with, sir?"

"I've got a bunch of suits. Some of them are in a little bit of a rough shape, but I'd like to off-load them. I'm also looking for steady access to alchemical materials and potentially even an alchemy workshop that I might be able to use."

Taking a moment to think over what Mark was asking for, Ivan slowly nodded. "Mana suits we can deal with, no problem, and I might even know an alchemical shop you can borrow time in. As for materials, that's a bit of a specialized field, and we don't handle it. I do know some people who do, and if I can get you into the shop, you can probably pull from their stock. Looking for anything in particular?"

"Not at the moment, no. I'll just be venturing out of the city, and I want to make sure that I have a steady supply of potions."

"I take it you have an alchemist on staff, then? Or . . ." Ivan trailed off, his eyes carrying a hint of confusion.

Waving his hand, Mark chose not to enlighten him. "I'll take care of the alchemist as long as you can provide the shop," he said.

Ivan was happy to let the matter drop. With a nod, he flipped through the ledger in front of him until he came to a blank spot. "Why don't you bring your goods in? Marco here can help you. Just deposit them in one of the bays. We'll do a quick inventory and get you a price."

"Thank you."

Heading back out to the truck, Mark helped Marco pull the suits out and put them in the empty bay while Ivan began assessing them. A couple of times, Mark saw him looking at the damage the suits had suffered and then peeking over at Mark. Ivan didn't let his curiosity get the better of him, however, and half an hour later, Mark was back in the van heading toward his apartment with the driver, a cool ten million credits richer.

In truth, Mark had been expecting half that amount, but the fact that the suits had already been scrubbed, as Ivan put it, increased the price. When Mark gave him a blank look, Ivan had explained that all mana suits had serial numbers and removing the serial numbers took considerable time and resources. So the suits already being outside the system made them much more valuable.

Ivan hadn't asked where Mark had gotten the suits, though he had casually inquired whether there would be more. To that, Mark could only shrug.

After being dropped off at his apartment and giving the driver a sizable tip, Mark headed back up to his room and settled in for the night, resuming his martial arts practice, as had become his habit.

The next morning, when he arrived at the Hunters' Association, he found Terra and the rest of the team waiting for him, eager to talk about what had happened after they had run away. Dragging Mark to a table in the cafeteria, Terra pushed a drink into his hands as Zem tugged on him from the other side. "How did you get out of there? I mean, there were so many of them."

"I'm quick," Mark said with a shrug. "Rather than try to run on the street level, I lured them into the building, went up the stairs, and then jumped out a window. I still had the Wraith Walk potion active, so I was able to lose them that way. It's really not nearly as exciting as you guys are imagining. What about you? Did you have any trouble getting back to the city?"

"One of the snipers took a couple potshots at us," Terra said, "but I was able to block most of the approaches, and we made it back without any trouble."

"Do you know who they were?" Mark asked, looking around at the group. "Do you think they were intentionally looking for us?"

"I don't think so," Terra said with a frown.

"Likely, they were just hunting for any teams who looked like they were returning to New Emery," Brightblade said, putting his drink down on the table. "I mean, it's fairly common activity, despite the fact that the association says it doesn't happen. The real question is, Are we going to run into them again?"

Holding his tongue, Mark turned to look at Terra like the others, causing the team leader to shift uncomfortably in his seat. "I mean, it's impossible to say we're not going to run into raiders again, but since we reported it to the association, I'm sure they'll lay low for a while."

Reaching under the table, Terra lifted a metal case and set it in front of them. "Here are the hearts, Apex. Do you need us to do anything with these, or can you handle it?"

"I can handle it," Mark said, grabbing the case and pulling it over. "After they're delivered, I'll send the money. Thankfully, this job went relatively smoothly."

"Much smoother than I thought it would," Apora said, "probably thanks to those Wraith Walk potions. If you have any more missions like this, definitely count us in."

"I will," Mark replied. "Speaking of missions, I might take a break for a couple of weeks. There are a couple of things I want to work on, including my suit, so I'm going to focus on that."

Exchanging glances with the rest of the group, Terra gave Mark a half-hearted smile. "I kind of figured that would be the case, but I'll keep you posted as we come up with things."

"Thanks."

Mark got up, grabbed the case, and left, waving to the others. He had already arranged to rent one of the suit workshops for the rest of the day, to see if it would be possible to not only modify his suit but also scan it for tracking devices. A few minutes after he arrived, there was a knock on the door, and Mark, upon opening it, found himself facing a cleaning robot. Without waiting for him to speak, the robot hummed and entered the room. When the door shut, a hatch in its chest opened up.

"Hello. Please deposit the box here."

Despite the fact that the voice was entirely mechanical, Mark recognized it as Maestro, and after retrieving the box that stored the mutated hearts, he stuck it into the large cavity. This time, it didn't vanish; instead, the robot simply turned and went back to the door, waiting for Mark to open it before rolling away.

It wasn't long before the reward arrived: 6,000 points and three million credits, which Mark divided up among the members of the team. An influx of 1,200 points to his account was enough to upgrade him to a level-three member of the association. The process was automatic, and Mark soon received a message outlining all the benefits of his new level, one of which was a discount on using the workshop.

After browsing through the rest of the benefits, Mark put it out of his mind and returned to working on his suit. He genuinely wasn't sure what to do with it, and after double-checking to make sure that no tracking devices were implanted in it, he began to sketch out some concepts.

The main trouble, he found, was that because the suit was separate from him, none of his powers worked well with it. In fact, he was realizing that he was genuinely better off just not wearing a suit at all. His body was tough, and between his mana shields and natural regeneration, the armor plating on his suit didn't add much. If anything, it actually made him less protected, rather than more.

The second major issue was that as soon as he put on a suit, his bone blade transformation was much harder to use because his hands were covered by gloves, reducing his offensive power. Stealth also became harder in a suit, as he had to compensate for the sounds it would make and the mana signature from the batteries. No matter how he sliced it, Mark was better off simply not using a suit. But while the Exlian wouldn't care one way or another, he had a feeling that walking around outside the city without a suit would get him on a watch list quite quickly.

After considering the situation a bit longer, Mark found himself puzzled. He knew that individuals with growth powers couldn't wear suits while using those powers, because activating them while encased in a layer of thick metal would result in a bloody disaster.

Tapping on his watch, Mark connected to the InfoWeb and pulled up information on the eighth-ranked empowered in New Emery. Going by the name Atlas, he used his size manipulation power to transform into a giant. This was completely incompatible with a suit, making Mark wonder how Atlas fought the Exlian. Upon looking up videos of the giant, Mark realized that Atlas had an absolutely massive suit of armor that he would put on after engaging his growth ability but before combat.

This got Mark curious, however, and he began to look through the lists of empowered, trying to find anyone with a similar problem. It became pretty clear that even those who could transform their bodies into other substances still preferred to use suits outside the walls of New Emery, though many of them wore modified suits that looked more like power frames than actual mana suits. This allowed them to use their bodies' natural defenses.

Biting his lip, Mark continued to scroll through the lists, looking for inspiration. When he got to the four hundredth spot, he paused, his eyes hovering on an empowered who went by the name Armored Sentinel. Dressed in what appeared to be a suit of black medieval armor that covered him from head to toe, as if he were some sort of dark knight, Armored Sentinel's power was the ability to manifest the suit of armor around him, which was completely incompatible with a mana suit. It was similar to the weapon manifestation that Mark's friend Danny had acquired.

Mark delved deeper, soon discovering a video of Armored Sentinel venturing outside the city to fight with Exlian, clad only in a summoned suit of armor. Closing the virtual window, Mark leaned back and stared at the ceiling, his thoughts churning. As long as he just said it had something to do with his power, perhaps it wouldn't be too difficult for him to walk around without bothering with a mana suit. He was unable to decide how to proceed, but then he suddenly slapped his forehead. "Why am I even wasting my time on this?"

He reopened his watch and spoke into the air.

"Maestro? Hey, this is Mark. I have a problem, and I'm wondering if you can help me with it. The situation is relatively straightforward. Because of my mana shields, I don't really have a mana suit that works well. Honestly, I don't feel like I need one, but I also don't want strange looks when I walk around practically naked. I'm wondering if you have any thoughts on this. I saw somebody who has the ability to manifest armor around them, and I remember Servo, my teammate in the Tomb, being able to autonomously deploy his suit. Do you have any thoughts on how I should approach this?"

Almost immediately, Mark's watch vibrated.

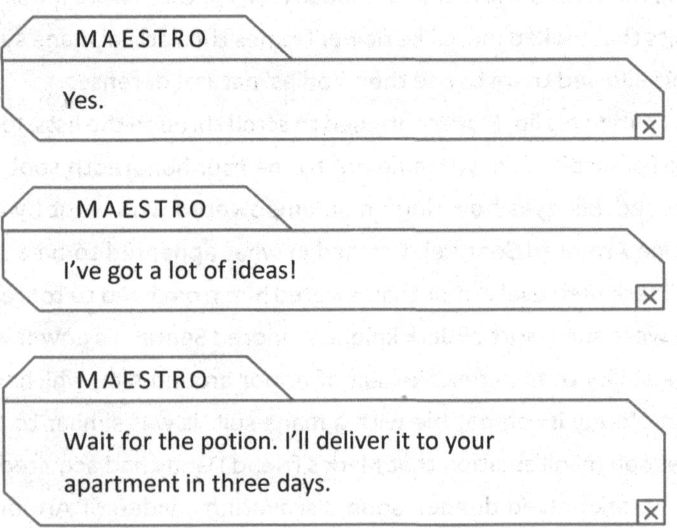

A chill settled on Mark, and he suddenly wondered if getting Maestro involved was such a wise course of action. Then again, if anyone could figure out a good solution to his problem, Maestro was it.

In the meantime, Mark had a few things he wanted to do. First, he needed to visit the alchemy workshop Ivan had arranged for him to use. Some of the potions he wanted to make, Wraith Walk among them, required controlled substances that it would be hard to get through the association without being a level-five member. He could make the more basic potions at the association, but having an off-grid workshop with access to rarer ingredients through the black market would make things a lot easier.

The second thing he wanted to do was head back out into the dead zone and try to find the raiders' base. He was fairly sure he knew where it was located, and he was curious to see if they'd left anything there. It seemed smarter to prep his potions first, however. So after grabbing a quick lunch, Mark hailed a cab to the address Ivan had given him. He was dropped off in front of a rather corporate-looking building among a lot of other corporate-looking buildings. Mark wasn't sure he was in the right place.

Walking in, he saw a secretary sitting at the front desk. After looking around at the well-worn upholstered seats and the plastic potted plants in desperate need of a dusting, he approached the secretary, who was simply watching him with a sort of idle curiosity.

"You look lost," she said. "Can I help you?"

"I don't just look lost," Mark replied. "I think I am lost. I was given this address by, uh, Ivan? I was looking for an alchemy workshop."

The secretary didn't react until Mark said the name Ivan, and even then, her eyes just shifted slightly before returning to normal. Reaching for the intercom, she pressed a button. "George, there's someone here to see you. About the empty lab."

"I'll be out in a second."

The voice on the other end of the intercom was rich, but when George walked out of his office and came down the hall toward Mark, he looked nothing like his voice suggested. Rail thin with long brown hair tied loosely at the nape of his neck and a pair of steel-rimmed glasses that drew two large circles on his face, George looked like a nervous scientist.

"Welcome. Ivan said you'd be coming."

In contrast to his appearance, his voice boomed, completely filling the space, and Mark caught sight of the secretary wincing from the corner of his eye. Reaching out to shake Mark's hand, George gestured for him to follow and led Mark down the hallway to an elevator. Rather than go up, they went down two stories into the basement.

"I bought this company some years ago," George said. "Our primary business is specialized Exlian research, solving particular problems for people with the money to pay for it. However, we don't do any of our own chemistry, so I've got a big lab that's been sitting idle. Two of them, in fact. Ivan says you're looking for a place where you can do a bit of alchemy. This lab is just the place."

When the elevator opened, they stepped into a large room, almost three hundred feet long and two hundred feet wide. It was packed with machines of all kinds, many of which Mark didn't recognize, and all of which were covered in a healthy layer of dust.

"Mind the dust. It's been some time since anybody's been down here. What do you think? Will it be sufficient for your needs?"

Looking around, Mark spotted an alchemy workstation in the corner. "I think so. He also mentioned you might be able to get me stock. If you guys don't do any alchemy here, is that still going to be possible?"

"Oh, sure. When it comes to Exlian parts, we have a good number of connections," George said with a grin. "Just tell me what you're looking for. Or rather, don't tell me. Tell Sarah at the front desk. If you hand her a list, she'll make sure that it's stocked for you within a couple of days."

"What about price? How much is all this going to cost me?"

"Well, considering nobody else is using it, I'm sure we can come to a nice agreement. But it'll be much more comfortable to do that up in my office. Come on, let's see what we can work out."

Forty-five minutes later, Mark left the office, strongly suspecting that he had just overpaid for access to a lab. Then again, George seemed entirely comfortable with less-than-legal activity. He had assured Mark that not only would the laboratory be clean when he returned the following day, but the many materials he needed for his various potions would be provided. Mark was also granted access to a side door that would allow him to enter and exit the building without anyone being the wiser.

As he took a taxi back to his apartment, he made a mental list of the various kinds of potions he was interested in. At the moment, Mark was flush with credits, thanks in large part to the mission his team had completed for Maestro. However, alchemy was known to burn through resources faster than almost any other profession. Mark knew that he was going to need a tremendous influx of both material and credits if he wanted to achieve his goals.

Thankfully, New Emery was surrounded by an ever-renewing resource in the Exlian, and Mark found himself growing increasingly eager to start hunting them. Of course, as a member of the association, he could always take missions, but a new idea was starting to bloom in Mark's mind. Rather than try to complete specific requests, why not just enter the dead zone and hunt for powerful Exlian? It would allow him to gather his own resources, as well as the bounties for killing the various monsters.

For the vast majority of hunters, a plan like this would be little more than suicide, but Mark was fully confident in both his ability to navigate outside the city and his ability to kill Exlian. The more he thought about it, the clearer it was that this was the best move. He spent the rest of the day meditating and practicing his forms, and all that night continuing to perfect the teleportation mana circuits.

Early the next morning, after receiving a notification that the lab was ready, he hurried back and entered through the small side door, which opened into a long sloping hallway. At the end of the hallway was a staircase, then a set of double doors that opened into the laboratory. As soon as he entered, the lights flicked on, revealing a scene diametrically opposed to what he had seen the day before.

The machines, which had all been covered up by dusty plastic sheets, now gleamed in the light, no hint of dust anywhere in the room. Against one wall were dozens of racks packed full of materials, each with a detailed label. Mark looked over everything, doing his best to categorize the various machines and spending a bit of time researching the ones he couldn't identify.

The laboratory contained not just tools and ingredients for alchemy but also everything he would need for building suits or performing experiments on Exlian. There were even machines that could be used for building out mechanical parts or tracing mana circuits into metal or plastic. The agreement that Mark had made ensured that he had full access to every piece of equipment in the lab, though most of it he imagined he wasn't going to use.

After he finished looking around, Mark took a moment to center himself, and then, focusing his mind, he split, two clones stepping out of his body and looking around. Though it was possible for Mark to create more clones, two was the number he could control comfortably while also operating himself. One clone headed for the alchemy lab to begin prepping for potion creation, while the second went to retrieve the materials he would need.

Mark sat down in the middle of the floor, his hands cupped together in front of him, palms up. Closing his eyes, he began to meditate, working on his mana control and at the same time directing the two clones to get to work. The contract Mark had signed specified that no one would enter the laboratory, which meant that unless he invited someone in, it was possible for him to keep his clones active permanently. Though each clone caused his biofuel to drain, Mark figured he could just make up for it by eating more, as the cost would be offset by the increased number of potions he could make.

He was quite adept at controlling his clones, but it still took him a few minutes to settle into a good rhythm, and soon, his two clones began working together to produce basic healing potions. Mark had long ago mastered these potions, and he quickly produced a set of twelve. After setting them aside, he began working on a number of utility potions, including Wraith Walk and Dead Man Walking, along with one called Night Sight that would give him thermographic vision. These potions were a bit harder, and he failed the first few attempts. It wasn't long, however, before he attuned himself to the machines he was working with and began to turn out potions one after another.

After a few hours of meditation, Mark let out a deep breath and stood up, stretching his muscles to shake the stiffness from them. While the clones could produce the potions, they lacked the ability to bleed, as any damage would cause them to simply vanish. This meant that they couldn't take advantage of Mark's alchemical blood ability, so he spent a few minutes adding drops of blood to the various healing potions. Then, with the help of one of his clones and a few breaks to allow his regeneration to kick in, he drew a few liters of extra blood and stored it so the clones could continue to use it.

Thanks in part to his regeneration, Mark didn't feel weak at all, despite having pulled multiple liters of blood from his arm. Instead, his biofuel simply depleted rapidly, an intense hunger awakening in him. Finding himself tempted to throw some of the alchemical materials into his mouth, Mark left the clones behind and went to find a restaurant to have a meal. After ordering his fourth plate of food, he realized that this wasn't sustainable and instead caught a taxi to a nearby grocery store, where he bought two boxes of nutrient pouches, all of which he consumed before making it back to the laboratory. Rather than head down to where his clones were working, Mark walked into the front office and greeted Sarah.

"Welcome," Sarah said with a bright smile. "How are you finding the space?"

"It's perfect, thank you," Mark said, glancing around the office. "I was wondering, though, would it be possible for me to arrange for a delivery of nutrient pouches? I'd like something to eat while I'm down there, as I'll probably be spending a significant amount of time in the lab."

"Sure, would you like me to add that to the list of materials to restock?"

"That would be great. I'd like to start by ordering a pallet."

"I'm sorry, did you say a pallet? Don't you mean a case?"

"No, I mean a pallet of cases. A case has twenty pouches, right? I need probably twenty to fifty cases."

"That's a lot of nutrient paste."

"It is a lot of nutrient paste," Mark said, scratching his nose. "But better to be safe than sorry."

Sarah clearly didn't agree, and it looked as if the thought of so many nutrient pouches made her want to gag. Mark, who by this point was completely immune to the taste, wasn't so sure what the big deal was.

After arranging for the pallet to be ordered, Mark thanked Sarah and headed back to his apartment, leaving his clones to continue their work.

The farther he went from his clones, the fainter the connection, and Mark had a feeling that if he moved too far away, they wouldn't be able to sustain themselves anymore. Unfortunately, he didn't know what that distance was. He hoped that his clones would be able to continue working even while he was out in the dead zone, outside New Emery.

The next two days passed swiftly, and at about noon of the second day, Mark heard a chime at the door. When he opened it, he saw a hovering drone that zipped into his apartment, dropped a package on his table, and then left just as quickly as it had come. There was no note or message from Maestro, but Mark knew exactly what was in the box and found himself quite nervous.

Taking a moment to settle his surging emotions, Mark opened the box and found a data stick lying alongside a vial of glimmering purplish-black liquid. Something about this serum looked different from the others Mark had taken before, so he slotted the data stick into his watch and pulled up the video it contained. Maestro's massive head appeared on the screen, and after a moment, he looked toward the camera and flashed a smile.

"I figured this would be easier, as I'll be quite busy over the next few weeks. I have too many projects in progress that can't be interrupted. Your request came at the most opportune time, as I've been looking for someone to test a new serum for me, and when you asked your question, a flash of inspiration struck. This serum is based on a powerful Exlian called a cataphract. The word 'cataphract' means a full-body suit of armor, which describes the Exlian in question exactly. Now, what makes this Exlian unique is that it is not, like most Exlian, an independent organism. Instead, the cataphract is more like a parasite that attaches itself to other, larger organisms.

"It was the comment about the late Servo's deployable suit that sparked the thought in my mind. The cataphract invades the spine of a creature and modifies its body by creating a special network akin to veins that runs parallel to a creature's nervous system, but closer to the surface of the skin. Normally, this network is completely hidden, undetectable even. But at a moment's notice, it can manifest a heavy chitinous plating that completely covers the creature from head to toe, transforming it into an armored version of itself. Originally, we believed the cataphract to be a specific ability of a large catlike Exlian, similar to a tiger, found far north of the city. However, despite killing many of these armored tigers, we were never able to extract the ability. It was only once I began to dissect them that I realized that the cataphract was a completely separate organism.

"I've managed to isolate its DNA and incorporate it into the serum I sent you, mixing it with the last batch of the war bear serum that you need to take. After this, you should find your war bear characteristics stabilizing. At the same time, I hope the inclusion of the cataphract will allow you to replicate its ability. Be aware, as always, that for every advancement a price must be paid. In your case, I'm not too worried, as you seem largely immune to the mental influence Exlian genes normally produce. If you have any questions, feel free to ask, though I likely won't answer them for the next week or so. Good luck."

As the video ended, Mark took another look at the purplish serum and swallowed nervously. Part of him was genuinely excited about the possibility of gaining a new ability, and being able to cover his entire body in a suit of armor sounded relatively cool. It would also allow him to avoid wearing a mana suit. Of course, there were downsides as well. He wasn't sure how strong the armor would be or if he could improve it.

Though he was hesitant to drink the potion, Mark was also aware that he didn't really have a choice. While Maestro didn't seem to want to force him, Mark had a strong feeling that their cooperation wasn't quite as optional as Maestro liked to make it seem. Then there was Mime, who was currently perched on the table, staring with anticipation at the purple serum.

"What do you think?" Mark asked, picking up the serum and shaking it. "Should I take this?"

Turning her bright eyes to him, Mime nodded emphatically and even licked her lips. With a defeated chuckle, Mark stopped hesitating and popped the cap on the vial. He winced slightly as a tangy metallic taste hit his tongue, but he swallowed the whole thing down with one swift gulp, then sat in the center of the living room, getting ready for whatever might come.

After taking the first serum, he had ended up in a mental battle with what seemed to be the spirit of the war bear. But to Mark's surprise, the mental battle he anticipated this time never materialized. Instead, he felt a freezing-cold shiver run down his spine, then intense pain that made him want to scream. It felt as if his spine were being peeled apart, disk by disk, but not wanting to accidentally alert his neighbors, he clenched his teeth, letting no more than a whimper escape his lips.

Mime jumped down from the table and padded her way to sit in front of him, her eyes boring through his body, as if staring at something that was working its way from the top of his neck down to his tailbone. The pain was intense and only grew stronger as the minutes passed. Mark could feel beads of sweat popping through the pores on his back, and a faint bloody stench began to rise.

Then the pain that gripped his spine began to spread, working its way like needles through his skin and toward his fingers and toes. Still, Mark didn't make a peep, though his teeth clenched so tightly that he began to taste blood in his mouth from his bleeding gums. Yet even as Mark's body suffered, he could also feel his regeneration kicking in, rapidly repairing the damage being done.

Wishing his transformation would end, Mark was forced to sit in place for hours as a terrifying battle was waged inside him. The entire time Mime hardly moved, and soon Mark began to feel a strange fear that rose up from his body, making him imagine that Mime was a terrifying apex hunter and, even more, a being whose will was absolute.

After two hours had passed, Mime suddenly moved, her body beginning to bleed outward, as if she had transformed into shadow itself. She darted forward, and rather than slam into Mark's chest, she simply vanished, merging into him. Almost immediately, Mark felt a sharp spike of pain, even more intense than everything he had been suffering up until that point. But then it was gone, replaced by a cool feeling that caused him to shiver. Suddenly, the strange, divided feeling in Mark's body was gone, as whatever modifications had been made melded into him completely.

Sufficient specialized genetic material acquired. Would you like to remember Cataphract Armor?

Cautiously accepting, Mark felt something deep in his body shift, and a new notification appeared.

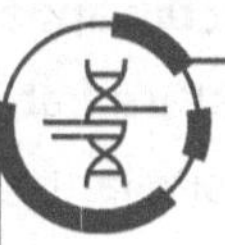

Insufficient genetic bandwidth to support four adaptations. Compatibility between Cataphract Armor and Bone Blade discovered. Merging abilities.

There was a hum deep in Mark's bones, and the feeling of unification grew even stronger.

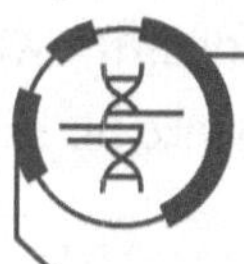

Bone Armor: Completely cover your body with a suit of Bone Armor.

Though the description was short, Mark could sense just how powerful the ability was. After taking a moment to catch his breath, he stood up and activated it. Immediately, he felt mana gather around him, and his body rapidly transformed. Plates of bone manifested above his skin and linked together to form a complete suit of armor that encased him from head to toe.

Feeling his vision shift slightly, Mark walked to the bathroom, astonished by how easy it felt to move in his new suit of armor. Glancing in the mirror, he saw that his face was currently covered with a full mask, one that looked exactly like the mask he had worn down in the arena.

As he stared at his reflection, Mark suddenly caught sight of something hovering over his shoulders, and his eyes went wide as two insectile, bladelike arms twitched. He was so startled at the sight that he reacted by instinct, launching an attack. Yet to his utter shock and more than a little horror, rather than his human arms moving, it was the new bladelike ones that darted forward, stabbing into the mirror and shattering it into thousands of pieces.

At the same time, he felt a slight movement from below his human arms and, looking down, saw two more insectile appendages extending forward. Freezing in place, Mark stared at the four arms that surrounded him. They looked quite similar to the insectile limbs of a war bear, though they were entirely made of bone blade, more like mantis blades, matching the material of his suit perfectly.

With a thought, Mark withdrew them and let out a sigh as he stared at the broken mirror and the two holes carved into the wall behind it. Stepping out of the bathroom, Mark concentrated and felt his armor retract, taking the four bone blade arms with it. When he focused, he could feel the arms slipping into his skin, nestling alongside his spine.

At something of a loss for words, Mark went and got a broom to clean up the shattered mirror. He then sat back down in the center of the living room to try to understand all the changes that had happened to him. Clearly, the cataphract serum had merged flawlessly with his body, but rather than the regular chitinous armor that covered most Exlian, Mark's new armored layer was composed entirely of bone. This meant that it was considerably stronger than most Exlian armor, and when combined with his mana shield, it made his defenses even more ridiculous than they had been before.

However, contrary to what he would have expected, he found his body remained completely flexible. It was as if the armor plates didn't exist at all. They could bend and twist, allowing his body to move as if he were naked. Realizing that this was likely a function of his characteristic absorption, Mark couldn't help but laugh at the absurdity of it all.

Getting to his feet, he settled into one of his katas and began moving through it slowly, executing each strike with gentle precision. Then, after he was finished, he returned to the starting point and began again, this time using the four bone blade arms that extended from the back of his armor. Though it was slightly awkward at first, he quickly began to find the knack of it and realized that he could execute his Cutting Palm technique with the bone blade arms as easily as with his hands.

As this meant he had just added the equivalent of four extra hands to his body, the thought of fighting an enemy using three times as many attacks was exhilarating, and Mark could hardly wait for night to come. He continued practicing all evening, and as soon as it grew dark, he hurried to bed. He was so excited that it took him a while to fall asleep, but when he finally did and appeared in the dream, he couldn't help but give an excited shout.

Almost immediately, he heard a rustle nearby and knew he had attracted the screamer's attention. That didn't bother Mark, as it had been his intent the entire time. With a thought, bone armor rippled around his body, and the four bone blade arms extended from his back, two stretching over his shoulders and two extending past his ribs, below his arms.

A moment later, the screamer's ugly head popped up over the side of the building, and it let out a familiar roar, its jaw opening wide as it prepared to unleash its sound blast. Though it would have been easy enough for him to dodge, since he had long since mastered the timing of the screamer's attack, Mark didn't budge. Instead, he stood stock still as he faced the screamer.

A moment later, a superheated blast of sonic energy rushed toward him, slamming into his armor. The mana shields sprang up first, blocking the majority of the attack, but ultimately, the intense vibration was too much for them, and they shattered, allowing a wave of superheated air to slam into Mark. He could feel the heat through his armor, but the force simply rolled off him, and as the attack faded, Mark emerged completely unscathed.

With a savage laugh, he darted forward, his blades stabbing out to pierce through the screamer's head. A moment later, the monster lay eviscerated before him, and Mark felt the savage desire to roar building up in his chest. Unable to contain himself, he threw back his head and let out a long howl, as if celebrating his newfound power. As the corpse of the screamer faded, Mark turned his attention to the wilderness. There were countless Exlian out there, and though they would provide no nourishment for him, they were the perfect targets to help Mark get used to his new abilities.

For six hours, Mark hunted relentlessly, not bothering to hide his presence as he threw himself into group after group of Exlian. What he discovered was genuinely terrifying. His cataphract armor completely negated the attacks of any Exlian C ranked or below. Even when they struck at full power, his body would barely shake. B-ranked Exlian that managed to get through his mana shields were able to leave deep gashes on his armor. But because his armor was an extension of himself, his regeneration would immediately kick in, allowing him to repair the damage within seconds.

This allowed Mark to completely ignore his defense and focus all his energy on attacking. The result was savagely spectacular, and Mark tore through groups of Exlian like they were paper, his bone blade arms ripping apart everything they touched. Soon, Mark was using not just his hands and feet but every part of his body, including the short horns on his head, to rip and tear his way through the enemy.

Most Exlian fell to his stabbing arms, which moved instinctively to cut through the enemy's defenses in rapid flurries. Because of the arms' flexibility, Mark found that he could fight in almost 360 degrees, allowing him to rush into the center of Exlian hordes without fear of being surrounded. By the time the dream came to an end, Mark had lost count of how many Exlian he had killed, and when he woke up, he realized that he had not died even once the entire night.

Shivering as the extent of his new power settled in his heart, Mark couldn't help but stare down at his hand, slowly clenching his fingers into a fist. There was no doubt in his mind that he had completely and irreversibly transformed. Whether he was a full-blown Exlian, he wasn't sure, but the last vestiges of his humanity had been buried. Of course, he still had his reason, lacking the insane bloodlust that consumed the Exlian. And when he wasn't manifesting his abilities, he looked human. But it was in the same way that Mime looked like a cat. No matter how catlike she appeared or acted, she was anything but.

The thought caused Mark's heart to tremble, but a moment later, reason won out and he calmed down. It was true that he was no longer human. It was true that he had transformed into something entirely other. But his choices were his own, and so long as nobody found out, what would it matter? Getting up, Mark took a shower, deciding to forgo his exercise that morning, and instead caught an early-morning taxi that dropped him off a couple of blocks from the alchemy lab. After walking the remaining distance, he entered the long hallway and soon arrived at the lab.

When he opened the door, his two clones turned and looked at him, strange expressions on their faces. Unsure what that was about, Mark commanded them to merge back with him, and a moment later, he felt his mind shudder as the two clones melded into his body. For a long moment, he simply stood in place, reviewing everything that they had done. To his astonishment, he discovered that he felt as if he had just spent the last few days working on his alchemy. It took him a moment to sort through exactly what he was feeling, but he quickly realized that the clone ability worked as he'd hoped.

The clones, though controlled by him, were essentially other versions of himself, and the longer they were apart, the more distinct they would become. As soon as they merged back together, however, their experiences would be added to his, granting him whatever advancements they might have made. Lacking true bodies, they couldn't make any improvements on the physical side, but they could gain new experiences and memories and improve their minds. The sheer flexibility of the quantum clone ability was mind boggling, and Mark was excited to start using it to its fullest extent.

Leaving one clone to work on alchemy and another to meditate in his apartment would essentially triple the speed of Mark's advancement. Not only would he be able to generate a steady income from the creation of potions and elixirs, but he'd simultaneously be able to work on his mana control and hunt for ingredients out in the dead zone or the wilderness beyond. He let out a deep sigh. He couldn't help but feel that being sent to the Tomb, where he could meet Maestro, was the luckiest thing that had ever happened to him. Remembering his master's note, Mark began to wonder if this was what Master Abrams had had in mind. There was no way to know, of course, but a part of Mark couldn't help but attribute it to him.

Of course, the help he had gotten from Maestro would have a cost, and Mark knew that one day the S-ranked genius would call in all the debts Mark had accrued. But that was fine, so long as he continued to grow in power. He was confident he would eventually stand on equal footing with even the strongest empowered, either in the city or under it.

Gathering up the potions that had already been made, Mark stored them in his shadow, split off a clone to continue working in the lab, and then stopped by his apartment to drop off another clone. Leaving two in the city would hamper his ability to split his body into multiple attackers, but he figured it would be easy enough, if the situation warranted it, to withdraw the clones in the city so that he could use them outside the walls. Mark was confident enough in his new armor, though, that he thought it was unlikely to be necessary.

Making sure he had the raider brute's watch with the map to the dead raiders' hideout, Mark headed for the city gate. To keep anybody from asking questions, he wore his regular suit. Though that turned out to be a mistake, as the guards immediately stopped him, asking him if he had a team going out with him.

Shaking his head, Mark handed over his association badge. "No, I'm on a solo trip. I'll just be collecting some materials, probably sticking pretty close to the city."

Frowning, the guard looked over Mark's profile. "You know it's not safe, right? I know you're B ranked, but it's not advised for anybody below the A rank to go out of the city solo."

"I understand," Mark said, trying to be patient. "I'm willing to assume all responsibility."

Though the guard didn't like it, he ultimately didn't have a reason to stop Mark, so after muttering that it was Mark's funeral under his breath, he handed back the badge and let Mark through the gate. After he had gone a couple of blocks, Mark ducked into one of the nearby buildings and removed his mana suit, tossing it into his shadow as his bone armor materialized around him. He took a deep breath, reveling in the clean air. Not wanting to be mistaken for an Exlian, he crept out of the building and swiftly made his way through the tangle of streets deeper into the dead zone, steering clear of the few Exlian drones he saw creeping around.

Most of them, upon noticing his mental signature in the network, were more than happy to avoid him as well, scurrying away whenever they got close enough to detect him. What he had discovered was that an Exlian's ability to sense the network was proportional to its strength, so the D- and E-ranked drones would only notice him if he got within around fifty feet of them. Any farther, and they were completely oblivious to his presence. On the other hand, Mark found himself able to spot them from almost five hundred feet away, more than enough to allow him to hunt them with ease, if he so chose.

A couple of the drones, however, upon discovering his presence, reacted differently. Stopping in place and dipping toward the ground in a strange sort of bow, they remained facing him as if waiting for something, and it was only after he moved out of their range that they turned and continued on their way.

Though the behavior puzzled him, Mark didn't pay it much mind, instead focusing on his surroundings, looking for landmarks that would show that he was close to his destination. He moved quickly, a pale shadow darting through the alleyways of the city, until he arrived at a wide-open square that he recognized from the map.

Orienting himself using the looming walls of New Emery in the distance, Mark began looking for the hidden base and soon came to a run-down bank. According to the directions, in one of the back vaults was a secret entrance that led to a secure room underneath the bank. It was here the raiders had established themselves.

Rather than rush forward, Mark entered the bank cautiously, looking for any sign of other people. Though he wasn't afraid of running into other empowered, he didn't think it wise to just rush into a raiders' hideout. Hunting through the bank, he found the vault and saw a scanning device attached to the wall nearby.

Scanning the raider's watch, he heard a faint chime, and the vault popped open, allowing him to enter. The vault itself was mostly empty, though he did find a few odds and ends shoved in one corner. He ignored them, however, and instead focused on the opposite corner, where he found a safe-deposit box that wasn't shut.

Following the directions outlined in the message, Mark stuck the watch inside the safe-deposit box, and a moment later, there was a hum, and the entire back wall shifted a few inches back and to the side, revealing a stairwell.

"I never would have found this place without directions," Mark muttered, shaking his head.

As he stepped onto the stairs, the wall shifted back into place, plunging Mark into darkness. With one hand on the rail, he walked down the steps, turned the corner, and descended another flight. In total, he walked down six flights of stairs before arriving at a door. When he scanned the watch again, the door opened with a hiss, and lights clicked on, revealing much more than the simple room Mark was expecting. Comprising a hallway with six rooms along the sides and a large room at the end, the facility Mark found himself in was clearly intended as a bunker.

Not only did it have a bathroom and a small kitchen, but there were rooms for sleep, storage rooms, and a large garage that had been converted into a suit workshop. As he walked into the garage, Mark saw thirteen gleaming mana suits lined up neatly by the wall. One, likely for the brute Mark had killed, was significantly larger than the others, but all of them looked to be in good shape.

Three different group markings were represented, and Mark, accessing the InfoWeb and logging into his Hunters' Association account, quickly realized that these suits represented the raiders' legal identities. All three of the markings were for official Hunters' Association teams, much like Terra's. Clearly, after leaving the city in their official capacity, the teams had changed into their unmarked suits here in this bunker and then headed into the dead zone to rob other hunters.

Mark didn't feel even a shred of guilt that he had ended their lives. Instead he set about dismantling the suits, absorbing them into his shadow so that he could sell them when he got back to the city.

After spending a couple of hours looking around the base, Mark hadn't found much else of value, though he was contemplating whether it would be worth using the base for himself. It had everything that he needed to live, and if he were to move an alchemy workstation from the city, a feat he could easily achieve thanks to his shadow's devouring ability, it would become much more convenient to hunt and process materials. His main concern was that other people knew about the base and might inadvertently stumble upon him. Deciding to play it safe, Mark left everything apart from the suits untouched. He would come back in a few days and see if anything had been disturbed. If nobody else had entered the underground bunker, he would consider using it as a base.

He was just as careful leaving the hidden base as he had been entering it, and after stepping out of the bank, he paused and looked around, considering what to do next. His original plan had been to hunt outside the city, but he could tell that there wasn't much room left in his shadow, which would make it hard to gather many materials.

After a moment of consideration, Mark decided to go back to New Emery, and soon he presented himself at the gate and greeted the same guard who had let him out of the city. Seeing that Mark was unharmed, the guard sighed in relief and gestured for him to enter.

Mark elected to go directly to Ivan's. Not bothering to rent a truck this time, he soon arrived at his destination. He was greeted by Marco, who directed him to one of the back rooms. There, Ivan was examining some crates of goods.

"Ah, Mark, so nice to see you again. Are you here to buy this time?" Ivan asked.

"No," Mark said, shaking his head. "I'm still selling. I was wondering if you'd be interested in thirteen more mana suits."

"Thirteen, you say?" Ivan raised his eyebrows and put his checklist away. "That's big business."

Unsure if Ivan was telling the truth or not, Mark shrugged. "I have them and want to sell. Currently, they're at my lab, and I'm wondering if you'd be able to pick them up."

"Of course," Ivan said. "What's the address? I can't give you a price until I've seen them, however, so we'll have to wait until they're brought back."

"Sure, that's fine," Mark said, waving his hand.

Though he had intended to go with the pickup crew, Mark was suddenly struck by a thought, so he concentrated on one of his clones for a moment. Back in the lab, clone Mark put down the beaker he had been examining and left the room, climbing the stairs and entering the long hallway, where Mark directed his shadow to deposit the thirteen mana suits in a neat row. He had never tried transferring material to his clones over long distances using his shadow and was honestly surprised that it worked.

Standing in the hallway, staring at the mana suits, Mark nodded in satisfaction and then went back into the lab, locking the door behind him and resuming his work at the alchemy station. At the same time, in Ivan's office, Mark gave instructions for picking the suits up from the laboratory.

"You can use the side door. I've set a temporary code for you, which will get you in. There's a long hallway there, and down at the end of it, you'll see the suits. However, these ones aren't quite as convenient as the previous batch."

"It's fine," Ivan said. "We'll make sure to cover them up while we're moving them. Of course, you know that this is going to mean a reduction in how much I can pay. After all, we'll have to wipe them from the system, get rid of their serial numbers, and repaint them."

"I understand," Mark said, getting up from his chair. "You can just deposit the money in my account."

"You're not concerned with how much you're going to get?" Ivan asked, a curious look in his eyes as he watched Mark walk toward the door.

Pausing in the doorway, Mark turned around, a smile slipping across his lips as he stared back at Ivan. "I'm sure you wouldn't cheat me."

With that, he turned and left, leaving Ivan staring after him thoughtfully. In truth, Mark wasn't concerned with whether he would be cheated. He considered the thirteen suits free money, and he wasn't about to complain, no matter how little it ended up being. Maestro had recommended Ivan, and since he was trusting Maestro with everything else, he figured it was fine to trust this recommendation as well.

What was more important was Mark's discovery that he could shift physical material between him and his clones using his shadow. This would completely eliminate the need to reenter the city to bring materials back; as long as his clones could remain in the laboratory, he could stay in the dead zone and hunt, which suited him just fine.

His only concern was that if he left through the gate, there would be a record of him leaving and not returning, which meant that he was going to have to find a way to get out of the city without alerting the system. His current plan was to use the gap in the southern wall that he had discovered when Sky had been kidnapped. So long as it had not been repaired, that would allow him to slip out of the city unnoticed. Of course, Mark was no longer so naive as to think that that area wasn't monitored. But if he didn't make too much trouble, he was confident that nobody would say anything.

He was about to head toward the southern wall when he paused, his mind turning to his friends. It had been some time since he had contacted Noah, even longer since he had spoken to Sky. They had sent messages back and forth a few times, but Sky was busy with her deployment and, according to her last message, was being run ragged as the Defense Force took full advantage of her ability. Noah was likewise busy, though with what, he didn't say.

Since Mark was about to leave the city for a long time and didn't know when he would have a chance to see his friends again, he quickly typed out two messages, asking if they had any time in the next day to meet up. Sky got back to him immediately.

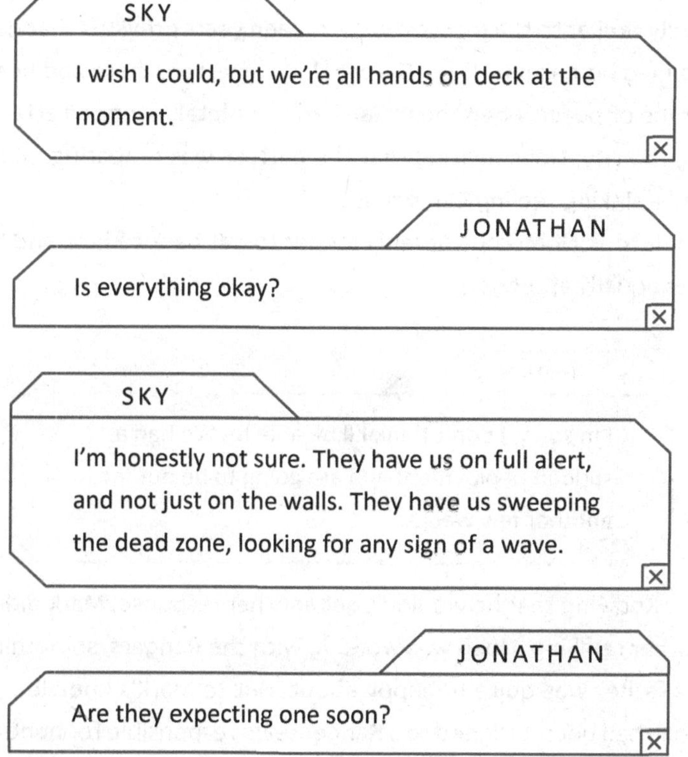

SKY

Yes. Apparently, they expected it months ago, but the fact that there's been nothing, not even small attacks, is putting everybody on edge. I'm not sure how long this mission is going to last, but hopefully I'll be back sometime next week, and it'd be nice to hang out then.

JONATHAN

Keep me posted, and stay safe.

Closing the messages, Mark frowned, thinking over everything that he knew about the waves. The current situation felt eerily similar to the massive wave fifteen years previous that had claimed his parents' lives. Before that wave, too, there had been a time of peace when the Exlian had completely stopped attacking the city. Now, hearing that the pattern was repeating, Mark had a sinking feeling in his chest.

It took Noah considerably longer to get back to him, and he was equally apologetic.

NOAH

I'm sorry, I don't think I'll be able to. We had a sudden deployment and are going to be out for another few weeks.

Knowing that he wouldn't get another response, Mark didn't bother replying. Noah was working with the Rangers, something his father was quite unhappy about. But to Mark's knowledge, Noah had been assigned to a Ranger team responsible for hunting

Exlian within the confines of New Emery. The fact that he had been deployed outside the city was strange and only added to Mark's sense that something ominous was on the horizon.

"All the more reason to improve my strength," Mark muttered, and felt a weight on his shoulder as Mime hopped up.

When he glanced at her, she gave him a firm nod and pointed toward the southern wall.

"I know, I'm going," Mark said with a laugh, and walked to the edge of the road to flag down a taxi.

When he arrived at the construction zone, it was just as empty as he remembered it. Climbing up the scaffolding, Mark stepped into the narrow passage and walked down the long halls, memories returning of the mad chase he had undertaken in this place. It was less than two years later, but he was a far cry from the young man who had been forced into desperate straits by the kidnappers. And if he were to be faced with a similar situation today, Mark was confident that eliminating the enemy would be as easy as snapping his fingers, a clear testament to just how much he had grown. Nothing had changed, so Mark slipped out of the city easily, hopping down to the ground and vanishing into the maze of buildings that made up the dead zone.

The dead zone was quiet, eerily so, but Mark found it strangely calming. As he paused to look around, habitually scanning the Exlian psychic network, he felt a deep sense of freedom, something he hadn't felt since he had been out in the wilderness at Felwer Mine. He wasn't sure if it was something in the genetic material he had absorbed, but the wide-open spaces of the wilderness called to him.

With a thought, his cataphract armor snapped into place, completely covering his body, as four segmented arms extended from his back. His scan had found nothing, but that was to be expected, as he was only a few blocks from the city wall. The farther from the city, the more powerful the Exlian would become. So Mark headed straight south, toward the territory of the murder scorpions.

He traveled quickly, keeping himself low and out of sight, his feet making hardly a whisper on the hard concrete. Eventually, tired of going around the buildings, Mark climbed up to the top of a three-story apartment complex and surveyed the landscape. Most of the buildings in this part of town weren't that tall, with only a few sticking up four or five stories. This gave Mark a good line of sight.

Glancing back, he saw the top of the city wall, with tiny figures patrolling along it. Hoping he was far enough away that he wouldn't attract the attention of the auto-targeting mana cannons, Mark took off running and leaped from the edge of the building, flying almost forty feet to land on the roof of the building across the street. He touched down lightly, shifting his momentum forward. As he did, a thrill raced through him, and after taking two steps, he leaped again, this time traveling even farther.

Moving across the tops of the buildings was much faster than running through the alleyways underneath, as Mark could take a more or less straight line toward his destination. Of course, it came with the risk that he'd be spotted by Exlian or even other hunters. In many ways, the latter would likely be more dangerous, as with his armor Mark could easily be mistaken for a humanoid Exlian.

Whether due to confidence or something else, Mark didn't worry about it too much, figuring he'd be able to take care of whatever came his way. A quick glance at the map on his watch helped him orient himself, and he continued to run. It took him almost two hours to travel nearly twenty miles from the city wall. The dead zone, which extended for almost fifty miles in every direction around New Emery, was divided into ten-mile bands. Within the first band, there were rarely Exlian stronger than E-ranked drones. Starting at the ten-mile mark, it was more common to see D-ranked Exlian warriors, and while racing over the rooftops, Mark had spotted quite a few.

The real prize, and Mark's target, however, lay beyond the twenty-mile mark, where the C-ranked Exlian could be found. This was where Mark intended to start his hunt. His goal was to kill and harvest as many C-ranked Exlian as he could while looking for B-ranked Exlian to hunt. As strong as he was, Mark was under no illusions that fighting a B-ranked Exlian would be easy. Still, given his current strength, he was confident that one-on-one he'd be able to hold his own. The challenge would be ensuring that the fight remained one-on-one . . .

Since he was going to be spending considerable time in the wilderness, Mark decided to take things slow, and after landing on the roof of a four-story hospital that had fallen into complete disrepair, he began scanning for prey. This far out from the city, drones moved in large groups, not bothering to hide their presence at all, and more than once, Mark saw small swarms of between twenty to fifty drones scuttling by. He ignored them, as he could tell that even the strongest drones were only D ranked, which wouldn't help him at all.

Just as he was getting ready to move and try a new spot, he picked up a group of four Exlian warriors heading his way. As he focused his attention on them, he suddenly found himself able to identify what type of Exlian they were, in addition to how strong: three D-ranked murder scorpions and a C-ranked one. Though Mark would have preferred a slightly stronger group, this was as good a group as any to begin his hunt. They had just entered the building he was resting on, heading for the second floor, so Mark dropped off the roof, his bone blade arms stabbing into the side of the cement building to stop his fall.

The sound echoed loudly, alerting the warriors to his presence. He could feel them probing the Exlian network, looking for any sign of him. However, he had shrouded himself using Mime's method. Despite being unable to spot him through the network, they rushed toward his location, drawn by the sound.

Mark remained hanging from the wall, curious as to what would happen when the Exlian realized they wouldn't be able to reach him. His assumption was completely shattered when one of the D-ranked murder scorpions burst out of a window and began rapidly climbing the side of the building. It ran so quickly it looked as if it were on flat ground. Three more murder scorpions rushed out after it, and Mark suddenly found himself facing off against four murder scorpions that seemed to have no trouble traversing the vertical wall.

As soon as they spotted him, they surged forward, their claws opening wide as their tails rose, ready to strike as soon as they came in range. Realizing he'd be at a disadvantage if he stayed where he was, Mark pulled his bone blades from the cement wall, pushing off with his feet at the same time to help him accelerate toward the ground and the incoming scorpions.

All of them were larger than he was, and as soon as he came within range of the first one, its tail darted toward his head. One of his bone blades rose to meet it, deflecting the blow, even as another blade slashed across the base of the stinger, severing it from the scorpion's tail. Letting out a horrific hiss, the monster tried to pinch Mark in half, but one of his other bone blade arms sliced into the nearest pincer, giving him just enough purchase to maneuver his body in the air, shifting past the incoming attack.

A moment later his heel drove into the monster's head, knocking the Exlian loose from the wall. With flailing limbs, it began to fall, and Mark fell with it, though only for a few feet. Stomping down again, he kicked off the falling scorpion, sending it down to splat against the ground, and threw himself sideways, transforming his vertical falling momentum into horizontal distance that allowed him to sink two bone blades into another of the monsters. It, too, hissed in pain, but before it could launch an attack of its own, it had been eviscerated by Mark's rapid stabs.

Catching a protruding sill, Mark's fingers sank deep into the cement wall even as he shook the now-dead scorpion free. The two remaining scorpions, one of which was C ranked, were utterly furious and almost upon him, closing in from two sides. Rather than try to fight them both, Mark pulled himself up and dove through the window, shattering the dusty glass.

He rolled as he landed in a hallway and sprang up just in time to meet a scorpion forcing its large body through the small opening. Taking advantage of the fact that it could only get two of its claws and part of its head into the window, Mark hacked it to pieces, tearing both claws off and striking its head half a dozen times in less than a second. With a wail, the monster fell backward, allowing dim moonlight to stream in through the smashed window.

There was a moment of stillness, and just as Mark started to scan the psychic network, he heard a loud rumble, and a massive section of the wall as well as much of the floor he was standing on began to crumble. The C-ranked scorpion, frustrated that it couldn't reach him, had just smashed in the side of the building, gouging out a tremendous amount of the wall, which caused the floor to tilt precariously.

Instinctively, Mark's arms pierced into the walls on either side and then flung him backward, farther down the hall. As the dust cleared, the scorpion, now able to force itself through the much bigger hole, chased after him, its tail stabbing repeatedly. Mark blocked each blow calmly, waiting to lure it farther into the building before launching his strike. With the death of each scorpion, Mark had felt the psychic network shaking, and since three had died so close together, the echoes were still ringing. Adding a fourth, more powerful scorpion to the mix would only amplify the Exlian death screams, drawing even more monsters to his location.

Once the psychic cry had finally faded, Mark didn't hesitate and struck immediately, jumping straight into the C-ranked murder scorpion's attacks. Its claws closed in on him, and its tail, venom dripping from the stinger, drove straight toward his heart.

Mark ignored the attacks, allowing the first claw to close in with tremendous force on his leg. When it was about to clamp down, a mana shield appeared, blocking the attack. Unfortunately, that meant he had no shield to block the second attack. The second claw snapped shut, sending cracks radiating through the armor on his arm, but he bore with the pain, his attention locked on the scorpion. Now that Mark was face-to-face with it, his blades were within range, and they stabbed into the claw around his leg, forcing it to release its grip. This only served to infuriate the beast, which pressed its third attack aggressively.

A loud crack echoed as the stinger aimed at his heart slammed into another mana shield that appeared over his chest, hitting with such force that the tip snapped off. In response, Mark's last two bone blades shot out, tearing through the scorpion's head and killing it instantly. Letting out a terrible wail, the creature started to thrash, but Mark lifted his leg and kicked hard, tearing the clamped claw free and sending the monster tumbling back down the hall.

It took almost half a minute for the creature to stop thrashing, but as soon as it did, Mark raced toward it. He could feel dozens of Exlian closing in on his position and wanted to make sure that he got to the corpses quickly enough. As he ran past, his shadow rose up to envelop the Exlian corpse, and a faint crunching sound echoed through the air as he leaped out of the hole in the side of the building and fell three stories.

When he was about to hit the ground, his bone blades stabbed into the side of the building, cutting deep gouges in the wall as he slowed down. He had already located the fallen corpses of the D-ranked scorpions, and his shadow eagerly swept them up, leaving not a drop of blood behind.

Mark's biofuel was rapidly filling, and he could feel a faint increase in his fortitude. The improvement brought by the three D-ranked murder scorpions was so slight that it was negligible, providing less than a thousandth of a percent of improvement. The C-ranked scorpion, though also only providing a tiny improvement, was closer to a hundredth, though that meant Mark would likely have to consume at least a hundred C-ranked murder scorpions before his fortitude would rise.

The thought didn't bother him at all. After all, he was planning on killing at least that many. As far as he understood it, the number of Exlian outside the city was endless, and any Exlian that he killed would only be replaced by another from the murder scorpions' nests.

Taking a moment to center himself and shroud his body with mental energy, Mark left, slipping past a few dozen drones that were rapidly closing in.

"This is gonna take a while," he muttered to himself.

It doesn't have to. Farther out from the city are more powerful Exlian. A B-ranked murder scorpion will have the same impact on your growth as ten C ranked, and an A-ranked murder scorpion the same impact as a hundred. Better yet, find their nests, and your growth will be endless.

Stopping, Mark reached out to brace himself against the wall, his fingers crushing the bricks as he forcefully prevented himself from turning and rushing toward the wilderness to begin hunting higher-ranked Exlian. It took him a moment to steady himself, and he only straightened when the nigh-overwhelming impulse had faded.

He wasn't sure if it was a side effect of the new armor or something else, but his desire to destroy and consume other Exlian had been magnified exponentially. Half afraid he might lose himself to it, Mark didn't hunt anymore that night. Instead, he retreated to an abandoned building to meditate. Sitting cross-legged in a dim room, Mark didn't retract his bone armor, not wanting to get caught without it. With his eyes closed, he focused on his breathing, forcefully calming his agitated spirit. It took him a few minutes to subdue the bloodlust that had permeated his mind, and when he did, he was left with nothing but cold clarity.

It wasn't that Mark was opposed to hunting more powerful Exlian. In fact, that was part of his plan. But he knew that rushing headlong into battle against them was a terrible idea. He had yet to face off against an A-ranked Exlian, and his experience fighting the B-ranked brain in Felwer Mine had made it clear to him that a gap between ranks was just about insurmountable.

Had Captain Calder not brought the mine's entrance down, there was no doubt in Mark's mind that the B-ranked Exlian brain would have killed him, Kami, and Sergeant Fletcher. Had it not been confined, it likely would have killed Captain Calder and Sergeant Rogers as well, completely wiping out their team. At the time, Mark had been D ranked, and he had been entirely helpless against it. Even Lieutenant Kami had stood no chance.

Mark was now exponentially stronger than he had been in Felwer Mine, and he could feel his power continuing to grow. Yet despite his increase in strength, he was under no illusion that it would allow him to fight an A-ranked Exlian. Thankfully, outside of major waves, they were incredibly rare. As for B-ranked Exlian, Mark was confident in his ability to face them head-on. He had already proved that with the giant murder scorpion he had hunted with Terra and the others, as well as the two B-ranked earth rats.

Once he had calmed down, Mark checked his watch and logged into the Hunters' Association InfoWeb portal. The portal could provide much of what the association's kiosks could, but Mark was most interested in the information services. With a quick search, he pulled up information on B-ranked Exlian sightings and began to scroll through the results.

He realized that as long as he was beyond the third band, which would put him more than thirty miles away from the city, he would find what he was looking for. B-ranked Exlian were rare closer to the city but became much more common in the outer bands. Checking his position, Mark saw that he was a little less than twenty-five miles from the massive city wall, so he hopped to his feet and left the building, beginning to jog southeast, away from New Emery.

In the distance, he could see a group of high-rise buildings. Some appeared to be office buildings, while others looked as if they had been apartments. Mark was particularly interested in them, as they would provide good vantage points from which he could survey the fourth band. He moved quickly, not bothering to hide his presence, and soon stumbled upon a group of twenty drones advancing up a street perpendicular to his path.

Realizing that he was going to run into them at the corner, Mark slowed down slightly, intending to let them pass first. Yet to his surprise, when they reached the corner, the drones all stopped and turned toward him. He was about two hundred feet away and could see them clearly, and he came to a stop as well, watching them warily.

The drones had frozen in place, and they lowered their bodies to the ground in a clear gesture of submission. Unsure what to make of the situation, Mark tentatively took a step forward, fully expecting the drones to charge toward him. Yet they didn't move, holding their bodies absolutely still. It was then that he felt it: a strange, subtle feeling that seemed to leak through the Exlian network. It was hard for him to identify the exact feeling, but he sensed awe, veneration even, from the drones, along with a hint of excitement, as if the drones were incredibly pleased to see him.

Since the drones weren't moving, Mark's only options were to retreat and find a new path or to walk right past them. Trusting that he could handle a group of D-ranked drones with ease, Mark took another step forward, then another. Finally, there was movement among the drones, but only to shift slightly so they faced him. Unsure what to make of the situation, Mark sped up, breaking into a jog as he closed the distance between him and the group of drones. Even when he came within a dozen feet, the drones remained still as stone, simply watching him pass. Though he had noticed similar strange behavior in other drones, this was the first time Mark had seen it with his eyes, and part of him couldn't help but be unnerved.

Strangely, another part of him felt as if it were the most natural thing in the world. After all, he was more powerful than the drones. From his limited understanding of Exlian hierarchy, their subservience was instinctive. He had gotten twenty feet beyond the drones when a thought struck him, and he paused, turning to face them again. He was fairly sure Exlian didn't understand human speech, so instead, he tried to focus his mind, expressing his command through his thoughts.

COME.

Mark felt the psychic network vibrate as the word permeated his surroundings. The drones reacted with an immediacy that shocked him, rising from their prone position and rushing straight toward him. It took all his effort to suppress his instinct to lash out and slay them as they got close. When they were only a few feet away, they stopped and lowered themselves to the ground once more, clearly waiting for another command.

For a long moment, Mark just stood in place, a dozen drones hovering just out of arm's reach. Why these drones in particular were willing to follow him, Mark wasn't sure, because he had run across plenty of drones that, upon seeing him, reacted by fleeing or attacking. Unsure how to ask in a way that would get across to them, Mark settled for something else, trying to craft a mental question that the drones would understand.

WHERE ARE THE POWERFUL ENEMIES?

This time, the drones didn't react nearly as quickly, but after a few seconds, one that was noticeably larger than the others backed up a few steps, then turned and began to make its way down the street. The other drones followed it. Noticing that they were heading in a new direction, Mark cautiously followed.

The drones moved fast, but Mark had no trouble keeping up, and after traversing almost fifteen blocks, the drones came to a stop. The large drone that had been leading chittered and then pointed with one of its claws. Mark, who had been paying very close attention to the drones as they traveled, could feel their unease leaking through the psychic network. There was danger ahead, though precisely what the danger might be, Mark wasn't sure.

Glancing at his watch, he realized they were at the twenty-nine-mile mark, near the outer edge of the third band. This, at least according to most of the information he'd gotten from the association, was where the number of Exlian began to rapidly increase.

Sensing that the drones didn't want to proceed, Mark moved ahead alone. Yet to his surprise, the drones, seeing that he was moving forward, gathered up and followed. Stopping, Mark turned to look at them, and they froze. It appeared that whenever Mark directed his attention toward them, they simply stopped what they were doing, as if waiting for a command. When he looked away, directing his attention elsewhere, they acted more normal, shifting and twitching and letting out their harsh, chittering noises. Mark didn't really want a group of drones following him around, as it would render his stealth abilities useless.

GO BACK.

The command echoed through the network, causing Mark to wince. He felt as if he were shouting, and from the way the drones trembled, it appeared they felt the same. Watching as they rushed away, heading back the way they had come, Mark wasn't quite sure what to think. The rational part of his mind was screaming that the fact that he could command Exlian was horrifying, but to the rest of him it felt as natural as breathing.

"I really need to figure out how to whisper," he muttered to himself.

With a thought, Mark shrouded his mental energy, drastically dulling his presence in the Exlian network. He began to make his way forward, sticking to the side of the street, close to the buildings, in an effort to remain hidden. As he moved forward, he continually swept the psychic network, looking for enemies. Soon, he spotted six Exlian in a building ahead. Based on their signatures, all of them were warrior ranked: three D ranked, two C ranked, and a bright light that Mark could only assume was a B-ranked Exlian.

Though this was a stronger group than any he had hunted so far, Mark moved forward confidently. He kept his body low as he crept toward the building's entrance. It appeared that at one point, it had housed a number of department stores. The Exlian were spread out on the first two floors, with the B-ranked Exlian and one of the C-ranked ones on the second and the others on the first.

Slipping through one of the broken floor-to-ceiling windows at the front of the store, Mark concealed himself behind a counter. They seemed to be resting, as none of them were moving around, but just when Mark was about to jump out and attack, one of the Exlian began to make its way toward him.

A moment later, Mark saw it come around a tall shelf. It was a mantis, with four thick legs, an upright torso, and two long arms extending from its back that ended in blades. The mantis was just as ugly as Mark remembered, but considering it was only D ranked, he felt zero threat from the creature.

As he watched it from his hiding place behind the counter, Mark saw it stop and sniff the air. Clearly, it had detected him and was trying to pinpoint his location. He was just about to jump out and kill it when he felt a shift at his side. Mime appeared in a crouch next to him, about to pounce.

Just before she did, Mark felt the mental shroud around him extend outward, stretching to encapsulate the mantis. Almost immediately, the mantis reacted, attempting to turn and flee. But Mime had already launched herself, her claws raking down even before she arrived at its side. Three silver streaks shot through the air, rending the creature's body apart, killing it instantly.

Mark wasn't surprised at how easily she killed the Exlian warrior. Instead, what caught him off guard was the fact that its death cry hadn't managed to escape Mime's mental shroud. As the faint scent of blood began to spread, Mark saw that the other Exlian, though only a few hundred feet away, didn't respond to the kill at all.

Landing on the corpse, Mime barely stopped before leaping to the ground. As her feet made contact with the floor, Mark felt his shadow stretch, leaping forward, as if mimicking Mime's motion. The shadow quickly enveloped the corpse, devouring every drop of blood that had been spilled.

Mime, meanwhile, sat and looked at Mark, casually licking her paw, as if asking him if he understood what she had just done. In truth, Mark didn't. He had no idea how she had managed to extend the mental shroud, but the fact that she had gave him a new option for hunting.

Mark's biggest challenge up until this point had been that every Exlian he killed unleashed a powerful scream through the psychic network, drawing the attention of other Exlian in the area. Mime's mental shroud clearly compensated for this, and if he could learn how to do it as well, it would improve his hunting efficiency by an order of magnitude.

Scanning through the network, Mark spotted another D-ranked mantis a bit farther away from the others. He quietly made his way toward it, eager to try to mimic Mime's attack. Passing between the shelves, he kept himself low, peeking around the corner toward the location of the mantis. Thankfully, it was looking the opposite direction.

Standing in the open, between two rows of broken-down shelves, Mark quickly checked for the mental signatures of the other Exlian. He watched them for a moment to ensure that they weren't moving around. Keeping himself still, he tried to manipulate the shroud of mental energy, casting it forward just as Mime had done.

Whether he lacked the control or something else, Mark wasn't sure, but instead of stretching out the way it had for Mime, the mental energy simply jumped forward, only enveloping the Exlian halfway. Immediately the monster jerked in surprise, and at the same time, Mark's presence, now revealed, flared to life on the Exlian network, causing the other Exlian in the building to let out sharp shrieks.

Realizing he had been exposed, Mark lunged from his hiding place, crossing the twenty feet between him and his target in an instant. The mantis had just started to turn around when Mark arrived, his bone blades plunging toward the creature's head and chest. Though it tried in vain to back up, the mantis wasn't nearly as fast or strong as Mark, and its attempt to block his bone blades with its own was futile.

Wasting no time as he felt his blade sink into the Exlian's brain, Mark commanded his shadow to envelop it without devouring, then turned. Despite the fact that two mantises were closing in, Mark met them calmly, dodging a slashing blade even as his own bone blades tore into the monster in front of him, cutting it down in an instant. The C-ranked mantis, which was a step behind, fared no better, and a few seconds later, Mark was past it, heading for a hole in the ceiling that led up to the second floor. His shadow spread like a cloak behind him, dragging across the ground. As it passed, the two mantis corpses disappeared as if they were never there.

Mark reached the hole at the same time as the B-ranked mantis, which jumped down to face him. Its bone blades stabbed toward his head with blistering speed. Despite the fact that he had been prepared for a harder fight, Mark was caught off guard by just how fast the B-ranked mantis moved. With two blades headed for his throat, Mark was forced to dodge, shifting toward one of the blades so that it would strike first. At the same time, his own bone blades responded, parrying the attacks and striking back.

There was a sharp clang as the two bone blades intersected, and Mark was surprised to find himself on the losing side of the battle. Unlike the giant scorpion or the tiny earth rats, the mantis wasn't restricted by its size. Though larger than the other mantises, it wasn't so large that it was constrained by the space; nor was it too small to have the body mass to compete in a contest of strength with Mark.

Though he was B ranked himself, the mantis was clearly stronger and faster, and after exchanging a dozen strikes in rapid succession, Mark realized that if he didn't have better abilities, he would be completely outclassed. Thankfully, he did, and the war bear's mana shields saved Mark from at least three attacks that otherwise would have pierced through to his armor.

Still, Mark didn't retreat, instead pressing forward to try to overwhelm the monster in front of him with his greater number of bone blades. The B-ranked mantis, despite being physically stronger and faster than Mark, still only had two mantis blades, giving Mark a distinct advantage in close quarters. Leveraging his incredible defense, Mark pressed close and soon managed to land a couple of strikes on the mantis's chest.

With a shriek of pain, the mantis suddenly surged forward, clearly intending to smash Mark with its bulk. But just before it struck, Mark, moving by instinct more than anything else, seized control of the ambient mana behind it, rapidly condensing it into a complex pattern. At the same time, a circuit flared to life in his body, linked to the target circuit by a thread of mana, and with a faint popping sound, he vanished from in front of the mantis and appeared behind its back.

Mark found himself just as surprised as the mantis, as he hadn't consciously tried to teleport. Instead, his instinct, honed from thousands of fights in the dream, had kicked in. His body felt torn, as if portions of his flesh had been ripped from him and left behind, and there was a faint bloody mist where he had been standing before.

Caught off guard, the mantis rushed through the mist, dispersing it as it waved its arms wildly, trying to figure out where he had gone. Mark, nearly paralyzed by the pain the teleportation had brought, dropped to the ground with a clatter. Almost immediately, his regeneration kicked in, healing the damage he had just done to his body.

With a groan, he rolled over and saw the remaining C-ranked mantis staring down at him from the hole that led to the second floor. With a shriek, it dropped straight down toward him, its bone blades aimed for his chest and stomach, and it was all he could do to roll over. With a crash, the monster landed, barely missing him.

Alerted, the B-ranked mantis spun around, its eyes fixing on Mark as he tried to struggle to his feet. The C-ranked mantis, eager to claim the kill, lunged for him, and though his mana shield blocked the first strike, the force sent Mark, who hadn't yet regained his balance, tumbling backward. This proved to be a blessing in disguise, as it gave his regeneration just enough time to finish healing his body.

Thrown into a tangle of shelves, Mark opted for a different strategy, pulling his mental energy together and shrouding himself, even as he scrambled backward, out of sight. The two mantises went wild, having lost sight of him in the network, and began thrashing about, destroying everything in reach as they tried to find him.

Hiding behind a flimsy metal shelf, Mark kept utterly still as a mantis blade tore through it like paper. Just after the blade passed above his head, he jumped up, lunging forward to attack the B-ranked mantis from the side. He held nothing back as his bone blades slashed and tore, using his Cutting Palm technique to its fullest extent.

Unable to shift its bulk around in time to meet Mark's relentless assault, the monster was soon dead, its scream echoing through the psychic network. The other mantis, driven mad by the psychic blast, launched itself at Mark, but it was neither as fast nor as strong as its B-ranked companion had been, and within less than a minute, it too lay dead on the ground.

Out of breath from the frantic fight, Mark sat down on a toppled shelf. He could feel his shadow eagerly awaiting his command, and with a tired wave, he sent it to clean up the Exlian. Per his instructions, the C-ranked Exlian was absorbed but not devoured, while the B-ranked Exlian was consumed completely.

As his breathing returned to normal, Mark shuddered slightly, feeling his strength increasing. Devouring Exlian of the same rank was a powerful supplement, and Mark was confident that if he continued to hunt B-ranked mantises, he would soon find his strength ranking up. From his rough assessment, devouring ten more B-ranked Exlian would be enough to promote his strength from B to B+. He would need a lot more than that to get to the A rank, but Mark wasn't particularly concerned. As long as he didn't make major mistakes, hunting them wouldn't be too hard.

What concerned him more, however, was the way he had just teleported. While Mark could test his new teleportation ability in the dream, it didn't affect him in precisely the same way as it would in the real world. He had learned, through countless tests, to successfully move himself without instantly dying, as evidenced by what he had just accomplished in his fight with the mantises. The challenge was that in the dream, many of his sensations were dulled, preventing him from gaining a completely accurate understanding of how the move affected him. Remembering the faint cloud of blood that had been left behind, Mark realized that while the mana circuit he had drawn on his body had, in fact, successfully moved his body through space to the target circuit he had established behind the mantis, it hadn't been strong enough to bring every bit of him.

The result was that the majority of his body had been teleported forward, while some of his blood and insides had remained behind. Without his powerful regeneration, there was no doubt in Mark's mind that he would be dead, and he couldn't help but say a quick prayer of thanks to Sergeant Fletcher, who had given him that ability.

Thinking about it for a second, Mark reached out a hand and condensed the mana fifteen feet away into the target circuit. He hesitated for a brief moment and then shrouded his body in the teleportation circuit. The world warped around him as the circuits connected.

Mark found himself standing fifteen feet ahead. However, he didn't stand for long, as intense pain erupted throughout his body. His legs gave out, causing him to collapse to the ground. This time, he wasn't fighting for his life, so he lay in one place, allowing his regeneration to chew through his excess biofuel to heal the damage he had just caused to himself.

A minute later, as he slowly got to his feet, he caught sight of Mime, who was crouched on the broken shelf where he had just been sitting. Her eyes narrowed as she stared at him, clearly communicating that she thought him an idiot. Truthfully, Mark couldn't blame her. The testing of this new teleportation ability was clearly dangerous, something he probably shouldn't have done before being a hundred percent certain of its success.

In his dream, the pain he felt was slightly muted, and he had no fear of death, as failure simply meant respawning. He didn't have that luxury in the real world, so it had been rather foolhardy of him to use the ability in the first place. But despite Mime's glare, Mark couldn't help but feel excited. He had succeeded, and that success opened up a whole new range of possibilities.

Mark had done the impossible: moving himself through space. To his knowledge, there wasn't a single empowered who could do the same, or an Exlian for that matter. But as much as he wanted to continue testing his new ability, a thread of caution appeared in his heart. He knew that he was being monitored, and he hoped the data his watch had just sent to Maestro hadn't revealed this new ability of his. If it had, Mark had no doubt that he'd find himself back in the Tomb, undergoing tests in the Cradle.

Regardless, it didn't seem wise to continue using the ability, as the more information Maestro had about it, the more clearly he would be able to see what it was that Mark had just achieved. Resolving to only use it in the dream or in times of desperate need, Mark filed away his experiences for later. Thanks to the B-ranked mantis, his biofuel was nearly full, so he would have no trouble continuing to hunt.

Before that, he wanted to test a couple of other things. So he found a quiet, out-of-the-way spot and settled down, concentrating on his clones. He could only vaguely sense them, as the distance between them was too far for information to be shared. Still, he was able to prompt the one in the laboratory to pause what he was doing and summon his shadow. A moment later, two C-ranked mantises and three D-ranked mantis corpses emerged from the shadow onto the tables that had been prepared.

As the clone set about butchering them, Mark let out a sigh of relief. He had suspected that transferring Exlian corpses through his shadow would work, but seeing it actually happen was reassuring. It would mean that he could stay outside the city almost indefinitely for uninterrupted hunting while leaving a clone inside the city walls to process the corpses that he collected.

Materials could be left outside the lab in the long hallway, and he could contact a courier to pick them up and deliver them wherever they needed to be. With that and the clone he had left in his apartment, who was continuing to meditate and study both the Cutting Palm techniques and the null field, Mark's efficiency would shoot through the roof.

Of course, maintaining both clones did take a toll, in terms of both mental pressure and increased biofuel consumption. What Mark was finding, however, was that his will was more than sufficient to compensate. Maybe it was because of the baeloth's necroseed, but he found it relatively easy to maintain the clones, and so long as he kept hunting Exlian, biofuel was the least of his worries.

Of course, there was always the chance that someone would enter the lab or his apartment, dispersing his clone, but if that should happen, Mark could simply return to the city and peel off another.

As he stood up to get ready for his next hunt, Mark couldn't keep the grin from his face. Mime jumped to his shoulder as he stretched and set off.

When he stepped outside, he saw that the long shadows cast by the buildings around him had begun to stretch as the sun made its way below the horizon. All his training had told him that spending the night in the dead zone was a terrible idea and that if he was forced to, it would be best to find an out-of-the-way spot to hide. But rather than nervousness, exhilaration ran through Mark as the sun's last rays faded.

Rather than terror, the darkness of night brought with it a feeling of comfort, as if an invisible weight had suddenly been lifted from Mark. And it was with considerable lightness of step that he made his way out into the street, scanning for prey. When he didn't see any Exlian nearby, he began to make his way toward a tall building in the distance.

Almost immediately, he discovered a group of mantises and shrouded himself before they could locate him. This group was only three mantises, one B ranked and two C ranked. Now that night had fallen, they had begun to stir, getting ready to go out and hunt. Drones typically operated at all hours, but other Exlian were clearly nocturnal, resting during the day and hunting at night.

Of course, when disturbed, Exlian would always choose to fight, no matter the time of day. But now, as Mark got closer to the ones in front of him, he began to sense other Exlian emerging from underground. Rather than rush ahead, he paused for a moment in the shadow of a skyscraper as the city around him came to life.

The Exlian network had, moments before, been almost entirely barren. But within less than ten minutes, Mark counted over a hundred Exlian mental signatures appearing around him. Confident that they didn't have the same sort of shrouding ability that he did, Mark quickly realized that they must have been in some sort of passive hibernation state, burrowed underground.

Most were weak, the majority seeming to be drones. But Mark also spotted another B-ranked Exlian, as well as numerous C- and D-ranked monsters. His original targets had already started their hunt, and their prey were some of the Exlian that had emerged from underground.

As soon as the first B-ranked Exlian began to hunt, however, the new B-ranked monster, which had just awoken, let out a shriek, commanding the Exlian around it to intercept the hunter. Curious about what was happening, Mark made his way closer, being careful to stay out of sight. He found a vantage point on the second floor of an apartment building and crouched behind the railing on the balcony as the two B-ranked Exlian and their minions met in combat on the street in front of him.

The first one was a mantis, a type that seemed to be more active during the daytime, while the other, which had just emerged once the night fell, was a murder scorpion. At first, Mark was rather surprised to see both types of Exlian present. But then he remembered that he was in the southeastern part of the dead zone, smack between the two territories.

Though the B-ranked mantis was dwarfed by the giant scorpion, it still faced down its opponent without any fear, thanks in part to its two lieutenants, which outranked any of the murder scorpions the giant scorpion had brought along. The fighting started as soon as the two sides saw each other. But what Mark found curious was that the two most powerful Exlian completely ignored the others as they threw themselves against one another in battle. From his vantage point on the second-story balcony, Mark watched as the two Exlian engaged in a vicious melee.

The scorpion's powerful claws and venomous stinger did tremendous damage to the mantis as it closed in. However, as soon as the mantis was close, it gained the upper hand in the fight, as the murder scorpion was too big to bring all its weapons to bear at once. Dancing around its side, the mantis dodged the scorpion's strike as its blades hacked and chopped at the scorpion's claws. The fighting was fierce, and the smaller scorpions swarmed the other two mantises furiously, inflicting as many wounds as they could, even as they were torn apart under the mantises' bone blades.

Mark waited patiently, suppressing his urge to jump down and get involved in the fight. He gained no advantage from killing the monsters himself, so waiting patiently until one or both of them fell and then collecting the spoils afterward would save him tremendous effort. Within a few minutes of the fight's start, it was already over. To Mark's surprise, the mantis team had won out over the giant murder scorpion and its horde of smaller scorpions.

Letting out a triumphant roar, the mantis bent down to begin feasting. That was the moment Mark struck. Rising from his hiding spot, he stepped forward, hopped onto the railing, and launched himself into the air. Whether due to the darkness or the fact that he was still shrouded, the B-ranked mantis didn't catch sight of him. It wasn't until Mark was nearly on top of it that its senses triggered, causing it to whirl around.

By then, it was too late. One of its bone blades deflected off Mark's mana shield as he landed on top of it, all four of his blades piercing into the monster's chest. One reached its heart, ensuring its death. As it crashed to the ground, Mark sprang free, dashing toward the other two mantises, which had just discovered that their leader had been brought down by Mark's sneak attack.

With enraged shrieks, they charged toward him, but Mark was too quick. He dodged their attacks as his bone blades cut them to pieces with unerring precision. It wasn't long before both had transformed into corpses, and Mark began to sweep the battlefield, collecting his spoils. The B-ranked scorpion added to his fortitude, while the B-ranked mantis increased his strength. Less than five minutes after he had launched his attack, he was gone, leaving no sign of the titanic battle that had just taken place.

Mark was like a fish in water, passing unobstructed through the streets, hunting and killing Exlian whenever he found them. By the end of the night, he had killed three more B-ranked mantises. He was working his way north, toward the eastern side of the city, intending to complete a large loop that would bring him back to the raiders' base. He wasn't sure if others were aware of its location. If they were, there should be some sign when he visited it again. On the other hand, if they weren't, Mark was planning on using it as a base himself.

As he began to plan, he decided that setting up a few bases throughout the dead zone would enable him to hunt more effectively, giving him places where he could retreat when he needed rest. A steady supply of Exlian corpses meant that Mark's physical energy could remain close to peak at all times, but that didn't mean he was immune to fatigue. Hunting and fighting took a mental toll as well, and Mark was starting to feel himself dragging. The biggest danger was that as he accumulated mental fatigue, his instincts became more pronounced, and he found it harder not to simply abandon himself to them.

By the time morning had come and the first rays of dawn warmed his back, Mark found himself standing outside the abandoned bank that held the raider base. After taking a few moments to observe it, he cautiously made his way inside. There were no Exlian inside the bank or in the base beneath, and Mark didn't sense any humans either. Making his way down, he punched in the code and entered the base, cautiously scanning to see if anyone else had entered.

Before he left, he had scattered a bit of salt from the kitchen across the threshold. It wasn't enough to be noticeable, just enough to reveal if anybody walked over the area. He didn't see any footprints, which reassured him. After carefully stepping over the patch of salt, Mark made his way to one of the beds and prepared to sleep.

This wasn't the first time Mark had stayed up all night, and previously, sleeping during the day hadn't produced the dream, but what he had subsequently discovered was that the time of day didn't actually matter. So long as approximately a day had passed since he had last been in the dream, he would enter it once more upon going to sleep. As he crashed into one of the beds, he soon found himself standing in the wilderness.

To his surprise, however, the building he appeared on wasn't the run-down building from Felwer Mine. Instead, he found himself in a city, with a wide urban landscape, mostly overgrown, stretched out before him. It took him a moment to orient himself, and when he did, he realized that he was in the dead zone. Mark still hadn't figured out what prompted the dream to shift, but clearly, something had caused him to move from the wilderness to the dead zone.

Just like before, Mark was standing on top of a building, this one three stories tall. As he looked out around the dead zone, he spotted multiple Exlian closing in on his position. Rather than wait for them to gather, Mark jumped down, landed in the street with a crash, and rushed toward the closest one. As he skidded around the corner, he caught sight of a large murder scorpion, clearly B ranked from its size, rushing toward him.

Having already faced off against countless murder scorpions, Mark didn't hesitate. He drove his speed to its limit as they closed in on one another. The murder scorpion stabbed out with its stinger, but Mark deflected the blow at the last moment, borrowing the force to advance even more quickly as he dodged past its grasping claws. His bone blades plunged with perfect accuracy into the monster's head, piercing its skull and ripping apart its brain in one single smooth motion. At the same time, Mark's other bone blades dug into the scorpion's carapace and pushed, allowing him to vault over the monster's body, barely avoiding a reflexive stab from its tail.

Devouring the Exlian in the dream was pointless, so he didn't bother. Instead, he checked for the other Exlian that were closing in. Unlike the wilderness, the Exlian in the dead zone seemed endless. Even as the next two powerful Exlian closed in on Mark, he saw a swarm gathering around him. No matter which direction he turned, thick swarms of Exlian closed in, and he realized that he was in for a fierce fight. Rather than shy away from it, he flashed a savage smile and threw himself toward the enemy, eager to test the very limits of his abilities.

Mark died twice over the next six hours, buried under swarms of Exlian, but when he woke from the dream, he wasn't disheartened at all. If anything, he could hardly suppress his eagerness to hunt. The only way he knew to temper this feeling was to go out and hunt, which was exactly what he did.

Over the next few days, Mark's life fell into a very simple rhythm. During the day and then late into the night, he would hunt, ranging across the dead zone. In the daytime, when fewer Exlian were active, he focused on looking for alchemical materials, plants, and fungi hidden among the concrete rubble. Then at night, he would shift his attention to the Exlian that emerged, devouring every B-ranked Exlian he could find, while sending the corpses of the lower-ranked Exlian to his clone in the laboratory.

He discovered that he could transport the materials he recovered as well, providing his lab clone with a steady supply of alchemical ingredients for potions. What was incredibly convenient was that the lab clone could simply drop those completed potions into his shadow, allowing Mark to recover them out in the field. This only increased Mark's hunting efficiency, and after a week had passed, he found himself staring at two very welcome notifications.

> Your strength has increased from B to B+.
> Your fortitude has increased from B– to B.

Mark could feel his will improving too as the remnants of the baeloth seed continued to integrate into his body. His main constraint was now his speed, so Mark turned his attention to trying to find a type of Exlian that would improve it.

Since the hounds he'd killed out in the wilderness had added to his speed, Mark looked for other Exlian that might do the same. Unfortunately, there wasn't much around the city that seemed as if it would qualify, so Mark decided to begin testing the various kinds of Exlian one by one. He started with the only other B-ranked Exlian he was aware of: the earth rats. Finding their dens was a bit tricky, but he started by returning to the place where he had led Terra's team. There he found nothing but an empty den, but upon seeing his interest, Mime had sniffed around and then calmly trotted out into the street, pausing to look back to ask if Mark was going to follow. He did, and about half an hour later, they descended into a ruined stairwell that had been completely blocked off.

Staring at the wall of stone and dirt, Mark scratched his head and then looked at Mime, who gestured with her paw for him to continue. As she clearly wasn't going to help him dig a path, Mark grumbled to himself and then got to work, using his bone blades to dig his way through the earth that blocked the path forward. Two hours later, they emerged from the other side, entering the abandoned metro station. A powerful stench in the air caused Mime's nose to wrinkle and her hackles to rise. Mark took a step forward and then froze as he felt a strange sensation wash over his body.

It was as if thousands of tiny needles had pricked his skin, and remaining in place, he carefully swept the area, examining both the psychic network and the darkness, looking for the source of the strange feeling. Then he saw them. Hundreds of glittering eyes, barely visible in the darkness. The majority of them were concentrated in front of him, but as he continued to look around, he saw more and more emerging every moment. Within a few seconds, there must have been thousands of them, and Mark felt a cold bead of sweat run down his spine. He wasn't sure why the earth rats in front of him weren't showing up in the psychic network, but it was clear that he and Mime had just walked into an entire den of them.

None of the rats seemed particularly powerful. But having been buried under hordes of Exlian in the dream, Mark didn't dare underestimate their danger. Then, slowly at first, but with increasing frequency, Exlian mental signatures began to pop up in the midst of the horde as more powerful rats woke up and joined their companions, encircling Mark. When the fifteenth C-ranked Exlian appeared, Mark let out a small breath and took a decisive step backward, intending to retreat. Taking it as a sign of weakness, the earth rats surged forward, forming a massive wave that rushed toward him with incredible speed.

What was most eerie, however, was that they made not a single sound, neither chittering nor squeaking. Instead it was as if a silent wall of darkness, consuming everything in its path, were closing in on him. Mark retreated faster, not liking his chances, only to find that the path he had created through the earth had already been blocked in. Under his astonished gaze, dozens of large rats rushed out of the hole he had made, earth crumbling behind them. They had collapsed his tunnel, neatly trapping him underground.

Sparing a glance at Mime, Mark realized that she had

vanished, likely melding back into his shadow, leaving him to face the onrushing horde alone. Gritting his teeth, Mark could only turn and face the horde. Rather than continue to retreat, he stepped forward, his blades slashing out, instantly eviscerating a dozen rats. Yet that was but a drop in the ocean of vermin that engulfed him, and Mark felt thousands of teeth and claws gnawing and scratching at his bone armor as he was engulfed in the tide of rats.

Every one of his movements destroyed a rat, but despite that, they continued to come, flooding over him as they desperately scratched and clawed at his armor. Their attacks were so frequent and fierce that Mark's mana shields simply couldn't activate, but thankfully his bone armor was tough enough that the rats' attacks couldn't get through. Of course, Mark knew that that only counted for the weakest of the rats. He had no doubt that the tough teeth of the C- and B-ranked earth rats would chew straight through him, and once they did, his death was all but assured.

Practically blind because of the sheer number of bodies swarming over him, Mark paid special attention to the Exlian network, watching for the more powerful rats lurking in the distance, waiting for an opportunity to strike. At the same time, he continued to swing his bone blades while unleashing a storm of kicks and punches, obliterating his enemies as fast as possible. Yet for each he killed, it seemed as if two took its place, and soon the floor was slick with blood.

Sensing one of the more powerful rats making a move, Mark fell back to buy himself another second and then struck swiftly, his bone blade slipping past a swarm of rats to accurately pierce the skull of the C-ranked rat dashing toward him. As it died, it let out a shriek, and the rats around it were shrouded in a strange energy, their eyes glowing bright red as they attacked with increased vigor. Worse, their attacks actually got sharper and stronger, and though they still couldn't pierce Mark's armor, they were certainly more of a nuisance than before.

Another powerful earth rat rushed forward as well, and once again, Mark located it among the horde and killed it, this time with a well-placed kick. As he drove his heel into the monster's spine, it too let out a shriek that strengthened the rats around it. Immediately, Mark began to feel scratches appearing on his armor as the effect stacked, drastically increasing the rats' attacking capability.

Mark felt his regeneration starting to kick in, healing the armor. While that meant that even with these stronger attacks, the rat horde wouldn't be able to pierce it, it also meant that his biofuel was starting to drain even faster than before. Unsure what to do, Mark spun, tearing apart all the rats near him with fierce slashes from his blades, buying himself a brief moment of respite, looking for a way out.

Then he sensed his shadow's eagerness, and he realized how foolish he was being. With a command, his shadow rapidly swelled, becoming liquid as it surged to cover the corpses of the rats he had destroyed. As rats disappeared, more swarmed toward him, and Mark lifted his blades to meet them. Yet before they could reach him, they had to rush into his shadow, and when they did, they began to vanish in tremendous numbers. Mark, who had assumed that his shadow could only devour corpses, was stunned as a gleeful crunching rang out and he felt the struggling rats being torn apart. It was a bizarre feeling, but he quickly got used to it. Recognizing his opportunity, Mark didn't remain on the defensive. Instead, he rushed forward, heading toward the C-ranked rats in the distance.

Though confused about what was going on, they reacted swiftly, sending even more rats toward him. Soon, Mark realized he had a different problem. Before, his concern had been running out of biofuel. Now, he could feel his shadow growing satiated.

As it did, it seemed to become lethargic, taking longer and longer to devour the new rats.

Realizing he needed to do something to burn through his excess biofuel, Mark pushed himself to the absolute limit. He leaped over the swarm of rats to attack the C-ranked rats behind them, yet even as he flew through the air, the swarm rose up to meet him, knocking him down. With a crash, he smashed into the ground, crushing dozens of rats underneath his body.

Immediately, the swarm descended upon him, completely covering him in a writhing sea of flesh. Mark struggled to get up, but the constant pressure from the rats leaping on top of him made it impossible. So began a fierce tug-of-war as Mark's shadow rapidly devoured the rats around him, transforming them into nutrients to boost his regeneration, while the rats clawed at his armor, trying to scratch it to pieces.

For longer than he was comfortable, this tug-of-war persisted, until one of Mark's slashing blades ripped through a C-ranked rat that had approached. Its death knell sent the already frenzied rats into pure madness, and the crimson glow that shrouded their eyes began to extend to their claws. One particularly fierce swipe against Mark's ribs tore through his bone armor and raked across his skin.

This was the first time during the fight that Mark had actually been wounded, and though his regeneration kicked in to seal the wound immediately, the jolt of pain sent him into overdrive. Knowing he couldn't survive against the fierce onslaught of rage-empowered rats, Mark unleashed his null field, blanketing the area in the strange energy that could not coexist with mana.

Two things happened simultaneously, leading to a result completely outside Mark's expectation. The first was that the rats snapped out of their madness and began instead to shriek, their voices laden with fear. The second was that Mark's shadow abruptly expanded, growing even larger than before, filling the mana void his ability had formed, and instantly devouring all the rats that fell into it as they attempted to flee.

At first, Mark wondered if his null field had somehow empowered his shadow, but he quickly realized that the actual problem was that it had caused his shadow to completely lose control of its form, failing to contain the drastic increase in biofuel it had been absorbing. Carefully withdrawing the null field, Mark willed his shadow back into place, and it retreated, returning to its typical shape at his feet. There was an uneasy silence as Mark looked around and saw that the rats, which appeared no fewer in number than before, had withdrawn to a safe distance and were watching him warily.

Feeling a shift at his feet, he glanced down and saw Mime step out of his shadow. She sat and gave him an exasperated look, as if annoyed at what had just happened. With a half-hearted shrug, Mark took the moment of calm to gather himself. In many ways, he was the rats' natural nemesis, able to consume them directly and use that power to fight them for longer. In theory, so long as he could avoid being instantly killed, Mark had nothing to fear from a battle of attrition with them. The only danger lay in their amplification ability, which Mark could counter.

Of course, this might change if Mark's shadow reached satiation. The proximity of so many bodies that wished him harm made his mana shield useless, and if their claws could get through his bone armor, Mark knew he'd lose the fight quickly. The problem now was how to retreat, because the path leading up to the surface was completely blocked, and as he looked at the caved-in entrance to the metro system, he saw a sea of rats waiting for him.

Mime's paw tapped on his armored boot, and when he looked down, she pointed deeper into the tunnel. From the hunger in her eyes, it was obvious that she was still fixated on their original goal of finding B-ranked Exlian. With a groan, Mark reached down and picked her up before slowly walking deeper into the tunnels. The rats in front of him scurried away, clearly not interested in entering his shadow, which was still eagerly flowing underneath him, occasionally stretching out long tendrils to see if it could snag a rat.

The swarm kept well clear, and Mark found his way unimpeded. At the same time, he could feel them stacking up behind him, forming an impenetrable field that carried with it a faint pressure that grew stronger with each step. Mark walked forward in the complete darkness and soon arrived at the end of the station platform. Since Mime was clearly expecting him to proceed farther into the tunnels, he hopped off the platform, causing a tide of rats to flee, and began trudging deeper into the earth.

Mark had long been aware that the metro system ran underneath the entirety of the dead zone, but it was considered a no-man's-land, a place completely controlled by the Exlian, and the Hunters' Association strictly forbade hunters from entering it. Yet here Mark was, casually strolling through one of the tunnels, his cat in his arms, thousands of rats surrounding them. The absurdity caused him to chuckle, and the sound echoed long in the confines of the tunnel, causing the rats to retreat even farther.

After walking for almost a mile, Mark came to a fork. Glancing down at Mime, he saw her pointing to the left, so he took that passage, noticing how immediately the rats grew stronger and more plentiful. To his knowledge, an earth rat wave had never attacked the city. Typically, earth rats were considered among the weakest Exlian, but now, seeing the countless rats before him, Mark began to seriously wonder if New Emery would be able to survive such an attack.

He had but to turn his head to see thousands of D- and E-ranked earth rats, with hundreds of C-ranked ones dotted among them. He was even beginning to see the odd B-ranked earth rat, and the sight sent shivers down his spine as he imagined a solid wall of earth rats climbing over New Emery's walls and swarming through the city.

Though Mime seemed confident, Mark wasn't sure that he shared her feelings. The sheer number of enemies around him made him wonder if he'd ever make it back to the surface. But despite the remnants of his human mind screaming, Mark walked calmly through the tunnels, making two more turns and heading down a long slope before he reached a massive natural cavern, where the remnants of the rail line ended.

There was a faint glow, and Mark saw a massive pool of glimmering liquid, pure mana so concentrated it manifested physically. He looked past the mist that rose from the glowing liquid and saw a large black blob—an Exlian nest—shivering in the center of the pool. Hearing hundreds of plops, he saw rats swimming across the mana pond toward him. Their fur glowed as they rose out of the pool and merged into the ranks of their brethren. When Mark stopped, Mime hopped down from his arms and began to calmly walk toward the nest, gesturing for him to follow. He took a step forward and felt the rats around him bristle, as if they were about to attack. Then the nest in the distance quivered, and the rats calmed down, retreating half a step to give Mark and Mime more space.

The nest extended a tendril and made a gesture that looked suspiciously like a wave, then settled down again. Mark, unsure what else to do, followed Mime. The closer he got, the more clearly he could feel the presence of the nest. It sat in front of him, a massive blob of physical, mental, and mana-infused presence, occupying all three spheres with equal weight. Mark would have assumed that such tremendous mental pressure would be hard to face. Instead, he found the opposite. A strong desire to dive forward and consume the nest was growing in him. The nest seemed to sense it and responded by shrinking slightly, fear emanating from it.

"Are we here to eat it?" Mark asked Mime, his eyes fixed on the massive blob in front of them.

As if sensing his hunger, the swarm rippled, and hundreds of B-ranked rats pushed their way forward, clearly intending to attack. When Mime shook her head, the nest relaxed slightly and began to wave its tentacles, causing the swarm of rats to reluctantly pause their aggression.

"If we're not here to eat it, then what are we here for?"

To his surprise, the nest responded, its massive mental presence reaching out to him, shrouding him as it tried to communicate. Though the mental energy surrounding him was completely alien, Mark was surprised to see images begin to flash through his mind, too blurry to make out but infused with feelings, colors, and sounds that formed a discordant kaleidoscope.

Mark soon began to piece together a rough sense of what the creature wanted. As he concentrated, a cohesive picture emerged, one of intense danger, fear, being hunted, and a desire for protection. Though dim, the pictures and sounds coalesced to form a clearer image in Mark's mind, one he found surprisingly familiar: a tall creature that walked on two legs, with four long arms that hung down below its knees and a long whipping tail. What allowed him to recognize it, however, was the smooth bone face and the pair of twisting horns atop its head. Though the figure didn't look exactly like the strange humanoid Exlian Mark had seen in Felwer Mine, it was clear that this Exlian was in the same vein, and the feeling of power that its image exuded caused Mark to tense up.

The nest expressed that this creature, this threat, was hunting it, and it wanted Mark to step in, to slay the monster and keep it safe. Stunned by the intelligence the nest showed, Mark saw the images shift and change, transforming into a being that looked much more like him, still humanoid, but with four extra waving arms extending from its back. In the broken images, Mark saw the figure that represented him consuming rats, one after another. It took him longer to puzzle out what was happening, and the nest patiently continued projecting the same image.

"Wait, are you saying that you'll let me eat rats, as many as I want, if I kill the apex hunter who's hunting you?"

There was no change in the images that the nest was projecting, and Mark smacked his forehead, realizing he had spoken out loud. Projecting the same question with his mind proved more effective, and the nest signaled its agreement. Mark had entertained the thought of communicating with Exlian in the past and had even sensed the will to survive expressed by the last nest he had faced. Yet the fact that he was actually communicating with one left him bewildered.

"What do you think?" he asked Mime. "Should I take this deal?"

Mime considered for a moment, then nodded emphatically. It only took a moment for Mark to agree, and a subtle ripple spread from the nest, extending out over the swarm, which rapidly dispersed, leaving a dozen B-ranked rats behind. Once their comrades were out of sight, they crept, trembling slightly, in front of Mark and lowered their bodies to the ground, clearly waiting for him to consume them. A complex feeling rose in Mark's heart at the sight, and he seemed to see the men and women of the city's three armies, willingly putting themselves in harm's way to ensure the safety of the whole. As he was trying to convince himself that it was different for the Exlian, Mark's shadow leaped forward, enveloping them one at a time and devouring them. Unsure if he should be annoyed that his shadow had acted without his command, Mark was distracted enough by the notification that popped up that he didn't let it bother him.

> Your speed has increased from C+ to B–.
> Your will has increased from B to B+.

Mark felt his will expanding even further, though it stopped just short of breaking through to the A rank. Seeing Mime turn and walk back toward the passage, Mark glanced back at the nest one last time and then followed her out.

They didn't see another rat the entire way to the surface, and when they finally arrived at the platform, Mark found that the entrance tunnel he had dug had been reexcavated. As soon as he walked out and up the stairs, he heard the scurry of feet and the sound of dirt collapsing as the tunnel was resealed. Suppressing the shudder that ran through him, Mark crouched and looked at Mime.

"It feels wrong to leave the nest alive," he said. "I'm not saying we could have fought our way through that horde, but a nest so close to New Emery is incredibly dangerous. If, during the next wave, the rats decide they want to get in on the action, I . . ." His voice trailed off, and he turned to look at the massive city wall in the far distance. "I genuinely don't know how we're going to stop them."

Mime regarded him for a moment, her head tilted to the side, and then, with something approaching a smile on her face, she walked over and rubbed herself against his leg. Though she didn't make any noise, Mark could tell that she was comforting him. Even as he reached out to scratch behind her ears, he heard the now-familiar voice in his heart.

The apex hunters are a much greater threat, and we can use the earth rat nest to grow stronger. If it ever steps into our territory, we'll have a reason to kill it. Attacking now would only lead to complications. Better to face one problem at a time.

"Can we trust the Exlian, though?"

For a moment, Mark thought he saw Mime laughing at him.

The Exlian are what they are. Some of them are intelligent enough to have strategy and cunning. But they have no guile. They do not know what it means to lie. That is something only humans are capable of.

The answer echoed clearly in Mark's heart, and he found himself relaxing. If that was the case, then he would trust the nest, at least for the moment. It had asked him to hunt the apex hunter, and according to the images, the apex hunter was currently located northeast of the city, near the edge of the dead zone.

Despite knowing roughly where his enemy was located, Mark had no desire to rush straight there. He still had no clue how strong the apex hunter was, though it clearly was strong enough that the nest feared it. He had a hard time believing that it was stronger than the rat swarm, however, and as he reflected on the feeling that the nest had given him, he realized that what it feared was the apex hunter's intelligence, rather than its raw power. That was the only thing that made sense, considering that the nest had asked Mark, who was only B ranked, to hunt it down and kill it. Surely it wouldn't send him on a wild-goose chase to attack an enemy overwhelmingly stronger?

Then again, there was no guarantee of that, so Mark thought it best to proceed with caution.

Just then, he felt his watch vibrate and looked down, seeing dozens of notifications. For a moment, he was confused, but then he remembered that one of the other reasons that the Hunters' Association forbade hunters from entering the metro system was that the entire thing was shielded, making it impossible for watches to connect. No doubt his watch had just reconnected to the network and, in doing so, downloaded all the messages he had received while underground.

When he opened the first one, Mark's eyes narrowed, and he quickly scanned through the others. One was from Noah and contained nothing but coordinates and a simple phrase.

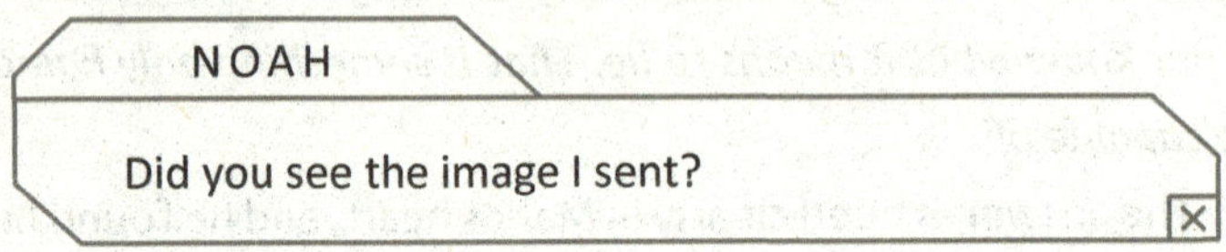

No image was attached to the message, but Mark didn't need one.

Noah was in trouble.

The rest of the messages were from Sky, asking where he was and if he had seen Noah's message. He sent off a response and then checked the coordinates Noah had sent. As the map zoomed in, he realized it was a spot roughly fifteen miles from his current position. Without waiting for Sky to respond to his message, Mark took off, heading straight there as fast as he could.

He had run four miles when his watch vibrated and Sky's call came through.

"Mar—I mean Jonathan—where are you? Did you see Noah's message?"

"I did," Mark said, not stopping, even for a moment.

"What's that on your face? I mean, doesn't matter. Where are you located?"

"I'm actually not too far from Noah's position," Mark said. "About eleven miles out. I can ping you my location."

"I'm on the opposite side of the city at the moment, but I'm heading that direction to see if I can get eyes on him."

"Do you know what's going on?" Mark asked.

"It seems like Noah's Ranger unit is under attack by a swarm, and their retreat to the city has been cut off," Sky said.

"Shouldn't the Defense Force be coming out to rescue them?"

A frustrated look flashed across Sky's face, even as she skimmed past a cloud, her hair flowing straight back in the wind. "I already checked the network. If they put in a distress request, the system would register it, but I haven't been able to find one. When I tried to raise an alert, it didn't work either. It seems like everything related to that unit is being suppressed."

"Either they're on a secret mission or somebody is intentionally sabotaging them," Mark said, his tone hard. "I'd guess the latter over the former. It sounds suspiciously like what happened to the Cerberus Battalion before. Let me send you my position. Be careful as you get close. There might be enemy fliers."

Ending the call, Mark slowed to a jog for a moment as he tapped on his map and shared his location with both Noah and Sky. Noah's name was grayed out, and Mark saw his earlier message hadn't gotten through. Closing his map, Mark took off running again, praying that Noah could hold on.

With her incredible flight speed, Sky reached the coordinates Noah had sent before Mark did, and once she arrived, she called him from the rooftop of a nearby building.

"It looks like his team is being besieged. I've never seen this kind of Exlian before," she said as soon as the call connected. "Let me see if I can feed you my cam."

A moment later, Mark saw another window pop up, this time with the camera feed from her helmet. As someone who patrolled the city wall, it was normal for her to record everything that she was seeing. Though whether she would get in trouble for sharing it over her watch, Mark wasn't sure.

She appeared to be on top of a seven-story building, looking down at the ancient remains of a park nestled between other tall buildings. The park was overgrown, but Mark could catch flashes of mana blades and the angry screeches of Exlian through the trees. It wasn't clear whether the Rangers had been ambushed on their way through the park or had been driven into it by the enemy.

There was an old playground near a large fountain, and it was here the Rangers had set up their perimeter. There only looked to be about twenty of them, which spoke of horrific casualties, as the team should have been at least fifty. The Exlian currently assaulting the Rangers came in all shapes and sizes, deformed amalgamations of arms and legs, with blades and hooks protruding from their bodies at all angles. They seemed to fight by simply throwing themselves at the enemy and flailing, relying on the sharp protrusions from their limbs to take down their opponents.

For their own part, the Rangers were doing their best to keep them at a distance, deploying their powers to full effect. Mark could see multiple energy controllers providing the main resistance, conjuring shields and occasionally blasting away an enemy that got too close. The other Rangers operated with the efficiency Mark had come to expect from the highly trained military, combining forces to cut down Exlian as they charged.

"Have you spotted Noah?" Mark asked, taking a corner at full speed.

"I think he's down there, in the gray. I mean, they're all wearing gray, but gray, black, and red, at four o'clock."

As soon as Mark's eyes landed on the figure Sky was referring to, he knew it was Noah. His brutal movements were faster, stronger, and considerably smoother than those of everyone around him. To say nothing of the fact that he occasionally thrust his hand forward and unleashed a powerful blast of mana that sent the enemy tumbling back. As a paragon, Noah had well-rounded abilities, making him a practically perfect fighter. Yet it was clear that the enemy knew this as well, and the majority of their forces seemed to be concentrated on that corner of the Rangers' formation, clearly trying to overwhelm him with superior numbers.

"I'm going to go down and help," Sky said, taking a step toward the edge of the building.

"Hold on," Mark said. "Don't move."

"What's wrong?"

"Look across from you, at the fifth floor. I thought I saw some movement there."

Crouching, Sky concentrated, and after a moment they both saw something shift in one of the broken windows. It was moving too quickly for her to catch a good view, but Mark gritted his teeth. "You need to get out of there. Get back to the city. See if you can get someone to send reinforcements."

"What? Why?"

Before Mark could answer, a figure darted out of the broken window, wings spreading wide as it rose above the park. Out of other nearby buildings, more flying creatures emerged, their wings flapping heavily as they shot toward Sky.

"Oh, that's why," she said.

While Sky was tremendously quick in the air and had an incredible degree of control, her abilities did not extend to aerial combat. She was unable to maintain her flight with more than fifty pounds on her body, which meant that an opponent simply had to grab onto her to turn her flight power off. Of course, she was so quick that catching her was nearly impossible. The enemy had already spotted her and now rushed toward her as fast as their wings would carry them.

"How close are you?" she asked.

"Probably ten minutes out."

"All right, I'll try to keep them distracted as I make my way back to the city."

"If nothing else, you should be able to get a Hunters' Association team. In fact, as soon as I get there, I'll set off my SOS."

Though Sky looked as if she wanted to respond, her opponents were already on top of her, so she ended the call as she moved to evade. Mark, taking a deep breath, sped up, not bothering to conserve his biofuel as he raced through the city. His additional speed, gained from the B-ranked earth rats he had consumed, came in handy, and seven minutes later, he saw the building where Sky had been a few minutes earlier.

Rather than rush straight into the fight, Mark sprinted to the building and scrambled up it, his bone blade arms cutting into the cement wall as he hauled himself up to the rooftop. Even as he jumped over the ledge, he was reaching into his shadow and retrieving the high-powered sniper rifle that he had pulled off the raiders.

Settling down at the edge of the roof that overlooked the park, Mark cradled the sniper rifle in his arms and scanned the fight below. The Rangers had lost two more men, though from the looks of it, both of them were simply wounded and had retreated to the center of the formation. Noah continued to fight, though his movements seemed much more sluggish than before.

Seeing an enemy closing in from Noah's side, Mark took careful aim, let out his breath, and pulled the trigger, holding the gun absolutely still despite the heavy recoil. The bolt of concentrated mana flew out of the barrel, crossing the distance in less than half a second. Mark's shot had been slightly low, and instead of hitting his enemy between the eyes, it blasted apart his chin and ripped through his throat.

Despite the grievous wound, the monstrosity didn't immediately die and instead began flailing violently. One of the Rangers, taking advantage of the sudden attack, reached out and lifted the monster from a distance, throwing it back into its companions, where its fierce struggles entangled three others. Feeling rather annoyed he hadn't killed the creature outright, Mark peeled off a clone to remain with the rifle and stood up. Running toward the side of the building, he vaulted over the edge and slid down the outside, using his bone blades to slow his fall, at the cost of ruining the building's wall.

Mark was about to rush toward Noah when a sudden movement caught his eye, and he quickly ducked, barely avoiding a massive fist that slammed into the ground where he had just been. Rolling backward, he bounced to his feet and found himself facing a strange-looking man with a massive left arm bigger than the entire rest of his body. His other arm was abnormally long and flexible, and it shifted like a snake, raised half above his head as he stared through slitted eyes at Mark.

Seeing the attacker up close confirmed a suspicion that Mark had had all along. Noah's attackers weren't Exlian, or at least not completely. Despite the faint threat the man in front of him gave off, Mark's attention turned to a figure who had just emerged from around a corner. A figure he had only seen once before, when he had escaped from the Tomb.

"Hello, Mark," the Prophet said. "This is our third meeting."

"Of five, right?" Mark growled, getting ready to attack.

Chuckling, Dallas held up his hands. This time, the nondescript man was dressed in a neat suit, looking like a run-of-the-mill businessman, though a shimmering scarf was around his neck. His clothing was entirely out of place in the ruined dead zone, but he appeared completely at ease, as if he were simply out for a stroll.

"Once again, I must reiterate, I have no desire to fight with the

Savior. Especially since it's clear you're working hard to become what you need to be."

Mark had no interest in getting involved in whatever crazy fantasy the Prophet of Salvation was immersed in. Yet something about the way that he said the words gave Mark pause.

"Oh yes," Dallas said, "you are developing wonderfully. It's amazing to witness the very pinnacle of our ambition emerging before me. The perfect fusion of Exlian and humanity. Tell me, what is your secret? Actually, don't. The mystery is better left intact. Instead, I'd invite you to witness the power of our movement."

Glancing at the warped imitation of a man between them, Mark scoffed. "You can't be talking about this freak."

The mutant's eyes widened, and a furious expression crossed his face, his muscles tensing as if he were ready to leap.

More than happy to get the fight started, Mark shook his head. "I thought Salvation's plan was to improve humanity. You'd have to be blind to think this was an improvement."

To Mark's surprise, Dallas just gave Mark a small smile as the mutant lunged forward, his massive left arm reaching for Mark's head. Though Mark was confident in his newfound powers, the mutant in front of him gave him a faint sense of danger, so he didn't dare underestimate his opponent's strength. Rather than meet the massive hand head-on, Mark shifted to the side, intending to rip through the arm with his bone blades. Yet even as he did, the mutant's flexible right arm shot toward his leg, wrapping around his left foot before he could react. Though Mark's mana shield flared, the mutant wasn't trying to pierce through Mark's armor; he was only trying to slow Mark down long enough for his other hand to arrive.

Mark ducked under the grab, two of his bone blades shooting toward the mutant's right arm while the other two attacked his left, aiming for his wrist, only to skid off the thick armor that covered both limbs, leaving bloody scratches but failing to deal significant damage. Mark's eyes narrowed as he realized he was in for a much tougher fight than he had anticipated.

Jerking himself free from the mutant's entangling grip, Mark hopped backward, even as his opponent continued to advance. He used his massive left arm as a battering ram that drove straight toward Mark, while his right arm attacked like a striking serpent, dancing around as it tried to pierce through Mark's defenses or entangle him. Forced to defend, Mark continued to give ground, using his bone blades to deflect his opponent's attacks as he gauged the mutant's strength and speed. Though the mutant himself was barely as strong as a C-ranked empowered, the speed of his right arm and the fortitude of his left were a step above, matching Mark's stats.

Though straightforward, the mutant's attack pattern was hard to defend against, and Mark had no doubt that once the mutant grabbed him, he would find it even harder to shake his enemy off. As he defended himself, his eyes drifted to Dallas farther back. The Prophet was watching with bright eyes, clearly curious as to what Mark was going to do in this situation.

Mark got the feeling that Dallas was looking for something, some sign that Mark truly was the so-called Savior. Just then, Mark heard the crack of his mana rifle firing again, and then a moment later, a second shot. He had ordered his clone to only attack when the situation was dire, and now he finally ran out of patience.

Instead of continuing to retreat, Mark pressed forward, directly attacking his opponent's massive left hand. His bone blades left gashes across the giant fingers, but the mutant didn't even seem to feel the wounds as he roared and closed his hand around Mark. Mark didn't bother to block it. Instead, his bone blades stabbed straight into the mutant's wrist, preventing him from pulling his hand back. At the same time, Mark planted his feet and lifted, using his superior strength to lift the mutant off the ground. Startled, the mutant attacked with his right arm, but Mark simply ignored it, trusting his armor to deal with the whipping attacks.

Devour!

The mental command caused Mark's shadow to boil, and tendrils of pure darkness began to creep up his body, swiftly engulfing the arm that surrounded him. At first, the mutant didn't realize what was happening, his focus entirely on trying to crush Mark. It was only when his pinkie and a large chunk of his hand were torn off by the devouring shadow that he let out a shriek of pain and tried to jerk himself free. Yet Mark wasn't about to let him go. The bone blades dug deeper, locking him in place as Mark's shadow continued to spread, now creeping across the mutant's massive left arm toward his torso.

A panicked expression crossed the mutant's face, but no matter how he yelled or thrashed, he couldn't get free. As the shadow spread, Mark dropped the mutant to the ground, where he crashed onto his side as his arm, completely covered in darkness, rapidly vanished into the endless abyss of Mark's shadow. The mutant was only visible for a few more seconds, but Mark had already turned his attention to Dallas, who looked quite satisfied.

"You know, compared to you, these poor men really are rather pathetic. But if you worked with us, we could change that. With your abilities, Salvation wouldn't need to hide in the shadows. We could fulfill our mandate, rising up to sterilize the corruption and rot that so infects New Emery."

"Is that why you're attacking the Rangers?" Mark asked, walking forward as the last lumps of the mutant vanished behind him.

"In part, yes," Dallas said, his hand rising to clutch at the shimmering scarf around his neck. "Among them is a specimen that could drastically improve our success rate in creating hybrids to fight against the city council. The corruption in this city goes far further than you probably realize, Mark, and we're not the only ones with plans for the city's fair citizens. In fact, if you want to hear true madness, you should talk to your friend's father. Ask him what the council or, more specifically, their scientists have been up to. They do far worse than us on a daily basis."

Mark thought he did a good job controlling his body language, yet Dallas must have seen something, because his eyes gleamed and he nodded sagely.

"Oh yes, I know about your relationship with Noah Javesi. Such things cannot be hidden. After all, wasn't he the one who came to save you when you escaped from the Tomb? It was a cute stunt but one that didn't fool anybody. At least, anyone important."

"Yet here I am," Mark said, spreading his hands as he continued to move closer to where the Prophet stood. "If everybody knows, then why am I walking free?"

"Because it serves their interests, of course. Now, as much as I've enjoyed this conversation, I can see that you're not ready to take our relationship to the next level, so I'm afraid I'm going to have to bow out."

As soon as Dallas finished speaking, Mark leaped, his powerful legs driving him forward as he grasped for the Prophet. Yet even as he closed in, the shimmering scarf unleashed a blinding silver burst, and Mark slammed into a wall that appeared between them, as if a curtain of pure steel had been drawn in front of him. Frustrated, Mark unleashed his null field, causing the obstruction to melt away, but even as it did, he realized that Dallas was gone, no doubt through the same bloody portal he had used to escape from Mark previously.

Suppressing his anger, Mark turned and darted toward the park, where the battle still raged. It only took a few seconds before the fierce fighting came into view, and he heard the heavy crack of his rifle, causing a mutant in his way to stumble. Seconds later,

Mark was on top of the wounded enemy, his bone blades piercing through the mutant's back and finishing the job. Though the mana rifle was powerful, the mutants had an unnatural level of fortitude, allowing them to survive even the most grievous wounds. The only thing that seemed to be able to keep them down was damage directly to their hearts, brains, or, as in this case, spinal columns.

Brushing past the mutant he had just killed, Mark caught sight of a Ranger desperately fighting a mutant with six long spiderlike limbs. The Ranger rolled across the ground, dodging the mutant's stabbing limbs, leaving a bloody smear on the ground from the jagged gash on his back. Bumping against a tree, the Ranger came to a stop and braced himself, clearly expecting a limb to pierce through his chest. Yet the limb never fell, and when he looked up, he saw the mutant lying in pieces not far away. Gripping the tree, he pulled himself weakly to his feet, only to see a strange dark shadow bubbling up around him, tendrils of darkness starting to creep up his limbs.

Mark, who had torn the mutant to pieces and moved on, felt his shadow's hunger and recalled it with a stern command to behave. With genuine reluctance, his shadow peeled away from the wounded Ranger, contenting itself with gobbling up the mutant's dismembered body as it retreated.

As he continued to work his way toward the Rangers' defensive line, where Noah was continuing to fight valiantly, Mark encountered more wounded Rangers fighting for their lives against the mutants. Each time he did, he struck quickly, ambushing the mutants from behind and eliminating them before they had any sense of their doom. More than once, the Rangers caught sight of him, and every single one reacted with fear and intense wariness, pulling back to defend themselves from his attack, only to be stunned when he ignored them entirely and continued his hunt of mutants.

Their expressions didn't go unnoticed, however, and Mark realized just how odd he must look to them. It was unlikely that they had ever seen a suit like his, since as far as Mark knew, only one other empowered had this sort of ability. Realizing that if he rushed straight into the mutants' battle line, the Rangers might mistake him for an enemy and attack, Mark shifted his approach, continuing to hunt around the outer edge of the battlefield, slipping through the trees and killing every mutant he came across.

The Rangers he rescued rallied quickly, gathering together and rushing out toward the main fight, providing much-needed support for their besieged comrades. By the time Mark had cleared three-quarters of the forest, the mutants had begun to sense something was wrong, and rather than continue their fight, they turned and fled, rushing out of the park and into the abandoned buildings that surrounded it. Four of the mutants were unlucky enough to pass by Mark's location, and he took them down, tearing through their reinforced bodies with ease and feeding the corpses to his shadow.

The Rangers seemed hardly able to believe that the fight was over, but to their credit, instead of collapsing to the ground to rest, they formed up, creating an even stronger defensive perimeter.

For a moment Mark considered retreating rather than showing himself. He honestly didn't particularly care about the Rangers and would have had little interest in helping them out if not for Noah.

But after a moment of thought, he realized that this would be a fantastic opportunity to reveal his new armor to the world. He currently had three clones active, and the toll was significant, requiring quite a bit of mental power to keep active. But he didn't feel safe without someone watching his back, and if it was himself, all the better.

Closing his eyes, Mark concentrated, and slowly the bone blade arms retracted into his armor, leaving only the tips of the blades protruding from above his shoulders and below his arms, forming an X across his back. His helmet retracted as well, melting away to reveal his face. He could feel a faint headache forming at the base of his skull from the sheer amount of mental power he was expending, but he needed to ensure that he wasn't mistaken for an Exlian.

Walking slowly out of the woods, he kept his hands open, facing the Rangers. When they saw him, they reacted swiftly, a group of them peeling off from the main team to approach him, their weapons drawn. At the same time, he could feel the mana around him starting to solidify, falling under the sway of one of the energy controllers. Resisting the urge to fight back, Mark came to a stop, staying still despite the threat the Rangers presented.

"Who are you?" one of the Rangers snapped, glaring at Mark through his helmet's faceplate.

Before Mark could respond, he heard a shout.

"Apex!"

Glancing over, he saw Noah running toward him, his gray-and-red armor badly battered. The Ranger who had barked the question at Mark glanced at Noah. "Lieutenant Javesi, do you know this man?"

"I do, Captain. His name's Apex. He's a freelance hunter, registered with the Hunters' Association. Level three, if I remember correctly."

Mark nodded along, confirming everything Noah said, though he kept his hands in the air to be safe. The captain looked at Mark again, his eyes sweeping over the unusual armor plating that covered Mark from his neck down. His eyes lingered on the bone blades, and it looked like he wanted to say something, but just then, one of the wounded Rangers hobbled forward, clutching the shoulder of one of the other Rangers for support. He had suffered a nasty gash across his leg, but before the mutant who had dealt the wound could capitalize on it, Mark had decapitated the monster, saving his life.

"Captain, he's the one in the woods that I was telling you about."

Visibly relaxing, the captain waved for his men to put down their weapons and gave Mark a stiff nod. "Appreciate the assistance, hunter. You said your name was Apex?"

"Yes, sir," Mark said, snapping a salute.

"And you just happened to be wandering around in this area and came to help us?"

Sensing the leading question in the captain's words, Mark peeked at Noah from the corner of his eye and then shook his head.

"I served as one of Lieutenant Noah's bodyguards, sir, before going freelance." He tapped his watch. "The lieutenant knew I was operating in the area and sent out a message."

"Hmm. And that Defense Force scout? The one who lured away the fliers?" the captain asked, turning to look at Noah. "Was that one of your bodyguards too?"

"No, sir," Noah said, his expression calm. "Just a friend."

"I see. While it's inappropriate for you to share our location, it may very well have just saved all of our lives. Apex, thank you again. Excuse me, I've got to go see to our unit's wounded."

Following the captain toward the Rangers' perimeter, Mark saw numerous wounded soldiers being tended to by the team's medics. One Ranger was in an especially dangerous state, his belly ripped open, causing his intestines to spill out of his suit. The medic working on him looked grim and glanced up when the captain approached.

"We're out of potions, sir. We used most of them in the last fight. I've given him a sedative and homeostatic shot, but he won't last more than a couple minutes, tops."

Cursing under his breath, the captain stared down at the wounded Ranger, his fists clenching so tightly his metal gloves groaned.

Reaching for his pouch, Mark pulled out a vial with ruby liquid inside. "I might be able to help, sir," he said, holding out the potion. "I've got a few top-of-the-line healing potions."

In fact, Mark had more than a few. His pouch was stuffed full of them, all deposited by a little tendril of shadow that had crept up the back of his leg.

Taking the potions from Mark with a grateful look, the medic rushed back to feed them to the most critically wounded. The result was drastic and immediate; as she poured the crimson liquid onto the gaping wound in the Ranger's belly, flesh knit back together. Mark knew his potions were more effective than the average, but he hadn't realized just how effective they were. The result was so surprising the medic actually gasped, looking first at the captain, then at Mark.

"What *are* these?!" she asked, still holding the vial with half of the potion in it.

"They're a specialized type of healing potion. They come from a new lab," he said, crouching down next to the wounded soldier.

Cradling the man's head, he took the potion from her fingers and helped the wounded Ranger drink it. No more than thirty seconds later, the man was able to sit up under his own strength, grimacing as the wound on his belly closed completely.

"How many more of these potions do you have?" the captain asked. "We have quite a few wounded."

"Enough," Mark said, taking out one potion and then handing the pouch to the medic.

The pouch held twenty-five small vials of healing potion, and revealing them raised more than a few eyebrows, but Mark didn't bother explaining. All of them had been created in his lab, infused with his blood to upgrade them, and then sent through his shadow. They cost him practically nothing, considering he had gathered most of the ingredients over the last week and still had plenty more. In his estimation, it was better to make sure that the Rangers were in good fighting shape, just in case the mutants decided to launch another attack. Standing up, he walked over to Noah, offering him the potion he had plucked from the pouch.

Noah shook his head. "I don't need it. Give it to somebody else. My recovery is pretty good on its own. A little bit of rest and I'll be fine."

As the Rangers bustled about getting their wounded back on their feet, Mark and Noah withdrew a few steps. Reaching out, Noah tapped the armor plates that covered Mark's chest. "What's this?"

"New suit," Mark said, lifting his hands in front of him and turning them over.

"Looks like carapace to me."

"It is, based on an Exlian called a cataphract. It's a new skill I picked up."

Giving Mark a long look, Noah nodded and didn't ask any further questions, and Mark didn't volunteer any information either. Both kept silent as the captain walked over.

"Lieutenant Javesi, we're about to head out. Are you able to provide scouting for us?"

"Of course, sir. Happy to do it. If it's okay with you, I'll bring Apex here with me. He's got a good nose for Exlian."

"Hopefully he's got a good nose for whatever those monsters were as well," the captain said, shaking his head, "because they certainly weren't Exlian, or at least not any sort of Exlian I've seen."

"They're not, sir."

Noah's confident response earned him a look from the captain, one that clearly conveyed annoyance and frustration. Still, whatever the captain wanted to say, he kept it to himself, and giving Mark a nod, he turned and went back to the main group.

"What was that all about?" Mark asked, watching as the captain walked away.

"My last name," Noah said, his lips twitching into a grimace. "It seems to follow me wherever I go."

"What does that have to do with getting attacked by mutants, though?"

Noah didn't meet Mark's searching look, instead gesturing for Mark to follow as he began to make his way out of the park and into the tangle of buildings, heading back toward New Emery. As Mark followed him, he directed his clone, who was still perched on top of the building, to toss the sniper rifle into his shadow. As soon as it had disappeared, the clone popped, fading away into nothingness, bringing a hint of relief to Mark's weary mind.

Noah clearly didn't want to talk about the situation, and Mark didn't press him. Instead, the two of them cleared the way for the Rangers, leading them past a few small Exlian swarms Mark spotted on the psychic network. Ten miles out from the city, they saw a dot appear on the city wall. It rapidly grew larger, and less than a minute later, Sky came to an abrupt stop right above them. Her suit was badly scuffed, though it didn't have any holes in it, and Mark could see the clear relief on her face through her suit's faceplate.

"Oh, thank goodness you are okay! The Defense Force is sending a recovery team. They should be here within the hour."

"I'm glad you are okay as well," Mark said, reaching out to rest a hand on Sky's shoulder once she'd descended to the ground. "How did you shake the enemies chasing you?"

"I just lured them back to New Emery. They were crazy and determined to catch me. As they got close to the wall, the automated defenses took them down. I've never seen Exlian like that, though. They looked . . . I mean, they looked almost human."

"Not Exlian," Noah said, tapping on his watch to inform the captain about the rescue team. "They were mutants, humans who had merged Exlian DNA with their own, similar to that friend of yours. What was his name?"

"Friend? Who are you talking about?" Sky asked, her face a picture of confusion.

"He's talking about Craig," Mark said quietly.

Sky stiffened, a pained expression flashing through her eyes.

"Oh, they're likely not friends of yours," Noah said quietly, clearly trying to comfort Sky. "It seems like those experiments have been going on for a while and maybe still are, but now is not the time to talk about it. Let's wait till we're back in the city, somewhere away from prying ears."

Getting a handle on herself, Sky nodded and took to the air again. "I'm gonna return and let the Defense Force know that I've made contact, and then I'll do sweeps so I can warn you if there are any enemies around."

While that wasn't strictly necessary, as Mark had access to the psychic network, he still nodded and let Sky go, figuring it was better for her to keep herself occupied than to hang around and dwell on the problem of the mutants.

Within a couple of hours, they had met up with the Defense Force battalion the city had sent out to rescue them, and returned to the city. Mark's strange armor suit drew a fair bit of attention, but after Sky, Noah, and the captain all vouched for him, the guards at the gate didn't give him too much trouble, only asking that he register his ability at the Hunters' Association.

Since both Sky and Noah had to debrief, Mark headed back to his apartment. The first thing he did after arriving was merge with his clone. This brought a tremendous rush of information to his mind and a slight strangeness to his body. Closing his eyes, he began to work through his kata, recentering himself and getting used to the changes.

Nothing was physically different, as his real body was much stronger, faster, and tougher than his clone's. Instead, the changes were the result of the clone's tremendous amount of practice and refinement, causing minute shifts in muscle memory that Mark now had to become acquainted with.

After running through his kata a few times, he finally felt whole again and headed for the shower, where he washed away a week's worth of grime from his body. In truth, he had barely noticed the dirt while out in the dead zone, but as soon as he returned to New Emery, his human mind had begun to protest about the smell more than anything else.

Changing into some comfortable clothes, Mark sat down on his couch and, as was his habit, began to ponder everything he had just experienced. As tense as some of the moments out in the dead zone had been, he found that he had genuinely enjoyed it: both the freedom of being outside the walls and the hunt. Mark could clearly feel that his Exlian side was growing stronger, and he had to be careful not to give in to it.

Of all his experiences in the dead zone over the last week, one, however, stood out the most. Not only had he directly communicated with an Exlian nest, but he seemed to have agreed to go hunt a humanoid Exlian. Mark had no idea if it was a distinct species or something else, but in lieu of a better term, he'd decided to refer to it as an apex hunter, since that was the primary image the nest had communicated to him. If he had understood the nest correctly, these apex hunters were Exlian without companions, solo hunters whose entire existence revolved around hunting nests. They cared nothing for other Exlian, though Mark had no doubt that, presented with an opportunity to kill one, an apex hunter would take it in a heartbeat.

He had even gotten that sense from the apex hunter he had seen out near Felwer Mine. Had Mime not been there, the apex hunter would undoubtedly have attacked him. For a brief moment, Mark wondered if the two apex hunters were the same, but then, remembering the image the nest had projected, he dismissed the thought. Though similar in body shape, this apex hunter had different horns upon its head and four extra-long arms, as opposed to the two arms on the body of the first apex hunter Mark had seen.

Sitting alone in his apartment, Mark stared at the blank wall in front of him. He could have opened the InfoWeb and watched something, but he found his thoughts were too tangled at the moment.

"You know, for a long time here, I thought I was going crazy," Mark said, speaking into the empty room, "but I genuinely think the Exlian can communicate. I mean, I have to believe it, right?"

Glancing down at Mime, who had appeared next to him and was nuzzling his hand with her nose, Mark cracked a grin. "I mean, you seem to communicate just fine, but I wonder, when I meet the apex hunter, is it going to be able to communicate with me too?"

Sitting back on her haunches, Mime stared up at Mark with her dark eyes. *Only those with a strong enough will can hear the voice.*

Startled by the unexpected response, Mark scratched his head. "You mean it has to do with my will? But hold on. If my willpower is now strong enough to allow me to understand the Exlian, then why can't anybody else?"

For the same reason the Exlian can't understand humans. You, however, are unique and have a claw in both camps.

Wincing at her words, Mark nodded. "Yeah, I guess that's true. Anyway, I'm curious to see what this apex hunter is like. Before that, though, I need to go to the association and register this new ability. Then I have a feeling that I need to have a conversation with Noah, and maybe not just Noah. It's time to get some real answers."

Early the next morning, Mark headed for the association and spent some time demonstrating his new ability. The assessment officers were astonished and quite curious where Mark had gotten it from. When he only provided evasive answers, they could only conceal their disappointment and record his information.

He still hadn't heard from Noah or Sky, so Mark caught a taxi to the laboratory and let himself in the side door. After walking down the long hall, he went down the stairs and stopped outside the locked laboratory door. A moment later, there was a hiss, and it slid aside to reveal him standing on the other side. The clone didn't say a word, but Mark wondered if he detected a hint of annoyance in his double's expression. Before he could look closely, the clone merged into him, and a rush of new knowledge flooded through his mind.

In order to fully digest it, Mark headed for the workstation and began to make potions. The process was smooth, almost second nature, and his body quickly adjusted to the full week of experiences the clone had just granted him. After working his way through all the potions he knew how to make, Mark spent an hour making more healing potions and drawing and storing more blood so the clone he would leave behind would have a steady supply. The Exlian corpses he had sent over had been stored in the freezer, and after double-checking to make sure everything was in order, Mark walked to the door, separated another clone, and sent it to work. He had just walked out of the building when his watch vibrated.

NOAH

Why don't we meet at my apartment? It'll be easier to talk there.

The address followed, and Mark responded, asking if he could bring anything or pick up food along the way.

NOAH

No need. I'll have the kitchen whip something up.

SKY

I'm not one to turn down food. I'll be right there.

Thanks to her handy flight power, Sky could go anywhere in the city in a couple of minutes, tops. For Mark, travel was much slower, and it was a full forty-five minutes before he was standing outside the door to Noah's apartment. Though in this case, *apartment* was entirely the wrong word, considering Noah had the top three floors of a skyscraper all to himself.

The door was answered by an attendant, who gestured for Mark to come in and informed him that Noah and Sky were in the living room. Walking up the grand staircase, Mark saw a breathtaking view of the city laid out in front of him, separated by floor-to-ceiling glass windows. He paused for a moment, his eyes sweeping the city and the wall that ringed it. His gaze was drawn beyond the wall, to the gray and shadowed dead zone, then out farther still, to the mountains far in the distance.

"It's rare that we get a day this clear," Noah said, walking over to stand beside Mark, his arms crossed over his chest. "Normally, you can't see the mountains."

"This isn't typically a view someone on a Ranger's salary can enjoy," Mark said, glancing at Noah.

If Mark's implicit question bothered him, Noah didn't show it. "You're right, it's not."

With half a shrug, Noah turned and gestured for Mark to follow him, leading the way into a beautifully decorated living room easily three times the size of Mark's entire apartment. "There are perks to being a Javesi. My family owns this building, among others, and when I informed my dad that I was going to move out, he gifted it to me."

Raising his eyebrows, Mark looked around. "Aren't you afraid that . . ."

His words trailed off. He looked back at Noah, who smirked and shook his head. "No, I've had this place completely stripped down and rebuilt from the ground up. We went all the way down to concrete and then encased that in soundproofed material. It's clean."

Just then, Sky strolled into the room, holding a plate piled high with food and a glass with a sparkling white wine. "Mark, glad you finally joined us."

"Not all of us are as quick as you, Sky."

She responded to Mark's half-hearted complaint with a grin. "It's my one redeeming feature. Get some food. As pretentious as this place is, the cooks are fantastic."

It wasn't long before the three of them had settled down on the couches, food and drink in hand. They spent the first few minutes chatting about nothing significant, but eventually the conversation turned to what had happened the day before.

"I'm not sure that there's much to tell," Noah said when Sky asked about the attack. "My Ranger battalion was out on a mission, and we were returning when, all of a sudden, our equipment got jammed. No outgoing communication or even internal communication. Thankfully, I still had my preprogrammed emergency message. I practically fried my watch, because I had to overcharge it to get the message out. But thankfully, the two of you got it and came."

"You called them mutants yesterday," Sky said. "And now that I think about it, they really did look like those monsters that Craig became. All twisted arms and strange body shapes. But why would mutants be attacking a Ranger battalion?"

"I'm not sure," Noah said, a frustrated expression flashing across his face. "I won't lie to you: Ever since the encounter with Craig, I've been having people look into the mutants, but I really haven't been able to come up with much of anything. The best that I've gotten is that they're the results of experiments. Experiments that should have been shut down years ago. They might have attacked me because they found out I was trying to uncover information about them."

He glanced over at Mark, who was quietly looking down at his plate. It was only after the silence stretched for almost a minute that Mark realized nobody was talking and looked up, only to see both Sky and Noah staring at him.

"You're awfully quiet," Sky said, reaching over to poke him lightly in the shoulder. "What are you thinking?"

"I don't have an answer to this situation, but I might have some pertinent information." Biting his lip, Mark glanced out of the floor-to-ceiling window, staring into the distance. "I ran into an organization down there, in the Tomb. They called themselves Salvation, and they seemed to be made up of these mutants. I didn't just meet the members of the organization, though. I also met their leader, a man named Dallas."

"Dallas? Are you sure that was his name?" Sky asked, her eyes going wide.

"Yes. I mean, that's how he introduced himself. Why?"

Taking a deep breath, Sky shook her head. "Dallas was the name of one of the doctors at the orphanage."

"Might be the same guy, or it might not. This Dallas was middle aged, looked maybe forty-five at the most."

"Huh, that can't be right," Sky said. "That's how old he looked when I was there."

"Can you draw a picture of him?" Noah asked, and when Mark nodded, Noah went to fetch a piece of paper and a pen.

Thanks to his high degree of muscle control and excellent memory, Mark wasn't half bad at drawing, and he had soon sketched out a portrait of the Prophet. Even before he was finished, he could tell that Sky was unsettled.

"Yes, that's him. That's exactly what he looked like, but that was ten years ago. It's like he hasn't aged a day."

"It might have something to do with the fact that he's mixed Exlian genes into his body," Mark said, putting the pen down with a sigh. "That's what the mutants are doing. They're trying to evolve themselves without skill gems. Instead, they forcefully merge Exlian DNA with their own. The result is these monstrosities that you see. So far, it doesn't seem to have produced anyone very strong."

Eyes narrowing, Noah shook his head at Mark's statement. "You can't use yourself as a standard to measure against, Mark. You cut through them like a hot knife through butter. I had a much harder time against them. I actually wanted to ask you about that. How come your attacks were so effective?"

Thinking for a moment, Mark extended his hand and transformed his fingers into bone blade.

"It has to do with this stuff," he said. He tapped his forefinger against his thumb, producing a clicking sound. "It's harder than a mana blade. Cuts better too. But I'm not surprised that you had difficulty. Most of them seemed to be C ranked, with tougher skin than normal, though you certainly held your own."

"The advantage of having mana blast, as well as superior combat abilities," Noah said quietly. "But the big concern is that these mutants were much stronger than Craig. I mean, we fought him when we were what, D ranked? Any one of these mutants would have wiped the floor with him and us. In fact, any one of them could have taken all three of us on without breaking a sweat. Either he was a defective product, or they're getting better."

"My guess is the latter," Mark replied, standing up and beginning to pace back and forth next to the couch. "Salvation's whole goal is to transform humanity into something of a cross between a human and an Exlian. They think that humans are weak, that as a species we've reached a dead end. The leader, Dallas, calls himself a prophet, says he's had visions of the future, and in that future, the Exlian are going to overrun the city. According to him, the only way humanity survives, that any of us survive, is if we embrace this change."

"Did he say how the change is going to happen?" Noah asked.

The question caught Mark off guard, and for a moment, he hesitated, not wanting to admit that he played a central role in the Prophet's insane plan. Taking a deep breath, Mark shook his head. "Not precisely, no. He said something about a mother rising from the depths and transforming everybody."

This time, it was Noah's turn to look like he had swallowed a fish bone.

"Now that's the face of somebody who knows something," Sky said, staring at Noah, her eyes large with expectation.

"Just some things I've heard," Noah said. "I told you I'd been digging into these mutants, right? Well, while I haven't been able to unearth anything about Salvation, or whatever it's called, I have picked up plenty of other rumors, and the craziest one is about an Exlian called the Mother."

"You mean like a matron?" Sky asked.

"No, not a matron. Matrons are more like Exlian commanders.

What makes them dangerous is their absolute control over the Exlian around them. The Mother is something more . . . According to the rumor, the Mother is an incredibly powerful Exlian, something between a matron and a nest, who is trapped below the city, and the waves that we face are the result of Exlian swarming our walls in an attempt to break her free. I know it's crazy, but it's possible that this Salvation group believes it."

"Not just possible, almost certain," Mark said, rubbing his forehead. "But what's worse is that that doesn't actually sound that crazy at all."

"What do you mean?" Noah asked.

Sitting back down on the couch, Mark looked at Noah, then at Sky. "I'm not sure how much you two know about nests, but nests are not mindless. They're intelligent, and they know how to defend themselves. Their primary means of defense is gathering Exlian around them. Now, they typically only gather Exlian that they've created, which wouldn't necessarily fit this situation. But there's another scenario where Exlian gather around a nest. That's when one nest is launching an attack against another. If there is a nest trapped somewhere in this city, then it's possible that other nests outside the city are trying to launch attacks in an attempt to consume it so that they can grow stronger. If this Mother, and I'm just calling it that for a lack of a better name, but if this Mother nest is particularly powerful but doesn't have any Exlian defending it, then the other nests might think it's easy prey, which would explain why they keep sending their forces out to attack."

"But instead of finding the nest, they find New Emery," Noah said, leaning forward and resting his forearms on his knees, "and they are not just finding New Emery, but they're also being beaten back by our defenders. That would explain why each wave gets stronger than the last. They're gathering power to try to defeat us, almost as if they think we are the Exlian defending this nest."

"When you guys talk about it this way, it sounds like it's true," Sky said quietly, looking between Mark and Noah. "It's not true, is it?"

"Well, I mean, at this point, we only have rumors to go on," Noah said with a shrug.

"And the mutterings of a crazy, self-proclaimed prophet," Mark added. "So I wouldn't put too much stock in it."

"Yeah, but how crazy would it be if it was true," Sky said, sitting back, her eyes drifting to the sky outside the window. "I mean, imagine if there was a nest here in New Emery. If there was, it would have to be controlled. Otherwise, we would have been attacked from inside the walls."

As soon as the words escaped her mouth, she blanched and fell quiet. Mark didn't need to hear her say a word to know exactly what she was thinking, because he was thinking it as well. Despite the fact that the dead zone outside the city was meticulously maintained and that Exlian rarely made it anywhere close to the city wall, a surprising number of Exlian attacks occurred inside the city. In fact, he had nearly been the victim of one himself right before he had awakened his powers.

Typically, these attacks were explained away, attributed to terrorists like Green Line. But Mark knew the truth. An uncomfortable number of Exlian seemed to lurk inside the city's walls. If there was a nest somewhere in the city, then no doubt it was producing Exlian. And given how cunning nests could be, Mark sincerely doubted that it was entirely contained. Of course, Exlian attacks weren't direct evidence of a nest's existence, but they certainly added weight to the argument.

When the Prophet had spoken of his vision in which the Savior called forth the Mother, Mark had dismissed it as lunacy. Now, he was starting to wonder if maybe there was a bit of truth to it.

Though he didn't completely believe the Prophet had the ability to see the future, he did appear to know when he and Mark were going to meet. Unable to make heads or tails of all this, Mark rubbed his forehead again, wishing that it would all just go away. Unfortunately, it didn't seem that it would anytime soon, so Mark could only let it go.

"You know, we still haven't answered the question," Sky said suddenly.

"What question?" Mark asked.

Picking up her glass, she took a sip and pointed at Noah. "Why the mutants attacked Noah."

Realizing he had gotten sidetracked, Mark coughed lightly. "According to the Prophet, they were there to further their ambition of perfectly mixing human and Exlian DNA."

"Wait, do you mean the Prophet was there?" Sky asked.

"For a little bit. He ran away like a coward before I could attack him," Mark said with a disgruntled snort. "I know that doesn't give us specifics, just that something about the Ranger team, maybe something they were carrying, was targeted by Salvation. Because Salvation thought it could bring them a step closer to the perfect human-Exlian hybrid."

Unfortunately, that didn't clarify anything, and after talking about it for a few more minutes, Mark and the others had to conclude that it was a mystery they simply weren't going to solve, at least not now.

"What are you going to do next?" Mark asked Noah after their drinks had been refilled.

"We lost nearly thirty people," Noah said, shaking his head, "so we'll be doing some reorganizing. We're an investigation team typically stationed inside the city, and all of us have some pretty unique skill sets, so it'll take a little bit of time to get the unit back up to full strength. Until then, we'll be resuming our investigative responsibilities. I expect it'll take a couple months, though. What about you? Are you going to keep hunting?"

"I am." Mark glanced down at his hands, which flickered between bone blade and flesh. "I'm finding that it suits me really well."

"Yeah, but it's dangerous. You don't need to do that. You can stay in the city. If it's a matter of money . . ."

Holding up his hand to stop Noah's words, Mark shook his head. "It's not about money, believe me. My alchemy is good enough that I could earn as much money as I need. I genuinely enjoy hunting in the dead zone, gathering materials, things like that. As long as I stay fairly close to the city, I'll be fine. You saw me at work. Most Exlian don't even stand a chance."

Noah's lips twitched as if he wanted to refute Mark's statement, but they both knew full well that he couldn't. Mark had torn through the mutants like they were straw dolls, his bone blades cutting through them in an instant. Most Exlian, though slightly stronger, would fare similarly. This meant that Mark was largely safe, so long as he stayed within the fourth band.

"Fine, but don't hesitate to let me know if something goes wrong. Now that I'm stationed in the city, I should be able to deploy a rapid-response team to get you out of any jams you get into," Noah said.

"I appreciate that, Noah. I really do." Mark smiled.

Rolling his eyes, Noah tapped on the table. "Speaking of your alchemy ability, however, I've had multiple requests, mostly from the unit's medics, but one from the captain as well, for more of those healing potions that you handed over. The potency of these things is insane, close to four hundred percent of the average potion. They're wondering where you got them."

"I've got an alchemist friend who makes them," Mark said, his expression carefully blank.

That caused Sky to laugh. “A friend, huh? That’s why you rented a whole laboratory for yourself.”

“Hey, I told you that in confidence,” Mark said in mock outrage.

Rolling her eyes, Sky turned to Noah, jerking a thumb back at Mark. “You’ve gotta watch this guy. He’s slippery.”

“He can be an eel for all I care, so long as he supplies our unit with more of these ultrapotions. That’s what the medics have taken to calling them, by the way.”

“Ultrapotion, huh?” Mark said, scratching his chin. “I like it. Well, you can tell them that there are more for sale. However, there’s a limited quantity, and the price is going to be high. In fact, because of the failure rate on these potions, not only will the price be at least three times—”

“Five,” Sky cut in. “Five times as high.”

“Fine, five times. But I’ll also need two batches of materials for a regular potion. I can supply the other special ingredients necessary to make them.”

Thinking for a moment, Noah shook his head. “The price needs to be at least ten times as high.”

Sky let out a whistle, but Mark furrowed his brow and shook his head. “Ten times? That’s a rip-off.”

“It’s not. Mark, I don’t think you understand just how strong these potions are. Abbott, the Ranger whose belly was cut open, was moments away from dying of blood loss. A normal healing potion, even if it did manage to patch up a wound, wouldn’t be able to replace all of the blood that was lost that quickly. The potion you gave him didn’t just heal his wounds; it gave him a lingering regeneration effect. According to our tests, the effect fades within a couple of hours after taking it, and it’s not nearly as strong as the initial rush of healing, but it still allows someone to heal two to three times faster than normal. You know that empowered heal more quickly than normal people, and this, well, this just supercharges it.

They shouldn't be called healing potions at all. Really, they should be called regeneration potions, and we should sell them for at least ten to fifteen times what a normal healing potion would cost."

By the time he was finished speaking, Noah had risen to his feet and was practically shaking his finger in Mark's face, causing Mark to laugh and hold up his hands in surrender. "Okay, fine. You've convinced me. We'll do what you say."

"Good," Noah said, looking slightly embarrassed as he sat back down. "And as your agent, I have exclusive rights to sell them."

"Ha, there it is." Sky chuckled. "I knew there was an angle."

"I just think we need to handle these potions sensibly," Noah protested.

Before Sky could reply, Mark agreed. "It's true. I knew they were more effective than normal healing potions, but I didn't realize just how much more effective they were. The last thing I need is for some powerful company to decide they need to get their hands on the potion at all costs and come after me. Letting Noah handle them will provide a layer of protection for me, and I'm happy to not only give you exclusive rights, Noah, but give you some of the profit as well."

"Profit is the last thing I care about," Noah replied, some of the tension draining out of his shoulders as he sat back. "There are a lot of Ranger teams that would benefit from having potions like these. The question is, How many can you make?"

"The ingredients aren't particularly rare but do require some specific circumstances," Mark said, scratching his cheek. "My guess is that I could probably turn out a couple hundred potions a week, as long as I have all of the materials I need. Of course, I don't really want to let potion making interfere with my hunting, so much more than that is going to be difficult."

"That's already enough, maybe even too many. Apart from the potions you're going to be using yourself, my suggestion is that we stick to selling a max of fifty or so in a week. Of course, stockpiling the extras is always a good idea. That way, when the next wave arrives, you'll be able to distribute them quickly. Like I said, let me handle distribution, and I'll ensure that there are no issues."

"Speaking of the next wave," Sky said, "weren't we expecting to see a wave in a couple of months—a couple of months ago? Yet there's no sign of it."

Mark shared a glance with Noah and then shrugged. "People have been saying that for years. Actually, just before the training camps started, Dr. Graham was all over the InfoWeb, talking about how the next wave was going to be the biggest yet. Even then, they said it was only a couple of months away, but the wave just never materialized."

"What do you think happened?" Sky asked.

Her question was met with more shrugs, and soon their conversation shifted to other topics. Overall, Mark had a wonderful afternoon with his friends, and he felt quite refreshed as he made his way back to his apartment that evening. Whether it was due to his experience in the Tomb or the changes his Exlian powers had wrought in him, Mark sometimes forgot how important it was to interact with other people. He found himself becoming more and more of a recluse, willing to spend long periods of time without talking to or even seeing another person. Seeing his friends and having the chance to just spend time with them and talk brought tremendous relief to his soul.

That got him thinking about some of his other relationships, and after getting back to his apartment, he headed into his bedroom to hunt through his bags. Despite having lived at this new apartment for a few weeks, Mark still hadn't unpacked all his things. Even now, he felt a strange reluctance to go through his bags, as if opening them up would force him to face the drastic changes he had undergone over the last two years.

Eventually, however, he knew he had to face the past, and

now seemed as good a time as any. Dumping out one of his bags onto his bed, he sorted through the odds and ends until he found a picture set in a simple frame. It was one of the few things he had brought from his house, and after picking it up, he spent a long moment staring at the happy-looking family it displayed.

Any vestige of the peace that the image represented had been stripped from his life, and Mark was more disappointed than sad when he looked at it. The majority of his disappointment revolved around the fact that staring at those faces that had once filled him with all sorts of feelings barely stirred his heart at all. It was a clear sign that in embracing his Exlian side, he had lost some core part of his humanity.

Letting out a long sigh, Mark flipped the picture over and undid the back, peeling away the frame to reveal a stack of images. The one on the bottom had a number scrawled on the back, and Mark quickly punched it into his watch. He had no idea whether the call would connect, and after a few rings he was about to hang up, but then there was a click, and it went through.

"Hello? Who is this? How did you get this number?"

Mark recognized the voice immediately. It was Emily, his brother's friend.

"I need to speak to Joe. Have him contact me." Mark hesitated and then added quietly, "This is Mark."

"Wait, what?"

Before Emily could say anything that might get flagged, Mark ended the call. His hope was that Emily would relay the strange call to Joe and that Joe would come track him down. This was the simplest way, in Mark's mind, for him to get in touch with his brother. Of course, he was sure that if he asked Maestro, tracking down the Green Line terrorists would be easy, but he was hesitant to connect them.

Doing his best to put Joe out of his mind, Mark spent the rest of the evening as he normally did, practicing his meditation and martial arts, before heading to bed to immerse himself in fierce combat against an endless swarm of Exlian. He woke refreshed, and after getting a bite to eat, he went for a run. It was early enough that the sun wasn't yet up, and the cool morning air energized him. After running for two hours, Mark came back to his apartment and took a shower, feeling quite refreshed in both body and spirit.

He had had plenty of time to think through the tangle of confusing thoughts that had plagued him the night before, and he felt as if he had regained his focus. The things he couldn't control were put aside. The things he could, he had made plans for. Of utmost importance was continuing to stay under the radar. Mark didn't want to do anything that might negatively impact his chances of survival. Of course, he always had the option of leaving the city, heading out into the wilderness, and starting a new life. But this wasn't an option he took lightly, as doing so would mean forever separating himself from his human side.

Opening his curtains, Mark stood in his living room and looked out the window toward the wall that surrounded the city. He had often wondered if any other humans lived beyond the wall, sequestered in other parts of the world, trapped in their own cages, just like the citizens of New Emery. Mark had been taught that there were no other humans, that nobody else had survived the onslaught of the Exlian, that New Emery was it. But more and more, he was learning to distrust what the rulers of the city said.

Of course, Mark's life was here, and rushing out to explore the wilderness didn't seem wise. He had no doubt that there would come a day when he could move unhindered through the land, and when that day came, maybe he would take a trip beyond the walls to explore the wider world. Until then, he had other things to do: hunting an apex hunter and improving his stats, to say nothing of figuring out what sort of madness Salvation was fomenting.

After redrawing the curtains, Mark left a clone behind and headed down to the street to catch a taxi. He directed the driver to the Hunters' Association and spent the next twenty minutes watching the city slip by. When he arrived, he greeted the guards at the front door and took the elevator up to the third floor. His first stop was the kiosk, where he began to look for hunting missions, paying particular attention to the types of Exlian the missions were targeting.

He had discovered in his hunts a couple of challenges. The first was that finding groups of B-ranked Exlian was hard. Most of them operated alone, at least within the fourth band. Though they often had weaker subordinates hanging around, it was rare to find more than one B-ranked Exlian in the same place. Of course, Mark was confident that if he ventured farther from the city, he would start to see them gathered in greater numbers. The problem was that in order for multiple Exlian of that rank to gather together, they typically needed a stronger force to keep them from fighting, which meant that if he found a group of them, the likelihood of encountering an A-ranked Exlian was even higher.

Though Mark had grown powerful over the last year, he still

didn't fancy his chances against a terror-ranked Exlian. The earth rats had proved to be an exception rather than the rule, as their small bodies didn't allow them to grow beyond the B rank, at least as far as Mark was aware. This was particular to the earth rats, and they more than made up for it in sheer volume. Even now, the memory of millions of rats swarming around him caused a shiver to run down Mark's spine.

Looking through the missions, he didn't find anything that particularly stood out, so instead he headed for the information desk. After purchasing as much information as he could about the fourth band, including maps, resource locations, and potential gathering spots for Exlian, Mark went to the cafeteria to get a bite to eat.

He had just sat down when he felt a faint prickling sensation, as if someone was watching him. He didn't pay whoever it was any mind, instead just steadily eating his food. Once he had finished, he threw away his trash and left the Hunters' Association, walking down the street instead of getting a cab. He didn't have a particular destination in mind but just wandered through the city.

Occasionally, the feeling of being watched would disappear, but after he'd walked another block, it would emerge once more, confirming that someone was indeed following him. Mark had been keeping a close eye on the psychic network and felt as if he had managed to locate the individual tracking him, despite the fact that he hadn't turned to look once.

Speeding up slightly, Mark stepped around a corner and shrouded himself in mental energy, dampening his presence as much as possible. Plenty of powers allowed someone to track a target from a distance, but the fact that Mark could feel the other's gaze meant that whoever was tracking him was keeping him in sight. That meant they likely weren't using any sort of power.

Sure enough, no more than a minute later, a young man hurried around the corner, his eyes darting this way and that as he scanned the street ahead for Mark. Whether it was due to Mark's mental shrouding or the fact that he was standing absolutely still, the young man completely missed him, walking right past. Furrowing his brow, Mark reached out and grabbed the young man's shoulder, scaring him quite badly in the process.

"Ah! What? How?!"

"Calm down."

Mark's words were heavy and cut through the young man's panic, causing him to lapse into a frightened silence. Maintaining his grip on the man's shoulder, Mark pulled him over to the side so they weren't in the middle of the sidewalk.

"You seem particularly interested in me," Mark said, his gaze boring into the young man's face. "Mind telling me why?"

Doing his best to calm down, the young man swallowed and nodded, his head jerking up and down nervously. "I . . . I was asked to follow you by one of your friends."

"Seems unusual for a friend to want me followed. Who might this friend be?"

Mark's question only made the young man even more nervous. Before Mark could press him, however, he felt a faint ripple of mana under their feet. His instincts screamed at him to jump away, but Mark recognized the ripple, and rather than escape, he simply activated his armor as the ground underneath them transformed into a liquid, and they plunged down into the street.

It was a strange experience to fall through six feet of concrete and earth, and it wasn't exactly the same as sinking through water. The fluctuations of mana around Mark made it feel as if the ground had simply been shifted into a different dimension, one faintly separated from Mark and the young man by a strange undulating mist. A moment later, they slipped out of the phased earth and landed in an open tunnel. Feeling danger locking onto him, Mark held up his hands and quickly opened his mask to reveal his face.

"Hello, Perry," he said, meeting the gaze of Joe's teammate, a powerful earth controller, who was about to try to crush him.

"Mark? Wow, you really are alive. But what's with that suit? You look more like an Exlian than a human."

"Still human," Mark said with half a smile. "At least last time I checked." With a wave of his hand, he dismissed his carapace, which sank back into his body. "Are you here to pick me up?"

"Yeah, I am. By now, somebody's probably noticed the disturbance. Let's go."

Turning, Perry began walking straight toward the wall, which parted before him like a wave. As Mark and the nervous young man followed, he realized that the earth was closing up behind them. Somehow, Perry was forming a bubble in the earth and moving it forward by shifting dirt from in front of them to behind them.

Though it didn't seem like they were moving very fast, it was only a few minutes later when Perry stretched out his hand and touched a cement wall. The wall phased out, and he gestured for Mark to go ahead of him. After the three of them had stepped through the wall into the concrete passage beyond, the wall solidified once more, and glancing down at his watch, Mark realized that they had traveled more than halfway across the city.

"Joe's waiting for you down below," Perry said, giving Mark a long look. "Cut him some slack, though. He's been under a lot of pressure."

"Oh, has he?" Mark replied, his tone bland.

In truth, he wasn't quite sure how he was going to face his brother. His feelings were complicated, while at the same time, he found himself relatively detached. Still, he left Perry and the other young man and walked down the hall, taking a set of stairs deeper into the earth. When he came to a set of double doors, he paused, and then, after calming his spirit, he pushed them open, stepping out onto a balcony that ran all the way around a massive man-made cavern. Lights set in the ceiling, two stories up, provided ample illumination, revealing hundreds of buildings with a labyrinth of passages between them.

Stairs in front of him led down to the buildings, and at the foot of them, Mark saw Joe waiting. Although their last meeting had gone poorly and they had left each other on bad terms, Mark found that he was excited to see his brother. As he walked down the stairs, Joe examined him carefully, just as he examined Joe in turn.

His brother looked older, his face thinner, more haggard. His hair had started to turn white, frosting at its tips. Despite the fact that he wasn't that much older than Mark, there was a frailness to his brother that Mark had never seen before, and it made his heart lurch.

"Hello, Mark," Joe said, his voice quiet.

Mark didn't reply until he had reached the foot of the stairs. Then he opened his arms, stepped forward, and hugged Joe. He was unsure what to make of the tumultuous emotions inside him, so he elected to just not bother with them at all. "Hello, Joe. It doesn't look like life underground suits you."

With a rather strained smile, Joe nodded. "Less life underground and more mitigating circumstances," he said, holding Mark at arm's length. "You, on the other hand, look like you're thriving."

Mark flashed a mirthless smile. "I guess that's one way to put it."

"Why don't we go inside?"

It was only then that Mark noticed Emily standing nearby, waiting for the brothers to finish their reunion. Though Mark didn't really have any reason to dislike her, he found himself irrationally irritated by her presence. But he carefully controlled his expression and looked at Joe, waiting for him to make a decision.

"We have a lot to talk about," Joe said, gripping Mark's shoulder. "From the little bits that I've gathered, it sounds like you've had quite the adventure. I'd love to hear about it. Come on, let's sit down."

Joe led the way into a nearby building, which he introduced as his home. It was small but neat, and from the familiarity with which Emily started hot water for tea, it was clear that this was her space as well. Joe directed Mark to the couch and took a seat in a chair he pulled in from the kitchen. The house wasn't that different from Mark and Joe's old one in its layout, and from the living room, Mark simply had to turn his head to see the kitchen where Emily was working.

Seeing Mark looking at Emily, Joe coughed. "I know you've met Emily, but it wasn't under the best of circumstances. I had hoped to introduce you two more formally at some point, but the timing never seemed to work out."

Emily carried cups of tea over, and Mark stood up to take his. He had had time to settle the flash of irritation, and he greeted her with as much equanimity as he could muster. After giving Joe a cup, Emily quietly withdrew, leaving the brothers to talk alone.

Joe watched her leave, a wistful look in his eyes. "We met during high school and kept in touch over the years. Emily is a whiz when it comes to science. She was a researcher while I was in the Rangers."

"Is she how you got involved with Green Line?"

Joe's lips twitched at Mark's blunt question. "We sort of fell into it together," he said. "What started us down this path was actually looking for a cure, a cure for burnout, which had affected one of our friends. Well, one thing led to another, and . . ." Joe let out a long sigh. "Here we are, I guess. But what about you? It seems as if you've experienced a lot since the last time we talked."

"That might be an understatement," Mark said, taking a sip of his tea. "When did we last talk? Almost a year ago, right? Right before I deployed?"

"A bit over a year now," Joe replied, glancing at his watch.

"Wow, time sure is flying. But what I'm more surprised about is that you aren't shocked I'm alive. I thought for sure that would catch you off guard."

Smiling slightly, Joe placed his cup down on the table and leaned back in his seat. "Jason mentioned something to me. I hunted him down shortly after you went to Gray Rock. He didn't have exact details, but he was able to tell me enough that I could guess what was going on. You're not the first person the military has done this to, and you certainly won't be the last. I must admit I am surprised to see you walking around on the surface, as I had assumed that the next time I saw you would be when we broke you out."

"You were planning on breaking me out?"

Flashing a wry smile, Joe faced Mark's skeptical look squarely. "Once we had the ability, yes. Unfortunately, we're pretty far from that point."

"Further than you know," Mark said gravely. "They sent me to the Tomb, which is a secondary prison underneath Gray Rock. It's full of incredibly powerful empowered, including a couple of people that you know. In fact, I've been tasked with delivering a message to you by one of the people I met in the Tomb, a woman who goes by the name of Winter Wolf. She controls ice."

From the way Joe's expression twitched, Mark knew that he had recognized Winter Wolf's name.

"She asked me to tell you that Ambrosia exists."

Joe had just picked up his cup, but when he heard Mark's words, he clenched it so tightly his tea spilled out onto the table. Caring nothing for the hot liquid that had just splashed all over his fingers, Joe stared at Mark with burning intensity. "She said what?"

"She told me to tell you that Ambrosia exists. I assume it has something to do with burnout? When I met her, Winter Wolf was an S-ranked empowered, wielding absolute mastery over ice, to an uncanny degree. I saw her completely freeze and then destroy a five-story building with no apparent effort. Obviously, I don't know how powerful the top ten empowered in the city are, but my guess is that she would give any one of them a run for their money."

His face white, Joe put his cup down in the puddle of tea on the table, his eyes downcast as he gathered himself. Mark waited in silence until his brother looked up, his calm restored.

"Ambrosia is the name of a secret project, the secret project that Emily and I were working on, are still working on. You're right, it has to do with burnout. Over the years, many of our friends have burned themselves out trying to protect the city and we were looking for a solution. Let me call Emily. She'll do a better job of explaining it than I would." About to stand up, Joe paused and looked at his brother. "Is that okay?"

"Yeah, sure. Why wouldn't it be okay?" Mark said quickly, trying to erase the subtle annoyance he felt.

He had no idea why even Emily's name irritated him, but he felt that it was immature, so he pushed the feelings aside as Joe went to get her. By the time Joe and Emily entered the room, Mark was in full control of himself and eager to hear about this project they had been working on. Emily seemed surprisingly nervous, but she gained confidence as she began to explain the Ambrosia Project.

"After school, rather than enter the Defense Force, I took the researcher route, and I interned at a laboratory studying disease. Our work was only tangentially related to empowered because, as you know, empowered are largely immune to diseases. The question was, Is it possible to create that same effect in regular people? As the research continued, however, I began to notice a troubling pattern: DNA sequences in our empowered samples that matched Exlian DNA I had seen in textbooks in high school. At first, I thought it was just a mistake, but the more I dug into it, the more I realized that both Exlian and empowered shared specific characteristics. When I brought this up, I was told that I was crazy, and then they moved me to other projects, ones that didn't have anything to do with genetics."

Pausing, Emily glanced at Joe, who nodded for her to continue.

"Well, I continued studying on my own, curious as to the connection. About that time, a good friend of ours burned out. She had been deployed alongside the Cerberus unit and, during a particularly bad fight, was forced to overcharge her ability. When she came back, I helped her with her medication, and driven by curiosity, I did an analysis on it, only to find that it carried some of those same Exlian DNA sequences. The medicine that she was taking to keep her body from breaking down was made from Exlian DNA, but it was also intentionally designed to be shed from her body. This is, of course, typical with a lot of medicines. They can do more harm than good if the genetic material contained in the medicine stays in your body long term. So it made absolute sense that this would be the case."

Emily paused again to gather her thoughts, then continued slowly.

"Ultimately, I began to research whether it would be possible to use Exlian DNA to repair the damage that had been done by overcharging, instead of simply mitigating the effect of that damage. We called it the Ambrosia Project, trying to perfect a serum that would actually cure burnout rather than just prolong the life of someone who'd overcharged their ability. We've had some success, but we haven't achieved our goal yet."

"From the sound of it," Joe said, leaning forward and fixing his eyes on Mark, "somebody has succeeded, and they've given the serum to Winter Wolf, not only repairing her ability but actually improving it."

Mark didn't jump to respond. Maestro was a sensitive topic, and it wouldn't do to go blabbing about him to just anyone. After all, the mad genius was ranked at the very top of the military's list of dangerous villains. According to public record, he had been executed. So letting others know that he was not only alive but still practicing his human experimentation down in the Tomb seemed unwise.

After thinking for a moment, Mark nodded. "I'm not sure of the exact details, but she certainly had full control of her powers. She just said that you were the one who had captured her."

"She didn't mention that she burned out during that fight, did she?" Joe said, frowning. "Her power had gone wild, and she had killed close to two dozen people."

"Mostly people who deserved it," Emily cut in.

"Well, yes, but just because they deserved it doesn't mean that she could get away without punishment. Besides, there were innocents involved, and they were frozen along with everybody else. Her power was out of control, so they called me to counter it."

"Well, she doesn't seem to hold any grudges," Mark said, "and in fact has probably benefited from it, at least when it comes to her power."

Sharing glances, Joe and Emily didn't say anything. Mark could tell that they were curious and wanted to ask more questions, but for whatever reason, they remained silent. To keep things from getting awkward, he tried to shift the subject.

"Emily, Joe said that you are still working on your version

of Ambrosia. Do you mind if I ask you a couple questions about it? I'm an alchemist and have a good bit of interest in any sort of potion or serum."

"Sure, what do you want to know?"

"Is it correct to assume that you are approaching this from a repair angle? I mean, you're identifying the damage caused by overcharging, then working to repair that damage to restore the target's powers?"

Emily looked at Joe, who nodded, and then tapped on her watch, projecting a virtual window that hovered above the coffee table. "At a basic level, yes. That's the plan. Here are two strands of DNA, one from an empowered before burnout, and the other from an empowered who has burned out. Actually, these are both from your brother, Joe. The strands that are similar to Exlian DNA are tagged in blue. The damage is tagged in red."

Studying the image, Mark pointed at a section of the helix that had been broken. "Was there a mana overload here? It seems like the damage started from the center of the strand and spread outward, almost like a fire."

"Correct. It's exactly like a fire. One that is continuing to burn. Left alone, the mana will chew through the rest of the strand, attacking the sections that are purely human. The result is weakness and eventually death. The medicine provided to those who burn out is designed to make the target's DNA mana resistant, preventing the damage from spreading. Obviously, that isn't a permanent or even long-term solution. We're mainly focusing on finding better mana insulators, to try to make the remaining strands of DNA entirely mana immune."

Reaching out, Mark manipulated the screen, turning the helix to look at it from a different angle. Emily's explanation made sense, but he couldn't help but think about how different Maestro's approach was. Though he had never talked about it with the scientist, he knew that Maestro wasn't at all concerned with repairing damage that might have been done to someone's body. His entire focus was on improving the human body's performance by combining human and Exlian DNA. Rather than worry about the potential danger, Maestro used serums to leverage the incredible mutability and rapid mutation cycle of Exlian genes. If Mark had to guess, Maestro's method of solving burnout was to simply evolve the target past it, trusting that the newly introduced Exlian genes would naturally repair the damage.

Of course, this was an incredibly dangerous approach and was liable to kill or permanently disfigure the target. Though so far Mark had only been helped by Maestro's serums, he had a feeling that had more to do with his body's natural adaptability than with how safe the serums were. The mutants running around all over the city were clear examples of how the process could go wrong.

As Mark looked at the virtual screen, both Emily and Joe watched him quietly. Emily started to say something at one point, but Joe put his hand on her knee and shook his head, causing her to lapse back into silence. A full five minutes passed before Mark straightened up and looked over the screen at Joe.

"I have two potential solutions for you. The only requirement is that you don't ask me about where or how I got the information."

A small smile tugged at the corners of Joe's lips, as if he had just won a bet. "Sure. What are the solutions?"

"The first one is the easiest. I can introduce you to the person who helped Winter Wolf. But I can't guarantee the safety of this path. In fact, I would bet that it's only got a forty percent chance of working. Maybe less. Regardless, you'll come out of it different. If it succeeds, your power will not only come back but get stronger. If it doesn't, you'll turn into a monster."

Mark held his brother's stare for a long moment as he let Joe process his words.

"Is that what happened to you? You don't look like a monster to me."

"My situation is different, Joe. I am not burned out. And . . . well, let's just say my situation is different. If you take this first path, you might not be able to come back to the surface. Ever. I have no idea what the end result will be."

Emily held up her hand, her face white and her mouth set in a grim line. "What is the other solution? This one won't work for us."

Raising his eyebrows slightly, Mark nodded and reached for a regeneration potion. "I mentioned that I'm an alchemist, right? Well, I have a recipe for a potion that could help as well. One of the main features of empowerment is that the surge of mana optimizes the human body, healing it in the process. If you can become empowered again, that might fix your problem."

Her expression relaxing, Emily looked at Joe and nodded. "That sounds like a much better solution. Is that the potion?"

"No, this is a potion that will boost your body's natural regeneration. I doubt it will do anything about the destroyed genes, but it will help preserve the rest of your DNA, to keep it from deteriorating. However, the effect only lasts for a few hours at most."

Placing the vial on the table, Mark pushed it over to Emily. "I can get more of these for you, and you can decide how to use them in conjunction with the medicine you normally use. As for the Second Awakening potion, I can give you a list of materials. Unfortunately, I have no idea where we'll find them. If we can get the materials, I can make the potion, but until we have them, we're stuck."

"That's better than taking the other route," Emily said. "If you provide the ingredient list, we'll do everything we can to find them."

Though he didn't have the recipe book that Master Abrams had given him, Mark remembered all the recipes by heart, and it only took him a few minutes to write down the five ingredients that the potion required. Two were crystals, another was a plant, and the final two were a type of venom and the heart blood of an Exlian Mark had only the name of. In truth, he didn't have much confidence that Joe and Emily would be able to gather the material, and from the frown that appeared on Joe's face, he didn't either.

After handing over the list, Mark stood up, intending to take his leave, but before he could go, Joe stopped him. "Mark, I have a favor to ask."

Mark took a small step back and shook his head. "Sorry, Joe. I don't want to get involved."

"You don't know what I am going to ask."

"Do I need to? You're going to ask me to get involved with Green Line in some way. But I'm not interested. You made your choice when you decided to go with a terrorist organization, but that was your choice. I am staying clear of all of this."

Stepping forward, Joe half blocked Mark's path to the door, forcing him to stop. "This isn't about being a terrorist, Mark. There are people who are in trouble with the corrupt government. People who are suffering. This is about helping them. This is about fighting back against the people who put you in jail. Who tried to kill you."

Mark's eyes narrowed slightly as he stared at his brother, stifling the harsh words that came to his lips. He had been happy to learn that his brother was still okay, even though he didn't look like he was in good health. But this attempt to drag him into the fight only made him angry.

Keeping his temper firmly in check, Mark shook his head. "No. I'm not getting involved. I'll help you with the potion, or if you are desperate, I'll connect you with the maker of Ambrosia in the Tomb. But I just want to be left alone. And I'm serious about that, Joe. Don't send your men to sneak around me. I'm in enough trouble, and I can't afford to get caught up in any more. If they do show up, I am not responsible for what happens."

Though clearly disappointed, Joe just took a deep breath and stepped aside. "I understand."

When he reached the door, Mark stopped and glanced back over his shoulder. "If it's a matter of life and death . . ."

The frown on Joe's face melted away, and his lips curled into a smile. "Don't worry about it, Mark. It's not."

"Good. But if it is, you can call my number."

"Thanks, Mark."

Nodding heavily, Mark left, heading out of Joe's house and walking up the stairs to the double doors. Continuing up the next flight of stairs, he met Perry, who was leaning against the stone wall of the tunnel. Perry straightened when Mark appeared, his eyes dropping to Mark's fist, no doubt checking for some sign of a fight.

"How was your chat? You talk about what you needed to?"

Mark kept silent, offering only a short nod.

"Good. I can put you back anywhere in the city you want to go. What's your pleasure?"

Glancing at his watch, Mark calculated. It was still afternoon, so he had more than enough time to slip out of the city. Then again, he would raise fewer eyebrows if he waited until the next morning to leave New Emery.

"Can you take me to my apartment?"

"Sure, what's your address?"

No more than ten minutes later, Mark was standing in his apartment, staring at the rippling wall as it slowly solidified. He had assumed Perry would bring him to the apartment building, but it was entirely beyond his expectations that the earth controller could use his ability to climb up the wall and let Mark out in his actual apartment. After leaving his number, he had vanished back into the wall, leaving no sign he had ever been there.

"Huh, a good reminder not to underestimate anyone," Mark muttered, shrugging off his shirt to begin exercising.

32

Dawn found Mark already in the dead zone. He had left New Emery before first light, slipping out through the gap in the southern wall. The morning was spent circling north, moving ever farther from New Emery until he was well within the fourth band.

When he ran across Exlian, Mark hunted them indiscriminately, wiping out every monster he saw. It didn't matter whether they were drones or warriors. He swept everything in his path, and by the time the sun reached its zenith, he had arrived at the earth rats' territory. From there, he set his face to the northeast and began moving much more cautiously toward the territory where the apex hunter was located.

Mark's primary goal wasn't to hunt the apex hunter. He was still unsure whether he was strong enough. Instead, like any good hunter, he would start by gathering information, doing reconnaissance on both the apex hunter and its chosen hunting grounds to try to find some sort of weakness that he could exploit. Mark's only experience with apex hunters had ended peacefully, which left him unsure how a fight would go.

Soon, the buildings around him began to grow denser, more

tightly packed, the streets getting narrower, with old trees whose gnarled roots made the cracked concrete uneven. This was an older part of the city, and the disorganization and lack of clear planning demonstrated that. Mixed into the buildings were estates where the wealthy had once resided, walled compounds now completely overgrown. Mark moved through these areas cautiously, paying careful attention in case there were hibernating Exlian. He had still not forgotten his first night out in the dead zone, when hundreds of Exlian had appeared as if from nowhere all around him.

As Mark pushed farther north, he began seeing a new sort of Exlian, one that he had never encountered alive before, though he had dissected a couple of them when studying with Master Abrams. They were called gorehounds and looked like large, stocky dogs, with heavy, carapace-covered shoulders and insectile mouths. Rising from each gorehound's back was a sharp spike that angled forward, and by lowering their heads when they charged, they turned into living spears, though they hit more like battering rams. Their bodies were packed with muscle, and they were known for short bursts of speed, generated by their frog-like hind legs.

Spotting a small group of them waddling down the street, Mark hesitated for a moment, considering going around. He didn't really want to create a big stir, especially if the apex hunter was anywhere nearby. Checking his map, he saw that he was still on the edge of the apex hunter's territory, making it unlikely that he'd draw the creature's attention and alert it to his presence. Keeping himself masked, Mark stayed low as he worked his way along the edge of the street, hiding behind some rusted-out old cars as he waited for the gorehounds to get closer.

There were three in the group, each the size of a pony, and when they had drawn even with him, Mark launched his attack. Leaping over the rusty car he had been hiding behind, he threw himself at the gorehound in the middle, his bone blades stabbing into its shoulder. Startled by his sudden attack, the gorehound responded as he'd anticipated, its powerful legs tensing and then launching it forward. As it accelerated rapidly, it ran straight into two of Mark's bone blades, skewering itself on them. The force of the impact spun Mark around, and his blades ripped free of the gorehound as its weight rotated around him.

To his surprise, the creature wasn't dead yet, though it was bleeding profusely from the two massive wounds in its shoulder and chest. Though their speed when traveling in a straight line was impressive, gorehounds lacked sideways mobility, in large part because of how their bodies were shaped. So Mark took advantage of that, staying to the side of the other two gorehounds, forcing them to shift in place until they were facing him. Both let out loud roars, lowering their heads and brandishing the heavy spikes on their backs.

Just before they leaped forward, Mark caught sight of their muscles tensing and dodged away, delivering three rapid stabs to the downed gorehound. Two of them caught the creature's flailing limbs, while the third pierced through its eye, scrambling its brain and killing it.

There was a rush of wind as one of the gorehounds flashed past Mark, moving so quickly he almost couldn't keep up with it. The other gorehound had taken the time to reorient itself, shifting again to aim directly at Mark. But even as it charged toward him, he kicked up the body of the gorehound he had killed, throwing it into the charging gorehound's path. With a loud crash, the monster slammed into its companion's corpse, slowing its charge enough that Mark could attack.

One of the most dangerous things about Exlian was that, unlike most empowered, their abilities didn't come from the direct use of mana, which meant that Mark's null field was practically useless. Instead, Exlian relied on pure biological attributes, pitting their strength, speed, fortitude, and will against Mark's. The gorehounds outclassed Mark in both strength and fortitude, in part due to the sheer mass of their bodies. But Mark had the advantage of agility, allowing him to shift around the battlefield and stay out of the gorehounds' path. This rendered their heavy spikes almost useless, and it wasn't long before the gorehounds shifted to a new mode of attack, leaping toward Mark and attempting to savage him with their claws and teeth.

Their flurry of melee attacks was met by an equally ferocious swarm of bone blades that cut through their defenses with ease, tearing their bodies to pieces before they could manage to land a solid blow. All in all, the fight only lasted a couple of minutes, mainly due to how aggressive the Exlian were. By the time it was over, Mark had burned through ten biofuel but had come out of it otherwise unscathed.

After devouring the corpses, Mark continued on his way, patrolling just outside the apex hunter's territory. Of course, there was always a chance that the earth rat nest's information was wrong, but it seemed to have a very detailed understanding of the apex hunter's typical stomping grounds. From the little bit that Mark had been able to glean, it normally hunted at night, rarely making daytime appearances. It seemed wary of the massive city in the distance, and Mark couldn't blame it. At the same time, the earth rat nest presented an irresistible temptation, keeping it from retreating and hunting elsewhere.

Mark wasn't quite sure how the apex hunter would overcome all the earth rats, but clearly the nest was convinced that it could, which was why it had recruited Mark to eliminate it. Mark still didn't know exactly how he felt about the whole situation, as a single apex hunter was likely less troublesome for New Emery than a nest with a massive horde of superpowered rodents. Then again, if the rodents had any desire to attack New Emery, they would have launched an assault already. The whole situation was rather confusing, so Mark just put it aside and focused on what was in front of him: finding and eliminating the apex hunter.

Continuing to work his way around the edges of the territory, Mark found more gorehounds. They seemed to prefer groups of three to five, though occasionally Mark would see a pair of them moving together. Regardless of their numbers, he eliminated them all, throwing himself into the fights with mad abandon and consuming the corpses after he had slaughtered them. He could feel his stats increasing bit by bit and was rather surprised to find that the gorehounds contributed to both his strength and his speed. The more gorehounds he hunted, the more explosive his abilities became.

By the time he was on the cusp of another breakthrough, Mark paused and retreated to a large mansion. It had been abandoned for years and was now overgrown by thick vines. Finding his way in through one of the broken windows, Mark took a seat on an old couch, only to have it crumble underneath him, its wood so rotten that it failed to hold his weight. Grumbling under his breath, Mark cleared away the debris and settled cross-legged on the marble floor.

He had a feeling that if he simply forged ahead, continuing to consume gorehounds, it might produce a problem. He had no doubt that he'd be able to increase his speed and strength. The question was, How much were the gorehounds influencing him? All their power was highly optimized for charges, allowing them to cross short distances at an incredible speed. Mark wasn't sure that was the sort of speed he was looking for. As with everything, biology was about trade-offs, and by increasing his muscles' explosiveness, he was potentially decreasing his ability to maintain exertion over a longer period of time.

As he sat and meditated, Mark focused on the changes in his body, doing his best to shape them into what he wanted rather than passively absorbing the gorehounds' traits. As he continued to press deeper, he felt a hint of resistance. Something in him, something he had absorbed along with the bodies, was building to a crescendo, pushing his evolution in a certain direction.

Mark wasn't unfamiliar with this feeling. He had experienced it before: the intense, residual will contained in Exlian genes that drove toward a specific evolutionary path. When faced with the war bear's imprint, it had only been Mime's help that had allowed him to avoid simply transforming into a war bear. Similarly, he had been forced to overcome the cataphract's imprint. Now he could feel the same sort of pressure, albeit weaker, from all the gorehounds he had consumed.

When he had been devouring lower-ranked Exlian, the pressure hadn't been as strong. But now he was eating C- and B-ranked Exlian by the dozen, and their residual will was combining to form a fierce pressure. It was a strange feeling, but he could sense that if he blindly continued down this path, the bone blades on his back would likely combine, forming one heavy spike that he could use to ram his enemies.

While Mark had no desire to transform into a gorehound or even adopt any of their traits, it brought up a curious question. Could he exert his will, pushing himself into new paths of evolution, by maintaining an image of what he wanted to become? While he wasn't sure whether it would be possible, one thing was certainly true. He needed to erase the gorehound imprint before consuming more of the creatures, lest it overwhelm him.

For the next two hours, Mark didn't move an inch, simply remaining in his meditative state as he systematically crushed the gorehound imprint with his will, smashing it repeatedly. Every time he did, it re-formed, pushing back against his will. Through repeated attacks, he began to get a sense of what exactly this imprint was. The mental energy that made it up wasn't any different from normal mental energy. It simply naturally returned to that specific shape when left undisturbed.

Mark found that it wasn't that hard to crush the imprint, though that likely had to do with the strength of his will compared to the fractured amalgamation of imprints. Every time Mark dispersed the imprint, a bit of the energy it contained diffused into him, further reinforcing his willpower. It was only a tiny amount, barely more than a few grains of sand in volume, but more and more started to slough off, merging into Mark's mind, even as the imprint grew weaker.

After two hours, it finally broke apart completely, blending into Mark's mind, as the impulse to evolve into a living battering ram faded. Letting out the breath he had been holding, Mark regulated his breathing and stood up, his four bone blade arms flexing.

"There must have been some residual will left from that war bear," Mark muttered, looking down at his hands.

A war bear, in addition to the mana shield, had six insectile arms that extended from its back. Mark hadn't consciously desired to have similar arms when he formed the cataphract armor, but clearly something unconscious had been guiding his evolution. In fact, he had never consciously considered how he wanted to evolve. But now that he was consuming a significant number of Exlian, it was clear that that was exactly what he needed to do. Evolving willy-nilly would turn him into a mutant monstrosity. Mark had no desire to take that path, no matter how much strength he might gain on it.

Of course, there were no free lunches. If he wanted to continue gaining power, he would have to evolve, which meant making changes to his current human form. Jumping into the air a few times to test his agility, Mark found that the explosive power he had been building had largely dispersed. Of course, his speed was still there. It was simply more refined than before, focused less on sudden bursts and more on how quickly he could move overall.

Night was coming when Mark finished testing his abilities, and after considering his next course of action, he elected to wait. He had a feeling that this part of the city would be overrun once night fell, and getting caught in the streets as Exlian swarmed around him didn't seem like a good idea.

Settling down for the night, Mark continued to ponder the evolutionary path he might like to take. There were a number of options, and one by one he considered and rejected different sorts of evolution. He thought wings might be interesting, but they would no doubt be cumbersome, making it hard for him to fight in close combat, which was his current strength.

Besides that, Mark had a secret suspicion that he might be able to learn to fly on his own. After all, powerful energy controllers could fly by controlling the mana around them. Mark just needed to figure out how they were doing it. Unfortunately, the only powerful energy controller he knew was Phoenix, and she didn't have any idea that he was alive.

That brought a twinge of guilt that caught in Mark's throat, derailing his thoughts of growing stronger. He had been wrestling with whether to reach out to Phoenix, but considering how long it had been since his death was announced, he found himself strangely hesitant. Would she blame him for lying to her? What if she was hurt that he was still spending time with Sky and Noah? The brief interactions he had with them felt like tenuous tethers keeping him from falling into the abyss of loneliness, and he feared they might snap at any time. The farther Mark strayed down this new evolutionary path, the greater the gap between him and his friends would grow, and the thought stabbed his heart like a sharp claw.

As the sun went down, the compound around him began to come alive, and Mark's face grew ugly when he saw just how many Exlian were appearing on the mansion's grounds. A few were inside the mansion itself, but Mark was more concerned with the nigh-endless lights popping up in the psychic network. The majority were D ranked or lower, but the sheer number made his scalp crawl.

There was no way Mark could sneak out without being seen, so he stayed put, keeping himself hidden, hoping the Exlian wouldn't come into the room. For the next few hours, he watched curiously as the Exlian milled about. He couldn't figure out why, but sometimes two Exlian would suddenly begin ripping each other to shreds while their companions simply watched with idle curiosity. Otherwise, nothing happened until close to eleven o'clock in the evening, when another wave of Exlian surged over and launched a fierce assault.

Even before they had arrived, Mark felt a heavy pressure growing in his chest. Seeing them, he immediately realized why. Leading the second group of Exlian was a gorehound whose mind gleamed so brightly it was like a bonfire among a thousand candles. Mark couldn't tell if it was truly an A-ranked Exlian or just a B-ranked one incredibly close to evolving, but it tore through its opponents with ease.

Cautiously peeking out one of the windows, Mark caught sight of it rampaging in the garden. Unlike the other gorehounds, this hound had two large spikes extending from its back, and its forelegs were even heavier than normal, with thick claws that it wielded with impunity, tearing apart any creature that came near. Suppressing the instinct to rush out and attack, Mark remained hidden, his hands clenched tightly, as the Exlian outside ripped through each other.

He watched through a sliver of window, peeking past the ivy as the powerful Exlian let out a roar and leaped forward, its front claws grabbing the next-strongest Exlian in the yard. Massive teeth bit down, tearing out the Exlian's throat, and as Mark watched, its body was rapidly consumed. That seemed to be the last push that the powerful Exlian needed to evolve.

With a muted roar, its body began to shift and change. It happened quickly, bones beginning to shoot forth spikes that burst from its skin, covering its body in blood. Yet the wounds healed just as fast, and scales began to emerge on its skin, reinforcing its defenses. Mark wasn't quite sure how the creature's body was growing, but from the rush of mana, he surmised that it was drawing in the ambient mana at an increased rate.

Because he was watching the movement of mana, Mark saw it suddenly twist. One moment, the mana surging into the Exlian was like soft clouds being sucked up. In the next, it twisted into jagged spears that rammed into the Exlian's body. Though it didn't halt the evolution the gorehound was undergoing, the shift in the mana did considerable damage, wreaking havoc as it was pulled into the creature's body. The spiky spears ripped apart muscle and cracked bone before shattering and transforming into ugly spiked chains that fused with the monster, causing it to weaken precipitously.

Shrinking back, Mark reinforced his shroud and stayed as still as possible, his eyes fixed on the now-wounded Exlian. Despite having risen to become a true terror-ranked Exlian, the monster in many ways seemed even weaker than it had been before. Jumping into the A rank was supposed to be a qualitative change, but something had gone terribly wrong, and Mark didn't understand what or why.

That question was answered a moment later, when the sound of fighting drifted into his ears and he saw a large team of humans in mana suits charging into the Exlian lines. They slaughtered indiscriminately, ripping their way through the horde of Exlian as they closed in on the now-wounded terror-ranked monster.

Mark recognized the crests on their armor immediately and caught sight of Hex, the S-ranked energy controller, moving with them. Hex hovered in the air, her hands stretched toward the terror-ranked gorehound, manipulating the mana it was still trying to absorb to strip its strength, speed, and fortitude while causing it to bleed vitality. Taking advantage of the Exlian's instinctive urge to pull in surrounding mana to aid it in its breakthrough, Hex had transformed what should have been its new strength into a terrible curse.

As her soldiers cleared the way, Hex continued to manipulate the mana around the terror-ranked Exlian, bending more of it to weaken the Exlian even further. By the time she reached it, it could hardly move, its limbs barely twitching as it glared up at her, too weak to even growl. Her face impassive, Hex lowered herself to the ground, landing next to the Exlian, and pulled a long, slim blade from its sheath on her back.

Staring at the terror-ranked Exlian for a moment, as if waiting to see if it would mount any resistance, she shook her head and pierced the creature's skull with her mana blade, driving it into the monster's brain to kill it. Normally, an Exlian, upon dying, would begin thrashing about, but her hexes still shrouded its body, and it barely twitched as its life fled. Pulling her blade free, she flicked the blood from it and sheathed it in one swift motion.

"Let's clean up quickly," she shouted. "Sora's got an entire list of places for us to stop tonight."

Mark hardly dared glance at her and kept himself as still as humanly possible. At the same time, he peeled back his helmet, revealing his face, and retracted his blade arms as well, not wanting to be mistaken for an Exlian. He was hoping that Hex and her team would simply kill all the monsters in the yard and move on, ignoring the mansion.

Unfortunately, they were much too professional for that, and they began sweeping the building room by room. Realizing that he was going to be found, Mark sighed and jumped out the window, badly startling a soldier standing nearby. With a shout, the soldier activated his mana sword and swung, more out of instinct than anything else. Mark stepped forward, getting inside the swing, and caught the man's hand to prevent himself from being cut.

Unfortunately, that turned out to be the wrong move, as the soldier flicked his wrist to reveal a second blade implanted in the arm of his suit, which he used to punch toward Mark's chest. At the last second, Mark's mana shield appeared, deflecting the blow and giving Mark the chance to retreat.

"Hold on, hold on, I'm human!"

Though it wasn't precisely true, Mark's lack of Exlian features convinced the gathering soldiers that he wasn't a monster, and they quickly surrounded him, staring at him suspiciously. Attracted by the commotion, Hex flew over to see what was going on. She skimmed over the soldiers' heads and landed in front of him, looking him up and down. As he met her gaze, Mark felt his eyes stinging, unable to compete with the raw power hers contained. She had the calm grace of someone who believed herself capable of handling anything life threw at her, but Mark could sense a subtle tension in the set of her lips.

"Who are you?"

"I go by the name Apex," Mark said, carefully retrieving his association badge. "I'm a freelance hunter with the association."

He held out the badge, and one of the soldiers took it, lifting it to hand to Hex. She waved him off, and after checking it to make sure it wasn't fake, the soldier handed the badge back to Mark. As he put it away, Hex frowned and glanced at the window Mark had emerged from. "What are you doing so far out from the city? Are you alone? Where's your team?"

"I'm a solo hunter," Mark said with a shrug. "I've been hunting in this band, mostly during the day, and then laying low at night."

"That's awfully risky," Hex said, her eyes returning to Mark.

Though her tone was even, Mark could tell that she was still suspicious. He couldn't blame her. Staying outside the city overnight was something only the most powerful people did, and despite his higher-than-average abilities, Mark didn't yet rank among them.

"Hold on a second," she said, and then tapped something on her watch, no doubt sending a quick message.

Less than a minute later, a small team arrived, led by Sora, the Seer. When she caught sight of Mark, her eyebrows rose, but she didn't say anything, simply looking at Hex and waiting for her explanation. Hex moved away from Mark, lowering her voice slightly, though it didn't stop Mark from hearing what she was saying.

"We wiped out the Exlian that you said was going to transition to terror ranked. Got here just as it evolved and put it down. We were sweeping the building when he popped up. Says he's a hunter that is solo hunting in the fourth band, goes by the name of Apex. Do you mind checking him?"

After hearing the details from Hex, Sora took a closer look at Mark, her eyes flashing with a rippling blue light. Mark felt a strange presence surround him, as if a giant eye had opened in the sky above and was peering down at him. For a brief moment, Mark felt as if he were an ant being examined under a magnifying glass, and great terror welled up in him. It was met by equally strong anger, a flash of fury so strong it completely shattered any fear Mark had.

The strangest thing was it didn't feel as if the fury had come from him; instead, it was as if it had been channeled through him. His body shook as the two forces collided, and then both were gone. Mark was left reeling, wondering if he had just experienced anything at all, or if it had all been in his imagination. Sora staggered back as well, the blue ripple shattering as she winced and reached up to clutch her helmet.

"Sora!" Hex cried, her hand clenching as she seized control of all the mana surrounding Mark.

"Hold on, it's not him," Sora said through gritted teeth, clearly in pain. "I've probably just been using my ability too much and got some backlash."

Looking relieved, Hex relaxed her tight grip on the mana around Mark, allowing him to breathe more easily. It took a minute for Sora to recover, and when she did, she looked at Mark, her expression haggard. There was a certain blankness about her gaze, almost as if she were looking beyond Mark at something no one else could see, but then a thread of fear appeared in her eyes, snapping her back to the real world. What she might have seen, Mark had no idea and was honestly too afraid to ask. He tensed, fully expecting a fight to break out, but Sora just shook her head slightly as she turned away and spoke to Hex. "He's fine. We're on a tight schedule, so we should move to the next location."

"And leave him here?"

"Yes," Sora said, her voice emphatic. "Just ignore him."

A spark of interest appeared in Hex's eyes, and she glanced over Sora's shoulder at Mark, who wasn't quite sure what was going on.

"Finish up, we're moving to the next location," Hex yelled, her eyes still locked on Mark.

As the team gathered, Sora and her small group of soldiers moved out first, with many of the larger force trailing behind them. Hex lingered a moment, stepping closer to Mark as she looked him over, the way a child might look over some new and interesting toy. "You might not know it from first glance, but Sora is incredibly pragmatic."

Unsure where Hex was going with her words, Mark didn't say anything, cautiously watching the S-ranked empowered as she got closer.

"There are only two kinds of people Sora treats with this sort of disregard. People who are guaranteed to die soon, and people who are so dangerous they'll bring about unmitigated disaster if messed with. Reason says you're more of the first. After all, a B-ranked empowered sleeping out in the dead zone speaks of a death wish. But my instincts are telling me you're the second. Unfortunately, I don't have time to find out right now, but I'm curious to know which camp you fall into. It was nice to meet you, Apex. I'm sure we'll meet again."

Mark's lips twitched as Hex chuckled to herself and flew off, rapidly vanishing from his sight. Though she didn't give him as clear a sense of raw power as Winter Wolf had, her methods were much more sinister and, judging from what he had witnessed, almost impossible to guard against. Even without her mana control, Mark got the feeling that she could snap him in half with one hand tied behind her back, probably with ease. The gulf between the S rank and the B rank was tremendous, and even if she hadn't weakened the terror-ranked Exlian with her spells, she likely could have simply removed its head with her bare hands.

The encounter put a serious damper on Mark's enthusiasm, and he spent the rest of the night resting in the mansion. His recent growth had brought with it a feeling he'd seen as confidence, but Mark was starting to realize that it was actually arrogance. Even the terror-ranked gorehound was at least a dozen times stronger than he was, and if it had finished evolving and caught him, Mark wasn't sure that he would have had any way to escape. Almost every rank was ten times stronger than the rank before it, which was one of the reasons Mark had no trouble killing C-ranked Exlian.

He was strong enough to take on multiple B-ranked Exlian at the same time, but a single blow from an A-ranked Exlian would likely shatter his defenses and deal tremendous damage to his body, to say nothing of the force someone like Hex could unleash. It was with a rather subdued attitude that he rose the next day and continued his hunt, eliminating Exlian as he worked his way around the edges of the apex hunter's territory.

That afternoon, he was resting in a three-story office building when his watch vibrated, and he saw he had a message from Sky.

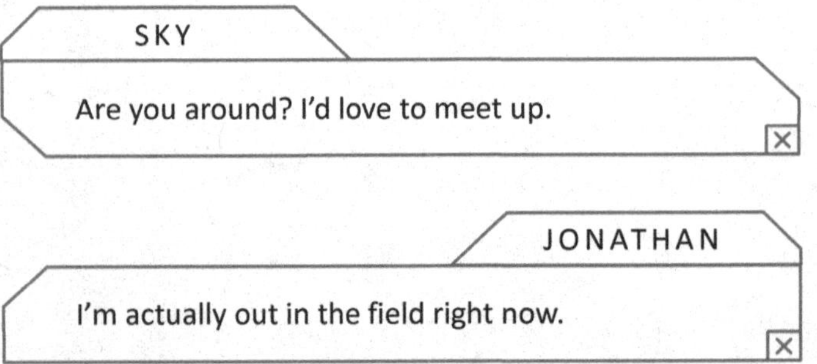

After sending the message, Mark pinged his location, and a moment later, he received a message back.

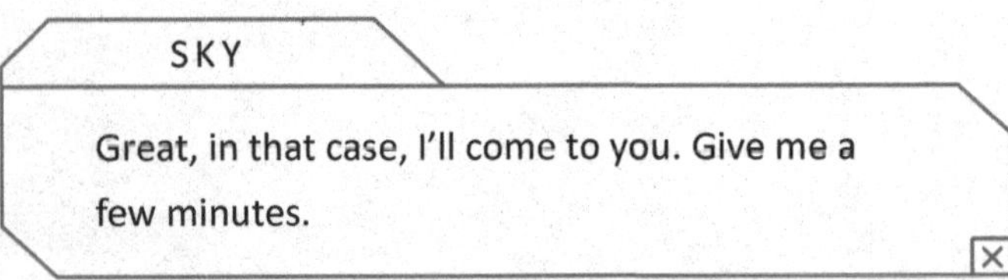

A few minutes turned out to be fifteen, but Mark didn't mind. He headed up to the roof and sat down, and not long after, Sky zipped through the air before coming to a graceful stop next to him.

"Wow, you're pretty far out here," Sky said, looking around. "We're almost at the fifth band. What sort of prey are you hunting?"

"Gorehounds," Mark said. "Their hearts, lungs, and the tendons in their back legs are all alchemical materials." What he didn't mention, of course, was that he had been eating his prey directly, and so despite having hunted eleven of the monsters that morning, he had no materials to show for it.

"Sounds good. Do you mind if I join? I've got some time off and thought it would be fun to hang out."

Despite the confidence with which Sky spoke, Mark could tell she was nervous from the slight shift in her pupils and a faint tension in the way she held her arms. His awareness was more instinctive than anything else, but he assumed it had to do with his ever-improving will, which made him much more observant.

"Yeah, I'd love to hang out. If you'd like, we can head back to the city and spend time there."

"No, no, it's fine," Sky said, waving her hand. "You're hunting, and I don't want to disrupt you. I don't know how much help I'll be, though. Fighting's not really my thing, but I can at least provide distraction."

"Do you even have any weapons?" Mark asked, looking over Sky's incredibly light suit.

"Of course I do," she responded scornfully.

With a flick of her wrist, two small mana pistols emerged from her suit, slotting neatly into her hands.

"They don't pack much of a punch, so heavy armor is a problem, but as long as I target weak points, they're pretty good. I've also got a mana blade, though that's not my favorite to use. Of course, if you think I'll get in the way, then we can go back to the city."

Staring at the two pistols, Mark shook his head. "No, you'll be fine. I'm actually really interested to see you use those. How long do they take to recharge?"

"Depends on the setting," Sky said, lifting one of the pistols to show the switch on the side to Mark. "They've got a single-shot mode, which is the most powerful blast and takes roughly five seconds to charge. They've got a multishot mode, which can release a shot every second for a sustained fifteen seconds. Then it needs twenty seconds to recharge. There's also a stun that releases a continuous beam, but that's only really useful on regular people. Most empowered can shrug it off just fine, to say nothing of Exlian."

"Well, like I said, I'm interested in seeing you in action. I've seen you zip around a good bit, but I don't think I've ever seen you actually fight."

"That's because I don't," Sky said with forced cheerfulness. "But maybe you could show me the ropes. You know, explain how you do it?"

It was then that Mark realized Sky's actual objective. Something was unsettling her, and it seemed she wanted to learn how to defend herself. He didn't let his realization show on his face, maintaining his calm smile as he jumped up and brushed off his butt. "All right, in that case, let's get going. We'll start working our way back toward the city a little bit. Most of the Exlian this far out are pretty dangerous. In fact, in the last fight, they nearly got me when I wasn't paying attention. Thankfully, my armor is strong, and it held."

Walking to the side of the building, Mark casually stepped off and plummeted down to the ground below. Sky kept pace with him, watching him curiously as he accelerated. When he reached the first floor, his bone blades stabbed into the side of the building, forcefully slowing his descent, and he jumped from the cracking wall to land lightly on the street.

"Keep close."

Mark took off running, moving at his normal speed. Sky had no trouble keeping up and appeared to simply be standing in the air next to him as she followed, always staying within a few feet, no matter how quickly he ran. This part of the city wasn't very dense, with wide streets flanked by overgrown trees, and shorter buildings that were little more than rubble. Normally, one would travel cautiously through such an area, since getting surrounded by Exlian was a sure way to die, but Mark's connection to the psychic network ensured he could see any Exlian coming well before it could detect him.

Spotting a group of Exlian ahead, Mark changed direction, cutting between a ruined car and a building that looked like it had suffered a bomb blast. Though killing the Exlian wouldn't have been hard, Mark was hoping to start with some weaker enemies, since Sky was only D ranked at the moment. It took them a few hours to get closer to the city, but Mark didn't waste that time, instructing Sky on Exlian behavior and typical combat patterns. By the time they found a small group of drones that Mark felt was a good challenge, Sky had a strong theoretical understanding of how the fight would go. Of course, theory was just theory, and Mark didn't blame her for her nervousness as they approached the resting drones.

"They're through the window, in the back of the main room. Looks like this used to be a storefront, so expect some sort of counter. If I had to guess, they are probably tucked down behind it."

Staring at the window, Sky touched her pistols hesitantly. "And I'm supposed to go in after them?"

"Yup. You can walk or fly in. Once you see them, start shooting. They'll try to catch you, but you should be fast enough to keep out of reach."

"Okay, that sounds easy enough."

Flexing her fingers, Sky hesitated for a moment and then, with a jerk, grabbed her pistols. Her body leaned forward as if to take off at full speed, but before she could, Mark grabbed her shoulder, stopping her. "Calm down, Sky. Rushing in like this is a great way to make mistakes. While you won't always get to dictate the pace and timing of a fight, you should always try to exert as much control as you can."

His voice had a calming effect, and Mark felt Sky's shoulders relaxing. She took a couple of deep breaths and then crept forward, her guns held high. Mark was confident that Sky could handle herself, or at least escape if things got hairy—he had never seen anyone or anything move as fast as she could—but that didn't stop him from paying close attention. Unexpected situations could happen at any time in the dead zone, and it was always better to be cautious.

Sky entered through the doorway, her body a few inches off the ground to avoid the shattered glass spread over the threshold. Once inside the building, she sped up slightly, moving in perfect silence like a sort of specter. Mark saw her flinch when the Exlian came into view, and the motion drew their attention. Her sudden appearance seemed to startle the monsters, buying Sky enough time to aim and fire one of her pistols. Unfortunately, in her haste, she squeezed the trigger too early and the mana blast went wide, missing the Exlian's eye and glancing off its carapace. The shot left a gouge in the Exlian's armor but didn't scare it one bit, and together with its companions, the Exlian lunged forward, mouths wide.

Mark expected to see Sky come flying out of the building as fast as possible, but to her credit, she simply floated back and fired her other pistol. This time she landed a shot in the closest monster's throat, burning through the soft flesh. One of the drones jumped over the counter, but Sky slipped to the side, moving so quickly it looked like she'd teleported. At the same time, she shot the drone from close range, her mana blast piercing through the monster's eye and frying its brain. As the drone crashed to the ground, Mark monitored the psychic network, just in case its death scream attracted any attention.

Sure enough, Mark saw more Exlian beginning to emerge, woken from their daytime hibernation by the death of their comrade. When the second drone fell after swallowing a barrage of shots, six more Exlian were heading their way. Rather than distract Sky, who was locked in a valiant struggle with the remaining drone, Mark did a quick sweep around the building, killing four of the incoming drones. The other two he left for Sky after estimating she'd be able to take down the drone she was tangled with soon. Slipping back into the building, he saw her firing two shots at point-blank range into the back of the drone's head.

"You've got more enemies incoming, Sky."

Mark's words must not have registered, because Sky stared at him blankly as the drone she had just killed collapsed to the floor.

"What?"

Mark just pointed as a drone came barreling through the front door, its claws skittering across the polished floor. It was moving so fast it slammed into the dead drone in front of Sky, pushing it into Sky's legs and causing her to fall forward. Just before she would have face-planted into the drone's waving claws, her entire body rose into the air. She was moving so quickly her back slammed into the ceiling, cracking it and knocking the breath from her lungs. Worried that she would fall back on top of the drone, Mark started to move forward, getting ready to intervene, but Sky surprised him by keeping her grip on her pistols and landing an accurate shot on the top of the drone's head. Though it didn't kill the monster, the blast drove it down into the ground, buying time for Sky to regain her bearings.

Mark caught a glimpse of her face through her clear faceplate and saw a crimson blush on her cheeks, but the look in her eyes was determined, and she threw herself back into combat, killing both the wounded drone and the second one that entered the room a moment later. When the second collapsed, Sky retreated to where Mark was, her eyes still locked on the doorway, anticipating another enemy.

"Well done. You've got great instincts, Sky. There are more drones coming, but we don't want to cause too much of a commotion. When hunting Exlian, it's better to kill a couple and then retreat and hunt elsewhere. If we kill too many in one spot, we might inadvertently start a wave, which won't be good. Let's go out the back."

Rushing to the back door, Mark cut through the lock with a flick of his bone blade and kicked it open, crushing a drone lurking in the alleyway. Jumping, he kicked off the wall and propelled himself up to the roof, catching the edge and leaping over. Sky didn't need to jump but simply followed Mark onto the rooftop. Breaking into a sprint, he headed for the roof of the building next door, clearing the gap easily.

"Your ability makes me so jealous," Mark muttered as Sky casually floated over the gap between buildings that he had just jumped.

"It could have been yours, you know," Sky said, the blush fading from her cheeks. "It's your fault I have it."

Mark didn't bother correcting her misconception, and together they continued their hunt, eliminating small groups of drones to help Sky get used to combat. After each fight they retreated, and Mark helped her assess how well she had done. The more she fought, the more confident she grew in her ability to evade the enemy, and the more comfortable she was with close proximity to the Exlian. This came to a head when Mark pointed out a single D-ranked murder scorpion lurking in the shadow of a rusted-out car. "That's your next target. This time, don't use your pistols."

"What? Are you crazy? What do you mean, don't use my pistols? How am I supposed to kill it without pistols?"

"You've got a knife, don't you?"

"Sure, but that means I have to get close enough to touch it. It'll rip me apart!"

"*If* it can touch you, which it won't be able to. Here, let's do this: I want you to touch the wall over there, then touch my back as quickly as you can. When I turn around, don't let me touch you."

Though she didn't look happy about it, Sky nodded and vanished in a blur, reappearing next to the wall in the distance. As soon as she touched it, she disappeared again. Even though Mark knew that she was going to appear behind him, it still took a moment for him to register that she had even moved. He felt her finger poke the back of his right shoulder, and even before he had spun, she was back at the wall in front of him, watching him with a smile on her face. Gawking at Sky, Mark glanced over his shoulder, wondering if the touch he had felt was some sort of trick. He had expected her to be able to move quickly, but what genuinely astonished him was the fact that her movement had been nigh undetectable. It was as if she moved through space without disturbing the air, or anything else.

"Did you teleport?"

Chuckling and shaking her head, Sky drifted toward Mark. "Nope. But my flight works by shifting my absolute position, which is why I'm not impacted by the air around me. My top speed is pretty fast, but I can't keep it up for a long time."

"What is a long time?"

Sky's forehead wrinkled as she thought about it. "I think I could go top speed for about ten minutes or so, but then I'd be useless the rest of the day. But as long as I'm not pushing to top speed, I can fly all day."

"Sky, this is crazy. You should just use a mana sword. I was already thinking that you could sneak up on your enemy to attack with a knife, but this is so much better. Just fly up, cut their head off, and then retreat before they know what hit them."

Sky's face paled at the thought of shifting to a close-combat fighting style, and she shook her head. "I . . . I can't. I'm already at my weight limit. If I add more weight to my kit, I won't be able to fly."

Scanning Sky, Mark looked for things on her suit that could be eliminated but quickly realized that she was already highly optimized for weight. If she wanted to add a five-to-ten-pound mana sword, she would have to ditch other equipment.

"I'm not saying you have to do it," Mark said, "but I think it would make a really effective fighting style. Rather than a sword, you could even use a spear, though you'll have that same weight problem. It's something to think about. For now, try to kill the murder scorpion with your knife. Or if that's too scary, at least wound it. It's got a weak point about six inches behind its head. There's a small gap in its carapace, and if you stab hard enough, you should hit its brain."

"But then I would need to get close to it."

Seeing the paleness of Sky's face, Mark didn't push the issue, and the two of them began looking for the next group of Exlian.

It was starting to get late, but neither of them was worried. Thanks to her flight speed, it would only take Sky a minute to make it back to the city, and Mark was planning on staying in the dead zone overnight. He liked to look for enemies from higher vantage points, so they had just climbed a building when, in the distance, they saw a bright flash and then heard the clang of weapons clashing. The fight was taking place a dozen blocks away, but due to the buildings between them, Mark couldn't see what was going on.

"Want me to go check it out?" Sky asked, deep curiosity in her eyes.

With a curt shake of his head, Mark turned away. "No need. It's not our fight, so let's stay clear."

"I'm going to see who it is. It will only take a moment. I'll be right back."

Sky was gone before Mark could respond, leaving him alone on the rooftop. He stared after her for a moment, and then, with a groan, he threw himself down from the top of the building, using the wall of the building across the street to slow his descent. He had just landed when he heard Sky's voice over their voice channel.

"Uh, Mark, it looks like the Borner family, and I think Phoenix is with them. They are being attacked by raiders. I'm going to help!"

Hearing that Phoenix was in danger sent a thread of fear racing down his spine and caused his heart to tighten. Before he knew it, he was darting down the street at top speed, holding nothing back. Yet no sooner had he rounded the corner than he picked up a large number of Exlian rushing over. There were at least three dozen, and a number of them were fliers, skimming low over the buildings.

"Hold on! Don't just rush in, Sky! There are Exlian coming. At least five are flying, and they're closing in on you fast!"

Hearing a muffled curse, Mark rounded the corner just in time to see Sky evading two winged Exlian. Her pistols both let off sharp blasts, though only one of them hit, scorching a hole in the wing membrane of one of the monsters. More Exlian were rushing her, so Mark skidded to a stop and crouched, his hands reaching down into his shadow and then emerging with his already assembled sniper rifle. Lifting it to his cheek, he braced himself and took aim, tracking an Exlian that had not yet closed in on Sky. She was currently playing a deadly game of tag in the dusky sky, but Mark was confident she would be able to hold her own so long as he could clear a couple of the enemy.

He was about to fire when a large insectile monster with a segmented carapace and a dozen legs skidded around the corner and let out a sharp shriek. It threw itself at him, but instead of taking his eyes off the flying Exlian, Mark simply stood up, leaving a clone behind. His hope was that it would last just long enough to pull the trigger, but as he met the insect Exlian, he was pleasantly surprised to discover that the clone remained in place, taking its shots.

The monster was on him in a blur of claws and sharp mandibles, but Mark wasn't intimidated in the least, even when the rapid-fire attacks broke past his mana shield and left gouges on his armor. He returned the favor with his bone blades, and while the Exlian's claws had only scraped him, he tore through its carapace with ease, spilling greenish blood across the concrete. A glance at Sky revealed that she was okay, so Mark stabbed the insect Exlian in the head and cut one of its legs off. As it thrashed, Mark turned and broke into a sprint, rushing toward the ongoing fight in the distance.

In the middle of a street between two squat buildings, fifteen fighters in brightly colored mana suits had formed a rough defensive line with a few badly smashed vehicles and some large shields, deployed by the four largest suits. Surrounding them were twenty others in pitch-black suits with no markings and a diverse array of weaponry. No words were exchanged, but attacks flew fast and furious as mana blasts and bolts crossed through the air. The two sides exchanged their arsenals with impunity, clearly bent on killing their opponents and bringing even more destruction to the already badly damaged buildings.

The black-suited raiders abruptly rushed forward, doing their best to dodge the Borner team's ranged attacks, but before they could get into melee range, a figure rose from the center of the Borner team, stretching out her hands and unleashing a powerful blast of mana that arced over her teammates' heads before exploding among the enemy. None of the raiders were hit head-on because as soon as they saw the mana gathering, they scattered, using a variety of movement abilities to rush out of the way. Yet just because they avoided the initial blast didn't mean they were safe. As if she had expected it, Phoenix controlled the exploding mana, forming dozens of smaller mana darts that shot off after the fleeing raiders.

But in exposing herself, Phoenix had made herself a target, and the raiders took advantage of that. A raider on top of one of the buildings, who had been shooting crossbow bolts down into the Borner team's lines, abandoned his crossbow and lifted his hands into the air. Out of the clear sky, a lightning bolt slammed down toward Phoenix's head, carrying devastating power that she didn't dare take head-on, despite her suit's built-in defenses. With a shout, she abandoned half of the mana darts and lifted her hand, summoning a shield to block the lightning.

This allowed the raiders to rush back toward the team, and it wasn't long before the two sides were locked in a fierce battle. One raider, upon reaching the team's lines, suddenly swelled up, his suit doubling in size. Another manifested sharp mana claws that glowed with a sickly green light. A third controlled half a dozen double-sided blades that spun in tight circles to swarm his opponent, forcing him into a defensive position. But the raiders weren't the only ones with powers, and the Borner team gave as good as it got, striking out with every weapon at their disposal.

Mark watched the fight breaking out, but he didn't charge in. Though it was obvious at a glance that Phoenix's team was the weaker side, Mark was confident that they could survive for at least a few more minutes, by which point the situation would have changed. He could feel the Exlian rushing toward them, and instead of turning to face them, Mark shrouded himself and waited for them to pass by. He only had to wait a dozen seconds before the first of the Exlian, an insect like the one he had killed earlier, passed him at breakneck speed, completely focused on the fighting humans. Watching it skitter across the street, Mark was struck by a sudden thought and quickly focused, bending his mind to project a clear mental thought.

EAT THE DARK ONES.

Mark wasn't actually projecting words; instead he was focusing on an image of the dark-suited raiders, trying to communicate that they were the prey that would provide the greatest boon to the

Exlian if consumed. Mark had no idea if it would work, and it could have been a coincidence, but the Exlian that had rushed past him shifted its trajectory and launched an attack on one of the raiders.

It seemed less like a coincidence when the second Exlian also targeted a raider, scrambling up a wall to attack one who was positioned on the nearby roof. As more Exlian joined the fight, the already chaotic melee grew even more frantic. It was one thing to fight empowered in mana suits, trading blows back and forth. It was another entirely to add frenzied Exlian to the mix.

The Exlian were bent on killing whoever crossed their path, but they seemed to have a particular desire to wipe out the raiders. As he watched the first few minutes of the fight, Mark was encouraged to see a number of the dark-suited raiders falling under Exlian claws. Of course, he wasn't confident that the Exlian wouldn't immediately go after Phoenix and her team as soon as the raiders were dead, so he began to prepare for that eventuality.

Sneaking closer, he caught sight of a raider struggling against an Exlian warrior. The raider was an energy controller, though a rather weak one by the looks of it, and was using mana shields to good effect to keep the Exlian's claws and teeth at bay. As Mark crept by, he pulled up his null field and, with a thought, extended it. Recently, he had been making good progress on his practice controlling the null field, and he was now able to manipulate its shape freely.

Like a strange, ethereal tentacle, his null field stretched out. As it approached, the Exlian reacted instantly, its body shifting away, as if it could sense the disturbance in the mana. The raider reacted only a moment later, instinctively picking up the void heading toward them. Sensing a weakness as its prey's attention wavered, the Exlian crashed forward, its limbs flailing as it tried to rip through the raider's mana suit. He responded by throwing up more mana shields, using both hands to block the storm of claws, only to find his shields sputtering and disappearing as the null field washed over him.

There was a brief moment of pure terror in the raider's eyes, and then he died as the Exlian's claws, now unimpeded, tore him to shreds. The Exlian was almost as surprised as the raider and hesitated for a moment, failing to sense Mark closing in from behind. When it finally did notice his presence, he was already too close, and his bone blades cut through its spine, sending the Exlian warrior to join the raider it had just slain.

Mark didn't stop, leaving the corpses for his shadow to deal with as he continued to circle closer to the battle. He sensed that Sky was finishing up her fight. A moment later, that was confirmed when her voice came through their channel.

"Fliers are down. I'm moving in to support."

Hunkering down behind a fallen sign, Mark kept a close eye on the fight as he waited for Sky. But the situation suddenly changed, and he heard Sky's voice once more.

"Mark, there's a large force heading toward Phoenix. It looks like reinforcements from her family, and they are kitted for war. They'll be arriving at your location within a couple of minutes."

Rapidly assessing the situation, Mark crouched lower and began to shimmy backward. "Let's retreat. The fight here is pretty much stabilized, and there shouldn't be any trouble in the next couple of minutes. We'll only cause confusion if we jump out now."

There was hesitation from the other end of the line, and Mark could tell that a number of questions were on the tip of Sky's tongue. She held them in, however, and simply acknowledged his words, agreeing to meet up with him a few blocks away. Mark jogged down the street, pondering his strange hesitance to meet with Phoenix. His worry wasn't about the fight itself but rather about the thought of having to face Phoenix once the fight was over.

When he joined Sky on the roof of a building six blocks away, his heart was still in turmoil, and he had no greater clarity. Sky was watching the fight.

"Things have pretty much calmed down," she said, glancing at Mark.

He plopped himself down next to her as he tried to observe the figures in the distance. For a moment, everything was quiet, though Mark could faintly make out the occasional clash of weapons, as well as Phoenix flying above the crowd, unleashing attacks toward the few remaining Exlian. Mark's gaze lingered on her.

"Why are you avoiding her?" Sky asked.

Her question was much blunter than anticipated, and when he turned, he found Sky staring straight at him, her eyes alive with curiosity. Finding his feelings difficult to articulate, Mark shrugged, causing the two bone blade arms above his shoulders to wave. "I don't think I'm afraid . . ."

"Really? How else would you explain it? I know she thinks you're dead, but shouldn't she get to know the truth?"

"I . . . I don't think that's a good idea."

"Okay, but even if you don't want her to know it's you . . . you could just keep your helmet up, and she would have no idea. Mark, you don't look anything like you did before. In fact, as long as you keep your helmet on, there's pretty much no way that she would associate you with the Mark she knew. You're obviously scared."

Feeling his cheeks flush, Mark was glad that he was wearing a full face mask. "That's . . . that's true. I mean, the first part. Not the being-scared part."

As he spoke, Mark turned to look at Phoenix in the distance and heard Sky giggle. "You really like her, don't you?"

"What?! No. What are you talking about?"

The words came out so quickly Mark didn't have time to stop them, and when he heard Sky's giggle turn into a full-throated laugh, he knew he was sunk.

"Ha! I knew it. Oh, that's so cute. Does Noah know? He's got to, right? If you like her, why don't you go say hi?"

Mark's shoulders slumped. "I'd like to, but as far as she knows, I'm dead. Apart from you and Noah, there are only a few other people who know I'm alive. I just . . . I don't know how to start that conversation. I mean, what am I supposed to say? 'Hey, Phoenix, remember how you thought I was totally dead? I'm actually not, but I've been keeping that information from you.' What if she's mad? I mean, I'd be pretty angry if someone I . . . someone I knew pretended to be dead."

"You were about to say 'liked,'" Sky said, leaning in to poke Mark in the shoulder. "Does she like you back?"

"I mean, yeah, I think so. We were supposed to go on a date before I got hauled off to jail. But I never made it."

"All the more reason you should let her know you're alive," Sky said, her voice losing its teasing tone. "I mean, you have to decide how you want to handle your own relationships. But if it was me, if I was her, I'd certainly want to know."

"You're right," Mark said with a sigh. "I just . . . Honestly, it makes me nervous."

"Says the man who will face down a horde of monsters without batting an eye," Sky said with a smile. "It's nice to know that you feel fear too. Makes you more human."

Mark didn't quite know how to respond to that comment, and thankfully, Sky quickly changed the subject after glancing at the sun setting in the distance.

"Well, I'm gonna need to get back to the city, and it looks like the fight over there is all done. Do you want me to find a chance to tell Phoenix?"

"No," Mark said, shaking his head. "If anybody's gonna tell her, it should be me. I think somebody else mentioning it would only make it worse."

Feeling a hand on his shoulder, Mark looked over and saw Sky staring at him with a gaze full of concern. "Mark, I think you need to talk to her. I know it makes you nervous, but you need connection. We all need connection. Life is so much easier with other people. Believe me, this is something I'm intimately aware of. Life has dealt you a bad hand. I get it, but isolating yourself out here in the wilderness, that's not going to help you. I don't want to pressure you, but if there's any way that I can help facilitate things with Phoenix, I mean, just let me know."

Letting his helmet peel back from his face, Mark flashed a smile. "Thanks, Sky."

For a moment, they just looked at each other, and then, to Mark's surprise, Sky stepped forward and wrapped her arms around him, giving him a squeeze. "I think you're great, Mark. I really do. Just remember that there are a lot of people who care about you. Well, maybe not a lot, but at least a few, and that's all that really matters."

Chuckling at her own joke, Sky let go, and a moment later she was a dozen feet above Mark, hanging in the air. "I've got to head back to the city, but thank you so much for helping me practice today. I have another day off next week, if you wouldn't mind me tagging along again."

"Anytime, Sky," Mark said. "Anytime."

"All right, I'll hold you to that. See you later."

Her body blurred and she was gone, drawing a streak toward the city wall in the distance. Mark sank into a crouch and rested his forehead in his palm with a light groan, his feelings in turmoil. There had been a time when Mark had fantasized about having a romantic relationship with Sky, but it was obvious that they were nothing but friends. Mark found he didn't mind it at all. His feelings for Phoenix were much more complicated, and it was with some embarrassment that he recalled the conversation he had just had with Sky.

Hearing a faint noise behind him, he glanced over his shoulder and saw his own head pop up over the side of the building. A moment later, his clone, still holding the sniper rifle, climbed up onto the roof and merged back with him, bringing memories of his ranged fight.

After hesitating for a moment, Mark lifted the sniper rifle, using the sight to get a clearer picture of Phoenix and her team. They were organizing to retreat, and Mark's gaze lingered on Phoenix, whose suit showed considerable wear and tear from the battle. Despite the damage she had taken, Phoenix moved with confidence, organizing her remaining men to coordinate with the reinforcements. Fifteen minutes later, their team began to retreat.

Mark had been watching them this whole time, wrestling with himself about how he should handle the situation. Though it was likely a coincidence, Phoenix seemed rather reluctant to go, and before turning back to the city, she scanned the dead zone, her eyes brushing past Mark's location not once but twice. Through his scope, Mark could see her confused expression clearly.

His involvement in the fight had largely been hidden, yet Phoenix seemed to have picked up on something. Lowering the sniper rifle, Mark slipped it into his shadow and stood up, letting out a sigh as he turned away. He knew that telling Phoenix he was still alive was the right decision, and he couldn't exactly explain why the thought of doing so made him so nervous.

Regardless, now wasn't the time. There were too many threats, too many enemies, too many dangers, dangers that would undoubtedly attach themselves to Phoenix once she was made aware of his presence. Of course, Mark knew that these were just excuses, reasons to avoid telling her the truth, but they provided at least a modicum of comfort to his unsettled soul.

Looking down at his wrist, Mark checked his biofuel and saw that it was full, thanks to the Exlian and raiders he had just chomped on. Dismissing the windows with a thought, Mark broke into a run, dashing for the edge of the building and leaping out into the air to land effortlessly on the roof of the building across the street.

His body was full of nervous energy, so instead of finding a place to rest for the night, Mark threw himself into hunting, slaying every Exlian he came across. A few of the fights were fierce, messy affairs, but Mark excelled in chaotic brawls and came out on top every time, almost never the worse for wear, using the punishing fights to work out his tangled emotions.

By the time dawn had come, peace had returned to Mark's heart. Though he still didn't know when he was going to let Phoenix know that he was still alive, the fights had sharpened his mind, clarifying for him that what he needed to be focusing on now was the apex hunter. By the time the sun had truly risen, Mark was back on the outskirts of the apex hunter's territory, looking for signs of where it might be.

The majority of the area comprised mansions that sat along

winding, wooded streets surrounded by large gardens, all overgrown after years and years of neglect. After taking a moment to survey the area, Mark plunged into the underbrush, weaving his way through the shade of the trees, while keeping his senses open for any sign of the apex hunter. The first thing he noticed was just how quiet everything was. Out in the wilderness, it was common to hear the faint sounds of insects and vermin. But the shaded streets Mark passed down were entirely silent, save for the faint sound of his feet against the crumbling concrete.

Whether this was due to the apex hunter or the presence of something else, Mark wasn't sure, but it caused him to slow down and pay careful attention to his surroundings. After about an hour of careful wandering, he discovered his first clue: an old sports car that sat not on the street but halfway into someone's yard, its once-sleek form marred by half a dozen claw marks.

From the looks of it, the car had been picked up and thrown before coming to a crashing stop in this spot. Of course, given the rust dotting the frame, it was possible that this had happened during the initial assault of the city, but the claw marks appeared to be more recent, potentially even from within the last year. There was no rust inside them, indicating that they hadn't been exposed to the elements for long.

After casting around for a while, Mark didn't find anything else, but he didn't give up. "Mime, can you track this thing?" he asked, running his finger over one of the sheared pieces of metal.

His black cat materialized next to him and began to do her own looking around before eventually sitting a dozen feet from the car. Looking over, Mark didn't see anything at first, since the spot was bare concrete. He crouched next to her, his eyes searching the ground, but it was only after he noticed her tail whipping back and forth that he realized there were faint scratches on the concrete, as if something had violently brushed over it.

"Is that the creature's tail?" Mark asked, his fingers lightly passing across the scrapes.

Mime nodded and stood up, beginning to trot away. How exactly she was able to track an opponent after so long, Mark wasn't sure, but he kept pace, jogging down the shaded streets between giant oak trees that had to be at least 150 years old. After close to half an hour, Mime came to a stop outside a massive mansion whose gate had been twisted off and lay in a heap between two large stone pillars shaped like lions. Taking a moment to examine the long driveway, Mark didn't see any immediate danger, and even when he swept the psychic network, he didn't sense anything.

That in itself was rather strange, as the dead zone was bursting with Exlian, though most of them hibernated underground during the daytime. That only convinced Mark even more that this was the home of the apex hunter, and with Mime on his shoulder, he began to make his way onto the mansion's grounds. Paying careful attention to the psychic network, he proceeded cautiously. The truth was that he had no idea exactly what he was walking into. He had faced off against an apex hunter before, but they had never actually fought. At the time, he had been much weaker, and he knew without a doubt that if it hadn't been for Mime's presence, the Exlian apex hunter could have killed him with a single claw.

Over the last year, Mark had grown much stronger, but that didn't mean that he'd fare any better now. He had a vague sense of this Exlian's fighting style from the scattered images the earth rat nest had given him. But even as he advanced onto the mansion's grounds, he was fully ready to turn and run as fast as possible if he found himself outmatched.

Despite how long it had been since the grounds had had any maintenance, the long driveway was mostly clear, with the occasional tuft of grass sticking up from the cracked asphalt. The driveway ended in a large circle with a dried-up fountain in the center and a wide staircase that led up to the front door.

The mansion itself was in relatively good shape, but Mark knew that appearances could be deceiving. He considered going through the front door, then thought better of it and elected to circle around the mansion, looking for another way in. He found two: a side entrance that led into what he assumed was the servants' quarters, and a back entrance composed of a dozen glass doors that led out onto a terrace.

Electing to use the side entrance, Mark carefully eased open the door and stepped into the mansion. Though he had no way of knowing, he imagined that he was the first human to set foot in the mansion since it had been abandoned fifty years ago. Though in his case, *human* was a relative term.

Pausing in the long hallway, Mark carefully examined the psychic network, looking for any sign of his enemy's presence. He found it more unnerving than comforting that he didn't sense a single thing. Glancing at Mime, who still sat on his shoulder, he saw that she had crouched, and the fur on the back of her neck was slightly raised. Her nervousness was a clear indication that there was an enemy about, but the fact that Mark had no way of finding it through the psychic network meant that, like Mark himself, it was probably shrouded.

Of course, he hadn't come this far to just hang out in the hallway, so Mark slowly made his way forward, his senses on full alert, checking the rooms he passed by. There was a door to the kitchen, another to a pantry, and still another that opened to a dark stairway leading to the basement. Hoping that he wouldn't have to go down there, Mark continued to the end of the hall, where a short flight of steps led up to another doorway, this one opening into the grand hall.

Cracking the door open an inch, Mark did his best to look through the gap. When he didn't see anything moving, he opened the door a little wider and slipped out, his eyes scanning the grand hall for any sign of the enemy. It was large, nearly forty feet high, and incredibly ornate, with detailed carvings and gold leaf covering almost every inch of the walls and ceiling.

Though it wasn't anymore, gold had once been of tremendous value to humanity, and the sheer quantity visible from where he stood indicated that whoever had owned this mansion had been among the richest humans in Emery before the city fell. Any other time, Mark would have enjoyed looking around, but at the moment, his nerves were too taut, and he found his eyes darting to the dark corners and the areas where thick shadow fell.

There were a number of statues in the room, and he found them unnerving, imagining that they might suddenly begin to move and even attack him. Shaking his head at the silly thought, Mark crept through the room, his feet making no sound on the thick rugs. A heavy layer of dust covered everything, and no matter how careful he was, Mark's feet caused little puffs to rise into the air.

At the end of the grand hall was another staircase, this one winding up a full two floors to the upper levels. The stairs were pure white marble, hardly touched by the decades they had sat unused. Mark had noticed that Mime's gaze had never once left the upper floor since they had entered the great hall, and he could only imagine that that was where he would find their enemy.

Fortifying himself with a quiet but deep breath, Mark put his foot on the staircase, intending to go up, when he caught a flash of movement above him and raised his head. He froze as he saw a long-limbed monster with no features, its head tilted toward him. He had already seen images of the apex hunter, but seeing it in person was completely different.

Vaguely humanoid, the creature had two thick legs that were clearly built for explosive speed. A long, hunched torso held four arms that draped all the way down below its feet as it crouched at the top of the stairs. Each long, sinewy arm ended in three curved claws with jagged serrations at their tips, optimized for tearing rather than cutting. Behind the monster, Mark could see two tails extending into the air, their tips pointing at him.

Mark stood stock still, his full attention on the apex hunter, and it stared back, its head tilted slightly to the side, as if curious. Like the other one he had seen, this monster had a featureless bone mask over its face, leaving Mark wondering how it could see him so clearly. He felt a slight weight on his shoulder vanish, and though he didn't dare look back, he felt Mime sink into his shadow. She clearly wasn't planning on helping him this time, which Mark found both exasperating and gratifying. He hoped that leaving him to fend for himself was at least a mark of her confidence in him.

For a long moment, Mark stood at the bottom of the stairs, one foot on the staircase and the other on the wooden floor, his gaze locked on the Exlian apex hunter above him. It didn't move either, remaining so still he might have mistaken it for a strange gargoyle if he didn't know any better.

Then a heavy mental presence descended, crashing into Mark's mind with the particular intensity he had come to expect from Exlian communication. At first, it was a tangled, jumbled mess, a torrent of thoughts, feelings, images, and sounds, forming a discordant explosion in Mark's mind. He winced as he tried to sort through everything, eventually picking up what he thought was the main thread of the apex hunter's thoughts.

MY HUNTING GROUNDS.

Mixed in with the declaration were a thousand other messages. The hunter was hungry, ravenously so, and desperate to improve its power. There was curiosity about Mark's form, along with a fragmented assessment of what his abilities might be, given how his body was shaped. There was a record of kills, a list of foes hunted and vanquished, including a number of nests. There was a sense of distance, and the images of countless mountains and the valleys between them, along with plains and a shimmering blue ocean. Clearly, the apex hunter had come far.

What Mark found most distracting, however, was a strident thought that carried deep fear and anticipation in equal measure, focused on something in the heart of New Emery.

The confusing tangle of thoughts and feelings subsided, giving Mark the chance to sort through them. The apex hunter remained perched at the top of the staircase, clearly waiting for some sort of response.

Mark wasn't sure how to answer. After all, he couldn't very well tell the monster that he was here to kill it, though he had a sneaking suspicion that the apex hunter already knew. After considering for a moment, Mark did his best to pull together all his memories from the dead zone and projected them toward the apex hunter, along with the clear feeling that all this territory was his.

The rejection was immediate, and for the first time, the apex hunter moved, its tails whipping behind it as it crouched. If it had eyes, they would undoubtedly be fixed on Mark. Instead, the creature just shifted its head forward slightly. Mark, for his part, doubled down, projecting his feeling with even greater intensity. At the same time, he began to recall his own victories: fighting the Exlian brain, killing the screamers, and devouring the baeloth.

Whatever effect he thought that the parade of victories might have, it did not. The apex hunter responded with scorn, clearly unimpressed by Mark's hunting record. Realizing that he might have inadvertently revealed weakness, Mark was about to back up when the Exlian struck. It flashed from the top of the stairs two stories above to a step in front of him. Its body created a stream of afterimages in the air like a line of quicksilver that only faded after it passed. It moved so quickly that Mark wondered if it had some sort of teleportation ability, but when its arm whipped into his side, activating his mana shield, he realized that it was pure speed.

The blow slammed into him with such force that Mark was thrown off his feet and tumbled head over heels back into the great hall. Unleashing a psychic scream that disoriented his senses, the apex hunter was on top of him before he had even come to a stop. Both its tails stabbed toward his legs. One of them was blocked by a mana shield, though the force of the blow caused the shield to crack. The other glanced off his bone carapace, leaving a deep gouge in his armor.

Seeing the apex hunter lifting its arms to slash him, Mark scrambled away, barely evading the attack. As he jumped up, his own bone blade arms slashed at the monster's chest. But almost contemptuously, it flashed backward, reappearing ten feet away from him. Its legs were coiled under it like a spring, and its four long arms were held out from its body, claws pointing toward Mark.

It was only then that Mark managed to catch his breath. The creature he faced couldn't have anything lower than A-ranked speed, though its strength didn't seem that much higher than his. In fact, as Mark mentally reviewed its attack, he realized that it was actually weaker, carrying significantly less piercing power. Of course, given the speed at which it moved, that almost didn't matter.

Shifting into a defensive stance, Mark watched the Exlian as it used two of its four arms to swing its body to the side. Its head continually pointed toward Mark as it began to circle him. Mark watched it carefully, only to find himself lulled into a strange trance as he anticipated its next movement. When instead it moved in the opposite direction so quickly that his eyes couldn't follow it, he found himself extra thankful for the mana shield, which deployed to block its slashing claws.

Once again, he was sent stumbling, though this time he managed to keep his feet. His counterattack caught nothing but air as the apex hunter once again darted backward. Mark had had all sorts of contingency plans in mind if he found his foe too strong, but the majority of them were now completely useless in the face of the apex hunter's overwhelming speed.

His best option, of course, was to retreat to an enclosed area, somewhere the predator would have less maneuverability. Yet even as he tried to edge toward the doorway leading down into the servants' hallway, the hunter seemed to anticipate his move and shifted to cut him off.

Letting out another psychic shriek, the apex hunter darted forward and unleashed a barrage of claw strikes, ripping and tearing at Mark in an effort to shred his armor. Thankfully, most of the attacks weren't simultaneous, which allowed Mark's mana shield to block the majority of them. The others scraped across his armor, leaving jagged gashes that soon began to heal up thanks to his regeneration.

Of course, Mark knew this wasn't a long-term solution. His biofuel was already draining faster as it was forced to both support his mana shields and repair his armor. He fought back as best he could, attacking with his own bone blades. Yet he found that he could barely touch the Exlian. Its movements were simply too fast, and anytime he counterattacked, it would simply shift its body out of the way.

For a tense few minutes, he and the predator fought back and forth, though to Mark it felt more like a one-sided beating than anything else. Realizing he couldn't continue the fight, he suddenly broke free and rushed toward the front door. The apex hunter followed, slipping past Mark to get in front of him, since it knew that attacking him from behind wouldn't help. Putting even more power into his charge, Mark dropped to one knee, sliding across the smooth wooden floor and raising a cloud of dust. Indifferent, the Exlian predator attacked through the cloud, only to find its claws failing to connect. Startled, it let out a psychic scream when it couldn't locate Mark.

Outside the mansion, on the other side of the closed door, Mark stumbled, nearly dropping to one knee as pain assaulted his body. He could feel his biofuel dropping rapidly as his regeneration tried to repair the damage teleporting had done to his body. He nearly missed the first step and half stumbled, half slid down the stairs to the driveway.

There was a sudden crash behind him, and the heavy wooden door that had stood undisturbed for fifty years exploded outward. Realizing he was about to have the apex hunter on his tail, Mark gritted his teeth and took off running, heading straight for the gardens. The driveway would have been a straighter shot, but he had no illusion that he'd be able to beat the apex hunter in a race. So instead, he opted for the tangle of vegetation in the overgrown gardens, hoping to use his stealth abilities to throw his pursuer off.

The hunter paused at the top of the stairs for just a moment before coming after him, but Mark was already scrambling into the underbrush, putting all his mental effort into shrouding his body. A moment later, the bush he had just dived through was shredded by a dozen fierce claw strikes. Mark had already scrambled away, and he quickly gained distance. Though the apex hunter was obviously faster than him, its senses didn't seem to be that well developed. Instead, if Mark was right, it relied almost entirely on its superior mental abilities, using them to identify and track its prey.

Now that Mark was out of sight and shrouded, it seemed to have lost him, and he continued to crawl away from the house, even as it destroyed the garden behind him. Having bought himself a respite, though likely a brief one, Mark tried to figure out what to do next.

The apex hunter was smart, at least as smart as him, and likely an even better hunter. Worse, its speed outclassed his by an entire rank, which meant that it would be nigh impossible for him to land a solid blow, unless he could somehow lull the Exlian into a false sense of security. That, Mark knew, was going to be impossible. Exlian didn't have a sense of security in the first place. They operated entirely on instinct, and the hunter's instincts were clearly much better developed than Mark's.

The only other option was forcing it to face him directly while restricting its movements. His only chance of doing that was to lure it into a confined space, which would likely be impossible, or to simply surround it with enough enemies that it couldn't easily escape.

All these thoughts passed through Mark's head in the few moments that it took him to crawl through the garden. When he arrived at the other side, he rose to his feet and took off, rushing toward the wall that surrounded the mansion. It was eight feet high, but Mark cleared it with a single leap and heard a heavy mental shriek behind him.

Gritting his teeth, Mark sprinted as fast as he could down the street toward the next mansion. He risked a glance over his shoulder and saw that the Exlian had made it to the wall. It must have caught his movement as he leaped, and now it was perched on the spot he had just crossed over, its eyeless gaze fixed on him.

Racking his brain for a solution, Mark hopped over the wall in front of him and tore through the grounds of the estate. He could feel the apex hunter closing in and knew that within a couple of minutes, he would be forced back into a fight, one that he likely wouldn't escape from.

Use all your advantages.

Mime's words rang clearly in Mark's mind, and for a moment, he had no idea what she was talking about. Then, at the edge of his consciousness, he felt the presence of more Exlian. Without hesitating, he sent out a mental message, commanding the Exlian to come toward him and protect him. Once again, he had no idea if it would work, and he was almost caught off guard when the nearest Exlian began rushing in his direction. He felt the apex hunter pause slightly, adjusting to the additional enemies, but Mark didn't stop, continuing his mad dash forward as his mental command echoed through the network. Dozens of Exlian that had been hibernating tunneled up out of the ground and took a brief moment to get their bearings before rushing toward Mark and the apex hunter, which was rapidly closing in behind him.

The nearby Exlian included weak drones and slightly stronger warriors, and though not all of them responded to his call, the majority seemed eager to defend Mark. It was bizarre to watch the Exlian stream past him, paying no attention as he ran among them.

It wasn't long before the first one attacked the apex hunter. Mark had been watching its mental signature closely and saw it wink out as the hunter tore it in half with a casual strike. The attack of a single Exlian hadn't slowed it down, but Mark was counting on the weight of numbers.

Reaching the other end of the property, he sensed a large distant group approaching to figure out what was going on. They had been awoken by the echoes of Mark's yells in the psychic network, and the residual echo of Mark's command caused them to draw near.

Mark was about to leap over the wall when there was a sudden flash, and he skidded to a halt as the apex hunter appeared on the wall in front of him. Its body carried a heavy tension, and Mark's mind was immediately assaulted by its powerful mental wave.

YOU CANNOT ESCAPE MY HUNT.

"Believe it or not, I'm aware of that," Mark muttered under his breath, "but I'm also not trying to escape."

Though the last part wasn't quite true, Mark still felt better after saying it. He didn't reply to the apex hunter's mental communication, except to command all the Exlian closing in to attack. Three-quarters of them did, speeding up as they launched themselves toward the apex hunter. The last quarter did the opposite, fleeing as far from the battle as they could. The apex hunter let out a mental shriek and launched itself at Mark, only for a drone to jump in the way, sacrificing itself on the hunter's claws to protect Mark from the blow.

Though such protection was unnecessary, Mark didn't let it go to waste, his shadow reaching out to devour the bisected halves of the drone. At the same time, he launched his own attack, lifting the crossbow that he had retrieved and unleashing a bolt at point-blank range. Unlike the sniper rifle, which required a few seconds to charge between shots, the bolt was immediately ready to go, and it ripped through the air with such speed that the apex hunter didn't manage to dodge entirely.

There was a shriek as the apex hunter fell back, blood spraying from its side where the bolt had clipped it. Backpedaling, Mark retreated as three half-centipede, half-rodent Exlian warriors, each the size of a small horse, charged his opponent. He feverishly reloaded his crossbow as he watched the warriors fail to land even a single blow on the apex hunter.

Though he hadn't expected them to do any real damage, Mark had been hoping that they would at least tie the monster down for a minute or so. Instead, he bought himself only twenty seconds before the last of the warriors fell to the apex hunter's flashing claws. It seemed to sneer at him, and even as he lifted the crossbow, one of its claws waved, and three blades of pure mana shot toward him.

One crashed into the crossbow, cutting clear through it and

causing it to fail to fire. The second and third slammed into his chest, shattering the mana shield that he had raised. The realization that the apex hunter could leverage mana for ranged attacks was terrifying, and Mark ducked a second set of mana blades, even as more Exlian launched their attacks.

It quickly became apparent to Mark that though his new tactic of swarming the apex hunter with friendly local Exlian wasn't going to work, it was at least buying him breathing room. Of course, what to do with that breathing room was the challenge, and to Mark it felt almost hopeless to launch any attacks, as the hunter would simply dodge everything that he or the other Exlian threw at it.

Mark, knowing that he was living on borrowed time, tried everything that came to mind, including a fierce mental assault intended to overwhelm the monster. It hardly flinched and responded with mana blades and slashing claws, forcing him into a desperate defense.

Even as they fought, more Exlian threw themselves into the fight, and more than once Mark found himself accidentally cutting apart one of his strange bug allies. Regardless of how they died, Mark absorbed all of them, devouring them with his shadow to replenish his rapidly depleting biofuel. At the moment, it seemed his only advantage, but to his dismay, the apex hunter seemed equally able to maintain its energy expenditures.

The one thing that seemed to be working in Mark's favor was that, due to the sheer number of bodies, the apex hunter could only get to him when it fought in close quarters. This gave Mark a slight advantage, as he had two more arms than the predator, though that was largely balanced by the creature's whipping tails.

It was only after they had been tangled together for a few minutes that Mark finally landed his first real blow, laying open a wide gash on the apex hunter's bony chest. The creature let out a shriek of pain and exploded into motion, its claws flying so fast

Mark saw nothing but a blur. He felt his mana shields shatter, attempt to re-form, and then shatter again under the relentless barrage, and soon he could feel his carapace starting to crack.

He responded with a heavy kick, attempting to knock the creature back, only to nearly have his foot torn off as the apex hunter reached out to grab it with two hands, intending to pinch through Mark's armor. Worried he'd lose a foot, Mark struck with all four bone blades, forcing the hunter to back off. Its claws left ragged wounds on Mark's ankle, but thankfully, they began to heal immediately.

As Mark's bone blades stabbed into thin air, completely missing their mark, the apex hunter lifted its claws and hacked down toward him, unleashing three more mana blades. Immediately, it flashed to the side and unleashed another three, neatly boxing Mark in and preventing him from throwing himself backward to escape the first set of attacks.

Mark, whose nerves had been stretched tight, felt an unprecedented sense of danger as the apex hunter crouched, the muscles in its legs tightening as it got ready to leap. Unable to avoid the mana blades, Mark could tell that he was locked into the path of the attack, and he had a sinking feeling that if it struck, it would kill him instantly.

As adrenaline spiked through his body, a deep calm flooded his mind, as if everything in the world had been wiped away: all color, all sound, all feeling and distraction. Mark felt as if he were observing the world through a completely new pair of eyes. Acting more on instinct than anything else, he took a small step forward and lifted his hand like a blade to face off against the charging apex hunter.

As the world grayed out, he found himself seeing everything around him as mana, including the apex hunter surging toward him. His instinct was to protect himself, so he began to extend his null field to block the incoming mana blades. At the same time, he knew that having the null field active when the main attack arrived would leave him without his mana shield, so he flicked his finger. A pulse from the orb of null energy at the back of his neck ran down his arm to that finger, where it was coated in mental energy and carried into the air.

His mind, sensing that it wasn't sharp enough, focused in further, causing even the black-and-white world to begin to fade until there was nothing but the sliver of null energy he had just projected. Then everything snapped back to normal, and the apex hunter let out a horrifying shriek. It was still a few feet away from Mark, but a terrifying wound had appeared on its mask, cutting from the top of its head straight down through its chin.

Stumbling backward, the apex hunter spasmed as it fell to the ground, and Mark felt his legs weakening, as if a tremendous amount of energy had just been sucked out of him. The Exlian surrounding them rushed toward the predator, clearly intending to finish it off, but before they could, Mime emerged from Mark's shadow, darting between his legs and leaping toward the apex hunter.

Immediately, the other Exlian veered away and rapidly vanished, clearly wanting nothing to do with the small black cat. Mark felt his biofuel meter surge as more of the corpses he had consumed during the fight were processed, and when he finally managed to stabilize his footing, he realized that he was alone with the apex hunter. His armor was in tatters, and he could feel a deep exhaustion in his soul, but that did nothing to dampen his excitement. He wasn't entirely sure how he had managed to wound the apex hunter, but he at least had an inkling of an idea and was confident that with enough practice, he'd be able to replicate it.

The apex hunter lay on the ground, still thrashing, but Mark could tell that it was already dead. His attack had been completely unexpected, and the Exlian had run headfirst into the strange blade he had projected. What was most bizarre to Mark was that the blade had not used mana at all but instead had borrowed power from his null field.

Somehow, his mental energy had refined it further, creating an impossibly sharp blade projected from his finger that had bisected the apex hunter's head by severing the mana it encountered. Glancing down at Mime, who was staring up at him with an eerily happy smile, Mark could only smile in return.

On an almost instinctual level, he knew what he needed to do next, and as the apex hunter's thrashing began to calm, Mark reached down and grabbed one of its limbs. His shadow eagerly surged up around it, swallowing both the hunter and Mime. For a moment, Mark thought he saw eight glowing red eyes appear in his shadow, but then it subsided, leaving nothing behind.

Getting to his feet, Mark headed back toward the mansion where he had originally discovered the hunter, trusting that he wouldn't be bothered in its lair. He could already feel his shadow working to consume the creature, and he wondered what sort of effect it would have on him.

It took him almost ten minutes to make it back to the mansion, and after picking his way through the smashed front door, Mark climbed the stairs at the back of the great hall and found a room on the second floor. Most of its furniture had been destroyed, torn to shreds to form a nest of sorts, and it was here that Mark settled down, sitting cross-legged in the center of the debris.

Remembering his struggle against both the war bear and the cataphract, Mark fully anticipated a mental struggle, but to his surprise, the apex hunter's imprint seemed to bear no animosity toward him. He could sense the remnant spirit of the creature clearly, yet it didn't seem to mind at all that he had just killed it and devoured its corpse. Instead, the apex hunter's remnant mental imprint seemed almost eager to join with him, and it melded into him flawlessly.

As soon as it did, Mark felt his muscles begin to twist and squirm as they were rapidly optimized to incorporate the apex hunter's improved speed. He could feel his mask starting to change as well, gaining the pair of long horns that had extended back from the apex hunter's head. After a moment of thought, Mark didn't stop them from growing, though he did work to guide them, shortening them slightly so they wouldn't get in the way of his bone blade arms. Those blades changed as well, lengthening slightly and gaining the jagged edge that the apex hunter's claws had carried.

Your speed has increased from B– to B.
Your speed has increased from B to B+.
Your speed has increased from B+ to A–.
Your will has increased from B+ to A–.

The greatest change Mark felt was the complete overhaul of his muscles, rebuilding them to give his entire body increased speed. He immediately knew that his speed, while not as fast as his foe's had been, had just gotten a drastic upgrade. But his attention was on something else. Along with the improvement in speed came a strange, instinctive understanding of how the apex hunter had formed mana blades using its claw attacks. To Mark, it felt that doing the same would be as simple as slashing the air. Yet he found when he tried it that no mana blades emerged.

It took him a few minutes to figure out why, and when he did, a broad smile flashed across his face. When the apex hunter had slashed its claws to produce a mana blade, it had drawn mana from a spot in the center of its chest where its mana gem had resided. Mark didn't have a mana gem, so there was nothing to draw power from.

Rather than be disappointed, Mark simply took a few minutes

to reorient his attack, drawing from the bead of null energy in the back of his neck instead of from the center of his chest. The result was astonishing: a blade of null energy that shot out from his finger and only dispersed upon hitting the door some twenty feet away. This was the basic form of the attack Mark had just used. He didn't know if it was genuinely the same as the third level of the Cutting Palm that Master Abrams had spoken of, the Body as the Sword, but he suspected that it was.

Mark could feel that his mind had broken through a shackle he had never even known had bound it, allowing him to more freely project his mental energy into the world around him. With enough practice, he had no doubt that he would be able to transform his mental energy into a blade, throwing it forward in the same way as the apex hunter had.

He could already project his null energy in the same way, and the two powers, when combined, transformed into an even more fearsome attack, forming an unstoppable blade that felt as if it could cut through anything. Whether that was true, Mark wasn't sure, but he had a sneaking suspicion that when he finally mastered the attack, he would find it his most potent weapon.

It took Mark a few hours to completely assimilate the apex hunter's body, and when he finally finished, he felt like a brand-new man. Or man-Exlian, as it were.

Getting to his feet, Mark stretched, his bone blade arms stretching as well. With a faint crackling sound, they extended another few inches, and Mark suddenly realized that he had gotten taller. Taking a step forward, he could immediately feel the difference. There was a smoothness to his movements that he had lacked before, though he had never realized it. It was as if a whole new world had opened up in front of him, allowing him to navigate his surroundings more freely. Mark had heard that some empowered took time to get used to their new abilities when they ranked up. His, however, were so fully integrated into his body that he found himself immediately understanding how to deal with his increased speed. He wondered if his improved will played a part in that.

Mark hopped up and down, then burst forward and crashed through the door that sealed the room in an explosion of wooden splinters, his bone blades tearing it to pieces. The sound echoed through the mansion, and Mark's sharp hearing caught an exclamation from downstairs. It was only then that he realized other people were in the mansion, and a frown flashed across his face.

With a thought, his cataphract armor extended to cover his head, forming his new mask. At the same time, Mark shrouded his presence and moved quietly down the hall, away from the stairwell. Less than a minute later, he heard the clatter of heavy metal boots on the marble staircase and murmured conversation.

"I'm telling you, there's something here. I heard a crash."

Slipping into a nearby room, Mark made his way to the window and peeked out of it, pausing when he saw a group of empowered in mana suits gathered at the front of the mansion. The improvements to his will had made his connection to the psychic network even stronger, allowing him to track the group of three currently walking up the stairs. The fifteen others outside the building wore crimson-and-black mana suits with no markings and the typical profusion of weaponry common to raiders.

Feeling a flash of annoyance, Mark considered simply leaping out the window and killing all of them. His hand was already on the window sash when he stopped himself. There was no guarantee that he was right about the group, and even if they were raiders, Mark hadn't seen them doing anything wrong, so simply wiping them out would make him no better than them.

After considering the situation for a moment, Mark decided to give them an opportunity and walked over to the door. He retracted his mask to reveal his bare face so they didn't mistake him for an Exlian, and then, after fumbling with the door handle, he stepped into the hall. He froze when he saw the three people at the top of the stairs. All three of them wore full face masks, tinted so Mark couldn't see their faces, but one of them, whose suit was slightly smaller than the others', stepped forward, leveling a crossbow at Mark's chest.

"Stay right where you are," she said, her voice crackling slightly as it came through the suit's speakers. "Who are you? What are you doing here?"

"I'm a freelance hunter," Mark replied. "The name's Jonathan Leeds. I have my badge and everything."

Sharing a glance with the others, the woman shook her head slightly. "You're pretty far out for solo hunting."

Mark shrugged and reached for his belt pouch, pausing when he saw the woman's finger tightening on the trigger of her crossbow.

"I'm just trying to get my ID," he said, his voice calm.

After hesitating for a moment, the woman gave a sharp nod, and Mark retrieved his ID with two fingers and held it out for them to see. One of the men with her stepped forward and grabbed it, taking a look.

"Looks to be in order," he said. "Hold on, let me run a scan."

Mark wasn't quite sure what he intended to do, but the others were still watching him, so he remained in place. After a moment, the man who had taken Mark's ID chuckled. "Looks like there is no record of him leaving the city, which means he must have sneaked out."

With a sinking feeling, Mark saw the woman's eyebrows rise, a ghost of a smile hovering on her lips. Though he didn't want any trouble, it was clear to him where this conversation was going.

Sure enough, the man holding his ID laughed and tossed it over the railing. "That means nobody will miss you."

At the same time, the woman who had her crossbow trained on Mark's chest pulled the trigger, and both of the men lunged forward, lifting their mana blades. To Mark, it looked like they were moving in slow motion, and with a wry smile, he realized how foolish he had truly been to try to fight the apex hunter. Now that he was on the other side, he realized that it must have been playing with him. Even the bolt shooting out of the crossbow was moving slowly enough that Mark was confident he could react. Not that he needed to, of course.

With a thought, his cataphract armor rose, encasing his head.

Four bone blade arms erupted from the back of his suit, two of them attacking the raider on the right, while the other two went for the raider on the left.

With the crossbow bolt heading straight for his chest, Mark just stepped forward, bracing himself slightly as the bolt impacted dead center. At such close range, the force behind the bolt was impressive, and it actually managed to shatter his mana shield. But by that point its momentum was so spent that it simply bounced off his armor, even as his blades stabbed straight through the two raiders.

The attacks were so fast they didn't have time to respond, and Mark knew enough about mana suits to pick their weak points. Both men died before they knew what hit them, and the female raider at the top of the stairs could only stare in astonishment as the tips of Mark's blades emerged through the raiders' backs.

Not wanting her to raise a fuss, Mark flicked one of his new blades of null energy at her, catching her in the throat just before her surprised exclamation burst from her lips. The blade ripped through her mana suit like it was paper, carried on through her throat, and cut through her spine, forming a neat slit. It only dispersed after sinking into the wood behind her as her body swayed and began to tumble down the stairs.

Before the corpse could fall, Mark was already beside it, grabbing the body by the shoulder. He was interested in examining the wound further but figured it would be a better idea to deal with the raiders outside first. As he walked down the stairs, his shadow rose up to swallow the three bodies. Rather than devour them immediately, he instead stored them, mostly to see if he could discover what identities they used in New Emery. The quality of their suits was impressive, though it was clear that they were built for speed and had relatively light armor.

When he got to the bottom of the stairs, Mark picked up his ID, stuck it in his pouch, and then considered what to do next.

Another fifteen raiders were outside the mansion, and as far as Mark was concerned, all of them were fair game. The fact that the scouts had immediately tried to kill him upon finding out his situation meant that none of them were worth keeping around. Plus he had a nagging feeling that he had seen some of these raiders before. Of course, where the feeling came from, he wasn't sure, since he had yet to see their faces.

After a moment of thought, Mark retreated back upstairs to the room he had hidden in before and got one of the corpses out of his shadow. It only took him a moment to unlatch the dead raider's helmet and exchange it for his own to see if he could listen to the team's conversation.

Taking the dead man's watch, Mark scrolled through the channels and chose the general one. Immediately, his headset was filled with chatter, none of it particularly important. A couple of raiders were discussing their plans for once they got back to the city. After a little while, Mark heard one of them complaining.

"What are we even doing out here? Did the boss say?"

Another voice joined the conversation. "Not precisely, no. All we're doing is dropping the device and then retreating. The rest will be handled by the mutants."

The first speaker, who showed up on the display as Karik, gave a disdainful snort. "You don't really think we can trust those maniacs, do you? They're barely even human."

Another speaker, identified on the display as Captain Rore, cut in. "Everyone, kill the chatter. Why haven't Clark and the others reported in?"

Immediately, the team went silent, and Mark saw a call coming through on a private channel. When he switched over to it, he heard, "Clark, check in."

There was silence, and then the voice came again. "Clark, check in."

Though he was tempted to answer the call, Mark ignored it and swapped back to the general channel.

"Team, we've got a situation. Clark is not responding. His devices are on, but I'm getting nothing back. He's been either incapacitated or killed. Prepare to move."

Pulling off the helmet, Mark tossed it next to the body and swallowed both with his shadow. He walked to the window and saw the raiders getting ready to breach the door. According to what he had heard, they were here to plant something. Something involving the mutants. Mark hadn't been too interested before, but now he found himself curious.

He waited until the raider team was inside the building before opening the window. It had been closed for countless years and jammed immediately, but he was able to force it open and squeeze outside without making too much noise. Dropping silently to the porch, Mark peeked through the door and saw the raiders checking all the rooms.

He hesitated for a moment, using the psychic network to identify the strongest of the empowered, then slipped inside, closing in on the raider closest to the door. He was hoping to take him out silently, but just before Mark reached him, the man turned to check the entrance, and his eyes widened as he caught sight of Mark.

One of Mark's blades shot out, piercing through the man's suit and deep into his heart. Though he didn't scream, the man jerked and his weapon clattered to the ground, causing the others to spin and look at Mark. Knowing he was in for a fight, Mark didn't hesitate and dashed forward, his blades tearing through three more raiders before anybody else could react.

All at once, Mark felt the floor underneath him buckle as if about to collapse. At the same time, beside him, stone rose and transformed into spikes that stabbed toward his ribs. Using a blade to parry the attack, Mark leaped into the air, only to get nailed by three crossbow bolts, which were immediately followed by a powerful blast from a mana rifle.

One of the bolts and the mana blast were blocked by Mark's shields, but the other two bolts got through, one deflecting off Mark's shoulder and the second cracking the armor over his stomach. Because he had been in the air, the impact of the four attacks sent Mark tumbling back toward the ground, but at the last moment, one of his blades punched into the wall, and he used the leverage to shift his momentum horizontally, slamming into another raider.

The raider tried to stab Mark with his mana sword, only to find it skipping off a mana shield that suddenly appeared. At the same time, Mark landed two solid blows on the man's chest, cutting straight through the armor of his mana suit. Though his strength was only B ranked, thanks to his Python's might, Mark could unleash one and a half times his normal strength, and his blow caused the man's suit to cave in. It was followed up by a sharp blade that tore through the collapsed defenses, killing the raider.

There was a loud shout, and a solid shield slammed into Mark, sending him tumbling backward. As he righted himself, he scanned the great hall, locating all his enemies. Of the fifteen, five were dead, leaving only ten remaining. A few of them had stepped into the rooms off the great hall and were only now starting to emerge.

Mark's main targets were the four near the back of the hall at the stairs. However, among them was the earth controller who had attacked Mark with the spike, along with two of the ranged attackers and a grizzled-looking man who appeared to be the team's leader. As soon as he saw the older man's face, Mark immediately knew where he had seen him before. He was a bodyguard who had accompanied Andre Javesi when he had come to talk to Mark in Gray Rock Prison.

Mark wanted to get to the bodyguard and beat the truth out of him, but first he would have to pass the massive, empowered brute currently standing in his way. As that raider was close to ten feet tall, with a suit made from thick, reinforced steel plates, Mark decided a head-on clash wasn't in his best interest. Still, he lowered his body as if about to charge, then shifted forward abruptly, causing the brute to settle into his defensive stance.

Instead of advancing, Mark dashed sideways, sprinting to the wall and running along it to evade the two crossbow bolts heading his way. He arrived at one of the side doors just as a raider stepped out, looking around for the source of the yelling he had heard. Mark hit him at full speed, driving him back into the room.

A few seconds later, there was a loud roar, and the doorway exploded as the brute smashed through it, taking out the jambs on either side in his haste. Looking around wildly, he didn't see anyone and froze in confusion.

Mark, upon entering the room, had used his blade arms to climb above the door, affixing himself to the wall while dragging the body of the raider he had slammed into. By the time the brute rushed in, Mark had stored the body. Too late, the brute sensed his presence and swung around, but Mark had already launched his attack.

He landed on the brute's back, two of his blades piercing through narrow chinks in the armor to help Mark keep his footing, even as his hands jabbed into the material that covered the back of the brute's neck. Normally, an Exlian in this position would simply rip and tear, trying to break through the tough armor, but Mark wasn't just an Exlian.

With deft fingers, he unclipped the brute's helmet, even as the man swung his body around with great force, attempting to dislodge Mark. There was a faint hiss as the pressure seal on the suit broke, and Mark's blades didn't hesitate, stabbing through the narrow opening into the brute's neck. With a scream, the massive man fell to his knees, and a moment later, he too was gone, swallowed up by the darkness of Mark's shadow.

The eerie silence that followed his choked-off cry caused those in the great hall to hesitate, unsure whether they should rush in to confront Mark. But even if they had entered, they wouldn't have found a thing. Mark had already slipped out through a window and scaled the outside of the house before reentering on the second floor.

On silent feet, he crept toward the door, fully intending to slip out and ambush those on the stairs, potentially even to steal away the bodyguard before anyone knew what had happened. He had just reached the doorway and grasped the handle when he caught sight of himself reflected in the silver edging of an ornate clock that had ceased to tell time long before Mark was even born.

A strange, featureless bone mask stared back at him, devilish, twisting horns rising from it. The sight was such a shock that Mark paused. Slowly, the mask melted away, revealing a pale face with six glowing red eyes. Mark could hear the commotion downstairs, but he remained absolutely still, eyes locked on his reflection.

Ever so slowly, he released the crushed door handle and took a deep breath, his features shifting back to normal. He could feel something deep inside him protesting, calling for him to open the door and hunt down the rest of them. Mark had assumed that the spirit of the apex hunter had simply given up the fight, but far from it—the monster had attached itself to him, strengthening his murderous urges substantially. Though Mark had given up his humanity, he could feel the danger of continuing down this path. Those he had killed might have deserved it, but the truth was he had no idea. He had simply seen them as enemies, seen them as prey.

Hearing a shout from downstairs, Mark closed his eyes,

scanning the psychic network. The raiders had entered the room below him, obviously searching for the dead brute. Mark, not wanting further conflict, ignored their shouts and exited through the window before climbing up to the roof of the building. There he paused, surveying the grounds, looking for other enemies. He didn't see any, so he leaped from the roof to a nearby tree and then from that tree to another, rapidly making his way out of the gardens and back to the street.

Though catching sight of himself had unnerved him, Mark's reason for leaving was more complicated. Once he'd stopped thinking of the raiders as nothing but prey, he had realized that simply eliminating all of them wasn't likely to achieve his goal. He wanted to know what they were doing, why they had come out to the mansion, and what association they had with the mutants.

As quickly as he could, Mark headed back toward the city, circling to the south to find the hidden entrance. His goal was to establish his presence in the city before the others returned. They had seen him in his cataphract armor, but his hope was that they had mistaken him for an Exlian, never thinking that he might be a human hunter.

Along the way, Mark didn't bother hiding his aura, and the Exlian he encountered either rushed to hide or stopped to pay respects. The closer he got to the city, the more often that happened, and the more unsettled he grew. Had he not been distracted, Mark would have stopped to investigate, but he knew that the clock was ticking, so he skirted around the bowing Exlian and kept running toward New Emery. On the way, he focused on his clones, connecting to the one working in the lab.

Ever since he had heard that the raiders had been tasked with setting up some device, he had been on the lookout for it, and as he hadn't seen it on the leader of the team, Mark had his clone pull the corpses out of his shadow to search them. Clipped on the back of the female raider who had tried to kill him with the crossbow, he found a large circular device with a series of antennae extending from it. It appeared to be a transmitter of some sort, and when Mark examined it more closely, he discovered a small box in the center of the device that was sealed shut.

When he picked it up, an intense hunger surged through him, and his clone nearly fell apart on the spot. It felt as if a powerful magnetic force were trying to pull the box into his hand, and the feeling was so sharp that he had to toss the box away. It bounced off the table where the body was laid out and clattered to the floor, sliding halfway under the table.

Crouching, Mark started to reach for the box, then paused. The intensity of the feeling had caught him off guard. He wondered if it would be better to wait for his main body to arrive before picking it up again. Leaving the box where it lay, Mark turned his attention to the rest of the device, trying to get a sense of its purpose.

It soon became clear that it was an amplifier of some sort, used to broadcast a signal. He had run into other devices that operated on a similar principle during his time on the base. As he examined it, he began to see similarities with the amplifiers used in computer terminals to broadcast to the network. This amplifier lacked the crystal a computer terminal possessed, and the spot where that crystal should have been located had been occupied by the sealed metal box. That led Mark to examine the box once more, though from a distance this time, occasionally pausing to check his main body's progress.

A few hours later, Mark stepped into the laboratory and merged with his clone, taking a moment to process all the clone's experiences.

It was clear that the device the female raider carried was intended to amplify some sort of signal. What was curious, though, was that from a distance, Mark couldn't feel anything from the box, as if it were entirely sealed. It was only when he'd touched it that he had had the intense feelings of hunger. As he reflected on the clone's experience, Mark realized that it was a particular kind of hunger as well. Rather than the hunger of having missed meals, it was more like the intense, instinctual hunger that consumed the Exlian, driving them to devour and grow.

Crouching by the table, Mark reached for the box and picked it up. Immediately, he felt his Exlian side bristle, as if all his cells let out a silent roar to express their desperate need. Whatever was inside the box was stimulating his body's desire to consume, and Mark had a feeling that if he smashed or otherwise opened the box, that desire would only grow stronger.

He could only imagine what would happen if the box were opened and then the psychic signal it gave off were amplified. It would drive all the Exlian in the area into fierce, frenzied madness. Whatever reason Councillor Javesi's men had for setting up the device, Mark couldn't imagine it was a good one. Driving the Exlian into a frenzy was a good way to get a wave. After all, the largest source of food for the Exlian was New Emery, and once the Exlian were driven mad, they would undoubtedly rush toward the city, throwing themselves against the walls until they had broken through or they were dead.

Mark still wasn't quite sure what the connection with the mutants was, but the device he had recovered was, without a doubt, a terrifying threat. Worse, if there were more devices like it and they were all activated at the same time, there was a genuine potential for a wave that would simply bury New Emery. Even now, Mark could barely suppress his hunger. Had his will not been as strong as it was, he had no doubt that simply touching the box would have turned him into a mindless monster, desperate to consume everything he could.

Placing the box next to the amplifier, Mark commanded his shadow to absorb the corpse of the raider and turned his attention to the nearby terminal. He first sent a message to Noah, asking him if he was free. Almost immediately, he got a response, and soon he'd arranged for Noah to come and meet him at the laboratory. When Noah arrived, he wasn't dressed in the typical uniform of a Ranger, and Mark could sense a rather thunderous mood lurking behind his calm expression.

"Is everything okay?" Mark asked as Noah looked around the room.

"I mean, there's always something going on," Noah said, flashing a smile that reminded Mark more of a wolf baring its teeth. "The unit I'm with is being dissolved due to our losses, thanks to my father's interference. I'm waiting on a reassignment, but it's taking suspiciously long."

"I'm sorry to hear that, Noah."

"It is what it is, and believe me when I say I've gotten used to it. My father is full of plans, most of which run counter to mine. My whole life has been a battle against his machinations. But you called me here for something, not to complain about my father. What's going on?"

"Well, actually," Mark said, scratching his cheek, "what I called you for might have something to do with your father. I'm not sure yet."

Gesturing for Noah to follow him, Mark led the way to the computer, where he'd pulled up a series of pictures. "I ran into some people out in the dead zone. They were attempting to set up a device, some sort of amplifier that will agitate Exlian, drastically increasing their appetite. I haven't figured out exactly how it works, but I have confirmed the effect. I was just wondering if you knew any of these people."

Noah didn't respond immediately, but from the way his jaw tightened, Mark knew that Noah recognized at least some of them. As it turned out, he actually recognized all of them.

"They're all Javesi hounds," Noah said quietly, his eyes

lingering on each picture in turn. "Thugs my father uses for various jobs. I've seen all of them. You said you ran into them in the dead zone? Do you know what they were doing out there?"

"Like I said, they were trying to set up this device to agitate the Exlian. What's more concerning is I overheard them talking about having some sort of deal with the mutants. They weren't very happy about it, but they were still working together. The team I ran into was supposed to set this device up, and then the mutants were going to do something else. My guess is it was the mutants' job to activate it. After all, when it's activated, it'll likely cause the Exlian to go wild."

Taking a closer look at the device, Noah reached out to touch the small box, and Mark watched without saying a word. When Noah picked it up and turned it over in his hands to examine it, Mark confirmed another theory. Despite having a tremendous impact on Exlian, the box was entirely harmless to humans, though a faintly disgusted expression crossed Noah's face, and he put the box down, unconsciously wiping his fingers on his clothes afterward. "What is that?"

Mark hesitated for a moment and then shrugged. "A great question. I'm not sure yet. Can you tell me how you felt when you picked it up?"

"Honestly? It felt kinda gross. Sort of slimy."

"It didn't feel dangerous to you?" Mark asked.

"Not really. Just like, I didn't want to get it on me. Which is strange, actually, because it's just a box."

"You were likely reacting to what was inside," Mark said. "I haven't opened it up yet, but my guess is that whatever is inside is some sort of powerful stimulant for Exlian but incompatible with humans."

After staring at the box quietly for a long moment, Noah turned and fixed Mark with a stare. "So why'd you call me?"

"Well, I can't really go to the authorities with this," Mark said with a wry smile, "and I kinda figured you'd be interested. More importantly, I'm thinking about putting a team together to go and find these mutants and crush them, considering they have some sort of tie to whatever Councillor Javesi is getting up to. I figured you'd want to be involved."

"You figured correctly," Noah said. "Let me do a bit of digging. I can start with this team of hounds and see what I come up with. This has my father's stench all over it, and I'd be more than happy to disrupt whatever he's planning."

"Then I'll wait to hear from you," Mark said, reaching out and putting his hand on Noah's shoulder. "We'll get to the bottom of this."

"Yes, we will," Noah replied. "Thanks for the call. I happen to have quite a bit of free time right now, so I should have something for you soon."

After Noah left, Mark cleaned up the laboratory and stored the box in one of the containment units. Splitting off a clone, he began to tinker with the amplifier while his real body headed back to his apartment. In truth, Mark didn't feel like he needed any rest, but he wasn't quite sure what to fill his time with while he waited for the results of Noah's investigation. If his past experiences were any indication, Noah would likely have a report within the day, and Mark wanted to be ready to go.

Once in his apartment, Mark merged with the second clone and felt his understanding of his powers clarify as the days of dedicated practice were integrated into his mind. Standing in his kitchen, he absently flicked his finger, causing a concentrated blade of null energy wrapped in a sheath of mental energy to fly out and clip the corner of the table. As the wood clattered to the ground, Mark snapped out of his daze and rubbed the back of his head, staring at the perfectly smooth cut he had caused.

The sight reminded him that he needed to go talk to Master Lemuel about Master Abrams's legacy and the Order of Blood. But the truth was that there were simply too many other things going on. So Mark pushed it to the back of his mind, turned around, and opened the fridge to look for something to eat.

Noah's call came at two in the morning, waking Mark from his sleep. Normally, he would have found the transition from fighting a swarm of Exlian in the dream world to sitting up in his bed in New Emery jarring. But thanks to his improved will, it was seamless. As soon as his eyes opened, he sat up and tapped the watch on his bedside table. Noah's face appeared on the screen, his brow furrowed. Mark could tell that whatever Noah had found, it wasn't good.

"You really stepped in it," Noah said, shaking his head. "I've only just scratched the surface, and already, it seems like we've found the main nest. I was able to dig up connections between the hound team you faced off against and the mutants, and in the process, I uncovered a number of hidden research projects. Projects going back years. They have my family's involvement painted all over them. I think I've located one of the main research facilities, hidden right here in New Emery."

"What do you want to do?" Mark asked, swinging his legs off the bed and grabbing the watch as he stood up.

"I want to go shut it down," Noah replied, his voice frosty. "It's well hidden, but because of its location, there aren't a huge number of guards. My guess is we should be able to swipe some data from the servers to get a better sense of just how big this whole conspiracy is. Once we've grabbed the data, I want to burn the place to the ground."

There was an intensity to Noah's voice that surprised Mark, but he quickly nodded. "I'm in. Is it just going to be me and you?"

"No," Noah said, shaking his head. "I'd like to pull some other people in."

"Who do you have in mind?"

"For one, Phoenix." Noah must have seen the grimace that flashed across Mark's face, because he suddenly smiled, his whole expression lightening up. "Sky told me that you kind of ran into her."

"Does it have to be Phoenix? I'm sure there are other people we can get who are just as strong."

"You might be, but I'm not. First of all, we can trust her. Second of all, since you 'died,' she's gotten a lot stronger. Strong enough that I'm not sure I can deal with her in a regular fight. She's been training like mad, and it's reflected in her mana control. Besides, I don't know any other B-ranked energy controllers."

For a moment, Mark was tempted to raise his hand—after all, he was both B ranked and able to control mana, allowing him to mimic some of the abilities of an energy controller—but he knew that Noah was trying to give him a good reason to let Phoenix know he was still alive, so he gave up arguing. "Okay, consider me convinced, though I'm going to have to work myself up to letting her know that I'm not actually a corpse. Who else do you have in mind?"

"I think we should grab Danny. He's gotten stronger as well, and I know he's on leave right now. More importantly, he's helped me with a couple other things, and he knows how to keep his mouth shut."

"What about Sky?"

"She'll be coming too. She has considerable interest in the mutants, given her background, and I think it's only fair to involve her."

"That puts the team at five," Mark said, plopping himself down on the couch. "Do we need more than that?"

"I don't think so. We're likely going to be facing off against empowered guards, most of whom won't be wearing mana suits. The five of us, fully geared, should be able to sweep the place relatively quickly. Of course, if we can do it stealthily, all the better. Once the alarm goes off, we'll probably only have a minute or two at best before reinforcements arrive."

Thinking for a moment, Mark nodded. "I might be able to arrange for a bit of help with our getaway, but it would mean sharing whatever we find with them. I reconnected with my brother, and I'm sure Green Line will be quite interested in whatever arrangement your father has with the mutants."

"Oh, you're talking about Perry, right? The earth controller? That's fine. I was going to suggest we travel through the sewers to avoid detection, but that's even better. I'll contact the rest of the team. Just show up to my house tomorrow by noon, and we'll go over the plan."

"I'll be there."

As Mark clicked off the call, he found himself equal parts excited and nervous. His excitement stemmed from the fact that they were going to break into a secret facility and find out what had been going on. The nervousness was that he would be facing two of his friends who currently thought he was either dead or locked in prison. Knowing that it would do him no good to sit around and stew on it, Mark called Perry's number and lifted his hand in greeting when the call connected.

"Hey, Mark. What's going on?"

"Hello, Perry. I was hoping I could ask for your help with something."

"Is it dangerous?"

Thrown off by the question and the straight-faced way Perry asked it, Mark froze, causing Perry to laugh.

"That's answer enough. You and your brother only ever call about dangerous things. What do you need?"

"Uh, me and some friends are going to check out a research facility where they're working on mutants. I was wondering if you'd be up to provide a quick escape route if the alarm goes off."

Staring at Mark through the screen for a long moment, Perry slowly nodded. "Sure, I can help with that. But in return, I'll need two things. A copy of whatever information you find, especially anything that links the project to the councillors, and a contact number for whoever it is you know that can resolve burnout."

"Can I ask why you want it? The contact number, I mean?"

"Because Emily won't let your brother ask you, but I can tell he wants to. Desperately. Mark, Joe isn't doing well. His case is worse than any of us knew, and if something isn't done, he'll be dead within the year. Maybe even a few months. He has been lying to all of us so we won't worry."

Without hesitating, Mark tapped his watch. "Maestro, are you on?"

Perry, unsure what Mark was saying, opened his mouth to speak, but before he could, another number joined the call, and a crackly voice sounded.

"Hey, Mark, nice to hear from you. I'm a bit occupied at the moment, so no video, but I can chat for a few seconds."

Ignoring Perry's astonishment, Mark waved his hand. "No problem. This is Perry, an associate of my brother, Joe. Joe burned out and has been hanging on thanks to the burnout medicine the city gives out. I wanted to ask if you could do the same thing with him that you did with me and Winter Wolf."

"She told you about Ambrosia, did she?" Maestro said, a hint of glee in his voice. "Sure, I'd be happy to take a crack at it. In fact, Joseph Fields is one of the people I was paying considerable attention to. I lost track of him when he got involved with that Green Line group, but I'd be happy to get up to date on his file. Can you have him come to the Cradle? That would be easiest, since it would let me monitor him directly. But enough about him. How is your experience with the new serum? Any major issues? It seems like you had a sudden spike in power recently."

Hesitating, as he didn't want to reveal his true abilities to Perry, Mark settled for an innocuous reply. "Everything is developing smoothly. I fought and killed a humanoid Exlian called an apex hunter. I'll fill you in later."

After setting up the contact between Perry and Maestro, Mark arranged to send Perry the details of the upcoming mission and then left the other two to talk. With their escape arranged, Mark threw himself into practicing his new abilities, working on capitalizing on his A-ranked speed and incorporating his new martial skill into his attack patterns. He had decided to call it Void as the Blade, since his method revolved around creating a void of mana and using mental energy to transform it into a deadly weapon. The more he practiced, the more natural it seemed, and Mark was soon immersed in his experiments.

Had his watch not vibrated with a message from Noah an hour before he was supposed to meet up, he very well might have completely missed going to Noah's house and instead spent the entire day obsessively perfecting his new attack. After answering the message, Mark took a quick shower, then caught a taxi to Noah's apartment. He was still thinking about his void attack and its various applications as the elevator rose to the penthouse.

As soon as the door opened, Mark stepped out into the grand entryway of the penthouse and found himself facing razor-sharp mana darts tracing tangled patterns through the air as they flew toward him from all directions. The attack was sudden, and Mark's instincts kicked in before he knew what was happening. A blast of null energy radiated outward from his body, forming a sphere around him. At the same time, his mental energy pushed out as well, manipulating the sphere into a thin shield that formed a wall only a few inches thick and wrapped around his whole body while still allowing Mark to deploy his cataphract armor.

Less than a second after he stepped out of the elevator, the first of the mana darts slammed into the barrier, and as soon as it did, Mark realized he was probably overreacting. Based on how quickly the dart evaporated, it likely wouldn't have hurt him at all, even if it had hit him directly. But he was already counterattacking.

Mark's armor completely covered his body, and he had crouched slightly when he deployed the null shield, getting ready to charge. By the time the next dart hit half a second later, he had located the attacker and was on the move, the marble floor cracking under him as he pushed off.

It was only when he was halfway across the hall that he recognized the person in front of him who had just unleashed the darts. Phoenix's eyes were red, as if she had been crying, and her expression was a mixture of anger and absolute shock. Mark barely had time to process any of it before he was right in front of her. His bone blades, which had been aimed at her vitals, shifted slightly to the side, slipping past her as Mark barreled into her. He tried to soften the impact as much as possible, but he still hit her with enough force to knock her back into the wall.

Realizing they were going to hit too hard, Mark slipped his arm around her waist and stabbed his blades into the wall. That still wasn't enough to slow them down, so he used his other hand to brace against the wall, trying to prevent himself from crushing her. As his momentum carried them both forward, he could see his mask reflected in her eyes, mixed with the confusion and shock. Grimacing as they came to a stop against the wall, Mark dismissed his mask, and the cataphract armor peeled back, revealing his face. For a long and breathless moment, the two of them simply stared at each other.

It was breathless for Mark because he simply didn't know what to say and could only stare at Phoenix's beautiful face in dumb silence. It was breathless for Phoenix because despite Mark's best efforts, he had hit her so hard he had knocked the wind from her lungs, leaving her gasping. Thankfully, her body was relatively tough, and she quickly recovered, only to find herself pinned against the wall with Mark's arm around her waist. She was dressed in casual clothes, which for Phoenix meant a dress, and though

Mark could feel only the pressure of her body against his because of his armor, it was like an electric shock that ran from the base of his spine straight up to his brain and then back down again, all the way to his toes.

By the time he realized how close together they were, Phoenix had recovered and was glaring at him with a complex look in her eyes. A soft blush stole its way up her cheeks as he returned her gaze, and Mark was suddenly hyperaware of the way that her hair framed her face. Seeing her lips parting, he panicked, wrenching his bone blades out of the stone wall as he tried to back up. He had hardly moved when Phoenix, her eyes still blazing with a mix of anger, embarrassment, and a whole host of other emotions, grabbed the arm that was wrapped around her waist, preventing him from pulling away. Her other hand rose, wrapping tightly around the back of his neck. Her touch brought a shiver that ran across Mark's skin, and his panic deepened.

"Phoenix, I . . . !"

That was all Mark managed to get out before Phoenix leaned in and their lips met in a fierce kiss.

"Well, that's one way to resolve the tension," Sky said from behind Mark.

"I told you," Noah replied, his tone practically gleeful.

Mark couldn't see either of them because Phoenix still hadn't let go of his neck, but he could just imagine the grins on their faces. The soft feeling of Phoenix's lips made him not care one bit. After what seemed like an eternity, Phoenix finally pulled her head back, her face now completely crimson. Her glare had softened somewhat, but Mark could tell she was still upset.

"Sorry," he said, feeling quite lame even as he said it. "I know I should have said something."

"Yes, you should have."

Phoenix's tone could have chopped iron and made Mark flinch. As he lowered his head, he saw her glare melting from the corner of his eye.

"Can you forgive me?"

"Do you think I'd be kissing you if I couldn't forgive you?"

A wide smile bloomed on Mark's face, and as he withdrew his armor, Phoenix brought her hand to his chest and pushed him back with the tips of her fingers. Mark could feel the heat of each fingertip through his shirt, and his heart jumped.

"Glad to see the two of you have figured things out."

Hearing Danny's deep voice, Mark turned and saw his massive friend holding a plate piled high with food. Danny had the power to grow into a genuine giant, but the large man seemed to have gotten taller and wider since Mark had seen him last.

"Hello, Mark. I'm happy to see you too, though I hope you're not expecting me to kiss you."

"Quite all right," Mark said, chuckling. "I'm content with Phoenix."

That earned him a sharp poke in the side, but as he winced, he caught Sky's wink and couldn't help but chuckle again. Tables covered in food had been set up in the living room, and Mark helped himself and then took a seat on the couch next to Phoenix. At some point, he knew that they would have to talk things out. There was still an underlying tension in her body, though she tried not to show it. The others took their seats as well, with Sky sitting next to Noah and Danny sitting on a couch by himself.

"What's the situation?" Danny asked. "Noah just told me to show up. Said we have some business to take care of, but he didn't give me any details."

"I didn't want to have to go over it more than once," Noah replied. "I'm sending a packet of information to your watches. It has both the location and the profile of the organization for you to go over. I'm just going to hit the highlights here. We'll have time to do a deep dive, since we'll be executing at night, but for now let me give you the overview of what I found. WrenTech Bio is, on the surface, a pharmaceutical company. They're massive, with plants all over the city."

"Are they our target?" Sky asked with a frown. "They've got clinics everywhere."

"No, not exactly. WrenTech Bio has a number of different divisions, and their bioresearch division is our main target. According to all of the documentation publicly available about the corporation, bioresearch is handled by the Chemir Group, a small company acquired about fifteen years ago."

With a flick of his finger, Noah projected the information from his watch onto the virtual screen that floated over the table in the center of the room.

"Chemir was a partnership created and funded by some influential members of the city, two of whom are important to our conversation. The first was my grandfather, Erol Javesi, and his primary partner in crime was Dr. Edward Graham."

"I hate to say it, Noah, but your grandfather and a famous Exlian researcher starting a company together isn't that suspicious," Phoenix said with a frown as she scrolled through the information Noah had sent over.

Unperturbed by her interruption, Noah simply smiled and put a new document up on the screen, this one showing a breakdown of the Chemir Group's organizational structure. "Just wait. The Chemir Group was primarily tasked with discovering whether there were any compatibilities between Exlian and human DNA, all under the guise of medical research. Their stated goal was to discover whether Exlian DNA could be used to repair defects in the human genome. Their own documentation stated that their initial research was purely theoretical, but eventually they launched projects to test their findings. When they attempted to go to trials, it was shut down by the city very quickly, mostly because of bad press around a certain human-testing story that had been recently uncovered involving some of the local orphanages. After their testing requests were denied, the company went quiet for a few months, and then WrenTech Bio bought them up."

"Okay, so I still don't see what the problem is."

"Since then, that group has done nothing. Not a single research project. Or at least, nothing on the books," Noah replied, changing the slide. "But I did some digging, and it looks like they've been receiving close to one hundred million credits in funding every year."

"For doing nothing?" Danny asked, putting his plate on the table and leaning forward. "That's a lot of money for doing nothing."

"Oh, it gets better. Chemir Group runs one of the largest social employment programs in the city. In fact, anyone who's on the down-and-out is pretty much guaranteed to get a job there simply by applying. This group, with no projects, is responsible for hiring over ten percent of the orphans in the city, along with practically anyone who finds themselves without a family. Every single time there's a wave, they step in to offer jobs to those who lose their parents, spouses, or children."

Glancing at Phoenix, who still had a frown on her face, Mark shrugged. "Okay, so that's where all the money's going. They're hiring lots of people."

With a mirthless smile, Noah shook his head. "Come on, Mark. You of all people should know nothing is that simple. It took some doing, and I had to burn one of my spies to get access to my dad's credentials, but what I found did not disappoint."

By the time he finished speaking, Noah was practically snarling. With more force than was necessary, he flicked his fingers, sending a file to the virtual screen. It began to populate names of individuals with information like their age, gender, and physical characteristics, along with a small picture. As the list finished populating, a red slash appeared over every single picture.

"Deceased. That's what the red slash means," Noah said quietly, his customary calm restored.

He began scrolling down, revealing an endless wave of red slashes.

"These are all people who were employed by the Chemir Group over the last twenty-five years. You want to know where the money is going? There's only one place it could be going. Bribes to the inspectors and members of the Defense Force to allow them to continue their human testing."

As Mark watched the hundreds of names scroll by, he couldn't stop the sigh that slipped from his lips. Though he had been playing devil's advocate, he knew full well that Noah was right. After all, Mark had heard from Maestro's own mouth that all empowered were the product of testing like this. Next to him, Phoenix had stiffened, her gaze fixed on the list and the pictures covered by red slashes.

"Noah, are you sure this information is accurate?" she asked, a barely detectable tremor in her voice.

Noah didn't reply but simply kept scrolling, causing an oppressive silence to settle over the room.

"All right, we get the picture," Sky said, standing up abruptly. "Turn it off."

Mark had never heard her speak so harshly and wasn't surprised when Noah hit a button on his watch, causing the virtual window to wink out.

Pacing back and forth next to the couch, Sky crossed one arm over her chest and bit the knuckle of the index finger on her other hand. Everyone waited quietly until she finally stopped and turned back to the group, her gaze sweeping over Mark, Phoenix, and Danny. "Some of those names were people who were with me in the orphanage. Supposedly, they died in work accidents. Or of health issues. My former neighbor is on the list. Her husband and son died, and she said she got a job on the other side of the city when she moved away. If she ended up being used for human testing . . . I want to get to the bottom of this."

"We all have our reasons for wanting to see this done," Mark said as Sky came to sit back down, "and we are going to see it through."

"Hold on there, Mark. You all have reasons for getting involved in this mess," Danny said. "I mean, I'm only coming because you guys are my friends. Honestly, if there was any way that, in good conscience, I could walk away right now, I absolutely would. I hope you guys understand what kind of storm you're about to bring down on your own heads. Our heads, I guess."

"But you're here," Phoenix said with a soft smile. "And that's what counts."

"Yeah, don't remind me. I knew it was a bad idea to accept Noah's call."

As harsh as Danny's words sounded, the smile on his face and the eager anticipation in his eyes communicated his real feelings clearly.

"So assume we're convinced," Phoenix said, turning back to Noah. "This Chemir Group has been hiring, experimenting on, and killing civilians for the last however many years. What are we going to do about it?"

"Well," Noah said, tapping his watch again to project the schematics of a simple-looking office building, "we're going to break into their offices, steal all their information, and then burn the whole place to the ground."

It took the five of them all afternoon and into the evening to finish planning out their mission. Noah had unearthed a considerable amount of information about the Chemir Group's main building, and after careful consideration, they planned out a multipronged assault. Noah wanted to hit three main targets: the control room, the head researcher's office, and the server room. The challenge was getting to the latter two, which required the permission of someone in the first. That made the control room the primary target. It was also the most heavily guarded part of the building, with both guards and automated defenses, and Noah handed the job of taking it to Phoenix and Danny. That left the researcher's office and the server room, which would be handled by Mark and Noah respectively. Sky's role was to watch for any sign of enemy reinforcements and to slow them down appropriately. After Noah told her her tasks, Sky grumbled a bit, complaining that she always got stuck outside.

"Because you're the only one who can do what you do," Danny said with a shrug. "We all play to our strengths. I mean, look at me. I think it'd be really cool to sneak into a server room and hack the mainframe. But Noah here has me bopping the guards."

"I'm not sure that you would fit into the server room," Noah said, shaking his head. "You might get stuck between the server racks."

Listening to his friends banter brought a warmth to Mark's heart, and for the first time in quite a while, he felt something approaching human. That feeling was immediately followed by a faint hollowness as he realized that this was what he was giving up to grow stronger. Peeking at Phoenix, he saw her wide grin, and the memory of their kiss washed away his tension. Even if he was changing, there were some things he wouldn't give up, no matter how much stronger it might make him.

After going over the plan in detail, Noah sat back on the couch, draping one arm elegantly over the back and resting the other on his crossed legs. "We have a plan, and we're going to stick to it as best we can, but unexpected things always happen. Be ready to shift as needed. We might need to rapidly redeploy our forces, depending on how challenging their defenses are. I've done my best to gather information, but it's always possible there's something I missed. So when we do this, keep a careful lookout. We don't need anybody getting killed."

"Deal," Danny said, grabbing his empty plate and standing up.

"I'm going to take advantage of this food while I can. I have a feeling I'm going to be using up a lot of energy tonight."

"You and me both, buddy," Mark said, standing up to join Danny. It had been some time since he had seen Danny use his ability, so Mark was quite curious just how tall his friend could now grow.

Mark didn't need a suit, but the others had specialized mana suits provided by Noah that took each of their powers into consideration while providing maximum stealth capabilities. As he watched his friends put them on, Mark gestured to Sky's state-of-the-art slimline model. "All of these suits look crazy expensive. Aren't you worried someone's going to wonder what you're doing with them?"

"No," Noah replied bluntly. "I don't like my dad much, but I have to admit there are some things that are really convenient about being his son. Our family has a black budget, one that we're all allowed to use. In fact, the last compliment I got from my father was because I had outfitted a team to do something nefarious. He'll probably call me to congratulate me, even if we do blow up his research facility."

"Your relationship with your dad is so weird," Phoenix said. "I just don't get it."

"Must be nice to have fathers," Sky chimed in with a smile. When everyone else's expressions soured, she laughed and waved her hand. "Sorry, I shouldn't make that joke. I know that things aren't always so simple. And Mark, he's an orphan like me. What about you, Danny?"

"Got a great family," Danny said. "My mom and dad run a small music company, recording patriotic songs. They like it, and it affords them a good living."

"Patriotic songs, huh? Can you sing any of them for us?"

"Believe me, the last thing you need is to hear me singing," Danny replied, shaking his head.

"What about those sisters of yours?" Mark asked, watching as Danny finished clipping his helmet on. "Didn't you say you have sisters?"

"I do. Four of them, all in the Defense Force. The oldest, Caroline, is a major. The other three are captains."

"That means your whole family is in the Defense Force?"

"For glory, for humanity," Danny said, flexing his fingers in his gloves. "I tell you, though, it's kind of a nightmare going home for holidays when everybody in the house outranks you."

Stretching out his hand, Danny summoned a massive mace made of pure mana. It dropped into his outstretched palm with a thud, and he swung it back and forth a few times, letting out a pleased grunt. "All right, looks like I'm good to go."

"I still think it's super bizarre that Mark doesn't need a suit," Sky said, flitting over to float next to him. "Are you sure your armor is tough enough to take a beating?"

"More than," Mark replied calmly. "In fact, it's probably stronger than all four of your suits combined."

"Now that I'd like to put to the test," Danny said, resting his mace on his shoulder. "Do we have time to do a bit of sparring?"

"No, we don't," Noah cut in. "Let's go."

Noah had arranged for a large vehicle that had been modified to carry Danny and his mana suit as well as the rest of the team most of the way to their target. After they piled into the van, Noah ran over the plan one more time. He was nothing if not thorough, and Mark could see the echoes of whatever training he had received bleeding through his words and actions. His time in the Ranger unit had only sharpened him, and Mark was as impressed as always with the meticulousness of Noah's plans.

When they arrived a few blocks away from the facility, the vehicle stopped, and Noah opened the door to jump out. As Mark followed, he heard a soft beep and his watch activated, a screen with Maestro's bulbous head popping up. "Mark! Come tell your brother he has to come to the Tomb!"

Blanching, Mark turned down the sound on the call, giving the others an embarrassed smile. Hurrying off to the side to get a bit of privacy, he crouched down by the wall and looked at Maestro. The genius was busy with something else, but Mark could see another call that had Joe's face open in the background.

"Wait, let me add you in," Maestro said.

The virtual window shivered, and Mark suddenly found himself in a call with both Maestro and Joe.

"Mark?" Joe asked. "What are you . . . ?"

Immediately, Mark sensed something wrong. Joe's skin was pale as a sheet, and his skin showed splotches of bruising. His gaze was listless and his reactions slightly delayed, but worse still was the slur to his speech. It was subtle, but Mark had never heard his brother like this before, and it made his heart clench.

"Joe, Maestro can help you, but you have to go down to the Tomb. He can help you get your power back."

For a second Joe's gaze sharpened, piercing through the screen with such intensity that Mark flinched, but then the moment passed, and Joe shook his head slowly. "I don't need a power that makes me a monster, Mark."

Stifling the hot anger that rose in his chest and taking a deep breath, Mark replied as calmly as he could. "But you do need to try to stay alive, Joe. For the people around you. For Marv and Kevin and Perry. For Emily. For me. There are forces trying to crush this city, and we need people with as much power as possible if we are going to survive. Don't give up on us. Please."

By the time he finished, Mark's voice carried a pleading note. He knew that he was asking Joe to go against everything that he had once stood for—and he understood the irony, since he had refused when Joe had asked him to do the same—but Mark genuinely believed what he was saying. The forces that were bent on New Emery's destruction, both inside and outside the city, were incredibly powerful, and without people like Joe stepping up to defend it, the city was sure to fall.

There was a long silence, and then a faint flicker appeared in Joe's eyes, like a tongue of flame reigniting. His chin rose slightly, and the intense weight that shrouded him fell away. "Okay. For you, and for Emily, I can become a monster."

The call ended abruptly, leaving Mark staring at the empty air, desperately hoping that he hadn't led his brother down the wrong path. Letting out the breath he was holding, Mark stood up and rubbed his forehead. There was a quiet chime as a message came through from Maestro showing a thumbs-up, but Mark dismissed it and silenced his messages so he could focus on the mission at hand.

After he rejoined the others, who were taking shelter at the corner of a building, Noah checked his watch and then pointed to the north. "Three blocks. Remember, we need to take down the guards at the front gate quietly. Sky, you're the only one who can hit the camera's blind spots, so we're going to need you to jam everything. We don't have long. Maybe a couple of minutes tops before someone in the control center realizes what's going on. We have no way of cutting their primary alarm. So, Phoenix, Danny, the two of you need to get there as fast as possible. Try not to make noise, because the last thing we need is for someone who's working late to spot one of you barreling down the hall and hit a panic button. The entrance to the underground part of the facility is located on the opposite side of the building. Mark and I will make our way there. Let's go."

Sensing a gaze, Mark looked over and saw Phoenix was watching him. Reaching out, he tapped the side of her shoulder lightly. "Don't worry. This is going to be easy."

"Well, if that's not the most inauspicious way to start a mission . . . I don't know what is," Danny grumbled.

Slightly embarrassed, Mark rolled his eyes at Danny and jogged after Noah, who had already begun moving down the street. Sky shot up into the air, her suit allowing her to blend almost perfectly with the night sky. If Mark hadn't had the psychic network to assist him, he was pretty sure that he would have lost sight of her almost immediately, in part because of how quickly she could move and the fact that there was almost no sense of motion when she did. Every time he saw her fly, he found himself curious about her power. But now wasn't the time to worry about that.

They had already done their mic checks, and Mark was extra grateful that his cataphract armor manifested over whatever else he wore, allowing him to keep an earpiece in. The facility they were raiding was a fairly standard-looking three-story office building with a chain-link fence that ran around it, blocking off a small parking lot at the front and a large one at the back. At first glance, that was all there appeared to be to the place, but Mark knew that there was a sprawling facility underneath the office building. The control room was on the northern side, while the entrance to the basement levels was on the southern side, which was why the team needed to split up. More importantly, cameras covered every angle of the entrances, which would have to be dealt with if they wanted to enter the facility unnoticed. That was where Sky came in.

As Mark and Noah made their way quietly to the southern side of the facility, Mark kept track of Sky, who approached the building from above. The only dead zone in the cameras that Noah had been able to find was on the roof. From there, Sky could deal with them one at a time. Her goal was to attach a small device to each camera that would cause it to loop a few seconds of footage until the device was removed. Of course, it would only take a few minutes for the device to be detected by the network sweeps. However, that was all the time they needed.

Mark scanned the psychic network, paying careful attention to the buildings around him. It was an instinct born of his time in the dead zone, where Exlian could be hidden anywhere. Though everything seemed normal during the first two scans, the third revealed a problem. They were still a block away from the target building, and Mark called for Noah to stop.

"Hold on, I think I spotted somebody. A guard."

Though Noah had no idea what Mark was talking about, he still stopped and told the others to stop as well. Sky was almost half a mile above them, well hidden in the darkness, while Phoenix and Danny were circling around to the other side of the facility. Focusing on the network, Mark tried to get a clearer picture of the person he had identified.

"There's someone on the top floor of this building," he said, pointing at a four-story apartment complex that overlooked the Chemir Group's building.

"Mark, it's an apartment building," Noah said, glancing at it in confusion. "Of course there are people there."

"No, this person has been sitting at the window on the fourth floor, looking out toward the Chemir building. I think we might have a watcher."

"That would certainly explain why they don't mind having a blind spot from above," Noah said, looking up at the top floor of the apartment building.

"Exactly. It might be a trap. If they show off an obvious gap in their security, that's where criminals will target. Let me double-check and see if it's actually someone watching."

"Sure, just be quick," Noah said.

Moving cautiously to avoid anyone who might be glancing out their window, Mark made his way to the wall of the apartment building and began to climb up it. Rather than use his bone blades to stab into the concrete, he simply gripped one of the windowsills and hurled himself upward, rapidly clearing the first two floors. Before he started to fall, he grabbed another sill, pausing for only a moment before launching himself straight up again.

Ever since Mark had devoured the apex hunter, he had entered an entirely new world when it came to his agility, and with his strength improved as well, he was finding himself able to do things he never would have dreamed of before.

Landing quietly on the roof, Mark made his way toward the metal hatch that provided access. Opening it was simple enough, as he could use his null energy to turn off the mana lock and simply pry it open with his fingers. Dropping to the hallway below, he located the apartment where the figure was sitting at the window. Admittedly, it had been less than a minute since he'd begun to climb the wall of the apartment building, but the figure still hadn't moved, reinforcing Mark's suspicions.

Blinking, Mark turned on his mana vision and located the alarm on the door. Had he attempted to enter by cutting off the mana as he had with the roof access hatch, he would have set off a silent alarm, alerting both the room's occupant and the security in the building across the street. But an alarm wasn't going to stop him. Rather than block the mana, Mark lightly touched the door, locating the thread of mana that formed the complete loop. Then he used his newly strengthened will to take control of it. He ran his finger up the side of the door, guiding the thread of mana that kept the alarm from tripping away from the door and into the wall. It was tricky work, but his practice was clearly paying off.

Once it was out of the way, Mark disengaged the lock and eased the door open, revealing a simple, carpeted hallway. There was a small galley kitchen to the right and a bathroom on the left. Straight ahead was the living room where someone was currently keeping watch. Once inside, Mark closed the door, being careful not to make a sound, and then split off a clone to keep the alarm in its new place, ensuring that it wouldn't accidentally go off. Suppressing the smile that rose to his lips at the absurdity of the situation, Mark crept to the end of the hallway and peeked into the room, where he saw a man sitting at a table that faced the window. Water and a few snacks sat next to him, along with a short-barreled sniper rifle and a pair of binoculars.

Wanting to ensure that his target wouldn't be able to send a message, Mark stretched out a null field bubble, neatly encasing the guard in it. To his credit, the guard reacted immediately to the abrupt dispersion of mana, one hand reaching for the gun on the table while the other slapped at his waist, no doubt hitting the panic button on his belt. It failed to activate, however, and before his hand could close around the stock of the rifle, Mark was on top of him. With one of his blades about to sever the man's neck, Mark thought better of it, suppressing his murderous impulse and instead landing a swift blow to the head that sent the man sliding off his chair, unconscious. Easily lifting the guard's body, Mark walked back over to the clone by the door and plopped the guard down. From his shadow, he got out zip ties, and soon the guard was tightly bound and gagged.

"Keep him here, don't let him get away, and make sure the alarm doesn't go off," Mark said to himself.

His clone nodded and then opened the door and gestured for Mark to step outside. It would have been a lie to say he wasn't slightly weirded out by interacting with himself like this, but Mark had come to understand that the clones were just versions of him that had opted to do something different. Of course, there was always the danger that the guard would wake up and see the clone, causing him to immediately disappear, so Mark had made sure to cover the man's eyes thoroughly. It would have been easier to simply kill him, but Mark was enjoying the renewed feeling of being human that he had gained from hanging out with his friends, and he was loath to break the illusion. Less than a minute later, he landed lightly next to Noah, who was waiting for him in an alleyway down below.

"What did you find?" Noah asked.

"A guard, paying close attention to the dead spot up there on top of the building. If Sky had flown in, there's a good chance she would have been seen and tagged by the guy's rifle."

"What'd you do with him?"

"Incapacitated," Mark said, his voice calm. "He won't be setting off an alarm anytime soon."

"Would have been easier to kill him," Noah said, his voice neutral.

Slightly surprised by his comment, Mark looked over at his friend and saw that Noah was watching him carefully.

"Yeah, it would have," Mark admitted, "but I'm trying to only do that when it's actually necessary."

"Good. Come on, let's go."

With the hidden guard taken care of, they got back to work, the two ground teams getting into position. Sky, who had been ready for quite a while, dropped down quietly to the roof and began the slow and careful work of looping the cameras. A few times Mark thought they might get busted by the guards that patrolled the parking lots, but Sky was careful and completely silent. Once, a guard even walked directly under the camera that she was above, forcing her to rapidly reset the loop she had just captured so it didn't replay him walking into the frame and then disappearing.

Noah kept careful tabs on the cameras as they were dealt with. As soon as the ones on the northern side of the building had been addressed, Phoenix and Danny moved, squeezing into the back parking lot through a hole Danny had ripped in the fence.

"Go quick," Noah said over the voice channel. "You only have forty-five seconds before the guard comes around the corner."

With the cameras looped and the coast clear, Danny and Phoenix headed for the building as fast as they could. They had just reached their entrance when, almost exactly forty-five seconds after Noah had spoken, a rather bored-looking guard stepped around the corner of the building, his light making a wide sweep across them. Danny had just reached for the door and froze as the light lit up his massive figure.

Before the guard could react, the mana around him froze as Phoenix seized control of it, locking him in stasis. Though Mark couldn't see Phoenix herself, he could see the camera feed from her suit and was able to identify what was happening immediately as the guard floated through the air toward her.

"Danny, grab him," Phoenix said through gritted teeth, clearly struggling to control all the mana as the guard instinctively fought back.

By the time the guard had crossed the distance, floating through the air, his feet a few inches off the ground, he had been knocked unconscious as the blood flow to his brain was restricted. Letting out a gasp, Phoenix relaxed her control, and Danny grabbed the guard's falling body before he hit the ground. Holding him with one hand, Danny tapped in the building's entry code, which Noah had acquired for them. The door unlocked.

This would be the most dangerous part of the operation, or at least the most likely to set off the alarm. After all, the command center was a few hundred feet from the entrance to the building, and Phoenix and Danny would have to cross that distance before the guards sounded the alarm. Mark held his breath as Danny stepped inside and began to rush toward the command center. Phoenix flew in after him, glowing mana gathering around her hands and feet as she shot down the hall.

As large as Danny's steps were, Phoenix was flying, allowing her to move a lot faster. She reached the control center in less than ten seconds. As soon as she got to the door, she thrust her hand forward, using her mana to melt straight through the lock. Normally, a highly secure location would have mana-resistant doors, but this was supposed to be a regular office with no need for any sort of high-caliber defenses.

Of course, that didn't mean those defenses didn't exist. As her mana burst through the door, a turret dropped out of the ceiling with a whir. It spun to face her, and Mark could see the faint glow gathering in its barrel through Phoenix's camera. Before it could fire, there was a bright flash as the ball of mana that Phoenix had sent ahead of her exploded, unleashing dozens of darts that traced irregular paths through the room. Six of them slammed into the turret, immediately disabling it, while the rest tore apart the guards, who had barely begun to react. A few seconds later, Danny arrived, skidding to a halt to avoid shattering the door. When he stepped into the room and saw the mess that Phoenix had made, he couldn't help but gulp.

"Don't just stand there. Help me figure out how to get these locks undone," Phoenix snapped as she tried to work the computers. "Noah, Mark, we've taken control of the command center. We should be able to wave you in."

"Well, that was fast. I thought that would be the difficult part," Noah said, gesturing for Mark to move in.

They hopped the fence on the southern side of the building and crouched behind a car parked at the edge of the lot, scanning for guards. Two were talking quietly at the corner, but Mark and Noah kept low, working their way toward the building while trying not to alert either of them. As they got closer, it became apparent that the guards weren't going to move, which would make it impossible to get to the doorway without being seen. Just as Mark was thinking about suggesting they attack, Noah did just that.

One moment, Noah was next to him, and the next, he had teleported behind the two guards and struck both. One of them fell as if all his bones had turned to jelly, while the other went as still as stone and then slowly toppled over. Noah grabbed both of them, lifting them easily, and gestured with his head for Mark to get the door. As soon as Mark put his hand on it, there was a soft click, and he heard Phoenix's voice.

"Should be unlocked. You're going to go into the hall, take your first right, and then your second left. The entrance to the basement is there."

"Thanks," Mark said as he pulled open the door and watched Noah carry the two guards in with no apparent effort.

"What was that?" Mark asked as they trotted down the hall after dumping the guards.

"What was what?"

"You just teleported. I didn't know you had that ability."

"I've got a lot of abilities," Noah said. "It's sort of my thing."

"What rank are you?" Mark asked, shooting suspicious glances at Noah.

"High?"

"Noah, that's not an answer."

"Fine, I'm low B ranked, but a lot of my powers are . . ." Noah paused for a moment as they reached the second passageway on the left. "A lot of my powers are really strong, but we can talk about all of this later. Right now, let's focus on the mission."

At the end of the hallway was a short flight of stairs and then a large metal door with a biometric terminal. Noah didn't hesitate, and after unclipping his helmet, he put his eye up to the scanner and let the light scan him. There were three soft beeps, and then Phoenix spoke again.

"We've got the request, and there, you're through."

The door shuddered slightly and then began to slide open.

"All right, we're all done here. I've installed the virus and locked the terminals down. We'll start planting the explosives, and then we'll come meet up with you."

Putting his helmet back on, Noah resealed it with a click. "Sounds good. We'll see you in a few minutes."

Maybe it was because of his experience down in the Tomb, but Mark had expected the basement facility to be much darker than it was. The hallways were all brightly lit, and as they jogged through them, Mark got the sense that they were well traveled. That sense grew even stronger when they turned the corner and saw a small group of scientists talking with two guards.

The scientists looked like they were clocking out, getting ready to leave for the day, and were making idle small talk with the guards, both of whom were wearing full mana suits and held mana rifles loosely at their sides. Each one was also armed with a mana sword, but Mark didn't get the sense that either was empowered.

Mark didn't need to glance at Noah to know what to do next, and he pushed off the ground, traveling the length of the hallway as fast as he could. But even with A-ranked speed, Mark couldn't beat instantaneous movement, and Noah had already arrived when Mark got there. Of course, Mark could have used his own teleportation, but that would have wounded him needlessly, and he wanted to be in top shape to deal with whatever they would find below.

The scientists started to yell, but Mark was already on top of them, and this time, he didn't hold back, figuring that anybody who worked in a human-testing laboratory was complicit. His blades flashed like a reaper's scythe, harvesting the scientists' lives, even as Noah pummeled the two guards into submission. Whether they had set off a silent alarm, Mark wasn't sure. There was always a chance that the guards' suits were rigged up to some sort of dead man's switch that would send an off-site alert, calling in reinforcements, so speed was of utmost importance.

By the time Mark had made it through the scientists, Noah had killed both guards, so Mark turned his attention to the metal door. Unlike the door to the command center, this one was reinforced, but with a thought, Mark coated it in a layer of null energy and then cut it to shreds with a few slashes of his blades. The sight of metal shards clattering to the floor left Noah, who had just pulled out a tool to hack the keypad, stunned, and he stared after Mark, who had already rushed through the opening.

"Talk about hiding powers," Noah muttered as he chased after Mark.

Though they had a rough sense of where they needed to go, Noah hadn't been able to get a precise layout of the underground facility, so they relied on a brute-force approach. Twice more, they ran into guards, who they eliminated quickly, relying on Noah's teleportation ability to get the drop on them each time. After clearing out that floor, they found the elevator to the deeper levels and jumped on it.

Running his finger down the floor guide pasted next to the

buttons, Mark spotted the offices on basement level three and hit the button. "The server room will probably be close to the offices. Everything else looks to be laboratories or holding cells."

As soon as he said the words, his eyes widened, and he looked at Noah, who was staring back with an ugly expression.

"I'm such an idiot," Noah said quietly. "They have holding cells. If they're running human experiments here, then obviously there are people in this facility. If we bomb the whole thing . . ." His words trailed off, and he didn't need to finish his sentence.

"We need to see if there are civilians present," Mark said, gritting his teeth, "and how many. If we can move them out, then we can stick with our plan to burn this place to the ground."

"And if there are too many to move?" Noah asked.

"I don't know," Mark said. "We'll deal with that when we get to it."

There was a soft ding as the elevator arrived at basement level three, and as the doors started to open, Mark grabbed Noah and pulled him to the side, barely avoiding a volley of mana bolts that melted through the back of the elevator. Tucked out of sight in the corner, Mark did a quick sweep of the psychic network, picking up two individuals in the hallway outside. There had been six mana bolts, four too many for a pair of people to unleash.

"Looks like there are four turrets," Mark said. "I'll deal with them if you can handle the guards."

At Noah's nod, Mark darted around the corner, his blades crossing in front of him to provide some extra defense, his eyes scanning the hallway. He could sense Noah was directly behind him, so he ignored the two guards who were crouched in the center of the hallway and dove over their heads, locking onto the four turrets that had extended from the ceiling and were now recharging their mana bolts.

Mark rolled as he hit the ground, then sprang to his feet and unleashed two void blades that tore through the air toward the closest turret. One caught the turret's barrel, while the other stabbed into its mass, wreaking havoc on its insides. The bolt it was about to fire exploded upon coming in contact with the severed barrel, transforming the turret into scrap.

The other three turrets, caring nothing for their comrade's demise, blasted away at Mark. One of them barely missed as he shifted to the side, but the other two slammed into him one after the other. His mana shield blocked the first, but the second arrived too quickly for it to recharge, and it punched a hole straight through his armor. As the bolt burrowed into his body, Mark gritted his teeth and flicked his finger again, sending out another void blade to eliminate a second turret.

The bolt of mana was still burning in his body, so he gathered some null energy and used it to surround the concentrated mana, crushing the bolt into nothingness. Staggering a step forward, he was thankful for his mana shield when two new bolts arrived. The first one hit the mana shield that appeared in front of his cheek and was deflected upward, while the second mana bolt punched a hole straight through his shoulder. Normally, such a wound would have been debilitating, but Mark's regeneration had already kicked in, healing the damage done in his chest before going to work on the hole in his shoulder.

Even as he sent out two more void blades toward the last two remaining turrets, the hole in Mark's shoulder was closing up. Like all his powers, his regeneration had gotten a noticeable upgrade since he had devoured the apex hunter, and now it worked almost twice as fast as it had before. Just because he healed, however, didn't mean that he didn't feel pain. The lingering sting of the two wounds caused Mark to clench his teeth.

"I might need to hunt more of those apex hunters," he muttered as Noah jogged over to see if he was okay.

"We really are gonna need to have a chat once we're done," Noah said, his eyes lingering on the spot where he had seen a mana bolt burrow into Mark's shoulder.

Any sign of the damage was already gone, and as Mark rotated his shoulder, it was clear he was none the worse for wear. The two of them shared a long look. It was clear that each had his secrets and didn't know the other nearly as well as he thought. Still, as curious as he was about Noah's powers, Mark trusted his friend implicitly. Reaching out, he patted Noah's arm. "Let's get through this first."

With the guards and the turrets destroyed, the way was clear, and Mark and Noah soon arrived at the main office, where they found the door was locked. Noah didn't bother to use his fancy lock-picking tool and instead simply kicked the door in, displaying a level of strength that Mark would have expected from an A-ranked empowered. As the door shattered, Mark caught sight of a figure ducking down behind a desk, and he darted into the room, vaulted over the desk, and grabbed a disheveled-looking scientist by the ankle. He dragged her out, only releasing her when they reached the center of the office.

She had graying brown hair, and a pair of round glasses sat askew on her nose. She was dressed in a lab coat, and from the bags under her eyes, it was clear that she didn't get much sleep. Mark also detected a slight jitter in her hands, and despite the threat she faced, she still glanced over at the desk, where a mostly empty bottle of purple liquid sat.

Crouching down next to her, Noah yanked her ID from her coat. "Mora Petterton. She is the lead researcher. We should be able to use her ID to get everything we need. I'll start that process."

Taking the key card with him, Noah walked to the desk and started up the terminal, pulling out a small black box to store the data they retrieved. In the meantime, Mark grabbed the bottle of purple liquid from the desk and examined it closely. "What is this?"

"Euphoria." It was Mora who spoke, a fanatical edge to her voice as she stared at the bottle.

"Euphoria is a drug. Keeps you from having to sleep," Noah said. "It's supposed to boost brain activity, but mostly it just makes you really addicted. It's banned on the surface." The entire time he spoke, Noah's fingers were flying as he combed through Mora's terminal.

Still holding the almost empty bottle of euphoria, Mark crouched down next to Mora. "Are you performing human trials in this facility?"

Mark fully expected Mora to deny it, but instead she nodded her head, her eyes never leaving the gleaming purple liquid. "Yes, all of the reports are in the weekly update. I've already sent them in."

Disconcerted, Mark glanced at Noah, who was staring at him from over the terminal's virtual screen. "And these human trials, where are you keeping the people who participate in them?"

"All Class C employees are held on the sixth floor while they are not actively participating in trials, as is protocol." When she had finished speaking, Mora licked her lips and swallowed, salivating at the sight of the remaining euphoria sloshing around the bottle.

"What's on the seventh floor?"

"All the live specimens we're currently running tests on and the Exlian we splice with."

"Is it weird that she's just answering all my questions?" Mark asked Noah.

"I mean, no, not really," Noah said, plugging in his device. "People who are addicted to euphoria are incredibly susceptible to suggestion. That's one of the reasons it's banned. What's strange is that they would let a euphoria addict run the program here."

"Huh, that is strange," Mark said, looking back at Mora. "Hey, why do they allow you to be in charge of the program?"

For the first time, a hint of clarity flashed through Mora's eyes. But then she caught sight of the purple liquid, and a dreamy look washed over her face again. "I can see the patterns. Increase the success rate of the splices. Make beautiful things."

Unsure what to say, Mark just stared at the drugged scientist, who was slowly reaching her hand out for the bottle he held. When he heard the elevator door ding in the distance, he stood up.

"Stay right here, okay?" he told Mora, who quickly nodded.

Unsure what to do with the liquid, Mark tossed it into his shadow, feeling strangely guilty when he saw Mora's stricken expression. She didn't seem dangerous, so he left her with Noah and went out to meet whoever was coming down in the elevator. It turned out to be Phoenix and Danny, both of whom looked slightly disgruntled.

"Why haven't you guys been responding to us?" Phoenix asked, her tone harsh.

"We haven't been getting any calls," Mark said, shaking his head as he double-checked his watch. "Nothing."

"This basement facility must be completely jammed," Danny said, tapping the wall with his mace, "which means we have good news and bad news."

"We've set up all of the bombs," Phoenix said, looking at Danny, "but if all the signals are getting jammed, there's no way we're going to be able to detonate them from here, not unless we can somehow get a message out to Sky."

"Even if we could, I don't think we want to," Mark said, leading the other two into the office where Noah and Mora were. "Turns out there are a lot of people in this facility who they've been running tests on."

"It's my oversight," Noah said from behind the desk. "For some reason, I was thinking about this place as simply a data-processing center, but no, they're actually running experiments on the lower floors, experiments that are probably going on right now."

"So what are we going to do about it?" Mark asked. "Do you have any solutions?"

"Yes, two. The first is to head down to the lower floors and hope we can let them out one by one. That carries the risk of setting off an alarm. Though if this entire place is jammed, my guess is that there are no alarms, which leads me to option number two. I found two protocols, one that'll bury this place and another that supposedly sets off an internal alarm so all the staff can be evacuated. My guess is that no matter which one we hit, the same thing's going to happen."

"When you say 'bury this place,' what do you mean?" Danny asked, glancing up at the concrete ceiling.

"I mean exactly that. My dad hates loose ends, and he cares for his reputation above all else. Rather than let this place get found, I'm certain he'd rather destroy it. As soon as I hit either of these fail-safes, the entire place is going to lock down and some sort of destruction protocol is going to go into place."

"That doesn't seem like a good plan at all," Danny said, the blandness of his tone causing Mark to crack a smile.

"No, Danny, it doesn't."

Biting her lip, Phoenix glanced at Mora. "Do we have any options besides running down there and hoping nobody else presses the button or pressing the button ourselves?"

"Not that I'm aware of."

Thinking for a moment, Mark tapped his watch to open up the virtual screen. "Maestro, can you hear me?"

There was nothing but silence, and he shrugged. "Eh, worth a shot."

"What was worth a shot?" Phoenix asked, looking at Mark strangely.

"We can talk about it later," Noah said. "Let's focus on figuring out our next move. Any other ideas? We've got most of the information downloaded. It'll only take another couple minutes, and then we could head back to the surface."

"No," Mark said. "As soon as they discover we broke in, this whole place is going to vanish. Whatever we're going to do, we need to do it now."

Considering, he walked over to the desk where Noah stood. "Okay, so help me understand these protocols. At what point should they be triggered?"

"They're fail-safes. They're supposed to be activated in cases of catastrophe."

"Mora," Mark called.

Hearing her name, Mora looked up from her slumped position on the ground. As soon as she saw Mark, her eyes brightened, as if remembering that he was the one who had taken the precious purple euphoria.

"Are the fail-safes activated in case of a containment breach?"

"No," she said, shaking her head. "We deal with containment breaches with the guards."

"In that case, I might have a solution," Mark said. "The goal is to keep the guards from killing the prisoners, right? Well, if there's a large enough containment breach on the seventh floor where the Exlian are kept, all of the guards are going to have to move down there. Then we should be able to eliminate the remaining guards on the sixth floor and start moving people out."

"Where are we going to move them? The elevator can only hold so many," Danny said, jerking a thumb over his shoulder.

"We'll have to rely on Perry, so we've got to get a message to him, but that means sending somebody back up to the surface. Whoever goes can take Mora here."

"I knew things were going to go sideways, but I didn't imagine they were going to go this sideways," Noah said with a frown. "But you're right: We can't just leave these people here. It looks like there are two elevators. Both will need key cards, however, so we will have to move as a group if we want to all go down to the lower floors. Unless we can find another one."

"Instead, what if you send me down to the seventh floor?" Mark replied. "I'll make sure the Exlian breach their containment and attack the guards. Monitor the situation from here and then move to the sixth floor to rescue those who are trapped once the fight breaks out. We won't have communication because of the jamming, but you should be able to follow my progress through the alarms."

"This sounds really dangerous, Mark," Phoenix said, stepping forward to grab his arm. "If you go down to the seventh floor and something happens, how are you going to get back to the surface?"

"I'll just dig my way out."

Chuckling at what he assumed was a joke, Danny shook his head, but when he saw Mark's serious expression, his laughter faded.

"I'm actually serious. And even if I get trapped, Perry will be able to find me before I die. We need to draw the guards' attention, and freeing the Exlian is the best way to do it."

Unplugging his device, Noah put it away and walked around the desk to stand with the others. "I agree with Mark. As dangerous as it is, I think it's the only way. However, I don't like the idea of sending Mark on his own. Phoenix, you go with him. Danny and I will take the elevator up to the surface to contact Sky and Perry, and then we'll try to rescue those who are trapped on the sixth floor. As soon as you've caused a disturbance, retreat to a safe spot, and we'll get Perry to pick you up."

Mark wanted to protest that he might not be able to protect Phoenix, but it was obvious from the look in her eyes that she wasn't about to let him out of her sight. Not that he could blame her. The last time they had agreed to meet up later, he had been thrown in prison and then faked his own death. "Fine, let's go."

Mark and Phoenix stepped inside the elevator and used Mora's key card to unlock access to the seventh floor. Before the door shut, Mark tossed the card to Noah and gave him a nod. "See you in a bit."

The doors closed with a hiss, and Mark and Phoenix were alone in the silent metal box. It plunged down into the earth, and Mark could feel the tension rise. Knowing they were in for a fierce fight, he took the chance to stretch out his body, limbering up. Glancing at him in the reflection of the silver door, Phoenix suddenly smirked. "How should we do this?"

"Attack the guards; leave the Exlian to me," Mark replied. "And let's try not to die. I've done it once, and it's not fun."

"Don't worry, I don't plan on dying anytime soon."

With a soft jerk, the elevator came to a stop and the doors opened, revealing a wide hallway and half a dozen guards staring at Mark and Phoenix in bemusement. It was unlikely that the guards had ever experienced a breach of the facility, and it showed in the way they failed to react to Mark stepping out of the elevator. He gave them a friendly wave as he spoke over his shoulder to Phoenix. "Glad to hear it. Do your best to keep up."

She opened her mouth to retort, but he was already gone, charging down the hallway toward the guards. As he moved, Mark unleashed a null field and then shaped it into a wave that preceded him, washing over the guards a moment before he arrived. Three of the six had managed to lift their mana rifles as he charged, but the mana that had been building up abruptly dispersed, and the rifles failed to fire, leaving them defenseless against Mark's blade.

The first two guards fell to Mark's stabs, but before he could attack the others, two dozen mana darts swarmed past Mark like a school of glowing fish, punching holes in the guards' armor and riddling their bodies with wounds. As the guards collapsed, Mark stared in bemusement at the neat holes in their face masks. At least one dart had managed to find its way into each of the guards' eyes, burning through to their brains. Considering that everyone had been moving, the accuracy of Phoenix's darts was rather terrifying. Mark turned to face her as she calmly walked down the hallway, a proud look on her face.

"I won't have any trouble keeping up."

"Clearly," Mark said, dismissing his mask and smiling at Phoenix. "You've gotten a lot better since the last time we raided an underground facility. It seems it's becoming a habit."

Though she tried to keep her impassive expression, Mark caught a slight quirk at the corner of her lips. "Just wait. This is nothing."

Letting his mask flow back into place, Mark took the lead again, pushing past a set of double doors to enter the main hall of the seventh floor. From the schematics they had pulled up on Mora's terminal, Mark knew that the floor consisted of a large hallway that enclosed a square mile. In the center of the hallway was a large, interconnected series of hangar-size laboratories and holding facilities. Mark's target was the closest holding room, where he could already sense hundreds of Exlian. The death of the guards had happened so quickly that no one had noticed it yet, but Mark expected the alarm to go off at any moment, and he wanted to cause as much chaos before then as possible.

Mark and Phoenix had just reached the entrance to the holding room when a strobing red light filled the hallway and a piercing alarm sounded. There was a click as the door Mark was reaching for locked, but he didn't care. His null field expanded, and the door simply fell apart under his blades, revealing a chaotic scene inside. The room was made up of countless small containment units, each barely large enough for the Exlian they held. Thick mana barriers kept the Exlian inside and prevented them from scratching their way out, but the barriers did nothing to contain the roars, growls, and screeches, filling the room with an overwhelming din.

"Well, what do we have here?"

The words cut through the noise, reaching Mark and Phoenix clearly. A broad-shouldered man stepped into the center aisle and began walking toward them, flanked by two nervous-looking scientists in white lab coats. The three of them had been hidden by one of the cages, preventing Mark from spotting them when he stepped into the room, but as soon as he laid eyes on the man in front, his heart clenched. It wasn't fear, exactly, but an instinctive recognition that the man in front of him was dangerous.

Though Mark hadn't expected to simply waltz through the facility without any trouble, he had to admit that he was surprised to have encountered this particular foe. The man in front of him was handsome, with a square jaw and long blond hair that flowed freely past his shoulders. His sculpted muscles were highlighted by the tight bodysuit that wrapped his body in silver, white, and gold, making him look a lot like a statue.

"Is that Cyrus the Warlord?" Phoenix whispered, just loud enough for Mark to hear.

He nodded, his gaze fixed on Cyrus. Like Noah, Cyrus had half a dozen known powers. Unlike Noah, Cyrus the Warlord was considered the most powerful paragon in the city and was the last sort of person Mark wanted to encounter. As an A-ranked empowered, Cyrus was a one-man army, capable of taking on an almost endless number of opponents. Even worse, the reason that Mark hadn't spotted him while scanning the psychic network was that Cyrus was giving off the same glow as the Exlian around him, a clear sign that he was a mutant. Completely at ease, Cyrus strolled down the aisle toward Mark and Phoenix, a small smile fixed on his lips.

"Something tells me that you're not supposed to be down here," he said, his rich voice cutting through the din. "Are you responsible for the alarm? You must be because I can smell blood on you, which means you probably killed the guards you've encountered."

Mark didn't see any sense in trying to deny it, so he just shifted back into a more defensive position. That caused the smile on Cyrus's face to widen, though the look in his eyes was anything but friendly.

"You should know that you've ruined yourself by coming here. But don't worry, I'll make your death swift, if not particularly painless."

"Capture them alive if you can," one of the scientists behind Cyrus said, his voice high pitched and nasal. "They look like they'd make excellent test specimens."

Masking the annoyance that flashed through his eyes, Cyrus gave a short nod and came to a stop barely fifteen feet away from Mark and Phoenix. "Well, I was going to do both of you a favor and just kill you, but it seems that you've caught Dr. Turen's attention, which means you have a much worse future in store."

Mark was only half listening to Cyrus's threats as he tried to remember everything he could about the A-ranked paragon. He had read a profile on Warlord when he was younger, though it was likely out of date, especially if Cyrus was participating in the mutant program. According to the profile, Cyrus's powers were well rounded and included enhanced strength, speed, flight, and basic energy control, typical fare for a paragon. His strongest power, however, was the ability to summon weapons and armor from thin air just like Danny could. This was where his nickname, Warlord, came from, and Mark had seen numerous videos of Cyrus using his ability to great effect.

Despite the fact that he was facing an enemy nearly ten times as strong as he was, Mark found himself quite calm. It was true that Cyrus was stronger, faster, and possibly even tougher than he was, but Mark had never backed down in the face of a fight and wasn't about to start now. Besides, even if he was outclassed, he had complete confidence in his own abilities.

Sensing a faint contraction in Cyrus's muscles, Mark shifted his blades and then stabbed out, meeting the sudden charge. Phoenix reacted half a second later, unleashing a wave of mana that hammered into Cyrus when he was only a few steps away. Phoenix had intended to blast him backward to buy some time, but Cyrus simply narrowed his eyes and summoned his armor, causing the blast of mana to roll right off him.

The armor was translucent, forming a thick green-and-gold carapace around Cyrus. It was dotted with spikes and blades and transformed Cyrus into a savage-looking knight. Though the mana blast didn't manage to stop Cyrus, he was still slowed by a step, giving Mark enough time to unleash his own attacks. Mark's four blades struck together, trying to pierce through Cyrus's armor, only to find the material was too hard. There was a grinding sound and sparks flew through the air as the blades skipped off it.

A moment later, Cyrus arrived in front of Mark, hammering a fist into his chest. Mark immediately shifted his weight backward to avoid the punch, even as a mana shield manifested in front of him. Though it looked just as thick as Cyrus's armor, Mark's mana shield only lasted a fraction of a second before shattering. Thankfully, the shield still served its purpose, robbing Cyrus's punch of most of its momentum, and when his knuckles connected with Mark's armor, he was barely shaken.

Beneath his ethereal mask, Cyrus's eyes widened in surprise, and then a fierce expression crossed his face. With Phoenix right behind him, Mark knew he couldn't back up, so he planted his feet and attacked again, only to find his bone blades barely scratching Cyrus's armor. He felt Phoenix readying her next attack and got ready to unleash his null field, hoping to neutralize Cyrus's armor. Before he could activate it, however, Cyrus waved his hand, and a long spear whipped out and slammed into Mark's side. Though his mana shield and bone armor absorbed the impact, it still sent him tumbling sideways into a cage, making his ribs ache.

Cyrus was about to follow up, but a bright glow in front of Phoenix distracted him, and he barely had time to react before Phoenix's mana blast flew toward him, giving Mark time to recover his balance. Clearly annoyed by the attack, the paragon snapped his fingers, and a shield appeared in front of him. The mana blast splashed onto it, sending rolling flames flying through the room, but Phoenix's attack was blocked, and when the flames vanished, Cyrus was entirely unharmed.

With a nasty grin, he rose into the air, the shield he had summoned hovering on his left and the spear on the right. "Your resistance is pathetically predictable, but it will be futile. If you don't want me to beat you within half an inch of your lives, it's in your best interest to surrender."

His words, bolstered by his power, carried a coercive effect, and Mark saw Phoenix take a step back, a hint of fear shining through her stubborn gaze. Mark, who had regained his footing, glanced behind him at the slavering jaws of the Exlian trying to gnaw its way through the mana barrier to get to him. Despite the fact that there were giant teeth only inches from his head, Mark simply looked back at Cyrus. He had expected to be outclassed in terms of physical abilities, and that was certainly the situation. The bigger problem was that the density of Cyrus's mana was higher than his and Phoenix's. Cyrus's attacks punched through Mark's shields with little effort, while his attacks could barely scratch Cyrus's armor.

"Now I know what it must feel like when other people fight me," Mark muttered, rolling his shoulders as he got ready for round two. "Phoenix, I need you to retreat."

Cyrus, still hanging in the air in the center of the aisle, watched with curiosity as Mark walked back toward him. Phoenix wasn't nearly as pleased, but before she could argue, Mark pointed back toward the door they had come through. "There are a couple dozen guards coming our way. The last thing we need is for them to involve themselves in the fight. I'll deal with Warlord while you take care of them."

Glancing at Cyrus and then back at Mark, Phoenix furrowed her brow. "You sure you're gonna be all right?"

"I'll survive," Mark replied, surprising himself with how calm he truly was.

After hesitating for a moment, Phoenix nodded and retreated toward the door. Cyrus simply watched her go, clearly confident that after dealing with Mark, he'd be able to capture her easily.

"So you do know who I am," he said, turning his attention back to Mark. "Here I thought you were completely ignorant. Though that does lead to an interesting question. If you know who I am, then what gives you any hope of being able to survive what's about to come your way?"

Stopping twenty feet from the floating paragon, Mark shrugged. "You talk an awful lot."

That caused Cyrus to laugh. "Do you think to anger me and take advantage of my emotions? A fool's errand."

"No, I really think you talk a lot. Clearly you like the sound of your own voice."

A smile of genuine amusement flickered across Cyrus's lips as he nodded. "And why shouldn't I? Like the rest of me, my voice is perfect."

Speechless, Mark stared at Warlord as Phoenix suddenly

threw up a mana shield behind them, blocking the doorway they had just come through. Half a second later a storm of rifle shots splattered against the barrier, causing it to dim noticeably. Twitching, Phoenix pushed more mana into the barrier as she looked back at Mark and Cyrus.

Taking a deep breath, Mark lifted his hands, getting into his Cutting Palm stance, and prepared for the hardest fight of his life. Once again, it was Cyrus who made the first move, stabbing his spear toward Mark's chest. The tip moved so quickly it caused a tearing sound as it ripped apart the air, but Mark simply shifted to the side, avoiding it and launching himself toward Cyrus. Before he made it halfway, Cyrus stepped forward and brought his hand down in a chopping motion. Mana swirled together, forming an ethereal axe that cut at Mark's head.

Knowing he couldn't block the attack, Mark activated his null field, creating a wide sphere where no mana could exist. The weapons that Cyrus had created immediately dissipated, vanishing into the air, along with Cyrus's heavy suit of armor. Mark, who was still moving forward, took advantage of Cyrus's surprise and stabbed him in the chest with two of his blades. They cut through the bodysuit and into Cyrus's flesh but only managed to sink a couple of inches in before Cyrus reacted. Mark's null field had robbed Cyrus of his ability to fly, so he had begun falling, and now he gripped the two blades and thrust them back, pulling himself free as he tumbled to the ground.

Turning over in midair, Cyrus lashed out with his foot, catching the edge of a cage, which gave him just enough control that he was able to flip and land on his feet. The cage, no longer reinforced with mana thanks to the null field, collapsed under the force of his kick, killing the Exlian inside. As the creature was crushed, it let out a loud wail in the psychic network, causing all the other Exlian in the room to go absolutely mad.

Despite having managed to score a hit against Cyrus, Mark actually felt worse about his chances after their exchange. He had severely underestimated the gulf between B-ranked and A-ranked powers. That realization was cemented when Cyrus flashed toward him and punched at Mark's head. Mark saw the attack coming and jerked his head back, but Cyrus was just too fast for him, and the edge of his knuckle grazed Mark. Pain radiated through Mark's head as his mask shattered, and he was sent stumbling back. Feeling the heat in his jaw as his regeneration kicked in, Mark realized that the glancing blow had not only broken his mask but cracked his jaw as well.

Seeing another punch coming, Mark threw himself backward but knew he wasn't going to make it. Miraculously, just before Cyrus's punch landed, an Exlian slammed into his side, disrupting his balance just enough that Mark was able to twist out of the way of the blow. As he fell to the ground and scrambled away, Exlian that had been freed from their cages by the null field swarmed around them. The slavering jaws he had seen earlier closed down on his arm but failed to pierce through his armor, but rather than shake the monster free, Mark instead focused his will and expanded his null field to its maximum. With a bit of mental effort, he flattened it out, transforming it from a sphere to an oblong shape that extended close to forty feet to his right and left. As the null field brushed past the mana shields that kept the Exlian contained, the shields began to collapse, freeing more Exlian, which immediately rushed out of their cages. At the same time, Mark sent out a mental command that echoed through the psychic network.

ATTACK.

Exlian of all shapes reacted immediately, rushing toward Cyrus and burying him in a giant pile of bodies. He roared with rage, but without his armor, the Exlian's attacks managed to get through, causing scratches to appear all over his body. With every move, Cyrus killed another Exlian, but hundreds more were rushing toward him, buying Mark enough time to grab Phoenix and flee. Seeing his battered state as he staggered toward her, she dropped her shield and grabbed his arm to support him. Mark's wounds were healing at a visible rate, and in a few seconds he was able to move freely once more.

"What's the plan? Do we retreat?" Phoenix asked, staring at the seething sea of Exlian.

"No. This is why we came. They'll tie him up for a moment, so we're going through there," Mark said, pointing at a doorway on the other side of the large room.

The door led to the seventh floor's main laboratory, and Mark figured that it would be the place where they could do the most damage. As for how to get through the Exlian, that was simple.

"Stay close!"

Mark broke into a sprint with Phoenix following close behind, heading around the giant Exlian dogpile on top of Cyrus. Some of the Exlian started to rush toward him, but under his incessant mental commands, they quickly turned to add their weight to the attack against Cyrus. Unfortunately, the null field also dispersed the mana Phoenix was using to bolster her speed, causing her to fall behind. Mark was about to turn around to grab her when he felt her hand latch onto his shoulder.

"Keep going!"

With Phoenix hanging on for dear life, Mark sped up, arriving at the door to the laboratory a few seconds later. He'd disrupted the rest of the containment units along the way, and the room was boiling over with Exlian, all of which were heading for Cyrus or toward the same doorway as Mark. Gritting his teeth, Mark hit the door with as much force as he could muster, using both his blades and arms to push it open. Transformed into shrapnel by the force of his charge, the door exploded inward, and Mark and Phoenix flew through. He canceled his null field at the last moment, and Phoenix let out a shout.

Two wings made of pure mana burst from her back, flapping to slow her and Mark down. When they finally stopped, they hovered ten feet off the ground, a swarm of Exlian pouring into the room underneath them. Ringing the room was a catwalk, and stationed every fifty feet was a guard, all of whom had their weapons leveled at Mark and Phoenix. But despite the threat from all around, the pair's attention was firmly fixed on the massive figure in the center of the room.

"Mark?" Phoenix's voice was quiet and laced with an entirely understandable fear. "Is . . . is that . . . ?"

Grimacing, Mark looked over the gigantic insectile Exlian that never should have appeared inside New Emery. Staring at them, it had entirely too much intelligence in its beady eyes for Mark's comfort. Its bulbous lower body spoke of limited mobility, but Mark knew that its power didn't lie in its physical ability, though any creature of its size was undoubtedly going to be powerful. Instead, its true power was hidden in the overwhelming mental presence that Mark could feel pressing in on his mind from all sides. Mental power that could forcefully take command of any Exlian in the vicinity, bending them to its will. Behind him, Mark heard a furious shout and a loud blast as Cyrus, no longer under the influence of Mark's null field, regained full control of his powers. Caught between a furious paragon and the most powerful Exlian he had ever seen, Mark swallowed.

"A matron? Yeah, I think it is."

"Does that mean we're . . ."

"In trouble? A whole pile of it."

To be continued . . .